About the Author

Richard L. Torch is a management consultant and has several management books to his credit. He presently lives with his wife and eldest son on a beautiful lake in Eastern Ontario, Canada.

This is his first fiction book, "A Younger Version of Yourself".
Richard describes his hero as Sean Little who now, using the "secret of the Pharaohs" with its billions of dollars, sets out to clean up our environmental problems. His hero, working outside the present political framework begins to solve the world's environmental problems, to the dislike of the US government. Mr. Torch proves that we have the technology, we have the money but it is our politicians indifference to the ever growing environmental and climate problems that are keeping us from a solution.

A Younger Version of Yourself

Richard L. Torch

A Younger Version of Yourself

Olympia Publishers
London

www.olympiapublishers.com
OLYMPIA PAPERBACK EDITION

A CIP catalog record for this title is
available from the British Library.

ISBN: 978-1-80439-991-0

This is a work of fiction.
Names, characters, places, and incidents originate from the writer's imagination.
Any resemblance to actual persons, living or dead, is purely coincidental.

First Published in 2025

Olympia Publishers
Tallis House
2 Tallis Street
London
EC4Y 0AB

Printed in Great Britain

Dedication

To CURTIS D. JOHNSON,
a quick mind
and a generous heart.
Thank you.

Contents

Historical Background and Information

This is the story of the most fantastic discovery to ever reach antiquity and modern science. A story that started with Napoleon's savants in Egypt to the modern-day miracle that we all know about today. A story that is still unfolding as I write.

On May 19, 1798, twenty-eight-year-old French General Napoleon Bonaparte, fresh from his victories in Italy with fifty thousand soldiers and sailors in 427 ships, set sail to conquer Egypt. This was his Armeè d'Orient, determined to first capture Malta and make it a French possession, and then on to Egypt to free the local fellahims (locals) from the oppressive rule of their Mamluk elite. Capturing Egypt, the French would have a stranglehold on the important British trade routes to Asia and especially India.

Napoleon included 167 "savants", scientists, architects, engineers, and other scholars to make a complete assessment of the ancient civilization he knew existed there. These were members of Napoleon's "Egyptian Scientific Expedition", not fighting men but intellectuals dedicated to their discipline and to understanding this strange ancient civilization.

For the next three years, while the French armies fought, the savants painted, drew, made measurements, and excavated dozens of large monuments in Egypt. All were fascinated by the strange picture writing that adorned all the monuments. Even the local imams (holy men) could not help them understand the nature of these buildings or the strange language inscribed upon them. When asked, they would say, "We do not know who built the pyramids, nor do we understand the strange drawings. They have always been there." Obviously, the knowledge of this ancient language and the people who built these amazing structures had died long ago, along with the people who had created them.

Shortly after arriving in Egypt, the British navy, under the command of Rear Admiral Horatio Nelson, on August 1, 1798, found the French fleet moored in Aboukir Bay and attacked. It was an outstanding victory for the British. With the French fleet now sitting on the bottom of the bay, the

British had undisputed mastery of the seas.

This meant that the French were now stranded in Egypt. Napoleon concluded a series of amazing military victories against the ruling Mamluk forces. But twelve months later, General Napoleon secretly returned to France. In the next two years, the French, after suffering a number of serious defeats in Egypt, General Menou formerly surrendered to the British in August 1801.

This is the first account of this amazing discovery, and the people involved. A discovery so fantastic that it could reshape the world as we know it today.

Chapter 1
With Napoleon's "Egyptian Scientific Expedition," 1798

Francois Lebelle, assistant to Napoleon's chief engineer, Nicolas-Jacques Conte, from Napoleon's "Egyptian Scientific Expedition" in Egypt in 1798, sat quietly in the market square, enjoying his thick black coffee. Francois was a tall man with glasses and a beard. He looked the intellectual type. Every morning in the marketplace, he enjoyed watching the hustle and bustle of the vendors setting up their stalls for the day's business. The market was noisy and crowded with the smells of the strange foods the locals ate. He felt that his morning coffee was the only time he could relax. *The life here is so different from France,* he thought.

A young fellahim or local of about twenty-two years of age approached him. He was a small youth, gentle and soft-spoken. Without saying a word, he sat down across from Francois. Francois had never met this person before and was not interested in what he had to say. But Francois was surprised at the young man's ability to speak French.

"Monsieur, my name is Syed, from an old and respected family. I know that you French fight the hated Mamluks who have overrun our country. I also know that you seek the treasures of the ancients and will pay well when necessary," said the young lad.

"Yes, you are correct. But we are not interested in the cheap trinkets sold in the shops here. We are under orders from the great General Napoleon himself to collect antiquities and make notes of everything we can from the monuments of your country," replied Francois.

"My family is the last of the descendants of the protectors of the secrets of Imhotep or Sankh, the one who gives life. His secrets are written on a sacred papyrus, protected by my family since the dawn of time. This I will sell to you for the list of arms written out on this paper." Syed then passed the note to Francois.

"Four pistols, eight rifles, two hundred shots, and five kilos of powder for a few scraps of papyrus—impossible!" Francois Lebelle exclaimed.

"But monsieur, what I am offering you is my land's most guarded secret, handed down generation after generation in a sacred trust. My grandfather is the last of the sacred guardians of the secrets of Imhotep, 'Sankh, the one who gives life.' Five thousand years ago, as the Chief Administrator to the Great Pharaoh Djoser, Imhotep was the one who brought learning, mathematics, architecture, and the knowledge of medicine to our people. He designed and built the first pyramid, the Great Stepped Pyramid of Djoser. His secrets have been guarded by my descendants up to now," replied Syed.

Francois Lebelle was not only astonished by the young man's fluent French but also by his knowledge of this ancient land. No other person, not even the best scholars, had any knowledge close to what he possessed. But here was a young man explaining its history in detail. He talked of events thousands of years in the past—Pharaohs, military campaigns—that took place before known recorded history. Knowledge that was obviously passed down from generation to generation—knowledge that even the greatest scholars in Europe did not possess. Francois hid his astonishment.

"You fakers are all the same, selling us proud French your worthless junk, claiming it is the work of the Pharaohs," he replied.

"But monsieur, these are no fakes. These are no forgeries. These are the sacred documents of Imhotep, 'Sankh, the one who gives life.' I am only offering you these papyrus because we need your weapons to defend ourselves from the Mamluks who raid our villages from the west. Please help us," explained Syed.

"But I must inspect the papyrus first. Getting my hands on the weapons you ask for is difficult, but not impossible," argued back Francois.

"If you insist, I will arrange with my grandfather to have the papyrus open for you to view. We can meet back here in the marketplace at sundown tomorrow night," suggested Syed.

Francois agreed, and then they parted company. Francois thought on his way back to camp, *These people are always trying to take advantage of us. When will it ever stop? But just maybe the papyrus that he speaks of is genuine. His knowledge of this ancient land is amazing and surpasses even the most respected scholars we have met.*

General Napoleon has ordered us to acquire all artifacts about this strange land. If these are real, he will be proud of my acquisition, but I will have to play down the guns I have to give up. I will face a firing squad if these weapons are ever used against us.

The next day, back at the excavations of the Great Sphinx, Francois thought, *Since the great defeat of the Mamluks at the Battle of the Pyramids, we have free rein to study these three monumental pyramids and the strange stone head sticking out of the sand. But it seems that everyone hates us in this strange land. Fortunately for us, to aid us in our work, General Napoleon has ordered the military garrison here to obey all of our requests and that we would be guarded while we work.*

Francois looked upon the hundreds of local workers manually hauling away the sand from around the Great Sphinx. After two days of digging in the intense heat, they uncovered the entire head and shoulders—a massive structure. And to everyone's surprise, the stone structure continues on with no one knowing how large it was. Francois and the other officers all wished that this monument to a long-dead civilization would be uncovered when the great General returned. He would be so proud.

Francois continued his work at measuring the three great peaked pyramids that existed behind the Great Sphinx. The largest of these, the Great Pyramid of Kheops, was his duty to measure and attempt to understand how it was made. The monument was huge, measuring 230 meters by 230 meters at its base and an estimated height of 147 meters. But this was only what they could see above the sand. Without excavation, they would never know how far down the Great Pyramid remained hidden.

The fellow savants or scientists asked, 'How did such primitive people move these stone blocks, many of whom must weigh over 15,000 kilos or more? What do they signify?' Francois and the others in Napoleon's engineering corps believed that these massive structures must be funeral temples for their past rulers. Napoleon himself was granted access into the pyramids with some artists who sketched the insides of this magnificent structure.

For the rest of the day, Francois continued to measure and document. After measuring the base stones, they set about measuring the height and estimated the depth of each base stone. Everyone remarked that the task of moving such stones from a distant location must have been enormous. Thousands of large stones were quarried from an unknown area. Where did they come from, and why were they here? Mysteries that the General had ordered them to find out.

The desert heat was unbearable. The French, not accustomed to the relentless heat of the direct sun, were constantly seeking water and shade. The workmen, covered in loose clothing and with their heads covered, had learned to work under the relentless sun's rays. They sang while they worked, a song that none of the French associates could understand. But they were happy to work and be paid.

They all work until sundown, and the French officers and native workmen went home. Only a few guards were left as there was little to steal. On his way to his camp, Francois thought about meeting Syed, who has promised to show him the ancient papyrus. *He's probably making it right now and hoping to fool me with his forgery,* thought Francois. *Likely, he'll want me to see it under a poor light so that I can easily be deceived. But not I, for I am a respected engineer in General Napoleon's "Egyptian Scientific Expedition."*

After a quick meal and some cheap local wine, Francois made his way to the marketplace and found Syed sitting on a stool. When approached, he gestured for Francois to follow him.

"Stay behind me about five meters, as it is best we are not seen together. In my country, the walls have eyes," whispered Syed.

With Syed leading the way, they walked through streets and alleyways with no names and no identification. At last, Syed led Francois up an ancient flight of stone stairs and knocked on a thick wooden door. The door opened, and a young girl let them in. Syed introduced her to Francois as Mirana, his distant cousin and caretaker for his grandfather. She was young and wore the traditional headscarf and face coverings of the locals. Nevertheless, you could tell from her beautiful eyes that she was a natural beauty.

There, sitting in the corner, surrounded by burning incense and candles, was the oldest man Francois had ever seen. Syed's grandfather sat there motionless, wearing a very beautiful Egyptian robe. The grandfather sat in a low-ceiling room with carpets on the walls and floor. Mirana continued with her duties in the kitchen.

In another language, different from that which is normally spoken here, Syed introduced Francois. Syed then motioned for Francois to sit. Francois bowed and sat on a large, elaborate cushion. Francois wisely did not speak while Syed explained to his grandfather that he must see the papyrus before bringing him the weapons to defend his village. The grandfather eventually looked at Francois and nodded. Francois sat motionless as a show of respect.

Syed then got up, went down a narrow hallway returning with a large alabaster-carved stone box with a similarly carved stone lid. The lid and box were covered in hieroglyphics, the strange, unknown picture writing of the ancient Egyptians. He handed the box to Francois. Francois immediately marveled at the intricate carvings. The work necessary to make such a beautiful alabaster stone box would be amazing. Obviously, this was not a commoner's box but must have come from a robbed tomb of a Pharaoh or a top official.

Francois thought, *hoax or not, inside this box are the articles I seek.* Francois smiled at the grandfather and gently opened the box. Like the outside, the inside was also beautifully carved into the strange picture writing. There, in front of Francois were the ancient papyrus that had been guarded by this family for thousands of years. Francois looked in amazement, wondering what secrets this ancient papyrus could hold.

"Do you know how to read these ancient symbols?" Francois asked Syed.

"No," replied Syed, "the knowledge of the ancient picture writing has been lost for thousands of years. No one knows what they mean."

Francois then replaced the lid on the box and nodded again at the grandfather. He gently handed the box to Syed, saying, "Yes, I wish to acquire this, and with your grandfather's permission, we will meet again two nights from now to make the exchange." Francois then stood up, nodding to the grandfather and left the apartments. After an hour of wandering, he finally found his way back to his camp.

The next day, Francois awoke, worrying, *"Have I been fooled?"* Francois mused to himself, *but I can tell the difference between the real and the forgery, so it must be real. The carved stone box is of such fine detail, far surpassing even the best artifacts we have yet to uncover. And the young man's knowledge is amazing. It must be real.*

That day, while continuing to measure the Grand Pyramid, Francois excused himself from his associates and went to the commissioner's building to arrange for the weapons. Upon entering, he was not friendly greeted but was given the respect deserving of his position. Francois knew that he could acquire the weapons he needed as a member of Napoleon's "savants." *We are to be given anything we need for our investigations,* he said to himself.

Francois approached the counter and clearly stated, "I need four pistols, eight long guns, two-hundred rounds of shot, cloth, and five kilos of gunpowder."

"And what do you need these for, starting your own army?" Laughed the unwashed attendant behind the counter.

"I need these to protect us on an expedition to the north in search of more buildings for the General Napoleon," Francois sternly replied.

After a few minutes, he returned back with four pistols, two-hundred rounds of shot, cloth, and five kilos of gunpowder.

"Where are my rifles?" Francois asked.

"Other than what you see in the arms of our men, all the long rifles have gone with Napoleon on his campaign to the Red Sea," replied the clerk.

Francois, knowing full well the disdain that Napoleon's fighting men had for the nonmilitary savants, Francois yelled, "I cannot go into the north with only four pistols! I need more."

The clerk, seeing Francois's anger again, went to the back and returned with two more pistols.

"Here, this is all I can spare you."

Francois left, thanking the clerk, and concealed his goods in a large blanket. He went unnoticed to his tent and hid his weapons. Francois then returned to his duties measuring the Grand Pyramid and worked until dusk. The next day, Francois continued to measure and remeasure the Great Pyramid. The structures were an obsession with General Napoleon, and he wanted everything recorded in detail.

Francois Buys the Alabaster Carved Box

Later that day, Francois returned to his tent, and after a brief meal and a short nap, he retrieved his goods and made his way to the bazaar. Being a savant, he was not questioned by any guards and was allowed to pass. There again sat Syed, waiting for him. Francois followed him a good distance back and again went to his grandfather's apartment. As before, his grandfather was sitting in the main room, and Francois was motioned to a cushion. Francois laid the weapons before the grandfather and explained to

Syed, "I could only get six pistols and no long guns, as they had already been taken by Napoleon to the Red Sea."

Syed seemed satisfied with my explanation. After a brief discussion with his grandfather, the grandfather eventually nodded and motioned for Syed to get the box.

Francois examined the box and the inner papyrus. It was exactly like it was before. Francois told Syed that he was pleased, and Syed said that his grandfather was pleased. Francois stood up and, using the blanket that he had wrapped the weapons in, wrapped up the box and left. But just as Francois was leaving, Syed motioned for him to stop. His grandfather said something in his foreign tongue, which Syed repeated to Francois, "My grandfather says that what you have has been guarded by our family for thousands of years. They have sworn their lives to protect it. He says he does know of the secrets that it holds, but the papyrus is the words of the Great Imhoptep himself, a god. You now hold words only spoken by the ancients. Go wisely." With that, Francois bowed to the grandfather and left.

Over the next few days, Francois and his men constantly measured and measured. Napoleon's orders were that everything be noted and drawn. Francois became so lost in his work and notes that he forgot all about the carved box he had acquired.

Three days later, with two of his associates, Francois attempted to visit Syed and his grandfather again. Francois had told them of the young man's amazing knowledge of the history of this land, and they were anxious to meet him. After hours and hours of being lost in these unnamed streets, Francois finally found the stairway to his grandfather's apartment. Up the steps, they went. Francois knocked on the door, and as the door was unlocked, they entered. The rooms were vacant. Whoever lived there was now gone, likely to their village in the west.

Talking to the neighbors was useless, as they believed that Francois and his friends were the French military, so they would tell them nothing. They would not even admit that there was an old man and a young girl living there. Francois's friends ridiculed him for having been dubbed by the local people.

"Francois, I hope you didn't give them any money for the stupid stories they told you. These people will tell you anything in order to gain your trust and your pocketbook." They laughed.

Fortunately for me, thought Francois, *I had not mentioned the carved box, so it will remain my secret.*

Surrender to the British (Convention of E-Arish, January 24, 1800)

Francois and his fellow savants knew that shortly after they arrived, their fleet had been destroyed at Aboukir Bay, now known as the Battle of the Nile, on August 3, 1798. They all agreed they were landlocked until replacement ships from France could reach them. Francois and his associates thought it best to avoid talk of the military campaigns and so engrossed themselves in their work. Francois thought a little more about his secretly carved box.

Everyone knew that after their naval defeat, Napoleon left Egypt twelve months later, and they had to fend for themselves. Francois learned later that Napoleon's replacement, General Kleber, signed a surrender to the British on January 24, 1880. But they still had to fight the Mamluk forces, whom they defeated at the battle of Heliopolis on March 20, 1800.

Later, after General Kleber was assassinated, the French forces were then under the direction of General Menou. And now, with the French troops being defeated at the Battle of Alexandria, surrendering Fort Julian, and then losing Cairo, General Menou again formerly surrendered to the British in August 1801.

As savants and scientists, they felt the conditions of the surrender were harsh.

The British agreed that:

a) They would ferry them back to France, and that all must be gone by August 30, 1801.

b) They must surrender all of their arms.

c) Article XVI specifically stated that the British had full ownership of all antiquities acquired by their expedition.

Word quickly spread among the savants that not only would they be seizing their weapons, but all of their findings, artifacts, and drawings. The savants were outraged, but under the circumstances, there was little they could do.

Upon hearing this, Francois knew that once the British searched him, he could not conceal the box. But he could hide its contents. Francois searched in vain where he could properly store the ancient papyrus without them being confiscated or destroyed. Looking over, he saw his table-top writing desk. This would be opened and searched for sure. Working with a thin knife, he opened the bottom panel, carefully placed the ancient papyrus inside, and resealed the box. Even Francois couldn't tell that the bottom had been opened.

Leaving Egypt and the Seizing of Antiquities by the British

So on that faithful day of departure, before boarding, all of the savants were set off to one side while the British checked the military men for weapons or anything else they could be hiding. Not only did they check their possessions, but they also made them remove their jackets, and they patted them down from head to toe. They were ensuring that no one brought a gun or a blade with them. All the time, the British had guns pointed at those they were searching. There was little that anyone could do but obey. Everyone was just tired of the fighting, the loneliness, and the disease and just wanted to get back to France.

Now it was savant's turn. But being nonmilitary personnel, they were not so roughly treated. The British did check their possessions, and Francois had to hand over his ornately carved box. Everyone wanted to bring something back to show for their years of hard work here. But as these items they confiscated were not weapons, the British were not alarmed; they simply took them. Francois and his associates speculated that many of the smaller items seized would never be handed in merely to become souvenirs on British fireplace mantels at home. But there was little anyone could do.

Then, to everyone's surprise, Francois's friend the naturalist, Etienne Geoffroy Saint Hilaire, a large, long-haired brash man, arrived with a large cart full of the paintings, drawings, sketches, and notes that they had labored years for. Etienne was angry and defiant that these notes, which they had spent three years collecting in this hot, desolate country, would be going back to France.

The British approached him and raised their weapons. Etienne was in a fury.

He lit a torch and, holding it close to the papers, proclaimed, "We are scientists, architects, engineers, and naturalists. We are not your enemy, nor have we engaged you in combat. We have been sent here to uncover the secrets of this ancient land, and the fruits of our work resides in this cart. I will accept your bullets and die here, but our notes will die along with me. I will not allow you to take these from me and my fellows. For this would be a loss equal to the burning of the Library of Alexandria, and the blame for this loss will be on the heads of you, the British."

The British officers talked among themselves. The British commander then said, "He is right. We have never fought these men and none of our men have fallen from their actions. Let them keep their notes and their pretty drawings. What does it matter to us? All their notes are in French anyway. We have all the valuable artifacts and antiquities that will soon be displayed in London as a tribute to our great victory over the French. Let them pass. Let them keep their papers."

The savants all stood in amazement as the British lowered their guns and Etienne extinguished his torch in the sand. Everyone was speechless. Then one of the savants started clapping, and everyone clapped, not only for their hero, Etienne, but for the British, who were allowing them to pass and keep their precious paintings, drawings, and notes. Everyone thanked the British and assured them for their generosity, they would have no trouble from them on the passage.

As the savants stood in line, the long procession of carts bearing the antiquities that the British had confiscated were loaded onto the ships. The British searched every tent and every building and dug in the sand for any other artifacts that may have been hidden. They searched everywhere. It was obvious they were under orders to return any and all artifacts back to England.

One soldier motioned to the commanding officer to come look at what he had.

It was a funny-looking stone that appeared to be inscribed in three different languages. The soldier asked if this too was to be collected, and the officer replied, "It is not ours to judge. We are to return with everything we can from this strange land. Load the stone. Maybe someday someone will know what it is."

Thus, this rock, later known as the Rosetta Stone, written in three ancient languages—Egyptian hieroglyphics, Egyptian demotic, and ancient Greek was sent to England. This was the stone that allowed the British linguist Thomas Young to identify some of the writing and eventually have the entire Rosetta Stone deciphered by the French linguist Jean Francois

Champollion in 1820. Now this strange picture writing of the ancients could be read, and the long-lost secrets of this ancient civilization could be realized.

Chapter 2
Returning to France, 1781

On the voyage back to France, the savants caused the British no problems and made sure that they were as polite and helpful as they could be. Francois took it upon himself to become a cook's helper and made sure that he cleaned and washed the dishes every night. As they were respected as learned men and not fighting men, the British didn't lock them up under the strict understanding that at the first instance of trouble, all of them would be treated as prisoners of war and locked in the barracks in the hold. A place none of them wanted to visit.

The savants were afraid that at the last minute, the British would not allow them to disembark with the paintings, sketches, and notes that Etiennre had threatened to burn in Egypt. Stored beside their drawings and notes were the many artifacts that the British had confiscated from them in Egypt. The savants agreed that they could not disembark with any of these artifacts under their coats, as the British would easily spot the theft.

"But these are ours, we found them," explained one architect.

Etiennre consoled the architect, "We all share your pain and frustration. But we must accept that, at this time, we are prisoners of war and held captive on this British ship. The British have the muskets, and we are their prisoner. They can do as they please. Best to not provoke them to cause them to hurt us or make them confiscate our work."

The savants agreed to not touch their notes on the passage home and to keep the documents out of sight. If they placed importance on them, the British would become curious and decide to return with them to England as further trophies. So the savants kept the documents under tarps under the watchful eye of each savant in turn. During the rough return home, the savants took turns making sure that their notes were not getting wet. Water landing on their pen and ink drawings would spell ruin and a waste of their precious three years in this hot, dry land.

Upon disembarking in France, the savants thanked the British men, officers, and captain for their kindness and generosity. They were all nervous as they brought up the thousands of pages of notes, paintings, and sketches taken in their three-year expedition to Egypt. They were very careful to keep the paintings and sketches hidden under their notes. Hoping the British would not become curious, as everything they saw was written in French.

Then everyone froze as the British captain walked up to a savant carrying documents and started flipping through the papers. He paused and then said with a sneer, "All in French, too bad. Of no use to us, proceed."

The savants sighed with relief, smiled, and continued emptying the craft. Once on shore, they saluted the British, who had shown them such respect and courtesy. The British then quickly set sail as sitting in a French port just after the conclusion of the war was not to their liking.

Francois returned home to his village of Batignolles, just outside of Paris. It was a small village of only three hundred people. He rejoiced at seeing the beautiful countryside, with its rolling hills and vineyards. Everyone knew one another, and everyone rejoiced at Francois's return. At twenty-seven years old, he was welcomed back by his parents in their cozy home to a home-cooked meal and rejoicing all around. But his mom and dad seemed older now. *Maybe it's that I'm getting older or has my three years away from them been that hard on them,* he thought to himself. His father now walked with a limp and used a cane when going upstairs or going outside. His mother, still beautiful, walked and talked a little slower now.

As an engineer in Napoleon's "Egyptian Scientific Expedition," his success assured him of a good job, and all of France was in a buzz over the paintings and descriptions of the ancient land of the Pharaohs.

This mania, for everything Egyptian, quickly over-shadowed the defeat of the French in Egypt. Francois, as a member of the team that brought back this information, like his friends, all basked in the glory and honor bestowed upon them. He could not travel or meet others without being forever questioned about the strange land that he had spent three years in. Even his old university professor was constantly asking him, "Please, Francois, come and speak to us. We wish to hear everything you have to say about this strange and foreign land."

It finally dawned on Francois. *Maybe this celebrity status was not so bad. I merely have to walk into a tavern, and all my food and drink are paid for as long as I talk about Egypt. My friends adore me, and the ladies love me. For I represent adventure and knowledge of a land so foreign that it defies the imagination.*

When he met with other members of the expedition, they all reported the same celebrity status.

"We cannot go out of our homes without people asking about Egypt and our exploits there," explained one architect. "Plus, with all the lies being told about the military campaigns, we should all agree that keeping our mouths shut and talking only about our efforts is the wisest thing to do. Little value in upsetting the military or General Napoleon."

Francois was delighted. With his reputation as an engineer with General Napoleon in Egypt, the job offers flooded in. Every firm of note wanted to have one of Napoleon's savants on their staff. Francois finally took a commission with a small firm building bridges. He enjoyed his work, especially being in the field supervising the work. Being outside reminded him of the open skies of Egypt, but without the intense heat.

As a treat to himself, he decided that he would buy a brass plaque for the writing desk he had with him in Egypt. So, upon his first salary, he approached a handler of brass and had a small brass plaque made up.

Francois Lebelle
Engineer
Member of General Napoleon Bonaparte's
Egyptian Scientific Expedition
1798 to 1801

After a few days, he picked up his brass plaque and attached it to the front of his writing desk. He cherished this writing box, as it had been his constant companion for his three years in Egypt. When not in use, he placed it proudly on his parent's table beside their fireplace for all the world to see. His parents were so proud, and they constantly brought friends in to meet Francois and see his writing desk and plaque. Francois was the talk of the village, and his parents enjoyed their new-found celebrity status.

Confrontation in a Bar

Not long afterward, with some money in his pocket, Francois agreed to join his friends at the tavern down by the docks. It was a smoky, dark establishment, frequented by dock workers and ship crews. Meeting his friends, they immediately started talking over the top of one another, asking questions about his trip to Egypt. As the wine flowed, their voices became louder and louder in their exclamations about what Francois saw and did while in Egypt.

Sitting nearby were three military personnel who had also been in Egypt. Big, heavy-set soldiers and along way into their drink, and upon hearing Francois brag about his exploits, they became angry. They spoke among themselves, "When we were in Egypt, we had to treat those lazy savants like gods. They could have everything they wanted and could go wherever they pleased. While we fought the Mamluks and the British, they sat back, made their pretty drawings, and measured everything in sight. If it wasn't for us, the Mamluks would have cut them down like wheat."

One of the military men, drunk and enraged, approached Francois and his friends, "You savants have nothing to be proud of. We are the fighting men of General Napoleon's army, and in Egypt, you were considered our inferiors. But in Egypt, we could say nothing but were under orders to let you have your way. But I warn you, be quiet and do not talk of Egypt. Too many of my comrades died there while you sat in your tents and made drawings. You insult me with your boasting."

Francois quickly replied with, "Yes, I too lost many friends in Egypt. Not to the British or Mamluks bullets, but to the dreaded plague. To all of us in Egypt, death was our constant companion."

"But you did nothing to honor France," the drunk soldier continued, "we fought for the glory of General Napoleon, and all you did was bring back your drawings and notes. Now all of France hails you as heroes, and everyone wants to hear your stories. No one wants to hear about our campaigns, the battles we fought, and our friends who died. If it were not for the dreaded British sinking our ships at the Battle of the Nile and stranding us there, Egypt would be a colony of France today. Now all that everyone wants to hear about is those stupid stone pyramids and the Great Sphinx, and nothing from us fighting men, the pride of France."

Francois again tried to reason with the drunk soldier.

"But we were not ordered to fight. We were there at the express invitation of General Napoleon himself, who wanted to know everything about this strange and ancient land. Besides my fallen comrades, my greatest regret is that the British confiscated all of the antiquities we had collected, which were to be on display in Paris. Myself and my associates spent those three years in the heat in order to bring the glory of ancient Egypt back to France and we failed. Now everything that we collected and many of my friends died for is sitting somewhere in a British museum in England."

But the drunken soldier would have none of what Francois said. He was still enraged over their defeat in Egypt, their surrender, and having to be transported back to France as prisoners of war. He witnessed no hero's welcome and no victory parades.

It was as though everyone wanted to forget about the war and their defeat by the British. All everyone wanted to talk about was the stone pyramids. His rage boiled over. He had had enough.

He then seized Francois by the collar and started to punch him. Francois's friends tried to hold him off, but once the other two soldiers joined in the fray, Francois and his friends were easily overpowered. Francois fought bravely and landed a number of punches to his assailant. Then another soldier grabbed him from behind and stuck his blade into his back. Francois stumbled to the ground, and everyone stopped fighting. The soldiers looked at one another and fled.

At once, a doctor was called for, but it was too late. Francois lay dead on the floor.

The police were never able to get a description of the soldiers, as all the patrons had either left and the ones who remained were nervous about testifying against members of General Napoleon's army.

"Tight-lipped" mentioned the investigating officer after interviewing the few tavern patrons who stayed behind.

"A man is murdered a few meters from where they sat, and nobody saw anything," the officer explained in disgust. That was the end of Francois Lebelle, a proud savant of General Napoleon's "Egyptian Scientific Expedition."

Francois's writing desk, his companion for his three years with Napoleon in Egypt, was all his parents had to remember him by. It stayed on their table, undisturbed, until they both died twenty years later. As there were no other relatives, the home and its contents became the property of the state and were auctioned off.

For the next eighty plus years, the box saw a succession of owners and eventually was found in an antique shop, where it was purchased by a descendant of Jean-Baptiste Prosper Jollois, chief engineer of Napoleon's Egyptian Expedition. To honor their ancestor, the Jollois family members made it a habit to pick up anything they could from Napoleon's expedition to Egypt. Thus, Francois's writing desk remained safe and protected while in their collection for the next one hundred and twenty years.

Chapter 3
Sean Little and Jennifer Sloan (Present Day)

The countryside around Crystal Falls, Michigan, is always peaceful and quiet in the summer. Sean Little's family homestead was a beautiful white-painted house with the white picket fence, the ones that always needed painting, along with fifty acres of farmland. Sean loved it here.

Sean was twenty-eight years old, six feet tall, of good build, an intellectual loner who had no problem being by himself. He was a blue jeans and tee shirt type guy and always felt cramped sitting in an office wearing a suit all day.

His greatest sadness is that both his parents were killed in a head-on collision on US Highway #2, leaving him the only child to inherit the family farm. Sean, having little interest in farming, allowed his neighbors, the Watts, to come and cut the hay off the property. They, in turn, would bring over some bags of steak and keep an eye on the property when he was away.

Other than his parents passing, he felt he had the perfect life. Sean was the chief architect for Hillsborough and Smith Inc., Architects, in Dearborn, Michigan. His firm specialized in new technology and energy-efficient buildings. Roger Hillsborough, chief partner of the firm he founded, liked Sean and admired his work. At first, the other partners thought that while Sean was talented, his ideas were far too radical and would never sell. Roger ignored their concerns, hired Sean right out of university, and regularly promoted his designs every chance he could.

Sean, an ardent environmentalist, saw his work as an architect as a beacon of logic in developing better and more environmentally friendly office buildings. Because of this, Hillsborough and Smith Inc., using Sean's designs, quickly developed a reputation for being at the forefront of environmentally friendly architecture. Clients loved Sean's insistence on using natural light and having a garden area on every floor. The other partners remained skeptical until a major construction company awarded them their first major contract for the new office tower in Seattle,

Washington, based on Sean's designs. Now, suddenly, everyone was on board.

Once completed, the building was an international hit. Architects from all over the world journeyed to see the Seattle Tower Building and its innovative environmental design. Sean's picture and that of the Seattle Tower Building appeared on the cover of every architectural magazine in the US. The orders started to appear for more of Sean's environmentally friendly buildings, to where they had to start recruiting more architects that shared Sean's vision. Sean was quickly promoted as their chief architect, with a large bonus.

But regardless of how hard Roger Hillsborough tried, Sean refused to buy into the company.

"I don't want to be an administrator. I want to design buildings and let people and nature try to get along," Sean would say.

Sean knew the owners wanted him to become a partner so that he wouldn't be tempted to leave and go elsewhere. Sean would allay their fears by saying, "I'm not going anywhere. You and I both know that my inbox is crowded with job offers, but I'm not leaving you or Crystal Falls. You do the administration, and I'll design the buildings. No problem."

At a large office party in Detroit held by a large Detroit law firm, Sean was introduced by Bill Fryer, a lawyer with the firm Todd and Todd Lawyers Inc., to a tall, beautiful, dark-haired lady named Jennifer Sloan, and they hit it off immediately. She was everything Sean was not. She was energetic and loved getting dressed up and going out. But it was her big eyes and her beautiful smile that got to Sean. He couldn't keep his eyes off her. She was a beauty.

Jennifer was working as an assistant at a large law firm. She liked hearing about Sean's innovative ideas on environmentally friendly office towers. They talked on the balcony overlooking Detroit, and Sean enjoyed every minute he spent with her. He gave her a ride home that night, and after a brief kiss at her apartment door, they bid farewell.

As promised, Sean called her the next day, and while Sean drove, she showed him the sights of Detroit. They went for a relaxing afternoon brunch at a Greek restaurant and opened up about their lives to one another. Sean was naturally the quiet, introverted type, but with Jennifer, he loved to talk.

As Sean's offices in Dearborn, Michigan, were only twenty minutes from Detroit, Sean made a habit of picking up Jennifer after work and going out for dinner. They would try a different restaurant every night while they got comfortable with each other.

He had just bought a new Lexus SUV and told himself that he needed to drive it to keep it in good running condition. He said this to Jennifer, and she just laughed.

He mentioned that he purchased the Lexus because driving his dad's Buick just had too many memories for him.

Sean nervously invited Jennifer to spend the weekend with him at his farm, just over an hour's drive from Detroit. She accepted, and Sean was delighted. Jennifer always got off work by three p.m. on Fridays, and Sean said he'd pick her up at work and drive her to her apartment to pick up her things. Two minutes after he arrived at the front door of their office tower, Jennifer came out. Entering his car, she immediately kissed him. They went to her apartment, gathered her overnight bag, and were on their way to his farm in Crystal Falls.

Arriving at the farm later, Sean gave Jennifer the tour. She loved it. What a difference from working in an office tower all day and going home to her apartment in another tower! Jennifer loved the open spaces, the fields, and especially the barn. She had never really been in an old post-and-beam barn before and was amazed at the size, the design, and the smell of the old hay. *How wonderful,* she thought. She was in love with the old farmhouse. She marveled at everything, from the wood floors to the wood trim to the metal-tiled ceiling in the kitchen.

"What a beautiful home," she said.

They immediately sat on the back porch, and Sean poured them both some wine.

"The view here is so peaceful. How can you ever bear to leave this to go to work?" she asked.

Sean explained growing up here as a boy and helping his dad around the farm.

It was a good life, he explained, and Jennifer agreed. Jennifer told Sean that she grew up in Detroit in a nice neighborhood in a modest side split house. She said that she was the only one who stayed when her parents and sister Emily all moved to California.

"They want me to come to California, and maybe one day I will," she said.

After some wine and some pork chops and veggies on the BBQ, Sean showed her the rest of the house. She loved the living room with the old fireplace.

"I hope we can have a fire here tonight. I so seldom get to sit in front of a real fireplace," she said.

Sean proceeded to carry her bags upstairs and show her the upper floors. He walked by a bedroom and placed her bags on the bed.

"This is your room," he said, and she just laughed.

A few feet down the hall, he showed her his room, at which point she grabbed him and threw him on the bed. That was it. They made passionate love and enjoyed being in each other's arms. Both slept well that night.

The next morning, Sean made her a farm breakfast of thick-cut bacon, toast, and eggs from his neighbor's farm.

"Who can resist the smell of bacon and eggs in the morning?" Jennifer said as she came down the stairs. They talked and talked. Both Sean and Jennifer enjoyed every moment of their time together.

Late Sunday night, Sean returned Jennifer to her apartment with the promise to call her on Monday. He was shocked himself, he just couldn't get enough of seeing her. It was pretty much a habit that he would pick her up at night after work and try out a new restaurant. In Detroit, there are lots of restaurants, so they had plenty of places to go.

Jennifer Moves In

After about a month of seeing each other, Jennifer hinted that living in Crystal Falls would be enjoyable. They talked about it, and they both loved the idea. Jennifer gave Detroit Lawyers Inc. her two-week notice and then moved in with Sean in Crystal Falls. Sean generously paid to break off her apartment lease and insisted on paying for the movers to move her things. He joked that he would find a way to make it a tax write-off, and they both laughed.

Sean had the run of Hillsborough and Smith Inc. During a manager's meeting, he suggested that he would like to start working from home. They quickly agreed, knowing that at home, he usually produces his best work. Plus, with a new girl in his life, they knew the request was coming.

Sean thought, *this way I can continue living in my parent's home and not have to sell it or rent it out. And I get to spend more time with Jennifer and enjoy the quiet life.*

Plus, it cuts down on my driving. He chuckled to himself. That night, he told Jennifer the good news, and she was delighted. They had an enjoyable meal together and then later fell asleep in each other's arms.

Everything was working out well. Sean already had an office in an empty bedroom all set up and started doing all his work from there. When he had plans to deliver, he and Jennifer would make a day of it. He would drop her off at the local mall and let her shop while he went to the office. Usually, he was there for 1–2 hours and then met Jennifer back at the mall. *Boy, does she love to shop?* thought Sean. Then they would go for lunch and then proceed home.

When the winter rolled in, Sean would send over his small designs and notes via email and his larger designs via FedEx. This worked out well, as Sean hated driving in bad weather and thought with using the computer and FedEx, I don't need to.

Jennifer moved in and adored the farm. She and Sean would walk the property and simply enjoy their lives together. After a couple of months of fixing up the farmhouse, it didn't seem that there was much for her to do. Sean was closed in his office most of the day, absorbed in his new designs. When working on something important, he disliked being disturbed, so Jennifer left him alone. He would emerge for coffee and lunch, but that was about it. *Too long being a bachelor,* she thought.

She started getting fidgety just around Christmas. Sean noticed this and took her down to meet her parents and sister Emily in California, and they spent an enjoyable two weeks and Christmas there. Sean enjoyed meeting Mr. and Mrs. Sloan and her sister Emily. This visit seemed to calm Jennifer's nerves. When they returned, they were greeted by Bad Man Winter with three-foot snowdrifts and a bad drive from the Wayne County Airport in Detroit back to the farm.

Now hemmed in by the snow and with Sean always working, she thought she was going to go crazy. *There is never anything to do here,* she thought. Sean would take her out to the only local restaurant, a highway roadhouse, but you can only go to the same place so often. Most nights, they would have a nice meal and then play Monopoly in front of the fire. This was great at first, but soon the excitement of living in quiet Crystal Falls was wearing off.

Somehow she got talking to an old high school friend, an airline stewardess, and she convinced her to apply online. She sent along a photo of herself, and along with her friend's recommendation, she was accepted. Jennifer did not know how to tell Sean, so she just simply told him over lunch one day and left. As simple as that. No long departure, no long discussions on staying. She just packed up her bags, got in a taxi, and drove off.

Sean was hurt. He blamed himself. Maybe the thought of living in Crystal Falls is just too boring. *Maybe flying the world is a better deal. It must be. She's gone.*

A month went by, and she never called. He tried calling her cell, but she must have gotten a new number. A couple of weeks later, he did receive one single postcard from Hawaii saying, "I love my new job, my new friends, and the exciting places I'm visiting. Thank you for all the good times. Goodbye."

No phone number, no return address. He wasn't even sure of the airline she worked for. He had to admit that he was lonely. The farmhouse just wasn't the same without her smile. He could fire up his computer and start working again on the new building in Hawaii, but when he left his office, there was no one to talk to and no one to laugh with. The office tower in Hawaii was complete on his end, and all his associates had to do was fill in the details. *I'm not needed until they finish their work,* he thought, *we are so far ahead that even with my Christmas holidays, we will finish the completed plans at least four weeks ahead of schedule.*

Invitation to New York

Sean survived a boring winter close to his computer and drafting table. One morning while he was making his morning coffee, the phone rang. It was his cousin and good friend, Jack Alair, who moved to downtown New York City. Jack was a fun-loving, beer-drinking numbers guy who had a brain for accounting. Sean glanced at the clock on the stove, and it said nine a.m.

"Sean, it's Jack. How are you?"

"Oh, you know, hanging in there, I guess," replied Sean.

"Sean, I've got some time off, and I know you're bored, so why don't you catch a flight and stay with me for a week? I've got plenty of room, and there is lots for you to do and see in New York. I know you love old architecture, and New York is full of one hundred-years-old and older buildings for you to wander through. You will love seeing the Empire State Building built in 1930s. What do you say? I'd love to have you come over."

"Jack. You hit me at just the right time. I need to get out of this house. It's so lonely here ever since Jennifer left. It's driving me nuts. When do you want me down?"

"The sooner, the better. Catch any flight you can, and you have my address, catch a cab, and if I'm not home, I'll leave a key for you at the front desk, and I'll let them know you're coming," replied Jack.

"You're on, Jack. When we hang up, I'll call the airport and arrange a flight. I'll let you know when I'll be arriving."

"Great news. Looking forward to seeing you," said Jack, and he hung up.

Wow, that's refreshing. A trip to New York. Always wanted to see the old buildings there, and now I can, thought Sean. He called the local airport and reserved a seat for a two p.m. flight to New York. Better get ready. He went upstairs and showered and packed a bag. No need to take a lot. If I forget anything, I can get it in New York.

The drive through the countryside was uneventful, and he arrived at the "Park Your Car Here" lot, registered, and caught the shuttle service to the airport. His tickets were ready when he arrived, and he checked in his luggage.

Chapter 4
In New York

The flight to New York was full, mostly of businessmen in their suits. In his heart, he hoped that Jennifer was on this flight. If only he could see her one more time. Upon his arrival in New York, Sean retrieved his bags and took a cab to Jack's apartment. Jack was away, and the clerk at the front desk knew of Sean's arrival and handed him the keys. The apartment was massive. Sean had expected a small apartment similar to those he designed for the new hotel in Detroit. But this was an older New York apartment building, obviously for the well-to-do in the 1930s. Lovely building, large foyer, vaulted ceilings and the vintage elevator. He loved the building.

Jack had obviously done very well for himself. He took a job with Swartz and Cooper Inc., the large accounting firm, and was promoted to being one of the managing partners, all in a space of five years.

Jack's apartment was full of antique treasures that he had collected after scouring the local antique shops and markets. Sean and Jack always shared a passion for anything old, especially when it came to anything about ancient Egypt or Greece. Sean, being an architect, had scores of books on Egyptian and Greek architecture and was always fascinated by how they could construct such massive and beautiful buildings with the limited technology they had. *Maybe one day I'll see them for myself,* he thought.

Sean contacted Jack and said that he would take a walk until Jack returned at five p.m. *Walking in New York is so different than in Crystal Falls. The buildings are so tall, the streets are always crowded, and the traffic never seems to move. What a place.*

He stopped for a bite to eat at a smoked meat sandwich outlet. *Boy, was it good? I guess if you only made one thing, it had better be the best, and it was the best smoked meat sandwich with a garlic dill pickle he had ever had. I can't even make one this good at home,* he thought.

Jack met up with Sean at five-thirty p.m. Jack was a big, burly, lovable guy who loved his life in New York and everything it had to offer. They went out for dinner at a restaurant across from Jack's building. It was an original 1950s diner that likely had not had a facelift in thirty years. The charm of the old diner amazed Sean. While you sat there, you could imagine the hot rodders and their girlfriends coming in for a soda in the 1950s. And because of this charm, the place was packed.

"I bet they must have a staff of forty people working here. Look how busy the takeout section is, and they must have six waitresses. What a place. Certainly puts to shame the restaurants in Crystal Falls, Michigan." Laughed Sean.

They chatted and caught up on old times as children. Jack talked glowingly of the times he would visit Sean in Crystal Falls and work on the farm.

"Those were good days," he said.

Sean agreed. The topic did eventually come around to his recent split with Jennifer. Jack had met her once on a business trip to Detroit, where they met up for dinner. He was sure that Sean and Jennifer would be getting married. *How wrong I was, though, Jack.*

"I don't think the quiet life of Crystal Falls and maybe getting married to a boring architect appealed to her any more," replied Sean. "She has a friend who is an airline stewardess, and she got her a job. Now she flies everywhere and has no time for me. I guess flying around the world for free is a lot better than living with me in Crystal Falls."

"To bad. I know some ladies I could introduce you to," said Jack.

"Please, Jack, no," replied Sean. I'm not ready to meet anyone else and would just like to chill out in New York if that's all right with you."

"No problem," replied Jack. "Keep the key you have and use my apartment as your home base. Now that my girlfriend, Nancy, has left and moved away, like you, the only thing I seem to do is work. Come and go whenever you want, and don't worry about me. I just found out that I still have work to do on a project I thought was finished a week ago. Clients, always changing their minds."

"Yeah, I know what you mean," said Sean. "In architecture, the clients phone every day thinking that you can design a new building in your sleep. I now have it that the clients cannot phone me directly, and the office relays their concerns to me via email. From home, I can work in peace, don't have to get involved in the office politics, and can address the client's concerns on my own time. Certainly, works for me."

So, Sean spent the next week relaxing and exploring New York as only a tourist can. He visited all the buildings and fell in love with the architecture of the Empire State Building. How this building was erected in 1930 amazed him. He had the famous photo of the workers building the Empire State Building all sitting on a beam, hundreds of feet above the ground, on his wall. *How can anyone be so unafraid of such heights?* he thought.

He marveled that in New York there is so much to see and do. He made a point of visiting a museum or art gallery every day. *Wonderful,* he thought. Plus, who needs a car in New York? Everyone takes a cab. Even Jack, who could well afford a car, doesn't own one and prefers to cab everywhere. Jack would always say that if he needed a car, the rental car companies, for a slight surcharge, would pick you up and take you back to their office. Then, when you returned the car, they would drive you home. Couldn't beat that. And Jack, being an accountant, would say, "And all my car rentals are paid for by my company what a deal."

So a pleasant week went by. Jack and Sean would meet for dinner at a different restaurant every night.

"Is there nothing but restaurants in New York?" asked Sean.

"Very few people prepare their own food in New York. It's just so easy to go out. Saves going to a grocery store, carting the food home, and then storing it in your kitchen. Plus, it saves on doing the dishes." Laughed Jack.

"What a different life you lead from mine. I'm a country hayseed architect living in the backwoods of Michigan, and you live here in the big smoke," stated Sean.

Sotheby's Auction

The spring day was bright and cheery. This has been so much fun living in my cousin's apartment in downtown Manhattan, thought Sean. *There are more people in one square block here than in the entire countryside around Crystal Falls, Michigan.*

Sean told his cousin Jack, "I've been here for one week now and haven't really bought anything to get excited about. You have lots here, and I've tried the antique stores and vendor markets, but everything I see I can buy cheaper in Michigan. Nothing really grabs me."

"Maybe this is what you should be looking at," said Jack. "There is a Sotheby's auction coming up in three days with artifacts from the collection of Jean-Baptiste Prosper Jollois (family), who was the chief engineer in Napoleon's "Egyptian Scientific Expedition" in 1798. Here, use my laptop and look it up."

"This looks really cool. It doesn't seem to have any ancient Egyptian artifacts, though, just things from the savants who went on the expedition," replied Sean.

Jack replied, "That is because, if I remember my history right, that's around the time of the Seven Years' War between England and France. Napoleon's Navy was defeated and sunk in the Battle of the Nile in 1798, and the troops were left stranded in Egypt. They fought on but were eventually defeated by the combined British and native Mamluk forces and surrendered by signing the "Convention of El Arish".

"Then, besides having to hand over all of their weapons, the British forced the French savants or scientists to hand over all of their ancient Egyptian artifacts before they would ferry them back to France. Remember, the French Navy lay at the bottom of the sea, and the French had no other way of getting home; they were stranded.

"If I'm also correct, all the artifacts the British confiscated were then taken and set up in the British Museum, which started the entire Egypt-mania craze in the early 1800s.

"The famous Rosetta Stone was one of these artifacts taken by the British. It was an ancient proclamation written in three languages: Egyptian hieroglyphics, Egyptian demotic script, and ancient Greek. From this, the French linguist Jean Francois Champollion, using clay impressions of the inscriptions, spent years working on and finally deciphered the hieroglyphics."

"Wow, you really know your stuff. How come you know so much about it? asked Sean.

"When I went to school in England, I lived near the museum that housed the Egyptian exhibits and would frequent it often. Plus, we learned about the British and French Seven Years' War and the sinking of the French fleet in 1798 by Lord Nelson. The British have almost made Lord Nelson into a saint, so you always heard a lot about him." Smiled Jack.

That night, Sean studied the fascinating photos of the upcoming Sotheby's auction. *This is the real deal,* he thought. The Wednesday before the auction, Sotheby's was open for a preview. He woke up early and took a cab to the auction hall. Getting there early, he only had to stand in line for twenty minutes before he and the other first twenty people were allowed in. What an interesting group of visitors! Some were dressed up, and many were in just casual wear. New York is so different from Crystal Falls.

All the artifacts were cleanly laid out with descriptive cards explaining what each item was and, where possible, to whom it belonged. Here you could see a factual description of the item, an explanation of its use, and who owned it, along with their name and position in the expedition.

There was everything from the French Expedition: canteens, mess kits, medical supplies, drafting supplies, you name it. Everything was collected by the Jollois family for the past two-hundred years to honor their relative, Jean-Baptiste Prosper Jollois, of the Egyptian Scientific Expedition. It was amazing how much was here. But like Jack said, there were no Egyptian artifacts to be found. Likely, even if there were, they would have had to be returned to the authorities in Egypt anyway.

Sean then found something he liked. It was an antique writing desk top that was about 20" wide, 13" deep, and about 7" inches high. This would have been used by one of the savants to write their notes. In the world of antiques, such writing desktops have little function and can be found in any antique store. But this one stood out. There in the front was a brass plaque…

Francois Lebelle
Engineer
Member of General Napoleon Bonaparte's
Egyptian Scientific Expedition
1798 to 1801

Sean thought, *Looks authentic to me, and besides, Sotheby's guarantees the authenticity of the items they sell, so I don't think it's a forgery.* As this was the only thing that caught his eye, Sean left the auction hall, trying to figure out what such an item would sell for.

On the day of the auction, Jack, having never attended a live auction before, said that he was coming along. Jack called the head office of the auction house to talk to Tana Toffler, the Secretary Treasurer of Sotheby's. Tana was a petite, intelligent person who basically ran everything at Sotheby's. As Jack's firm did all the major accounting work for Sotheby's, he got to know Tana very well and even went out on a few dates together.

"Tana, it's Jack Alair over at Swartz and Cooper. How are you?" asked Jack.

"Great, Jack. Good to hear from you. You're not calling me to take me to another terrible New York Rangers game, are you? Every time I go, they lose, and the last time it was six to two against Toronto. I must be a jinx or something."

"Yes, I would love to take you to another game, but no, that's not why I'm calling. I need a favor," asked Jack.

"Sure, Jack, what can I do for you?" replied Tana.

"My cousin Sean is down from Michigan, and we were hoping we could get some seats for the Egyptian Expedition auction you are having today?" asked Jack.

"No problem. I'll call down to the reception and put you and Sean's names on the list. When you arrive, tell them you're a friend of mine, and they'll sit you up at the front, where all the action is," replied Tana.

"Thanks, Tana. I really appreciate it," replied Jack.

"No problem, enjoy the auction and spend lots of money," said Tana, and she hung up.

Excited, both Sean and Jack showed up thirty minutes early in order to get a good seat.

"Will be interesting to see what everything goes for," stated Jack. He was fascinated and said he could feel the excitement in the crowd. Sean, on the other hand, attended plenty of his hometown country auctions, so he had a better idea of what to expect.

After Sean registered and gave his bidders information, he and Jack were approached by a Sotheby's employee.

"Excuse me, are you Jack Alair, friends of Tana's upstairs?" asked the gentleman.

"Yes, we are," replied Jack.

"Great, follow me. Tana called me and said you were coming and to seat you both near the front. She signs my checks, so I have to be nice to her." Smiled the gentleman.

Now seated in two seats, three rows from the front. Sean said to Jack, "Good deal, thanks for calling your friend."

"Are you kidding, Sean. This is so exciting. I'm really happy I came along," said Jack.

At exactly ten a.m., the auctioneer introduced himself and thanked the people for coming to today's auction. He went on to explain a little about Napoleon's Egyptian Scientific Expedition and that the artifacts returned started the entire Egypt-mania craze of the early 1800s. Then he started the bidding.

The bidding was done logically, starting with artifacts from known members of Napoleon's expedition. There was a considerable amount from the Jollois collection whose family was hosting this auction. After his artifacts were sold, the auctioneer moved on to other items that were associated with lesser-known members of the expedition. About halfway through the auction, the writing desk that Sean liked appeared.

"Here we have a writing desk from the savant Francois Lebelle, stated the auctioneer. "The brass plaque inscription on the front reads...

Francois Lebelle
Engineer
Member of General Napoleon Bonaparte's
Egyptian Scientific Expedition
1798 to 1801

The helper then showed the audience the box, opened it, and showed the writing compartments inside.

"Just a regular writing desk, all except for the brass plaque," Sean whispered to Jack.

The auctioneer offered the writing desk for five hundred dollars but the first bid was only two hundred dollars. Sean waited and jumped in once the auctioneer said $250 and the bidding was on. It proceeded in by increments of fifty dollars until the other bidder slowed down to a final bid of seven hundred dollars. The skilled auctioneer egged the bidder on, and he raised his hand for the seven hundred dollars bid, and Sean quickly replied with the $750 bid. Trying to get a bid of eight hundred dollars the other bidder shook his head and declined. The other bidder was done. The antique writing desk was now Sean's.

Jack was amazed that Sean would pay so much.

"Even with the buyer's premium and sales tax, I got this box for about one thousand dollars, a bargain. It's the only thing that really caught my eye. Now I have a great souvenir of my trip to New York," Sean replied.

After paying, Sean was handed the box and motioned to a table consisting of boxes, bags, and wrapping paper. After carefully wrapping his find, they journeyed back to Jack's apartment. Once inside, Sean removed the box, and they both inspected it carefully.

"What a find! An actual two-hundred-year-old artifact from General Napoleon's Egyptian Expedition I will cherish this forever," explained Sean.

Little more was said about the box, and for the next few days, Sean continued to visit museums, art galleries, and antique shops. The architecture of New York continued to fascinate him. *These buildings are even far more impressive than the ones in Detroit, and I thought they were big,* Sean thought to himself.

On his day of departure, Sean and Jack said goodbye with the promise to do this again.

"Maybe I'll take some time off and visit you in Crystal Falls," said Jack.

"Please do so. The house is so empty ever since Jennifer left. I could use the company," stated Sean.

They hugged as longtime cousins do, and Sean got in the cab.

Chapter 5
Back Home in Crystal Falls, Michigan

Now back home, Sean immediately began reviewing the plans for the new office tower in Hawaii. The associate architects were doing a splendid job, and everything was to Sean's liking. He sent off complimentary emails to his associates, telling them how proud he was of their work. The plans should be finished by the end of the month.

He liked the way that Hillsborough and Smith, Inc. did business. They refused to take on additional projects until the present ones were finished. Sean had friends that worked for other architectural firms and knew those firms would take on new projects all the while the building they were already working on was not finished. The company would switch all the top-level architects working on the present project and put them on the new one. This left the completion of the present project to fall on the new, less experienced architects. This, Sean felt, always resulted in shabby work and several lawsuits. Best to stay on one project at a time until it's finished.

Sean continued to fine-tune the new office tower in Hawaii. *Millions of dollars already spent, and they haven't decided on a name for it yet. Amazing!*

The house was lonely, so Sean thought of his pleasant trip to New York with Jack.

With these thoughts in mind, he took "Francois's writing desk" off the shelf by the fireplace and examined it. To think that this box was in Egypt with Napoleon, what stories it could tell. I wonder whatever happened to the owner. He tried looking up "Francois Lebelle, a French civil engineer" on the internet under several searches but to no avail. Just a minor-level engineer on the expedition.

He read and reread the brass plaque,

Francois Lebelle
Engineer

Member of General Napoleon Bonaparte's
Egyptian Scientific Expedition
1798 to 1801

As he always enjoyed reading about Egypt, Sean started reading about Napoleon's ill-fated Egyptian military campaign. More interesting was the success of the scientific expedition ordered by Napoleon to find out everything about Egypt. *To be one of the savants on this expedition would have been the adventure of a lifetime. To be there in the early 1800s before the influence of the western world corrupted their culture must have been fabulous. What sights they would have seen?* He loved the painting of Napoleon on horseback before the exposed head of the Great Sphinx. *Incredible.*

He enjoyed looking at the writing desk with the brass plaque proudly displayed. Whenever guests arrived, they were all invited to look at it, as this quickly became Sean's most prized possession. As a tribute to his late father, Walter, he kept his dad's wristwatch, pens, and a few more of his dad's precious items in the box.

Weeks later, after the final completion of the plans for the Hawaii project, Sean went to the office and went out with the other architects for a meal and drinks.

"To the completion of the now still-unnamed Hawaii office tower. My congratulations to you all. Upon completion, the building will be a marvel and talked about by every firm around the world. Our insistence on using as much natural light as possible and putting gardens on every floor has delighted the future owners of the building. I hope so; they've already paid us for the plans." Laughed Sean.

Everyone laughed. Sean sat down and enjoyed the rest of the evening with his co-workers. He decided to drive home that night, so he limited himself to only two drinks. *Best not to get arrested tonight; I like my new Lexus.*

On his drive home, he thought that his life was about as good as it could get, but he still missed having a companion around. *Oh well, maybe one day. Must join a health club or something to meet people. I'll wither and die in Crystal Falls all alone unless I meet someone.*

Sitting in the living room in front of a roaring fire, with the brandy bottle beside him, he congratulated himself and progressively got more intoxicated. *Ah, who cares? I'm home here all alone, in the middle of nowhere. Who cares how much I drink?*

Sean's eyes went to the writing desk and the brass plaque. *How cool it is!* He got up to examine the box.

Sean Finds the Papyrus

With the box in hand and sitting down, Sean stubbed his toe on the coffee table, and the writing desk went flying and landed on the floor. *Oh, no, what an idiot! I'm drunk,* he thought as he bent down to retrieve the box. *Oh great, I broke it, and the bottom has come loose. I'll have to take it to an antique repair shop and have it looked after. Stupid me, it's my own fault.*

Sitting with the box on his lap, he examined the damage. Even in his drunken stupor, he could see where the bottom had detached from the sides. The box had an opening, and there seemed to be something inside. Drunk as he was, he still took out his pen knife and opened the bottom. He could see some material inside, so he proceeded with opening the bottom.

He carefully removed the pages within. Here in his hands were twelve sheets of papyrus covered with Egyptian hieroglyphics. *What a cool find,* he thought. Thinking that they had little value or were fakes, he placed these papyri in the main section of the box and returned them to the shelf. Then he went to bed.

He consumed himself in his work on some new office tower designs he was thinking about. He was trying to figure out a way to place mirrors either on the top or on the outside of the building to ensure the natural light fell on all sides of a building at once. He had mentioned his ideas to his superiors, and they approved of his "brainstorming new ideas".

Taking a break from his work, he sat with a coffee in the main room. His eyes caught the writing desk and brass plaque. He retrieved it and examined the damaged bottom. After carefully removing his dad's personal effects, he then removed the old papyrus. Sean carefully put each sheet into a plastic page protector and taped them up. He had twelve papyrus pages of about 5" wide by 10" high. While in the page protector, he could examine both sides of the papyrus without having to actually handle the frail papyrus itself. Seeing no page numbers or any other identification, he numbered each page protector from 1–12, in the order that they were stacked in the box.

Pretty cool, probably an ancient formula for making home-brewed beer. But the ancient hieroglyphics intrigued him. Wonder what it means? For the next couple of hours, he read up everything he could about reading this ancient Egyptian language.

Deciphering the Hieroglyphics

Researching the internet, Wikipedia, the online encyclopedia, told him…

"Hieroglyphics are written in columns or in horizontal lines. They are generally read from right to left and from top to bottom. Sometimes the script is read from left to right. The reader can determine the orientation by looking at the animal and human figures, they face toward the beginning of the text. For example, if a figure faces right, the text should be read from right to left."

He also discovered…

"In AD 391, the Byzantine Emperor Theodosius 1st closed all pagan temples throughout the empire. This action terminated a four-thousand-year-old tradition, and the message of the ancient Egyptian language was lost for 1500 years.

"It was until the discovery of the Rosetta Stone and the work of Jean Francois Champollion (1790–1832) that the Ancient Egyptians awoke from their long slumber."

Sean thought, *Wouldn't it be cool to see what these pages mean? A message from the ancients.* He set about photocopying both sides of the papyrus, which left him with twenty-four clear copies of the hieroglyphs to decipher. He sat down and, using the internet, was able to start to make out certain symbols and words. *At least I have something other than buildings to occupy my mind.*

For the next four months, Sean enjoyed the relaxation of looking up the meanings of the hieroglyphic text. Little made sense. The symbols inside an oblong circle with a line underneath represented someone's name, so this is where he tried to start. *But it's like a jigsaw puzzle. Everything looks scrambled until you put in the last piece.*

After months of work, this is what he had deciphered from the first papyrus:

"I am Nebwenenef, high priest of Amun, servant to the great
Pharaoh Ramesses II. It is I who have been chosen to
guard the secrets of Osiris, god of the underworld, and
Imhotep, Sankh, one who gives life.

Oh, Imhotep, son of the great god Ptah, servant of the First Great
Pharaoh Djoser, allow me to follow your wisdom. Bring forth the
knowledge of mathematics and build the great pyramids to honor the gods.
Allow me to honor your wisdom and virtue. May the light you have shone
upon the world forever remain bright.

To the future guardians of these papyrus, yours is a sworn and sacred
trust.

I lay before you the secrets of the ancient gods. Here within lies the
secrets of long life. This may never be used except in the honor of the gods
themselves, the Pharaohs. No one else must know about these secrets, for
only gods can continue on with their lives."

Wow, this is pretty heavy stuff, thought Sean, *and I thought it would be
a beer recipe.* Little by little, Sean became able to understand the ancient
writings better, and he spent more and more time deciphering the
hieroglyphics. He tried in vain to limit himself to only one hour per day, but
the more he uncovered, the more it made him eager for more.

The Ancient Secret of Osiris and Imhotep

Then, after another three months, the text was complete.

"To prepare the secret of Osiris, god of the underworld, and Imhotep,
Sankh, one who brings life, you must have a long list of ingredients."

These were all foreign to Sean. *Maybe these are ancient names for
common things we have today.* The rest of the text told of preparation of the
chemicals and how long it had to sit to be effective. The next several pages
went on to describe how to administer the chemicals to the awaiting
Pharaoh or a member of his immediate family.

"The Pharaoh god to receive the secrets of Osiris and Imhotep must be
locked up in a room with only water to drink and no food and be alone for
two days. They must be then properly bathed in water and rubbed down
with olive oil. They are to be covered in a clean white cloth and lay flat
while the formula is placed in the back of their mouths.

"Now they must be taken to a room with no windows that has been washed. Here they are to remain locked in for two days with only bread to eat and water to drink. They are to see no one and talk to no one. It is how they can humble themselves and communicate with the god Osiris, the god of the underworld. Only Osiris, the god of the underworld, has the power to restore youth and prolong life. If chosen, Osiris will bless them with a longer life.

"After these two days of penance, they are permitted to leave. And if Osiris so wills it, they will have forfeited all their body hair as a testament to the gods, and they will be a younger version of yourself from an earlier time."

This is certainly heavy stuff, thought Sean. He thought of this for a while. *Maybe there is something here. The ancients had medicines that we are only learning about today. And what does "they will be a younger version of yourself, from an earlier time" mean?*

Chapter 6
The Experiment

Over the next two months, Sean did his best to research the names of the ingredients listed on the papyrus. The instructions on what to do with them seemed clear enough; he just didn't know what to get. He consulted historians and museums to find out what they knew about specific items mentioned on the list. After months of research, he ordered a number of the ingredients directly from sellers in the Middle East.

Finally, he was ready to experiment with the secrets of Imhotep.

The instructions were clear: the individual must fast for two days in a windowless room by themselves, then be shaved of body hair, washed, and then rubbed down with olive oil before administering the formula. Then they were to be put in a room with only bread to eat and water to drink for another two days. *But what does it all mean?* thought Sean.

Experiment #1: Walter, The Hairless Cat

Sean made the decision to follow the instructions on the papyrus and see what happens. But first, he needed a subject. He remembered enjoying the old black-and-white Frankenstein movies where Dr. Frankenstein was faced with the same problem. But Dr. Frankenstein needed dead bodies, and Sean needed one living creature with no hair. And one that wouldn't object or talk later.

After searching his brains for the types of animals he could use, almost all would object to having all their hair or fur removed. He thought of using a sea mammal, but keeping them alive in an aquarium would just be too much work. Then it finally dawned on him—a hairless cat. He once saw one at a friend's place in Dearborn and thought it was the weirdest cat he had ever seen. But wisely, he kept his opinion to himself. *No problem. I'll just buy one of those cats.*

The next day, he called around to the various animal shelters, and there was a hairless cat available for him. Cost: $150.

"No problem," he told the attendant. "I'll be right over. My name is Sean Little, and please hold the cat for me."

It was a short thirty-minute drive to the animal shelter, and there, in a cage, sat a hairless cat. Sean paid the lady, and when she handed the cat to him, she called the cat a "Sphinx Cat." He should have asked about the name, but he was so excited that he forgot.

The new cat he named Walter, after his dad, Walter was certainly friendly enough and took to Sean immediately. He stopped on the way home and bought some quality cat food and cat litter. That should do it.

Doing his best to follow the ancient instructions, Sean fed the cat very well over the next several days, and then stopped and placed Walter in a spare bedroom for the required two-day fast. He fed the cat all the water it needed—just no food. On the prescribed day, Sean removed the cat, washed it down completely with soap and water, and once dry, rubbed Walter down with olive oil.

And just like Frankenstein, he thought, he strapped Walter to a table to the point he could not move. *Walter took this all in good humor, likely because he's hoping that I will eventually feed him again,* thought Sean. Having made up the formula in advance, Sean did his best to figure out the small dosage that a cat would need as compared to a human. Calculations complete, he used an eyedropper to place one small drop of formula in the back of Walter's throat.

Nothing happened. He excused himself from Walter, and when he returned, still nothing. Wouldn't you know it? *All this work for a practical joke,* thought Sean. But as stated in the papyrus, he locked up Walter in a clean, sealed, windowless room and left him there "with only bread to eat and water to drink" for an additional two days.

Feeling guilty, Sean always made sure that Walter had enough bread and water. Then, at the end of the second day, Sean retrieved Walter from the room. He looked different somehow. Sean placed a bowl with some luxury cat food and milk for Walter, which he was happy to consume. As Sean watched Walter eat, he was convinced that this was not the same cat he had purchased about a week ago. *This cat seemed more agile and eager. Even its face seemed happier. What was this change?*

Walter was also more affectionate. He would enjoy rubbing himself up against Sean's leg and sitting on his lap. *Doesn't seem to be any side effects.* Then, looking at Walter, Sean realized… he has no hair! He held Walter up, and there was no hair, no hair anywhere. The soft, peach-like fuzz that all hairless cats have was all gone. He went to the room where Walter had resided for two days after receiving the formula and got down on his hands and knees. There it was. Walter's peach fuzz hair, still covered in olive oil, was all over the room. *Strange side effect, but Walter seems okay.*

Experiment #2: Alex, the Cat

He worked for a few more days on his new designs and waited to see if there were any changes in Walter. Nothing, just the same affectionate cat, but totally without hair.

Best to make sure. He called up the same animal shelter and explained that he needed a companion for Walter.

"Sure," the lady said, "we have plenty of cats, and seeing that you paid so much for your first cat, your next one is free. Come on down."

While at the animal shelter, he selected a nice cat that seemed to be quite docile.

Better get one that won't run away. He thanked the lady and left. No problem with the new cat, it just sat on the passenger seat and fell asleep.

He decided to follow Walter's original routine with the new cat. For the next several days, Sean fed both cats really well. *Yeah, that will do it. I'll call him Alex.* Sean said to himself. He picked up Alex and placed him in the spare bedroom. Here, Alex would fast for two days, as prescribed in the papyrus. At the end of the two days, Sean picked up Alex, washed him down with soap and water, and then rubbed him down with olive oil. *Must do this exactly the same as I did with Walter, or I'll never be sure,* he continued to tell himself.

Sean took Alex over to the table and strapped him down. Alex was not very excited about the prospect of being tied down, but he accepted it soon enough. Now tightly secured on the table, Sean administered the same dosage of potion that he had given to Walter. *So far, so good.*

He unstrapped Alex, picked him up, took him to the small room with no windows, and deposited Alex there. Sean had already laid out bread and water as prescribed. *Wonder what will happen next.* Two days passed, and he continued to bring Alex bread and water. No change, nothing.

Now, when Sean went to retrieve Alex, there was the cat, totally naked of any hair. *Must have just happened in the last couple of hours.* There was cat hair covered in olive oil all over the carpet. When Alex spotted Sean, he came running over and rubbed himself on his leg. Sean picked up Alex and Alex seemed a little more affectionate and cuddly. *Just like Walter, Alex seems happy and content. What is going on here?*

Sean kept an eye on both cats over the next few days. They became great friends. Surprisingly, Alex, who had originally taken no interest in the house mice, was chasing them and catching them. *Strange,* Sean thought, *when he first came here, he didn't have the energy or the desire to chase mice. Now he catches them, no problem.*

Experiment #3 Terry, the Dog

Best to try again. He decided on getting a dog this time, but from another animal shelter so as not to arouse suspicion. He called around and found one that had several dogs for him. After a forty-five-minute drive, he arrived. Viewing the dogs, he noticed a small older dog that looked like he didn't have many days left. He asked the attendant, and he said, "We have had that dog for months and nobody wants him. We will likely have to put him down." The attendant handed the small dog to Sean, and the old dog cuddled in his arms.

"I'll take this one." The sign on the wall said small dogs twenty dollars so Sean paid and left.

The new dog certainly seemed friendly enough, but he's old and has no energy. At least I'll feed him well and make his remaining days pleasant and enjoyable.

On his way home, he bought the best dog food he could find, telling himself he's going to allow the new dog to feast tonight.

Fortunately, both Walter and Alex didn't seem to be bothered by the new dog. *I need a name. I'll call him Terry, Terry the dog,* Sean muttered to himself. He let Terry have the run of the house, but being old, he didn't wander much. Sean checked his notes and was determined to follow the same routine that he had for Walter and Alex.

After days of Terry getting accustomed to his new surroundings and good meals, Sean picked him up and placed him in the spare bedroom. And just like the cats, Terry fasted in this room with only water to drink.

"Sorry, Terry, this is what I have to do," Sean said as he closed the bedroom door. And as with the cats, he laid down the newspaper, hoping that Terry had been potty trained.

At the end of Terry's fast, Sean picked him up and gave him a good bath with soap and water. Once dry, he rubbed Terry down with olive oil as prescribed. *Probably feels weird on a dog, but I have to do it.* Sean took Terry to the table and secured him down. Terry, being docile, didn't fuss much. With the cats and Terry being about the same size, Sean administered the same dosage of formula to Terry as he had with the others. Done.

Sean carried Terry over to the small, clean room without any windows. He laid out newspapers for him. Sean placed plenty of bread and water for him, and as with the others, he felt guilty about having to leave him there.

When bringing in more bread and water, Terry seemed to be okay. At the end of the second day, Sean went to fetch Terry. There was Terry, running around the room as if he was high on drugs. Terry had no fur, no hair, and nothing. *Wow, this is weird.* Terry's fur lay scattered all around the room, but that was not the strange part. Terry was probably excited about being allowed out, so he had a brief spell of excitement. No, Terry was now a new dog, running around the house and playfully chasing the cats. You could even tell that the cats were annoyed. Here was this old, docile little dog that barely moved, and now a couple of days later is a seemingly younger dog full of energy.

Sean picked up Terry to examine him. *Seemed okay, but just so much more energy. Almost seems like he has a new lease on life. Okay, this will probably wear off in a few days, and I'll get my lethargic dog back.* No. Terry had come alive, and there was no diminishing of his enthusiasm for running and playing.

Sean observed the three pets over the next two weeks. All seemed happy to be there, and they even began to enjoy each other's company. The cats continued to catch mice, so he didn't have a problem with that. *We have lots of mice.* He did observe that Alex's hair was starting to grow back. And then he noticed that Terry's hair was starting to grow back. He looked at Walter, the hairless cat, and because the hair was so fine, it's hard to tell, but yes, the peach fuzz hair was coming back. *Strange, there is really something going on here.*

Hillsborough and Smith, Inc.

Working day and night on his designs while attending to his pets, Sean produced some interesting designs for some environmentally friendly buildings. He decided that he would take his designs to the office and show them off. He called and said that he would be coming in tomorrow.

Arriving at the office, the senior partners greeted him at the door.

"We are all very excited to see the new designs," stated Roger Hillsborough, founder of the firm. Roger was an interesting fellow. In his late 50s. Roger was a tall, athletic African-American ex-military architect who started his own firm soon after leaving the service. He did try working for other firms but was fed up with just designing regular square-block office towers. His superiors thought his ideas of environmentally friendly buildings were just too radical for them, so he quit and formed his own firm with his friend Harold Smith, also a 50ish African American, ex-military architect.

Their business really took off after they hired new talent like Sean Little, who had a flair for designing visually pleasing and environmentally friendly office buildings. With Sean as their chief architect, Hillsborough and Smith Inc. were now in the forefront of environmentally pleasing office architecture, and Roger wanted it to stay there. So according to him, anything that Sean wanted, Sean got.

Besides, Roger and Harold had a weakness for owning and driving expensive automobiles, and whatever they could charge for Sean's designs, they could buy all the cars they wanted. Roger was so proud of his new Mercedes GLS SUV that he was anxious to show it off to Sean. Roger was always fond of saying, "Well, I can't trade in my wife, but I can get a new car every six months; that's okay," he would say with a smile. Even Roger's and Harold's wives took their husbands obsession with owning new cars with good humor.

"At least I know where they are all the time; they're either in the office or out looking at new cars," both would always say with a laugh.

With some idle chitchat out of the way, all the managers went into the boardroom, and Sean laid out his large folder. After coffee and some more idle chitchat, Sean opened his folder and produced the designs.

"Sean, this is great stuff. Once we figure out how to logically reflect the sunlight to the dark side of a building, we will revolutionize office building structures for generations to come. Fabulous," stated Roger and all the others in attendance concurred.

"How did you come up with such innovative ideas? Being home is good for you and for us," mentioned others.

"That's an interesting idea. What would you say if I relinquished my office and just continued to work from home? Obviously, I do my best work there. What do you say?" Sean stated.

"That's interesting," stated Roger, "we have been looking at your empty office for weeks now and could use the space to house our new architects. We didn't want to say anything for fear of upsetting you, but you can work from home from now on. If we need you, we'll just call. Please drop in once in a while so that we can remember what you look like." Everyone laughed.

Sean proceeded to clean out a few personal items and architectural awards from his desk. After putting them in his Lexus, Roger insisted that Sean and two other managers come with him in his new Mercedes and go out for lunch.

"Sean, how have you been keeping yourself busy out in Crystal Falls? asked a new manager at the firm.

"Oh, you know, when not working on my designs, I've taken up the hobby of trying to fix up the old farm. I have no intentions of moving, so I might as well dress it up the way I like it," replied Sean.

Everyone nodded. Some thought how lucky he was, and likely some others thought he was nuts for wanting to live by himself in the middle of nowhere. Once he left, Sean thought that the plans he left would keep them occupied for months.

Upon arriving home, all his pets were glad to see him. At least somebody loves me, and they cut down on my loneliness. Their loss of hair Sean could understand, but not their increase in energy. They seem like brand new pets, running around and enjoying life. Best to try again.

Experiment #4: Bruno, the Labrador Retriever

Freed from having to show up at work, he could continue on with his experiments. He called the animal shelter where he had picked up his last dog, Terry. Yes, they had a wonderful and quiet Labrador Retriever that he could have for $40.00. He said he'd be right over. The dog was big and old and seemed friendly enough.

"Great, I'll take him," said Sean. He paid and left with his new dog, Bruno.

Labradors are a friendly breed and will enjoy himself around the farm. I just hope the others accept him. If not, I'll have to keep him in the barn, thought Sean. Upon arriving home, the other pets pretty much ignored Bruno. They took no offense to him, and he took no offense to them. *Prefect,* thought Sean.

Sean had plenty of pet food and fed all his pets well. Bruno seemed very content with his new surroundings, and after taking a run of the place, he picked out a nice corner by the fireplace to lay down. Sean got him some blankets, and after a few pet hugs, Bruno went to sleep.

With Bruno, the same procedure was followed. After a number of days of feeding him well, Sean placed Bruno in the spare bedroom with only water to drink. Obviously coming from a kennel, Bruno was accustomed to being shut in.

"It's only for two days," assured Sean.

Then, when the required two days were up, Sean retrieved Bruno and gave him a good bath. Once dry, he rubbed him down with olive oil. This seemed to bother Bruno at first, but he eventually settled down.

Then Sean picked up Bruno and placed him on the table. He was a little more difficult to strap down, but Sean finally managed to attach the straps. Sean, measuring for a larger dog than his previous experiments, gave Bruno about four times the potion that he had given to the others. Now complete, Sean unstrapped Bruno and carried him over to the room with no windows. He placed plenty of bread and water for Bruno.

Sean would check up on Bruno and refill his trays with more bread and water. Being a larger dog, Sean would come in regularly and clean up after him. *No change. Maybe the formula only works on smaller animals,* Sean thought.

At the end of the second day, Sean went to get Bruno. there was Bruno, jumping up and down, all smiles, and not a single hair on his body. *How weird,* thought Sean. Being a big dog, there was oily dog hair everywhere.

Bruno was excited to be out and devoured the good meal that Sean laid out for him. *I guess it's just like getting out of prison, isn't it?* But like the others, Bruno was now a changed dog. Sean waited for the excitement of being free to wear off, but it didn't.

This seemingly docile dog was alive and full of energy. Sean let him and Terry, the little dog, outside together, and they both went nuts. Running, playing, and chasing everything that moved. Bruno liked chasing the birds and would jump into the air to try and catch them. *This is incredible. They seem to have a new lease on life. Their energy is boundless.*

He kept accurate notes on all his pets and their progress. Yes, their hair started to grow back, and he eventually noticed that Bruno's hair was also coming back. This went on for the next month as he let the pets have the run of the house. They all seemed to tolerate each other, so leaving them alone didn't seem to be a problem. He also noticed that their appetites had improved, and he was buying far more pet food. *Well, I guess they need something to help them burn off all that energy.*

After a month, there was no change. The pets all enjoyed going outside: the cats to chase and catch more mice, and the dogs to just run around and be silly. *Everybody seems to be enjoying themselves.*

Chapter 7
Taking on a Partner

After four experiments, Sean knew he was on to something. The animal's loss of hair was secondary to their incredible increase in energy. Even after two months, they still seemed healthy and full of life, and their hair was growing back just fine. It's like he transformed these docile animals into younger versions of themselves. Just to be on the safe side, he took them all to a vet, and she reported that all the animals were in perfect health.

Maybe this formula is a miracle "age reducer, energy enhancer" drug that I could patent and make millions. Isn't that how Viagra started? The chemist was trying to produce a heart drug, only to find that the test subjects would not hand over the rest of their pills. It not only helped their heart but also increased their sex drive and libido. Maybe, just maybe, this is like that.

This is too big for me to handle alone. I'll call Jack and see if he'd be interested in getting involved. Besides, Jack could handle all the business aspects, incorporation, and securing the patents. Seems like a logical fit. Sean called Jack at his office.

"Jack, I really enjoyed my stay with you a few months back," Sean said.

"It was pleasure having you down. Even though I live in the Big Apple, I get lonely sometimes, and your visit was a pleasure," said Jack.

"Jack, I've come across something really fantastic," explained Sean. "I can't explain it over the phone, and you wouldn't believe me anyway. I want you to get involved and come down and see for yourself. You will be amazed, I promise."

"Sean, if there's money to be made on it, I'm in." Laughed Jack.

"If I'm right, once patented, we will be richer than our wildest dreams. But you have to see for yourself. When can you come down?" asked Sean.

"If it was anyone else but you, I'd hang up. I've known you for a long time and never known you to exaggerate or get involved in wild goose chases. I have my work all caught up here, and as I have weeks of holidays saved up, I can be there next Monday," said Jack.

"Great, let me know when your flight arrives, and I will meet you at the airport. See you on Monday," said Sean.

Experiment #5: Andy, the German Sheppard

On Wednesday, Sean acquired another dog, an old German Shepard, from another animal shelter. This old dog was docile and would make a good fit with the rest of my pets. Likewise, he fed the new dog, Andy, well and kept him for Jack to see. Sean placed Andy in the spare bedroom for his two days fast. *Should be able to take Andy out when Jack arrives.*

Jack arrived on the Monday two-forty p.m. flight into Detroit, and Sean was there to greet him. Jack could tell that Sean was excited, but he remained tight-lipped about what he was going to show Jack. Back at the house, they tried to have small talk, but Sean was just too excited. Finally, Sean asked Jack to observe and not question. Sean removed Andy from the room and, like before, washed him thoroughly and rubbed him down with olive oil. Jack thought Sean had totally lost his mind, living alone in this farmhouse all by himself, but he kept his opinions to himself.

Jack was concerned when Sean placed Andy the German Sheppard on the table and strapped him down. He protested, but Sean again asked him to observe.

"I will not hurt him, I promise," said Sean.

After administering the formula, Sean picked up Andy and took him to the room with no windows. He laid out plates of bread and a bowl of water.

"That's all you're giving him after two days of starving the poor animal? protested Jack.

"Please, Jack, I must follow the instructions in the letter."

"Okay, it's your show, but I am starting to think you've lost your mind," replied Jack.

"Now, for the next two days, I feed him nothing but bread and water," said Sean.

Jack felt terrible about this, but Sean assured him that Andy was not being harmed. At the end of day two, Sean opened the door to retrieve Andy. There, like the others, was Andy, all smiles and jumping but totally devoid of hair.

"Wow! Great going, Sean. You've created a way to make animals bald when the real money is in trying to get them to grow their hair back. Lots of demand for "instant baldness" should be quite a hit." Laughed Jack.

For the next few days, they would sit and watch as Andy played, ran around, and playfully chased the other dogs. Sean tried to explain the increase in Andy's energy but as Jack had not seen the dog before, he remained unimpressed.

"You haven't shown me anything of value except in a way to guarantee instant baldness, and I'm sure it won't sell," said Jack.

Experiment #6 Rex: The Alaskan Malamute

"Okay, we'll do it your way. You get to select the next dog and follow me through the entire procedure," stated Sean.

Jack agreed, still totally believing that this idea had no commercial value whatsoever. The next day, they went to yet another animal shelter, and Jack picked them out a friendly older Alaskan Malamute that he named Rex. For the next five days, Jack helped Sean with the procedure, and he himself kept his own notes, just to be sure. When it came time to retrieve Rex from the windowless room, Jack stood in amazement. Here was Rex, as playful as a puppy but without any hair.

Likewise, Jack felt that Rex's enthusiasm for being released would quickly die down and he would return to being the big, slow dog from a few days ago. Rex continued to run around outside and chase the other dogs. None of the dogs exhibited any aggressive behavior and loved each other's company, but their energy was endless.

"This is amazing, said Jack. You would think that he was years younger; he's got so much energy. Let me stay for another week to find out."

"Great" replied Sean. I'm really enjoying having you around, and this project is far too much for me to handle."

So for the next week, Jack played with Rex every day. The dog had so much energy. This could not be the same dog I got from the shelter. But there he was, running and playing like a pup.

"Sean, we must keep this to ourselves," said Jack. "I don't know what you found or where you found it, but if we duplicate these tests in a lab and there are no adverse side effects and we patent it, we will be wealthy. But please appreciate that it will take years of clinical trials before being allowed to try it on a human subject, and then still more years before bringing it to market."

"Yes, I realize that. But don't you think this is fantastic? It's as if we've erased years from these animals' lives. Could you imagine if this were to work on humans? The idea of reversing the aging process sends goose bumps up and down my spine. We will have revolutionized medicine," said Sean.

Jack replied with, "I think I'm going to call you Ponce De'Leon. He was the Spanish conquistador who searched Florida for the fabled Fountain of Youth. Let's hope you found it."

Jack Returns to New York

Jack has trouble controlling his emotions. What he saw at Sean's farm amazed him. Could it be possible that Sean has stumbled upon what people have dreamed about since the beginning of time? Is there a way to reverse the aging process?

He returned to his office at Swartz and Cooper, Inc., and put his notice in for a leave of absence. As a managing partner, he had no problems but found it difficult to explain why he would be away. He implied that he had met a girl in Michigan, and they all nodded their heads in approval. With this explanation, the questions stopped.

Not knowing how long he would be away, he rerouted his mail to Sean's address. Who knows what will happen or how long I'll be away? I can incorporate a company while I am there and start researching the clinical trials right away. I have all the connections I need to get this ball rolling. He hurriedly packed his bags and left.

Back in Crystal Falls

Sean met him again at the airport. As Jack did not own a car, Sean said, "You can drive my dad's Buick anytime you want. It's in excellent shape with only a few miles on it."

"Great," said Jack.

Both Sean and Jack quickly decided that one more trial would have to take place. The next day, they returned to yet another animal shelter, and Jack selected an older Scottish collie. It seemed friendly enough.

Experiment #7-Kevin: The Scottish Collie

Back at the farm, they both followed Sean's written instructions to the letter. It was not hard to do as Sean had the instructions posted on the wall and made up into check sheets as they proceeded. They worked well together based on their friendship and trust from years of knowing each other as children.

But only Sean mixed the formula and applied it. As Jack was fond of saying, "I do the administration; you do the procedure. The less I know, the better." Because of this, Jack didn't want to know where this information came from and did not ask.

"Best that a secret always remains a secret." Jack would say.

Over the next few months, they did several experiments, all as successful as the first. Try as they might, they just couldn't find a flaw in the procedure or a negative consequence of the application. Yes, Kevin, the Scottish Collies's hair did fall out but quickly grew back. This was the only side effect that they could see.

All the animals acted as if they had been given a new lease on life. All of them loved being outside, with the cats chasing mice and the dogs running and simply enjoying themselves. Sean and Jack would sit in amazement at their energy. Would it ever stop? Their appetite was amazing, but what was one to expect? They spent their entire days playing outside.

Jack set about incorporating a company with both he and Sean being equal partners. He did insist upon putting in a clause that if one of the partners passed away, their share of the company would become the sole ownership of the surviving partner.

As both were healthy, they thought little of it.

Jack in Boston at Ralph Barns Laboratories

Now incorporated as Little and Alair Inc., Jack set about investigating and doing clinical trials. He contacted a former client of his who, along with other things, owned a laboratory testing facility in Boston. He spoke to Ralph Barns briefly and told him he would like to meet him to discuss some clinical trials on a new product he and his partner had developed. Jack declined to discuss it further over the phone, and they agreed that Jack would fly out to Boston and meet with Ralph and review the laboratory. Jack took Sean's dad's Buick out of the garage. *A beauty. Mr. Little obviously took very good care of this car. I'm glad I can borrow it.* He realized how special Sean's dad's car was to Sean, so he was touched by the offer.

He drove to the local airport and parked the Buick. The next day, Jack was in Boston. He loved Boston, which has so much history and a really good hockey team. But as there was work to do, he had no time for sight-seeing or going to a hockey game.

Jack checked into his hotel and contacted Ralph. Ralph came right over and took him to his research laboratory, Barns Laboratories Inc. just minutes from Jack's hotel. Ralph was one of those "wunder kinds" who was successful at anything he set his mind to. At about six feet tall and in his mid-50s, Ralph had a zest for life and got involved in new projects. His interests spanned from the scientific to aerospace engineering to gourmet cooking. To Jack, it seemed that there was nothing that Ralph wasn't involved in.

Knowing Ralph, he hoped for a full lab, and it was everything that Jack could hope for and more. Ralph's lab did the final live-person testing for the Federal Food and Drug Administration on cosmetics and oral medicines for large cosmetic and pharmaceutical companies.

"Yes," Ralph explained, "the cosmetic and pharmaceutical companies all have their own research facilities, but the government pays us to verify their findings and report our research. Nothing gets put on store shelves until we approve it."

Later that evening, over a good dinner, Ralph questioned him on the procedure he wanted testing. Ralph's questions were relentless. Finally, Jack broke down and told Ralph what he had experienced at Sean's farm. Ralph almost yelled in the quiet restaurant.

"Are you sure? Are you nuts? To be able to reverse the aging process would be the greatest medical discovery of all time! But even though I like you, I still can't believe you. I must see for myself. If true, my entire laboratory and staff will be at your disposal." Ralph's mind went to work. He continued, "The only way for this to work is for us to set up a number of live animal test subjects, have Sean administer the formula, and then we constantly test and observe the animals twenty-four seven. I have everything here imaginable to test live subjects. So the testing must be done here in my lab under the strictest of conditions. So you must return with Sean, and we'll set up the testing here."

"Logical enough. I'll call you when I get back and arrange for our return," said Jack.

"Great," said Ralph, "and I'll have the test animal subjects all lined up and ready to go. This isn't a joke, is it, Jack?"

"No joke, Ralph. If you had seen what I've seen, you would be as excited as I am," said Jack.

Jack returned to his hotel and caught the morning flight back to Detroit, Michigan. Upon arriving' he went to pick Sean's dad's car out of the airport compound and drove back to Crystal Falls.

Chapter 8
Sean and Jack Back in Boston

Jack was so excited to tell Sean the good news. He explained Ralph's laboratory and the elaborate testing facility.

"If we can do our tests there and they prove successful, we are halfway there to going into production. Could you imagine putting an "age-reversing drug" on the market? The world-wide demand for it would outshine any other product introduction ever. And the price we charged would be irrelevant; regardless of what we charged, we could still not produce enough," said Jack.

Sean agreed. The next day, Jack called Ralph back and asked when he would like them both to arrive. Sean wanted to know exactly how many test subjects there would be and their approximate weight. He had to be sure in order to arrive at the correct dosages.

"Anytime is good for me. We have extra space in our workload to accommodate the tests. My intention is to start out with two dogs and two pigs. The dogs will be Labrador Retrievers of about 80lbs each, and the pigs will be of the same weight. These should make good initial test subjects," replied Ralph.

"But why pigs?" asked Jack.

"Pigs have a very similar metabolism to humans, and some people even have pig valves installed to replace their own faulty heart valves. With two dogs and two pigs, these tests should give us a good idea of what you have," answered Ralph.

Jack put the phone on "speaker," and Sean added, "In order to speed things up, I will email you the complete instructions on having the animals fast for two days with nothing but water to drink and no food and then being properly washed and rubbed down with olive oil. You will need a table where the animals can be held motionless for me to administer the formula to them. After that, they must be placed in a clean room with no windows for two days and fed nothing but bread and water."

"No problem," answered Ralph. "I will await your email, and we will follow your instructions to the letter."

"Great, we'll let you know when we arrive," said Jack.

Sean set about itemizing the exact instructions as stated in the papyrus. He typed up the instructions, sent off the email to Ralph, and kept duplicates for himself.

He then burned the photocopies of the papyrus to ensure that no one would ever know where the secret came from.

Sean and Jack in Boston

Sean and Jack arrived by plane two days later. Sean had with him four plastic vials with the right dosage for any animal of about 80lbs. each. These he kept on him twenty-four hours a day. *Best to keep them safe,* he thought. They contacted Ralph and agreed to meet in the hotel lobby at eight a.m. tomorrow.

"Get a good night's sleep. Tomorrow is going to be a busy day," said Ralph.

The next morning, true to his word, Ralph was there in the lobby, and after Jack introduced Sean to Ralph, they called a cab and drove in silence to the lab. Upon entering Barns Laboratories Inc. Sean was impressed. First, they had to remove their clothes, shower, and then be sprayed with an antiseptic mist. They were then handed white lab jumpsuits that covered everything except their faces. A lab assistant approached Sean and Jack and introduced himself.

"Let's proceed. We have the test subjects in Room #1 to #4, all ready to go. We have followed your instructions to the letter. All four of the animals have fasted for two days, been properly washed, and been rubbed down with olive oil. Everything that you have requested."

Sean, Jack, and Ralph entered a large, perfectly clean testing laboratory that reminded Sean more of an operating room than a lab. The four animal test subjects were brought out individually and placed in large cages along one wall.

"Everything is ready for you to proceed," stated the assistant.

"Let's start with the dogs first," said Sean.

The assistant called in two other assistants, and they brought the first dog to the table and hoisted him up. This first dog had no trouble being secured in, and Sean opened the first vial and administered the formula. This dog was then removed to be placed in a clean room. The same procedure was performed on the next dog, with similar results.

Now to the pigs. Sean had never been around pigs before, so he didn't know what to expect. The assistants knew how to handle them and the three of them lifted the first pig up onto the table. As pigs were not accustomed to being manhandled the pig started squealing violently. Lying on his side, the three assistants held the pig down as Ralph secured it with the straps. *So far, so good.*

"You have to turn his head skyward and open his mouth," said Sean.

Without saying a word, the assistants turned the pig's head upward and, using a rubber wedge, kept his mouth open. Sean administered the formula and stepped away to let the assistants remove the pig to a clean room.

The same procedure was used on the second pig. So far, a complete success. Sean approached a sink, washed out the four vials, and returned them to his pocket. Ralph, upon seeing the final pig taken to a clean room, said, "The dogs and pigs will be monitored and observed twenty-four hours a day. And as stated, they will be fed only bread and water for the next two days."

Two anxious days passed, and Jack and Sean spent the time touring Boston and eating too much and drinking too much beer. Anything to pass the time while they waited. Then they were invited back into the lab.

As before, all test subject's hair now remained on the floor of their pens. The assistants all reported that upon their test subject's hair falling out, their vital signs improved. They then placed all four animals in their own separate, larger holding pens for further observation. *Pretty hard to tell about a pig's behavior, but the dogs seemed to be more lively and energetic.* Ralph had the animals remain in the larger pens for two more days.

"Well, all I can report to you is that all four of the test subjects appear to be in remarkable health and seem to have far more energy than before. But so far, we can only determine that your formula acted as a stimulant and that their hair fell out, nothing more. Let's take a month off and think about what we have seen. You and Sean return to Michigan, and we'll work on coming up with some more tests here. You may be on to something; I just don't quite know what it is," said Ralph.

Sean and Jack Back in Michigan

Sean and Jack agreed and caught the next flight back to Michigan. They sat silent on the plane, both lost in their own thoughts. Sean had asked the Watts to drop over and feed their pets. Upon arrival at the farmhouse, they examined all six of their pets, and you could see the remainder of the food the Watts had put out for them. What great neighbors! All the pets seemed perfectly healthy and happy to see them.

"Well, where do we go from here?" asked Sean.

"I think we have done everything possible on our end. I don't see any more tests that we can do, other than monitoring the health of our new family. Best to let Ralph come up with further tests that he can administer in his own lab. We need concrete proof of what this product does and have to determine if it is safe for human consumption. Then and only then can we apply for a patent and start production. But we have to wait for Ralph," stated Jack.

Jack, seeing little else to do, decided to fly back to New York. "Might as well be doing something that makes me money," he said.

The next day, Sean drove him to the airport. Sean consumed himself with some new office tower designs. *Little else to do. Such a letdown from the excitement of doing the experiments and going to Boston.* Two long, boring weeks went by, and the phone rang. It was Jack.

"Good news: Ralph and his people have come up with more test subjects and tests. He's convinced that we have something, but he's not sure what it is. He says that the test dogs are in superb health and as lively as pups. We are to meet him next Monday in the hotel lobby, like before. I'll fly out of here and meet you there," said Jack.

Sean was so excited. Then he hatched his plan. He would perform the procedure on himself and make himself available for Ralph to run tests on him. He scheduled in two days of fasting, weighed himself, and made up just enough formula for himself.

He also wrote a document stating that he and he alone is responsible for taking this formula and that Jack, Ralph, and his associates in no way encouraged him to take the drug. I produced it, so I must try it first, he wrote.

With the formula prepared and his bags packed, Sean spent most of his two-day fast in a clean room with just his notes and his computer. *Might as well work when I'm in there,* he thought. He only left the room to get water, use the bathroom, or feed the pets. With his work, the two days went by quickly.

He caught the morning flight to Boston and met Jack at the hotel. It was after six p.m. and Sean lied and said that he had already eaten and just wanted to go to bed. Jack had a sandwich brought up to the room. The next morning, Sean and Jack met Ralph in the lobby, like before. They hailed a cab and, in a few moments, were at the lab.

Sean and Jack knew the drill. They all stripped, showered, had themselves sprayed with an antiseptic mist, and dressed in the white garments laid out for them. They were directed toward Laboratory Room #2.

Sean Takes the Formula

Upon entering the lab, Sean stated in front of everyone present, "Before we proceed, I must tell you this. I have fasted for the last two days and consumed only water. I will be administering the formula to myself either here or back at my farm in Michigan. I discovered this drug, so it is only fitting that I be the first test subject."

With this, he handed over the signed statement absolving Jack, Ralph, and his laboratory of any involvement in his decision to take the drug. While the others stood in shock, Sean then walked over to the examination table, laid down, and poured the fluid from the vial into the back of his throat. He then got up, took the vial to the sink, and washed it out.

"I think I need to be washed and rubbed down with olive oil," Sean said with a smile.

Still seeing the others in shock, Sean undressed down to his underwear and motioned for the olive oil to be brought to him. Jack got it for him and handed him a washcloth. Sean rubbed himself down with the olive oil and, when finished, stated, "Now I want you to take detailed photos of my face and hands."

Once they got their cell phones, everyone started taking pictures. Now completed, Sean said, "Which examination room do you want me in? And remember, I am only to have bread and water for the next two days."

Ralph, coming out of his shock, finally said, "Well, everyone, our hands are tied. If we let Sean leave and he dies, we are responsible. As he has ingested the drug himself, let's proceed with the tests and observations and see what we have. We have little choice."

At this point, the assistants approached Sean and helped him get dressed back in the white lab garment. They then attached electrodes to his body and to his head and escorted him to a clean room that contained a bathroom.

For the next two days, Sean had nothing but bread and water. He took this all in good humor, as long as he had books to read. The team of six assistants rotated so that two assistants were monitoring his progress constantly. Nothing happened. Then, about one and a half days later, Sean's hair started falling out. Sean reported the sensation of this was like getting a good buzz from a cheap bottle of wine. With Sean's body hair now falling out, his two-day limit was up. They opened the doors to his sealed room, and he stepped out. Everyone was looking at his face.

"Sean, you look years younger," explained Ralph. "Here, look at yourself in this mirror."

Sean walked over to the mirror and laughed. "My, I do look good. What a handsome fellow."

They then showed him photos on their phones of this face from just two days ago.

A remarkable difference. They originally speculated that this was from him being sealed up and having plenty of rest. But no, the transformation was far more than that; it was as if five years of life had just been reversed for Sean.

They proceeded to do more tests—blood tests, heart tests, treadmill tests, everything imaginable. The assistants here were no slouches. This was an accredited government-approved testing facility with the finest staff and equipment. Everyone was amazed. It was as if a forty years old man had walked into the room and a thirty-five years old man walked out.

Staff from all over the lab came in to see "Sean the Miracle". He certainly didn't mind the attention from the pretty assistants. People continued to touch his skin and ask him how he had come across such an amazing discovery. He just remained tight-lipped and smiled. His common response was, "Ask Jack, he's my partner."

Sean and Jack stayed for another few days. Sean stayed in the lab, and they did dozens of tests. Every single test indicated that his body had gone through a transformation and that the cells themselves reversed their aging process. They tested and tested again. The same results.

Testing on Ralph's Uncle George

Ralph asked Sean and Jack to go to their hotel while he and his staff looked at their notes. The next morning, Ralph called and stated that if Sean could come up with some more formula, they could repeat the process on Ralph's sixty-eight years old uncle, George Barns.

"No problem. I will return home to get some," stated Sean.

So Jack flew back to New York while Sean returned to Crystal Falls. Sean waited for Jack's call.

Ralph and the assistants all agreed that they had to keep the results of these tests to themselves. They all agreed that secrecy was a must until they knew what they were dealing with.

Ralph then called and presented his plans to his sixty-eight years old uncle, George Barns. As soon as Ralph told his uncle what he wanted to do, his uncle said, "Are you crazy? If I have a chance to be five years younger, where do I sign? I'm taking the next flight to Boston. I'll be there tomorrow." Then he hung up.

Once admitted to the lab, Ralph and his team had a test subject they could monitor from the very start. Mr. Barns was a healthy, sixty-eight years old, physically fit individual who had a zest for life. All the lab assistants agreed that he would make a great test subject. He kept joking all the time he was there, and everyone felt he was a pleasure to work with.

While fasting for two days, the assistants took every test imaginable to determine Mr. Barns health level. They also photographed almost his entire body. Jack called Sean, and he arrived from Michigan just in time to administer the formula. Sean, after showering and being dressed in the white lab garments, introduced himself to Mr. Barns.

"How do you do, Mr. Barns? I am Sean Little. Do you know why you are here and what this might do to you?" Sean asked.

"Sure do, son. If there is any chance of being one day younger, I'm taking it. My wife passed away three years ago, so I've got nothing to lose. I've signed off on all the papers for Ralph, so the police can't say that he forced me to be here. You took the process yourself, didn't you? How do you feel?" asked Mr. Barns.

"Well, to tell you honestly, I feel great. I have more energy and jump to my step. Other than my hair falling out, I have no side effects. But it seems to be growing back," replied Sean.

"Well, let's get this show on the road. Give me your magic drug and make me young again," urged Mr. Barns.

With that, Mr. Barns laid back down, and Sean poured the fluid into the back of his throat. Then Sean went over and washed the plastic vial. Mr. Barns was led by the assistants to his clean room for two more days of observation. As he was being led out, he started saying, "Not too fussy about the only bread and water thing, but what the heck, I'll get over it and get me a big, fat, juicy steak when I get out."

So for the next two days, every test was run on Mr. Barns that Ralph and his team could think of. Almost like clockwork, a day and a half into his isolation, what was left of Mr. Barn's hair all fell out.

"No problem, I feel great. It's just that all of my hair fell out just like you said it would," Mr. Barns told the observing assistants.

When Mr. Barns was finally released from his observation room, the assistants continued to run every test imaginable. Quickly, they determined that, by a miracle, Uncle George was years younger than he was just two days ago. The real proof was in the photos. Comparing photos of his face now to those photos just taken two days ago, and you would swear these new pictures were of a younger brother, not the same man. Mr. Barns kept telling everyone how good he felt and wanted to get out for that steak.

Ralph talked to Sean and Jack in his office.

"We can't explain what has happened. We have compared every test result taken when my uncle arrived to those tests taken a few days later, and you would swear that we were testing a younger version of himself. I can't explain it, but you two are really on to something. The tests prove it."

The three sat in silence. These were not tests made in someone's basement. Ralph's lab was one of the most respected research and testing laboratories in all the US. Then, finally, Ralph broke the silence.

"Why don't you two go home, and we'll continue testing my uncle and get back to you? I can't see any other plan of action right now. I'll call you both when I hear something." With that, Sean and Jack left. On the way out, Jack said, "These people at Barns Laboratories don't make mistakes. They test and retest until all doubt is gone. They will keep Mr. Barns under tight observation and monitor his progress. Ralph will let us know when we should come back."

"I guess you're right. If I hurry, I can catch the last flight back to Detroit. Thanks, Jack; it's been a heck of a ride so far," said Sean as he stepped into a taxi.

Chapter 9
Secrets Out

Sean returned to Crystal Falls, and Jack returned to New York. Exciting times.

In the airport, Sean stopped into one of those "all we sell is luggage" shops and picked up a beautiful aluminum case with the foam inserts that the camera guys usually haul their expensive cameras around with. *Pretty cool. I look like a secret agent with this fancy case.*

Sean returned home, and as before, the Watts had been in and fed the animals.

His pets were all overjoyed to see him. It was too late to start anything, so he had a drink, happy that he was back home. The next morning, after attending to his pets, Sean started to assemble the ingredients he used and started labeling the bottles they were in and placing them in his new case.

He speculated if he should continue using the same vial to store the fluid or if he should use a new vial every time. *The vial never touches anything, and I wash it out every time, but I should start using a new vial and destroying the old ones. With that issue settled, I'll just get some the next time he's at a pharmacy.* He also left a copy of his list of ingredients and the procedure in the case. The original papyrus, in their protective plastic sleeves, he carefully hid in the secret space behind the fireplace. *Nobody could ever find them there.*

Life went on as normal for Sean. He did his designs and, when bored, played with his pets. *I was right, I can get more done in an hour at home than I can in four hours in the office with all the noise and the distractions.* His mind floated off to the pretty junior architects that the firm had just hired. *Architecture used to be a man's profession, but it seems that more and more architects now are women and pretty ones too.*

If I hang around the office too much, I'll start getting interested in one of the girls and then I'll never get any work done. Office romances never work out. Oh yeah, it's all fun when they start, and then everyone gets their nose in your business and talks behind your back. I'm staying at home. Besides, I still miss Jennifer. Hope she's okay.

Time to Run and Hide

Early one morning, the phone rang. It was Jack, and he was frantic.

"Sean, Ralph's Uncle George Barns couldn't keep his mouth shut. Ralph kept him in for a week of observation, and as soon as he got out, he started telling everyone that Ralph had the secret of eternal youth. Most people laughed at the beginning, but when George got back to Dallas, Texas, where people knew him, they believed him. Some lady he plays cards with has a son who is a reporter for USA Today, and she called him. The guy came down and talked to George. Now USA Today has printed a story, and Ralph says there are reporters and camera crews outside of the lab twenty-four hours a day. He's being harassed out of his mind. He says that he hasn't talked to the reporters yet because he refuses to leave the lab."

"What the hell are you talking about?" asked Sean.

"This is turning into a media frenzy. The newspapers have latched onto it and are speculating that Barns Laboratories has the secret of eternal life. With the election over, there must be nothing else to report on, so they are falling all over this. It's only a matter of time before it hits the TV networks. Because Ralph has not spoken to the reporters yet, our names have been kept out of it. It is only a matter of time before one of his assistants talks. The large networks offer money to get someone to talk and I bet they are offering the assistants cash as we speak. Someone will talk and tell them about us," said Jack.

"What should we do?" asked Sean.

"I don't know about you, but I don't want reporters showing up at my office and harassing me day and night. I'm leaving and going to my friend John Forrester's cottage in Maine and lying low for a while. It doesn't have cell service there, so you can't contact me there. I suggest you get out before your yard is filled with reporters and curious people. Once this hits the airways, we'll be public figures, searched out wherever we go," replied Jack.

"Okay, you win. A good friend of mine has a remote cabin in northern Michigan. I'll tell him the story, and I know he'll let me stay there, and he'll keep it to himself," said Sean.

"But you have to promise me you will leave today. This story might be on the five-p.m. news, and then our lives will become hell," pleaded Jack.

"Okay, I promise. It will take me less than an hour to pack and get going," said Sean.

"And one other thing, drop by an ATM or your bank and get out plenty of cash, I mean, like ten thousand dollars or so. Anyone can trace you on your debit or credit cards, but it's difficult if you're spending cash. Do it. In today's world, anyone can trace anyone just by looking up their phone records or transactions. The police and reporters do it all the time. Next, they can track you on the GPS on your phone and the GPS in your new LEXUS, so don't use your phone under any circumstances and ditch the LEXUS and take your dad's Buick," pleaded Jack.

"Good advice. I'll do it as soon as I leave," stated Sean.

"Okay, I'm leaving the office now, gathering what I need from my apartment, grabbing lots of cash, and then I'm out of here. Keep in touch." Then Jack hung up.

Sean was rattled. *What the hell is going on? Best to take Jack's advice.* He called the Watts and asked them to look after the pets and the house again.

"If you need anything, just buy it, and I will pay you back when I return," he said.

He then called his friend Bill Fryer, who had a cabin near Shanty Creek, Michigan. "Sure," he said, "you know where the key is. I won't be up there for at least two months, so you have the place all to yourself.

Sean then briefly told him what happened and that he needed to lay low for a while. Bill agreed, saying, "My lips are sealed, and I'll call the neighbor I pay to look after the place and tell him you're coming. I'll say that you're writing a book and do not want to be disturbed. Plus, the cabin is so remote that it doesn't have any cell service."

"Even better, thanks Bill; I owe you one," said Sean, and he hung up.

Sean grabbed his case with the ingredients in it, filled a large suitcase with clothes, grabbed some coats, and put them by the door. Being in the country, he kept some cash on hand, but it was only a few thousand dollars. He then laid out some food for the pets, got in his dad's Buick, and took off. *I'm so nervous. I think this is all stupid, but it is best to be on the safe side.*

He dropped by his bank and withdrew fifteen thousand dollars in twenty-dollar bills. He joked with the teller he knew, saying that he was buying a friend's tractor, and the guy insisted on cash. Seemed like a likely story. He filled up his dad's Buick gas tank before getting on the highway and paid by credit card. The teller there knew him, so he used his credit card to save his cash.

Now on the highway, Sean headed north on Interstate I-75. It was about a six-hour drive to the cabin, and Sean thought the drive would at least allow him to relax. He had to stop a few times for a nap. Once off the highway, he stopped at a small grocery store and bought everything he needed. He thought about using a credit card, but instead followed Jack's advice and paid cash. He wore a John Deere hat over his bald head and sunglasses, so no one paid any attention to him. An hour later, he was at Bill's cottage.

Sean Hides Out at Bill Fryer's Cabin

Nice place, totally private and totally off the grid, perfect. The cabin was an older pine log structure with a large porch on the front. The cabin was surrounded by approximately twenty acres of bush, and you could walk through the woods to the river where Bill kept his small fishing boat and an aluminum canoe. He retrieved the cottage key from under the rock in the garden and let himself in. *Cool place,* he thought. It was a cabin, so it was furnished like a cabin. Pine tables and chairs, old couches, and small tables. There was an icebox, not a fridge, and an old wood stove for heat and cooking. *No problem,* Sean thought. *I'll just eat a lot of canned goods while I'm here.*

In the shed outback, Bill had a generator and a hundred-gallon fuel tank full of fuel. Sean started the generator, and it started on the second pull. *Thank God,* he thought. Not needing the fridge, he could forgo using the generator for a long time. He was looking forward to cooking on the wood stove and boiling water for coffee. The cottage had an old RCA TV that picked up only three stations. *Perfect.*

Sean spent the rest of the day wandering the property and having a drink on the dock. *It's great out here.* Upon waking the next morning, he started a fire in the wood stove and then went out and started the generator.

Can't go without hot water and a morning coffee. Back at the cabin, Sean started bowling water for coffee and some slices of canned meat to be cooked on the stove. With this in hand, he sat down and turned on the TV. One of the few stations he could get was a sports channel and CNN.

Uncle George Tells All

After watching the sports channel for a while, when the program changed, he switched the TV over to CNN. After watching the troubles around the world, he sat in horror as the announcer said, "Ladies and gentlemen, I don't know what to make of this, but here it goes. Out of Boston, Massachusetts, there comes reports that the prestigious government-sponsored, Barns Laboratories, Inc. has developed a drug that reverses the aging process. This has all come to us from George Barns, the uncle of Ralph Barns, who owns Barns Laboratories, and he himself has undergone the procedure."

The TV now shows the laboratory and people and reporters mingling about.

The reporter continued, "Mr. Ralph Barns, owner of Barns Laboratories, has kept himself barricaded inside, and as of yet, has not talked to reporters. But what we do have for you is an interview with his uncle, George Barns. The so-called guinea pig in this experiment."

The TV then switches to a reporter standing outside of George Barn's home in Dallas, Texas.

"Hello, this is John Jefferies with CNN in Dallas, Texas, reporting. I am presently standing outside of George Barn's home. George Barns is the uncle of Ralph Barns who owns Barns Laboratories in Boston, Massachusetts. George Barns has experimented on with a new age-reversing drug. Mr. Barns has agreed to talk with us. Here he comes now."

Mr. Barns comes bouncing down the steps. Obviously delighted with his new celebrity status.

"Mr. Barns, tell me how this all started," asked the reporter.

"Sure, I got a call one day from my nephew Ralph, who owns the big Barns Laboratories in Boston. He said he needed a healthy test subject to try out this new age-reversing drug. He said it has passed a number of animal tests, and one other person has tried it with favorable results. They needed me to come in so that they could do tests from start to finish. And boy, oh boy, I jumped at the chance and was there the next day."

"Then what happened?" asked the reporter, obviously delighted that George wanted to talk.

"Well, I show up at Ralph's fancy lab. I undress, I shower, and I put on one of their fancy white outfits. On the first day, they do nothing but tests to determine how healthy I am. Then they put me in a room with only water to drink for two days. I had plenty to read and a flat-screen TV to watch, so the next two days went by fast. Then they take me out of the room and bring me back to the lab. Here I am introduced to a fellow named Sean Little, who has the formula, and his partner, Jack Alair. I lie down on the table, and Sean pours about a half-ounce of fluid down the back of my throat. Doesn't taste too good, but no matter.

"Then the assistants wash me down and cover my body with olive oil. I thought they were going to make me into a salad," joked Mr. Barns. "Then they take me into another room, where I am fed only bread and water for another two days. Tough way to diet, let me tell you. About halfway through the second day, all my hair falls out. I was told this was going to happen, but my body felt so good it didn't matter. Later that day, they bring me out, lie me down on the table, and do every test they can think of. Ralph must have ten million dollars in equipment hooked up to me. They keep asking me how I feel, and I keep telling them I feel great.

"Ralph keeps me there for another week for observation. They let me order anything I wanted, so my first meal was a big, juicy steak and potatoes. Let me tell you that after five days with little to eat, that steak tasted great. The funny thing is, years ago, I lost most of my taste buds. No reason; I just couldn't taste food all that well. When I bit into that first piece of steak, my taste buds exploded. My sense of taste has returned, and I thought I was going to eat everything in sight."

"How do you feel right now, Mr. Barns?" asked the reporter.

Mr. Barnes replied with, "Fantastic! Haven't felt this good in years. Ever since my wife passed, I just sat around the house with no energy and no desire to do anything. Now I've got so much energy, I can't wait to get up and do things. Besides my taste buds, my appetite has returned, and boy, oh boy, do bacon, eggs, and coffee ever taste good in the morning?"

"Mr. Barns, it's been about ten days since you completed this procedure. Have you noticed any adverse side effects?" asked the reporter.

"None whatsoever. Feel great and can't wait to get out of bed in the morning and get going," George quickly answered.

"Mr. Barns, in your opinion, is this procedure something you would recommend to other people of your age?" the reporter asked.

"Are you kidding? They made me five years or more younger. I haven't felt this good in years. I hope that Ralph will do this to me again. Just think, he could make me fifty years old again." Laughed Mr. Barns.

Now the reporter standing by himself said, "There you have it, folks. The first interview with George Barns, uncle to the owner of the prestigious Barns Laboratories in Boston, Massachusetts, Ralph Barns. George has been given an age-reversing drug that, to my eyes, seems to work. I'm not a scientist or a chemist, but it looks like Barns Laboratories is on to something big. What mankind has searched for since the beginning of time is a way to reverse the aging process and restore youth. Signing off, this is John Jefferies for CNN in Dallas, Texas."

While all this was going on, FBI agents were bombarding Ralph Barns with questions. They had him in one of his examination rooms, telling him to cooperate or all of his government funding would be pulled. He had little choice, especially since the two FBI agents questioning him had two guys with them who had so much firepower on them that they looked like gun store mannequins.

Ralph Tells All to the FBI

Monica Forsyth, a small, petite, high-strung woman, Special Agent in charge of this case was relentless in her questioning of Ralph Barns.

"You will tell us everything we need to know now. If you do not cooperate, the first thing is that your government funding will be pulled, and second, impeding a federal investigation is a federal crime with up to ten years in jail. So you better start talking now," demanded Monica as she turned on the portable tape recorder. Ralph Barns starts talking.

"Okay, here it is. An accountant fellow I know, Jack Alair of Swartz and Cooper Inc., calls me and wants to arrange a meeting. He says it's important. We meet, and he says that he needs me to do some clinical trials for him and his friend. I finally get him to tell me, and he says that he believes that his friend has a formula for reversing the aging process. I told him I thought it was a scam, but he persisted, and I agreed to arrange for some animal test subjects to be brought in.

"I acquire some animal test subjects and follow the instructions Sean emails me.

"Sean and Jack arrive a few days later, and we start. Jack's friend Sean is an architect from Michigan at a place called Hillsborough and Smith, the guys who design those environmentally friendly office buildings. It is obvious that he's the guy with the formula. After they enter the lab, Sean has vials of fluid that he pours down the throats of the test subjects. We then place the animals in clean rooms for two days of observation. Halfway through the second day, all the animal's hair falls out, and later that day we release the animals. Their energy level is amazing. The dogs especially started acting like pups. You couldn't settle them down. We tested the formula on some pigs, and the results were the same.

"Sean and Jack leave and return in a few days. Sean had to go back to Michigan to get more formula. When they return to the lab, we plan to resume our testing. Then Sean says something like, We need to test this on a human subject. He then hands me a file of signed documents, absolving me and my lab of any responsibility. And while I'm looking at these files, Sean lies down on the examination table and pours the fluid down his throat. There was nothing we could do so we continued with the tests.

"Like the animals, halfway through the second day, all of Sean's hair falls out, but he reports that he feels great. Once released, we do dozens of tests, and he appears to be a younger version of himself.

"Now knowing that we're onto something, I contact my sixty-eight year old Uncle George Barns in Dallas, Texas, and I tell him the story. He not only volunteers but shows up the next day, raring to go. Sean returns with more formula, and we do the same procedure on him, and the results are dramatic. His energy level is fantastic, and he feels great. We kept him for one week for observation, and he appears to be sixty-three years old again. That's the story," said Ralph.

Monica turns off the tape recorder and thanks Ralph for his cooperation. Monica then warned, "Best you stay in the lab here. The media frenzy ever since your uncle started talking is getting frightening. We will have anything you want—food, clothing, equipment, anything brought in for you."

"Okay," said Ralph, "you're the boss."

Chapter 10
Jennifer Gets Involved

The FBI quickly starts a search of everything they can find out about Sean Little and Jack Alair. Jack Alair's ex-girlfriend, Nancy, was nowhere to be found. They felt that she had either changed her name or left the country. That left the FBI looking for Sean's ex-girlfriend, Jennifer Sloan, who was now an airline stewardess for United Airlines. Monica Forsyth, the chief FBI agent in charge, quickly found out that Jennifer was in the air and was scheduled to land in Seattle, Washington, in one hour. Monica called ahead to the Seattle FBI office and notified them that Jennifer was to be detained and questioned. Jennifer's flight was on time, and once she disembarked from the plane, She was met by two men in dark suits.

"Jennifer Sloan?" asked the lead agent.

"Yes, I am Jennifer Sloan. How may I help you?" she answered.

"Could you follow me, please?" stated the same agent.

Now seated in an airport manager's office, the two men sit down across from her and introduce themselves as FBI agents. The same agent starts asking questions, "What can you tell me about your boyfriend, Sean Little?

"Well, for starters, Sean and I are no longer together; we split up about four months ago. And other than sending the occasional postcard, we have not spoken," replied Jennifer.

"What else can you tell us about him?" asked the same agent.

"Well, he's the top architect for a firm in Dearborn, Michigan, called Hillsborough and Smith, Inc. They specialize in environmentally friendly office buildings that Sean designs. Being the quiet creative type, he's kind of a recluse and lives on his deceased parent's farm in Crystal Falls, Michigan, about forty-five minutes from Dearborn. He doesn't have any friends and prefers to keep to himself," Jennifer said.

"Why did you two split up?" asked the agent.

"Believe me, the quiet life in Crystal Falls is quiet. Doing nothing all day while Sean attended to his drawings was driving me nuts. He was totally devoted to his work.

"Bored out of my mind, my girlfriend mentioned that I could become an airline stewardess, and so I jumped at the chance. So here I am," said Jennifer.

"What else can you tell us? asked the agent.

"That's all there is. He's a nice guy. Is he in any trouble?" asked Jennifer.

"No trouble. He's gone missing, and no one knows where he is. We just need to talk to him about something that happened in Boston, Mass. You are free to go," stated the agent.

Jennifer was totally confused. Sean would never do anything wrong; it's just not in him. Being in the air, she had not yet heard the news. Later that night, in the hotel the airlines had rented for their stewardesses, Jennifer sat horrified as she watched the evening news. There were videos of the media group outside of Barns Laboratories, the CNN interview with George Barns and Sean and Jack's pictures as the individuals who held the secret.

Upon seeing Sean's picture, she knew exactly what she had to do and knew exactly where he was. She was also smart enough to know that she couldn't reach him directly, and besides, they can track you on your phone, she thought.

Concerned about Sean, she called her supervisor and said that her mother was in the hospital in Detroit and had to go.

"No problem," said the supervisor. "Check the schedule and grab the next flight to Detroit. Hope your mom's okay." And then hung up.

Jennifer checked the schedule, and there was a flight to Detroit leaving in two hours. She made the call and had herself checked in. *A perk of the job,* she thought.

She flew courtesy of her airline as a regular passenger. Some of the attending stewardesses knew her, and as the plane was only half full, some took the time to sit with her and chat. Everyone was talking about the "new age-reversing drug" being tested in Boston. Jennifer let on like she didn't know and let her friends talk.

Arriving at the airport in Detroit, she hailed a cab and went to Bill's office at Todd & Todd Lawyers Inc. in downtown Detroit. Bill was a top-level lawyer at Todd & Todd and could do pretty much anything he pleased. Tall, dark, and handsome, he and Jennifer had dated briefly in university but broke it off, but they still remained the best of friends. Bill was a downtown type of guy who loved his job and even looked good in a suit.

It was Bill who introduced Jennifer to Sean at an office party, and once they "hit it off" together, he let them use his cabin whenever they wanted. Jennifer and Bill's girlfriend, Nancy, became friends, and in the summers, Bill would invite Sean and Jennifer up to enjoy the great outdoors with them. Unfortunately, Nancy eventually left Bill. But Bill still let Sean and Jennifer use the cabin whenever they wanted.

Jennifer decided to just surprise Bill and not call him on her cell phone. She knew that the police could track you via your cell phone, so she thought it was best not to use it at all. Getting out of the cab, she then took the elevator upstairs to Bill's office.

Jennifer walked into Bill's office, and Bill almost fell out of his chair.

"If I knew such a pretty girl was going to visit me, I would have worn a better shirt," he said as they embraced. Bill thought of Jennifer more as a sister than as an ex-girlfriend and would do anything to help her.

Jennifer started to explain the trouble Sean was in, and Bill said that it was all over the news, including Sean's and his cousin Jack's pictures. Bill told her that Sean had called, and he naturally offered him his cabin up north.

"They can never find him. No one can trace him to me, and besides, there is no cell service up there, so he couldn't make a call even if he wanted to," said Bill.

"Regardless, would you come with me to your cabin to make sure Sean's all right?" pleaded Jennifer.

"Well, my works all caught up here, and you know I'm a sucker for helping a damsel in distress. Sure, let's go. Just let me tell the office manager I'll be away for a few days. No one will question me after seeing a pretty girl come barging into my office. They'll all think I'm off on a weekend of flesh and sin." Laughed Bill.

In the elevator, Bill said, "Fortunately for us, I brought my 4x4 Yukon today. It's better on the roads, especially if it rains."

Jennifer agreed, knowing that she could use some shut-eye in the car while Bill drove. They arrived at the cabin in Shanty Creek, Michigan, in about four hours, stopping only for gas and some sandwiches. Jennifer slept most of the way.

They arrived at the cabin about seven p.m. and both Bill and Jennifer knocked and walked in. Sean was watching TV about the "new wonder drug" and couldn't believe it when he saw both Jennifer and Bill arrive. Sean immediately wondered if Bill and Jennifer were together until Jennifer jumped on him and embraced him. She was crying and couldn't stop.

"I've missed you so much. Being in the air was cool to start, but I feel so empty inside. There has never been anyone else but you, and because I left you like I did, I didn't have the nerve to contact you and say I'm sorry."

Sean just looked at her, and he started crying. They hugged and laughed and hugged and kissed some more. Bill, seeing how the water works, said, "I'm going fishing and will be back in three to four hours." And winking at Sean, Bill grabs his life jacket, tackle box, and rod and walks out the door.

It wasn't too long before their feet hit the floor and they found their way to the bedroom. Sean locked the door, and they made love as only long-separated lovers can. Sean and Jennifer both knew that this was it; they would be together forever.

Bill returned later and knew that both of them would be asleep. He ate a can of beef with a spoon and then slept on the couch. Being an early riser, he was up and out fishing before they both got up. *Nice to see the sunrise,* and two's company, three's a crowd, reminded Bill to himself as he left for fishing.

Chapter 11
Mercenaries in America

News like this spreads fast. Within hours, every single news agency in the world was reporting on this story. Politicians, businesspeople, and every bad guy knew exactly what this secret meant, and the power wielded by those who possessed it. Who could resist the story of a common guy finding the "fountain of youth?"

The news agencies ran this story 24/7. News announcers speculated that possessing this formula would make that person the richest and most powerful man in the world. No human being, politician, billionaire, or common man could resist the lure of being young again and would do anything to do so. Greedy, envious eyes watched the news and planned.

This must be ours at all costs, thought Amir, head of a large terrorist organization in the Middle East. Amir was an arrogant, cunning, and ruthless man who would stop at nothing to better himself. His phone rang. It was his master, the all-powerful, oil-rich ruler of his country.

"Amir, do you realize what this formula means? Whoever possesses it will be the most powerful person in the world. To be able to bribe world leaders with being years younger, no one could resist. You could charge millions per application, and the money would just keep pouring in. The rich and powerful would be at our feet, begging to make them young again. You must do everything to kidnap those who have the secret.

"I will transfer four hundred million dollars to you immediately. Do this now, and we will control the world." Then his master hung up.

Amir thought for a moment. *This has to be done immediately before someone else beats us to it.* Amir called Donovan, his trusted operative in the United States, who had done successful work for him in the past. Donovan was a hard-core killer, large and muscular, with tattoos all over his body.

Lucky for me, thought Amir, *Donovan's only loyalty is to the all-powerful dollar, and he knows to keep his mouth shut.* Donovan was ex-US military and like Amir, would do anything to advance his station's life. Donovan picked up his phone, and Amir, hearing Donovan's voice, quickly introduced himself and stated, "Have you heard about this age-reversing discovery out of Boston?"

"Heard about it. It broke on the airways today, and that's the only thing on the news," said Donovan.

"Listen very carefully. Are you prepared to go to work right now? asked Amir.

"Yes, absolutely. I have never failed you before. What do you want done?" asked Donovan.

"I am wiring you ten million dollars to your Swiss bank account immediately. You are to assemble your team. Later today, one of my associates will deliver $4,000,000.00 in cash in American funds for your expenses. Once you have assembled your team and they agree to join, give them each twenty thousand dollars cash and then wire them each $100,000 from your Swiss account that evening.

At the end of the successful mission, each of your men will receive ten million dollars was transferred to their accounts anywhere in the world. These payments should secure their loyalty and the successful completion of their duties. You will receive an additional fifty million dollars upon the completion of this mission. You must do this and do this now. Time is crucial," stated Amir.

"You are bribing me and my men with lots of money. Must be important. I will assemble my team today. What is our mission?" asked Donovan.

"You must kidnap the two partners, Sean Little and Jack Alair, who have the age-reversing formula. Ralph Barns, who heads the lab, states that they and they alone possess the formula, and his uncle confirms that it was those two who administered it, no one else. My sources in America have told me that both have gone into hiding, but they are not professionals, so they will have left a trail. Get them and get them now.

"You will be contacted by my associate, whom you worked with before, and he will deliver any information that we have. If there is anything you need, contact him. Plus, make sure that one of your men is a helicopter pilot. My associate is acquiring a large helicopter that I believe you will be needing." Then Amir hung up.

One hour later, a knock came at Donovan's door. It was an unnamed associate whom Donovan recognized. Without a greeting or saying a word, the Middle Eastern national placed a large goalie hockey bag in his hallway and handed Donovan two file folders. The associate nodded, turned around, entered the awaiting Mercedes, and left. Donovan opened the large bag, and there was $4,000,000.00 in American funds. *These guys sure work fast.* He smiled.

Donovan read the information. It would appear that Sean Little is an architect for the architectural firm Hillsborough and Smith Inc. out of Dearborn, Michigan, and is one of the two with the secret. The information listed includes Sean's home information, personal information, contact information and information on his new Lexus.

Next was the information on Jack Alair, who works for the accounting firm Swartz and Cooper, Inc., out of New York. New York is closer, so we'll go after him first.

Donovan hung up and called his associates. These men are all ex-military, and their loyalty is to anyone with lots of money. These were all large, tough ex-military guys who preferred the easy money of criminal activities over a regular nine to five job. They met Donovan at his home that night at seven p.m. Once all was assembled, Donovan laid out the plans.

"Guys, this is the big one. Anyone who agrees gets in cash right now, twenty thousand dollars with an additional $100,000 deposited by me into your numbered Swiss accounts later tonight. Once the job is finished, you will each receive ten million dollars wired to your account. This is no joke. Who's in?" Having worked for Donovan in the past and been handsomely paid, they all agreed.

"Good," said Donovan. "Once you are in, there is no turning back. I'm sure that our employers do not like to be toyed with. Here's the job: you know that a laboratory in Boston has uncovered a way to reverse the aging process. The two principals, Sean Little and Jack Alair themselves, hold the secret. According to all accounts, Ralph Barns, who owns the lab, does not know the formula, and it's only administered by Sean and Jack themselves. Sean is an architect and Jack is an accountant. These are the people we are being paid to kidnap and get the formula."

"That's it, just kidnapping two guys in suits? And what do you want us to do for the rest of the day?" joked Trevor, the tall, skinny ammunition expert. Everyone laughed.

"Return home and meet back here in two hours. All your gear, two suits, white shirts, ties, and black shoes for each of you. Myself, Trevor, Mike, and Randy are going to New York. Billy, Matt, Al, and Craig are going to Michigan. I will have the details worked out when you are back," stated Donovan.

Two hours passed, and Donovan finished his plans. He went to the barn and brought up a large white raised roof cargo van with the lettering "Ed's Electrical, No Job Too Big or Too Small, We Do Them All" plastered on the side. He had two identical vans. *An electrical service van is perfect. It can go anywhere at any time, and no one notices. Plus, the vans have no side windows to eliminate prying eyes.*

He even went so far as to actually have a dummy company and answering service set up if someone checked up on the company's name. The vans were registered under a fake company's name with a fake name on the ownership. *Good,* thought Donovan, *we may have to ditch the vans later on.*

Each van also had a false floor, and the compartment was fully equipped with 6-AK-47 assault rifles, 8–9mm Glock sidearms, twenty-four hand grenades, tactical gear, and enough ammo to start another war. Even the guns could not be traced back to him, as all the serial numbers had been removed. *You can never be too prepared.*

He brought the first van up to his house and loaded his case with his executive clothes and casual clothes, then loaded his tactical gear. *Always take too much equipment. You never know what to expect.* Donovan was fully loaded when the rest of his team returned.

"Billy, go get the other van out of the barn. The keys are in it," ordered Donovan. "Trevor, Mike, and Randy, place your gear in this van, and you others place it in Billy's van. Billy brought up the other van, and they loaded their gear and waited for their instructions.

"Men," said Donovan, "myself, Trevor, Mike, and Randy are going with me to New York to get Jack Alair. Matt, Al, and Craig are going with Billy to Michigan to get Sean Little. These guys are suits, not military people. They have gone to ground, but someone knows where they are. Guys like this always leave a trail. You are to kidnap your target and acquire anything that you think will help get the secret out of them. That could be a wife, kids, mom, dad, or someone they know or care about. If done properly, no one needs to get hurt.

"The sooner we get to them, the better. And yes, there will be others thinking the same thing. So let's get going. Billy, everything you need on Sean Little is in this folder.

"Here's an extra ten thousand dollars for expenses. Pay cash for everything—no credit cards, nothing. We don't leave a trail. Any questions?" Everyone shook their heads. Just as Donovan was entering his van, he joked, "after this, I'm moving to the Cayman Islands."

The men loaded themselves into the vans and departed. Donovan's group had a five-hour drive to New York, and Donovan thought that they could get in at about four a.m. and get downtown to the offices of Swartz and Cooper unnoticed. The others had a fifteen-hour drive to Michigan, so wouldn't be arriving until about three p.m. later that afternoon.

Chapter 12
Mercenaries Go for Jack Alair

On the drive, while Randy drove, Donovan, Mike, and Trevor changed into their business suits, shirts, ties, and black shoes. Donovan then issued them their fake FBI credentials.

"Might as well look the part," said Donovan. They easily located the offices of Swartz and Cooper Inc. on Lester Avenue in downtown New York.

"In an electrical van, you can park anywhere," Donovan joked with the guys.

Randy found a good spot to park, just off the back. They waited until 9:15 to make sure everyone was in the office. They exited the van and walked around to the front door. Three tall, handsome men in dark suits. No one noticed, and no one cared. They looked like executives going to their office. Perfect.

On the 12th floor, and entering the offices of Swartz and Cooper, Inc., Donovan approached the receptionist and requested to see the manager immediately. The operations manager came out and introduced himself. Donovan, waving his credentials, stated, "We are with the FBI and need to talk to Jack Alair and anyone who knows him."

"No problem," said the manager. "I've heard all about it on the news, but Jack has gone away, and I don't know when he'll be returning. You are, of course, welcome to talk to the other staff."

"Let me, into Jack's office, and I will meet with the others in there. This is a matter of national importance, so please bring me in the people who knew Jack the best," ordered Donovan.

The manager ushered Donovan and the two others into Jack's office, and all three started looking around. The first three people Donovan interviewed all said pretty much the same thing. Since his girlfriend Nancy had left him, Jack turned into a little bit of a recluse. He had his apartment in a luxury building off Charlotte Avenue, and that was about it. They mentioned that he was up to something with his friend Sean, but Donovan already knew that.

On the fourth person, they hit pay dirt. John Forrester said he was Jack's friend and was visibly nervous. John was a middle-aged, intellectual type who obviously disliked confrontation. Donovan could tell that John knew something and was determined to find out what he knew.

"Mr. Forrester, lying or withholding information from an FBI officer during federal investigation is a criminal offense and can get you up to five years in a very unpleasant prison. You must tell us everything you know right now, or my two associates will arrest you, put you in handcuffs, and take you away. What do you know?" yelled Donovan.

John, visibly shaken, said, "Jack contacted me and said that he needed to lay low for a while. I offered him the use of my cabin in Maine, and he said thanks and hung up. He knows where the key is."

John then grabbed a piece of paper and, while writing, said, "Here's the address to my cabin near the little town of Rockport, Maine, and directions to my cabin."

"Have you spoken to him since?" asked Donovan.

"No," replied John, "the cabin is in the middle of nowhere, and there is no cell service up there. The closest village is fifteen miles away." Perfect, thought Donovan. *No way that this guy can call ahead and warn him. Should be an easy capture.*

Donovan immediately stood up and thanked John on behalf of himself and the FBI. "Your friend is in danger, and he needs our help," Donovan said as the three exited the office.

Randy was in the van waiting for them downstairs, and they left. Donovan checked the directions on his phone and determined that they had a seven-hour drive. While driving, the three changed back into casual clothing and prepared their weapons. Mike opened the false floor in the van and distributed the weapons of choice.

"This should be no sweat," said Mike, and they all agreed.

Outside of Rockport, Maine, they filled up with gas and got sandwiches.

Mike went in alone and paid for everything with cash. He wore a large, brimmed hat in case the gas station had surveillance cameras. Can never be too careful, Donovan always said. They arrived outside of the cabin a little after five p.m.

"Everyone set, ready to go?" asked Donovan.

"Yes," they all replied.

"As he is not expecting company, I will walk up and knock on the front door. If questioned, I will say that my boat broke down and that I need help. Randy, you stay with the van, and when I signal you, drive up, and we will take Jack Alair with us. Mike and Trevor, you stay in the bushes until I signal you to come in," said Donovan.

Donovan knocked on the door, and Jack answered. Donovan, recognizing Jack from the photos, started to explain that his boat had broken down and needed to make a call. All the while, Donovan was waving to Mike and Trevor to come in. *Strange,* thought Jack, *this fellow has plastic gloves on.* As Jack started to reply that he didn't have a phone, Donovan stepped back, and Mike came around the door and put an automatic rifle up to Jack's forehead. Mike never said a word, deferring to let his boss speak.

"You are Jack Alair of Swartz and Cooper Inc. In New York. You will sit down and tell us everything you know about your age-reversing formula. You will tell us, or we will kill you. Now sit down."

Donovan pulled out a kitchen chair, and Jack nodded and sat down. Jack was stunned and had no idea what was happening.

Donovan then ordered Mike to tie Jack up. Mike took a strong plastic zip tie out of his nap sack and tied Jack's hands behind the back of the chair, plus he zip-tied each of his legs to the chair legs. The third man, Trevor, guarded the door. Jack could tell these guys were pros and knew what they were doing.

"This is no joke. There is no one coming to save you. You will tell me what I want to know, and you will tell me now. What is the secret of the age-reversing formula, and where did you find it?" ordered Donovan.

"I don't know that. Only Sean knows. After spending two weeks with me in New York, he goes home and, about a couple of weeks later, calls me and tells me that he has discovered something and we'll both be rich. I go down, and he does some tests on some dogs, and the results were impressive. The dogs were so active, they acted like pups," Jack answered, his voice trembling.

"We agreed that I would handle the administration and Sean would handle the procedure. Knowing that we needed accurate clinical tests, I contacted Ralph Barns of Barns Laboratories in Boston, whom I knew through our previous business dealings before. I eventually met him and told him the story. Of course, he thinks I'm nuts and that it's all a scam, but I convince him to let Sean and I come in and run some tests. We eventually do some tests on some animals, and the level of their energy gets Ralph's attention. He keeps the animals under observation for about two weeks, and they are still healthy and acting like pups.

"On our next visit, while walking into the lab to do more tests on animal subjects, Sean announces that it is time for a human trial, lays down on the table, and pours the chemical down his throat. There was nothing we could do. We were so shocked.

"Sean had already given Ralph signed papers, absolving him of any responsibility, so Ralph says that we might as well proceed. Sean disrobed, and we took photos of every square inch of his body. Sean then goes into a clean room for two days and emerged with no hair, but you would swear that he was five years younger.

"Comparing the photos, there was no doubt that Sean was a younger version of himself. Can't explain it, he just looked younger. Sean was fine. Ralph did every test on him known to man, and Sean was in perfect health. Then Ralph called his sixty-eight year old Uncle George and made him an offer to also be tested. George jumped at the chance and was at the lab the next day.

"Sean and I came back after George arrived, and Sean administered the formula. George emerged just like Sean did, apparently five years younger and full of energy.

"That's the guy you see telling the story to the CNN reporter. As soon as that interview hit the airwaves, the media frenzy began. Ralph called me, telling me he was holding up in the lab and that I and Sean better head for the hills. I borrowed this from my friend's cabin, and heaven knows where Sean is. All I know is that he's in northern Michigan, in a cabin somewhere. That's it, that's all I know," said Ralph.

"Bullshit," said Donovan. "You know, and you are going to tell us about the formula."

"But I don't know," protested Jack. "I don't know how he found out about it or what it is or why it works. Sean is the guy you need to see, not me."

This enraged Donovan, and he started beating Jack with the side of his Glock, 9mm. He just kept hitting and hitting Jack until Mike grabbed his arm.

"He'll be ready to talk now, boss," said Mike.

Through his bleeding lips, Jack kept saying, "I don't know, I don't know."

Donovan again started hitting Jack, knowing they had the wrong guy. By this time, Jack was already unconscious, and Donovan had put a bullet in his head.

"Dead men tell no tales," he said.

They walked to the awaiting van and left. Donovan was furious that they had picked the wrong guy. And as before, an electrical van in cottage country was not noticed, and they drove away undisturbed.

Chapter 13
Mercenaries Go for Sean Little

Billy, Matt, Al, and Craig traveled through the night, taking turns driving and stopping only for gas and food. They followed Donovan's instructions and only used small gas stations and paid cash for their purchases. They drove directly to the offices of Hillsborough and Smith Inc. in downtown Dearborn, Michigan, and after changing into their suits, they pulled the same charade of being FBI agents looking for Sean Little.

Try as they might, no one knew where Sean was. They all stated that Sean was a creative guy who did his best work away from the office. Few of the staff ever got to know him very well. Besides, he was their boss, so they left him alone. Even Roger Hillsborough, the owner of the firm, was glad to help but did not know where he was. They left with the only chance of going to Sean's house to hopefully find a clue to where he had gone.

They arrived at the farmhouse one hour later, and it was deserted. Prying open a back door, the four gunmen entered the house. They searched every room, every closet, every desk drawer. All they could find was hundreds of sketches for office buildings. Totally frustrated, the only thing they could find was an outdated phone directory from about five years ago. Everyone kept their friend's numbers on their cell phone. Nobody kept pocket phone books any more, but at least it was a start. Best to retire to a hotel, start making calls, and await news from Donovan. Phoning Sean's friends was not necessary, as Donovan got a text from his contact: "Sean Little is at a cabin in Shanty Creek, Michigan, on 56 Fairmount Drive."

These people are good, he thought. *Nothing you can't find out if you have enough money.* Somehow, they always know before we do. He immediately contacted Billy and gave him the directions. The hunt was on.

The police and real FBI were just behind the mercenaries. Monica Forsyth, the chief FBI agent on the case, was on her way to Jack Alair's office in New York. Monica was a career FBI agent who distinguished herself in any assignment she was given. She was a tall, dark-haired, steely-eyed, determined individual who made sure that her actions were respected in this man's profession.

She thought this was going to be an easy assignment until she visited Jack's office first, only to find that others posing as FBI agents had already been there. Jack's friend and coworker, John Forrester, told them everything and gave them directions to his cabin near Shanty Bay. The real FBI agents, hoping to get there before the impostors did, radioed ahead to their office in Maine and a helicopter with four FBI agents left. After a forty-five minute flight, they arrived about one hour after Donovan and his henchmen had already left.

They landed in a clearing at the T intersection off the road, and the FBI agents got out with guns drawn and started running for the cottage. When they arrived, two agents approached the front door, and the other two positioned themselves on either side of the cabin. It was evident what had gone on here. There was Jack, securely tied to the kitchen chair, obviously tortured, with a bullet hole in his forehead.

"Whoever is after these guys mean business," muttered the FBI supervisor. The supervisor immediately radioed back to Monica and explained the situation.

"We are sweeping the cabin for fingerprints, but I believe the guys who did this are pros. I don't think they left any clues," said the supervisor.

Monica Forsyth immediately notified the Michigan office and had Sean's cell phone traced back for the last two weeks. Excluding all the calls to the office, the agents in Michigan came up with a call made to Bill Fryer, a lawyer for Todd and Todd Inc. in Detroit. This call was made just before Sean went into hiding.

"I am on my way right now. Find this guy, question him, and do not let him out of your sight. That is an order," yelled Monica to her FBI associate.

At the airport, Monica had a plane waiting and flew directly to Michigan. There was no need to go to Bill's office, as they already knew that Jennifer had flown there to meet him, and they left in his Yukon together. The FBI agents on the ground also quickly found out that Bill Fryer had a family cabin a few hours north of Detroit. They also knew that there was a small, privately owned airstrip a few miles away. Monica told them to notify the owner of the airstrip to inform them they would be landing in two hours.

"Will do," replied the FBI agent.

Two hours later, the government plane with Monica and her other FBI agents on board landed. The local police and FBI agents gave them a ride to the cabin.

"Our men are in hiding and have the cabin surrounded," replied the FBI agent who had spoken to Monica over the phone.

"Good. Here is the plan. I will approach the cabin and introduce myself. I do not suspect any resistance. Remember, this guy is an architect, not a criminal," stated Monica.

Monica walked up to the cabin and knocked on the door. Jennifer answered, and this shocked Monica, thinking that she had the wrong cabin.

"I am Monica Forsyth with the FBI, and I am looking for Sean Little. Is he here?"

Jennifer, likewise shocked, called out, "Sean, I need you."

Sean came out of the bedroom, totally shocked at seeing a lady FBI agent standing before them.

"Yes, I'm Sean Little. How may I help you?"

"May I come in?" asked Monica.

"Yes, please do," said Jennifer.

Right then, two other heavily armed FBI agents entered the room and stood there, staring. Monica, seeing the look of terror in Jennifer's and Sean's eyes, said, "Guys, I have the situation under control. Wait for me on the porch, now get going." They walked out and took up positions on the porch.

"What's going on here? I'm up here to get away from the media frenzy over a discovery I've made, and now I've got armed FBI agents talking to me. I have done nothing wrong, and I have broken no laws. Why are you here, and how did you find me?" questioned Sean.

"We were able to track you through your phone call to your friend Bill Fryer, and we determined you were here. There seems to be some validity to your age-reversing discovery ever since it came to light that the government-funded Barns Laboratories has done tests on animals and human subjects. I think that once it hits the news and TV, everyone wants a piece of you, including Uncle Sam.

"Now, for the bad news, someone else is looking for you, and they are not as nice as we are. Someone wants your formula or whatever it is and will kill you to get it.

"I am sad to say that your friend, Jack Alair, has been found in a cabin

100

in Maine, obviously tortured and then killed with a bullet to his head," explained Monica.

Jennifer, overcome with emotion, started crying. This upset Sean, who then yelled at Monica, "Jack knew nothing. I made the discovery all on my own, and we agreed that the less he knew, the better. Being an accountant, he set up a company for the two of us to make money off my discovery. Jack was to handle the administration, and I was to handle the procedure. That's it. He knew nothing."

"That's likely why they killed him once they found out he had nothing to say. Whoever is after you two are professionals and killed Jack to ensure he couldn't identify them. They obviously mean business and will kill you both if you don't come with us," stated Monica.

"Seems we have little choice. Oh, this is my girlfriend, Jennifer, and where I go, she goes. And coming up from the dock is Bill, who is the fellow you traced my phone call to. He has to come too," stated Sean.

"No problem, I don't know how this will play out, but it would appear that every moment you are not in our custody, ' your lives are in danger. Likely, the people who killed Jack are on their way here now. Get your stuff ready, I have a plane at the local airstrip and we'll leave as soon as possible," Monica stated.

Bill walked past the two-armed FBI agents on the front porch and then saw Monica his jaw dropped. Sean quickly explained what was going on, and Bill agreed. *Best to agree,* he thought, *especially when the two guys on the porch had enough firepower on them to start a revolution.*

"Okay, anything you say, let's go. I have an allergy to lead, and I don't want to be here when the guys that killed Jack arrive," said Bill.

They quickly packed an overnight bag, and Sean grabbed his aluminum case out of his dad's Buick. Monica looked at Sean and asked, "Have you got everything you need?"

"Yes," Sean replied.

The three of them were escorted to the awaiting SUV's and driven to the airstrip. They boarded the plane, noticing all the while the other FBI agents had their guns drawn. Shortly, they were airborne.

Later that day, Bill, Matt, Al, and Craig arrived near the cabin. There were police and FBI vehicles everywhere. They drove down the road near the cabin, and Bill rolled down his window and said, "Excuse me, sir, what's going on?"

The local police officer leaning up against his car said, "Those people who discovered that wonder age-reversing drug were located just down the road here and have been removed by airplane. Seems that someone killed their partner, and they are all under police protection now. This is the most exciting thing that's happened here in a while."

"Yeah, I heard all about it on the news. I hope they keep enough of that stuff for me and my wife. We could use it," said Bill. The officer laughed, and Bill waved and drove on.

Hearing this, Bill immediately called Donovan and told him that the FBI had beaten them to Sean Little.

"I already know. My contact just told me," said Donovan.

Chapter 14
Back to the Laboratory

On The Flight to Boston

Once in the air, Monica tried to explain the situation to Sean, Jennifer, and Bill.

All three were visibly frightened. Jennifer started crying. *She cries when really upset, and she had every reason to be really upset,* thought Sean.

"This is what it looks like to me," stated Monica. "Because the initial tests on your formula have proven successful and Barns Laboratories has been involved, everyone believes you've discovered the fountain of youth. I'm not sure if you have, but it's not for me to decide. I am to escort you back to Barns Laboratories for you to conduct further testing. Ralph Barns is waiting for you."

"But we have done nothing wrong. We have not broken any laws, so you can't hold us," said Sean.

"That is not for me to decide. I'm just following orders. You are being detained under the National Securities Act, which pretty much allows us to do whatever we want.

"If what they say is true, your formula is a world-wide game changer. Whoever possesses it can dictate terms to anyone else in the world. No person can resist the prospect of being younger, no one. And for this reason, we know that some very mean professional people are after you and your formula and killing you to get it is the least of their worries," replied Monica.

"But I won't tell them. They can beat it out of me, but I still won't talk," protested Sean.

"Oh, no?" Monica questioned. "You're tied to a chair while they are cutting Jennifer's fingers off or taking a propane torch to her face. How long would you hold out?"

The gravity of the situation started to dawn on Sean. He finally realized that without the FBI's protection, they would be hunted down, forced to talk, and then killed. They had already killed Jack just so he couldn't identify them, so they would be next on their list. The three sat in silence for the rest of the trip. Sean tried to console Jennifer as best he could. There was little else they could do.

At Barns Laboratories

They arrived at night at a small airport close to the laboratory. The tarmac was covered in black FBI vehicles, and there must have been over thirty armed agents mingling about. Once they landed, a large black SUV pulled up to the plane, and they were escorted to it and told to get in.

They arrived at the laboratory forty-five minutes later. There were eight SUVs in their procession, and they arrived at the front door of Barns Laboratories. The agents got out and surrounded the vehicle Sean, Jennifer, and Bill were in.

"It's unlikely that anyone will try to kill you until they have your formula, but this protection is necessary nonetheless," stated Monica. "I am responsible for keeping you safe and alive. The building is surrounded by agents 24/7 and you will be living here for the time being. All your food and anything else you require will be brought in for you. It's not safe for you outside, and the additional tests must be conducted. My orders come from the highest levels of our government."

"Great," Bill said. "I went to help Jennifer find her boyfriend, and now I'm a prisoner of the FBI in a lab in Boston. I have no part in this and don't want to be a part of this."

"My orders are direct and clear. You three will remain in this lab until we tell you otherwise. It is highly likely that whoever killed your friend Jack will come after you, Bill, and use you to get to Sean. Jack was tied to a chair, beaten and tortured, and then shot in the head. I don't think whoever is looking to acquire this formula will hesitate in doing the same to you," stated Monica.

But Bill protested, "But I don't know anything. What value am I to them?"

"I don't think you see the whole picture here," stated Monica. "These people will stop at nothing to get to Sean and his formula. As Sean has no family and few friends, they will likely kidnap you, torture you, and send the videos to Sean saying, "If you don't tell us what we want to know, your friend dies." That is the least of what they will do. Just by you being with Sean for a couple of days makes you a target."

With that, an FBI agent motioned to Monica to proceed, and they exited the vehicle.

The FBI agents were so close to them as they walked up to the main door of the lab that they could smell their breath.

"Movie stars at the Oscars don't have this many people this close to them," joked Sean.

Ralph met them inside, and Sean introduced Jennifer and Bill. Ralph asked, "Did you hear about Jack?

"Yes, the FBI briefed us on the way here. If you know what's going on, please let us know. The last few hours have been a terror. Here we are at Bill's cabin, not hurting anyone, and the FBI surrounds the cabin and takes us away on an airplane, and now we are here," said Sean.

"Well," said Ralph, "the world has gone nuts ever since my uncle George was interviewed on CNN. With the election over, it seems it's the only thing on the news.

"I was asked by the FBI to give a statement to the press to try and kill some of the rumors of you discovering the "fountain of youth". I told them that you had approached me and we did some animal testing, and then, to everyone's surprise, you took the formula yourself and we did tests on you. And other than your hair falling out, you seemed okay.

"Then I took the risk, contacted my uncle and tested the formula on him. He's great and that's when all hell broke loose. Some lady he knows has a relative who is a reporter for USA Today, and they ran a story on George. CNN then got a hold of it and sent a reporter and a film crew to see him in Dallas, Texas. Once that interview hit the airways, it has been replayed a thousand times. Every newspaper and news outlet in the world is in Dallas talking to my uncle. And unfortunately for us, he's happy to talk and is enjoying his celebrity status."

"I understand all about that," stated Sean. "The media is playing this up big time. But do you really think that our lives are in danger?"

"Yes," replied Ralph. "If your formula does actually reverse the aging process, every government and every person in the world will want it.

Whoever controls it could dictate terms to anyone they wanted, using the prospect of being years younger as bait. Name me a world leader that wouldn't sell their soul to be five, ten, or twenty years younger. Or name a billionaire who wouldn't give up their fortune to be younger. The power of this would change the world."

At this point, Monica introduced herself to Ralph, "I am Monica Forsyth, the FBI officer in charge of keeping the four of you safe and alive. All of you, for the time being, are restricted to staying in this lab. Your apartments are well furnished, so you will be comfortable here. Anything you need for yourselves or for your work will be provided, anything. You will continue with your tests and find out what this formula actually does. But under no circumstances will you or any of your staff be allowed to leave, understood?"

"Yes, we understand," they all replied.

Sean then asked for his aluminum case. Monica sternly replied, "We will be keeping that safe for you until tomorrow morning, at which time it will be returned to you."

Sean knew full well that everything in that case would be inspected and that they would easily find his notes on making and applying the formula. But he knew that it was futile to ask again. Monica then said, "It's been a tough day for all of us. Let's get washed up, get some food in us, and have a good night's sleep. Agent Jones here will take your orders for takeout food, and it will be delivered to your room. Order anything you want, compliments of Uncle Sam."

Ralph spoke up and said that there was an excellent Chinese food restaurant around the corner, and everyone nodded in agreement. They all told Agent Jones what they wanted for dinner. At this one of Ralph's assistants escorted them to their apartments. They at once had showers, and then their food orders were dropped off at their apartment doors. We all fell into bed, exhausted. The next morning, Ralph and Sean got together and discussed what to do next.

"We just continue on with the testing," stated Ralph. "We have everything we need here, and what we don't have they'll get for us. After hearing what happened to Jack, I agree that our lives are not worth ten cents once we step outside of the front door. Best to stay here and be safe."

"Okay," said Sean. "Seems we have little choice. We must determine if this process is viable, safe, and can be marketed. I agree that further tests have to be conducted, and this is the place to do it. Just wish I didn't feel like such a prisoner all the time. I feel bad for Jennifer and Bill. They didn't need to be dragged into this."

"Yes, I agree," said Ralph. "But until we know what we have, they are safer here with us."

"Yes," said Sean, "what's the game plan?"

Ralph replied, "I have ordered in several pigs of various ages for us to continue testing on. As you know, pigs have a similar anatomy to humans, and they are the best to use, except for more human subjects."

"Okay, let's get started," stated Sean.

As they walked to the lab testing area, they walked by a window facing the main street. Where last night there were only FBI and police vehicles, now there were the police and FBI agents plus thirty or more news agency camera trucks, reporters, and hundreds of people outside the barricades the police had installed.

"I guess news travels fast," remarked Ralph. "Once they were done interviewing my uncle, news got out that you were here to resume testing, and they've all come out. What a circus." Sean nodded in agreement.

They continued walking and entered the laboratory, and Sean's case was there on the table. He knew it had been tampered with, and upon opening the case, his suspicions were justified. It was obvious that his notes had been removed, read, and photocopied, and the originals returned to the case. But there was little he could do about it. Unknown to Sean, the list of ingredients in the case and the instructions had been sent to two other government-funded testing facilities. These were secret labs that were charged with duplicating Sean's findings.

Over the next six days, a routine settled in. Bill and Jennifer read and watched movies. Ralph and Sean continued with their testing. Eating meals was their only true delight, so Bill and Jennifer ordered something special every evening.

"Might as well make the best of it, and besides, it's on Uncle Sam's tab," said Jennifer.

The tests on the pigs were all proceeding well, and Ralph and Sean were pleased. They retired to bed with the test subjects now under twenty-four-hour observation. That night seemed just like any other night.

Chapter 15
Attack on Barns Laboratory

No one realized that once news got out that Sean was at the Barns Laboratories to continue testing, plans for his capture were being made. Donovan called his contact and requested a blacked-out helicopter, a big one capable of holding ten people. The next day, he was told that a Bell Huey helicopter had been acquired and where it would be. He confirmed with Randy that he could fly it, and Randy said, "I could fly that thing up your ass without you even knowing it." Donovan considered that a yes and confirmed the helicopter.

At six p.m. that evening, Donovan briefed his men on their drive to the meeting place just outside of Boston.

"Listen up, we are to secure and kidnap Sean Little and his girlfriend, Jennifer Sloan. Here are pictures of both of them for you. Plus, there is an aluminum case that Sean Little keeps the ingredients of the formula and its directions in, this is also to be acquired. This is a straight "snatch and grab" operation. We land on the roof, we go in, we kidnap Sean and Jennifer and the aluminum case, and we leave."

"But why do we have to go after the girl if we have Sean and the case?" asked Billy.

"It's because if Sean is holding out on anything to do with the formula or doesn't want to cooperate, his girlfriend can be used to persuade him to help us," replied Donovan with a grin. Then Donovan continued. "My contact says that there is little or no security inside the building. All the cops are on the outside, and the doors are locked. There is a helicopter landing pad on the roof, and once we land and get what we want, we'll be out of there before anyone knows it. Put your silencers on your weapons, and don't kill anyone unless you absolutely have to. Let's get going."

Right on time, the helicopter landed in the secluded, designated landing spot just outside of town. The Middle Eastern pilot got out, and Randy got in. Parked off to the side was a large tour bus, which would later be their getaway vehicle. The helicopter pilot left the helicopter running and then handed Donovan the keys to the tour bus. Everything was going as planned.

Once in the air, in Boston, the sound of the helicopter aroused no suspicion.

Later that night, the blacked-out ex-military helicopter approached the roof of the lab and silently landed. Seven black-suited, heavily armed men jumped out and proceeded to the single door. Thinking that this "snatch and grab" operation should take less than ten minutes, Donovan had ordered Randy to stay on the roof and to be ready to take off as soon as they came up. None of the police or agents on the ground saw the helicopter, and even if they had, few would have thought much of it.

The seven men easily pried open the roof door and descended into the fourth-floor storage area. They knew what they were looking for and were determined to get it. Each man was equipped with plastic wrist restraints and duct tape for people's mouths. They slowly descended the stairs to the third floor, which housed the apartments they were looking for. Donovan's contact told him that Sean and Jennifer were in Apartment Room #3. Slowly, they walked down the stairs and knocked on the door. Jennifer answered and looked directly into the barrel of an automatic assault rifle.

"Do not say a word. If you cry out, you will die. Where is Sean Little, and where is the aluminum case?" asked the mercenary.

Jennifer, almost crying said, "Sean is still downstairs in the lab running some tests. The case must be with him. It never leaves his side."

The mercenary nodded, turned Jennifer around, put duct tape around her mouth, and then secured her hands with the plastic wrist restraints.

"If you do exactly what you are told, both you and your boyfriend will get out of this alive," whispered the mercenary.

He led her down the hallway to the staircase. The second-floor lab area was deserted. All seven of the kidnappers entered and searched around. They had been told that down the hallways were observation rooms and that the staff and Sean may be observing some test subjects. Just as Donovan was splitting up his men to check the hallways, a sound came from behind a wall.

"This is the FBI. You are completely surrounded, and you cannot escape. We now have men on the roof arresting your pilot. You cannot escape," yelled Monica.

Hearing this and thinking it was a lone guard with a single handgun,

Donovan opened fire against the wall where the voice came from. Matt, the mercenary holding Jennifer, threw Jennifer behind some cabinets and landed beside her.

All of a sudden, the room was full of gunfire from the fifteen heavily armed FBI agents as they cut down five of the seven mercenaries. Only Matt, holding Jennifer, and Donovan were left. Donovan continued firing, and the FBI riddled the area that he was hiding in with bullets. Donovan was dead.

"To the person holding Miss Sloan, you are completely surrounded, and your associates are dead. If you stand up and surrender now and hand over Miss Sloan unharmed, you will be taken into custody and given a light sentence. I witnessed that you did not fire on us, so you will be charged as being an accomplice to the crime, nothing more." Monica hoped this would work, and the agents waited patiently for a response.

Then they heard a voice. "I am going to surrender now. I was told that there would be no bloodshed. I was hired to do a kidnapping, nothing more. I do not wish to hurt Miss Sloan. I am going to stand up now with Miss Sloan, and once up, I will put my hands in the air."

Matt slowly stood up and helped Jennifer stand up. Matt had his hands over his head, and the FBI agents came out of their hiding places. Monica instinctively rushed to Jennifer while the other agents forced Matt to the ground and handcuffed him. Without saying a word, three agents proceeded with Matt to the stairs to the awaiting FBI paddy wagons.

Monica yelled out, "The area is secure, now you can come out." Several of the doors down the hallways to the observation rooms opened, and Sean, Ralph, and several lab assistants emerged.

Sean rushed to Jennifer, who was crying uncontrollably. Holding her tight in his arms, he assured her that everything was okay. A lab doctor approached Sean and said, "Give her one of these pills and put her to bed, and she'll sleep comfortably."

"Thank you," muttered Sean.

Sean went to take Jennifer back upstairs, and Monica said, "Best to hold off for about fifteen minutes while my men search the area."

"No problem," said Sean, and he retired with Jennifer to a couch in the lab.

The FBI agents came back and stated that the laboratory was secure. Sean and Jennifer then were motioned to go upstairs, but they were still accompanied by two heavily armed FBI agents. When they reached their apartment door, the two agents went in first just to make sure. They knew that the room had already been checked, but after another thorough search, they motioned for Sean and Jennifer to come in.

"Both of us will be right outside your door all night. Nobody will get to you, I promise," said the larger of the two agents.

While all this action was going on in the lab, four heavily armed agents came up a back set of stairs and proceeded to the roof. They burst forth from the unlocked door and, with assault rifles raised, approached the helicopter. At first, Randy thought it was Donovan coming back, but once he saw the rifles pointed at his head, he knew better.

The commander of the FBI agents said, "Your friends downstairs have all been killed, and you will be too if you don't turn off that helicopter and surrender. Don't even think of trying to escape, as we have orders to shoot to kill, and at this range, we can't miss. There are two Boston Police helicopters in the air above your head. You cannot escape."

Randy, the pilot, seeing that his situation was hopeless, turned off the key and emerged from the helicopter.

"Put your hands in the air," ordered the supervisor.

As soon as he did, two agents approached him and hand-cuffed his hands around his back. They frisked him and removed his 9mm Glock pistol, and all four agents proceeded to take him downstairs to the waiting paddy wagon to join his friend Matt.

The supervisor arrived on the second floor and reported to Monica that the pilot had been taken into custody without a fight and that the helicopter remained on the roof.

"I will arrange for the helicopter to be removed," she said. She then thanked the supervisor for his good work, and the supervisor nodded and left.

About an hour later, Sean left Jennifer sleeping and emerged from the apartment.

"Please do not leave your apartment, Mr. Little," said the taller of the two agents.

"There has just been an attempt on my life. My girlfriend is hysterical but is asleep now, and I'm going to talk to Agent Monica and see what is going on. Come with me if you like, and leave the other fellow here," replied Sean.

The taller agent, knowing that Sean was leaving, agreed, and they both entered the lab area together. At a table, Monica was assuring Ralph that he would be getting all new equipment to replace anything that was damaged.

Sean walked over and said, "Monica, I don't want any government bullshit. I want you to tell me exactly what is going on."

Monica replied with, "Yes, Sean, you have a right to know. Since Jack was killed, we knew that some highly paid professional mercenaries were determined to get to you and your formula. They are always one step behind us, and in Jack's case, one step ahead of us. They are getting their intel from somewhere. With the two surviving members of the group in custody and the six others dead, we should be able to track down who hired them. That's all I know for now."

"But how did you know they would be here tonight?" yelled Sean.

"We didn't know. Fortunately, a night watchman at the next building saw the helicopter land and saw the mercenaries get out. He called it in to the police, and they notified us. We were able to get to the lab just in time, as we heard them coming down the stairs with Jennifer. Fortunately, the lab was deserted, and you and the other lab staff were down the hall in the observation rooms. When I introduced myself as the FBI, the one guy opened fire, and all hell broke loose. After his associates were killed, the guy holding Jennifer surrendered. You know the rest," said Monica.

"That's it, that's all. My girlfriend is almost killed, and you don't know what's going on?" yelled Sean.

"Sean, I know one thing: the people who hired these thugs are not going to stop trying to get to you. These guys were highly paid professionals who could acquire an ex-military helicopter and pay for it in cash on a moment's notice. That takes some serious connections and some serious money. This is not the end of this. They and others will stop at nothing to get to you and the formula," said Monica.

The FBI Interrogates the Mercenaries

The two captured mercenaries, Randy, the helicopter pilot, and Matt, were both ex-military. Questioned in isolation, they both told the same story. Monica questioned Randy first and recorded everything he said.

Monica, after turning on the tape recorder, spoke, "You have been involved in the commission of a crime that has left seven people dead. If you cooperate and tell us everything you know, you will receive a reduced sentence. We know you were the helicopter pilot and were not involved in the gun fight in the lab."

"Seven people?" questioned Randy. "I know that you guys killed six out of the seven in the lab, but who is the seventh guy? Monica said, "Jack Alair, Sean's partner, was found in a cabin in Maine, tied to a chair, beaten, and then killed with a bullet to his head."

Visibly shaken, Randy started to talk. "No one told me what happened to Jack. They said they left him alive once they found out that he didn't know the formula."

"Well, you were told wrong. Now tell us everything you know, starting from the very beginning," said Monica.

"Okay, Donovan, my ex-commander in Afghanistan, calls me and asks me if I would like to fly a helicopter and make lots of money. No problem, I said. He told me to meet him at his home at seven p.m. that evening. When I arrive, I meet the rest of the crew, eight in total, including myself and Donovan. Four of the others I knew, two I didn't, but they were obviously ex-military and knew Donovan."

"What were the names of the others? asked Monica.

Randy replied with, "Well, there was Donovan and myself, Billy, who seemed to be Donovan's right-hand man, and Matt, Al, Craig, Trevor, and Mike. Eight in total."

"Then what?" asked Monica.

Randy said, "We all went into Donovan's living room, and Donovan explained the terms. This is the big one, he said. He said that those who agreed to join in would receive twenty thousand dollars in cash that night, with an additional $100,000 to be wired to our bank accounts later that evening. He said that at the successful completion of the mission, each of us would have ten million US dollars sent to the same bank account or any other bank account in the world. He said that he has worked for these people before and that they have very deep pockets, and they never let him down. Hearing about this money, everyone agreed to join. No one budged, no one quit.

"Donovan said that ours was a snatch-and-grab operation to capture the two guys with the age-reducing formula. He told us a little about Sean Little, the architect, and Jack Alair, the accountant, and said that they are just some guys in suits who have discovered some miracle drug and that his friends want it badly. All we need is their formula, and once we have it, these guys are free to go. We all thought it would be an easy operation, over in a couple of days, and no one needs to get hurt, no problem.

"I have never worked with Donovan since we left the military. But I guess he thought he could use a helicopter pilot, and I can fly them all. I was a helicopter instructor in Afghanistan and can fly any helicopter ever made. Seemed like easy money to just fly a helicopter."

Randy continued, "Donovan had two identical large white raised-roof cargo vans painted up to look like electrician's vans. Pretty smart, no one ever questions a work van, so you can go anywhere. These vehicles had false floors in them loaded with guns and ammo. Donovan took Mike, Trevor, and me with him to get Jack to New York.

Billy, Matt, Al, and Craig went to Michigan to get Sean.

I can't say about Billy in Michigan, but in New York, I sat in the van while the three others went up to Jack's office and, posing as FBI officers, questioned Jack's co-workers. Jack was not there, and a coworker said that he let Jack use his cottage up north. I ended up driving to the cottage and Donovan, Trevor, and Mike went in and questioned Jack. Thirty minutes later, they got in the van, saying that Jack was okay but does not know the formula.

Donovan's contact told him that Sean had been taken to Barns Labs in Boston and that we were to meet him ASAP at the Wandering Inn just off Highway #93, just outside of Boston. No problem. We drove day and night and finally arrived. The next morning, Donovan laid out his plans for entering the lab, kidnapping Sean, his girlfriend Jennifer, and his aluminum case with the formula and directions in it.

On the designated night, we met in a field outside of Boston, and a guy got out of the blacked-out military helicopter and motioned to Donovan that it was all his. There was also a large tour bus ready for us to escape in. Whoever Donovan is tied up with, these guys are pros. I was given directions to the lab and the rest, you know."

Monica then turned off the tape recorder and motioned for the two agents to escort Randy back to his jail cell. Across the hall, Randy's story matched up with Matt's. Matt confirmed that Donovan had recruited them at his house, that Billy was the head of his group, and that they were to kidnap Sean Little. Donovan always received intel from someone off his phone but would not talk about it.

Not knowing where Sean was, we got some hotel rooms and awaited further instructions. All we had was an old personal phone book of Sean's that we were going to start making calls from when Donovan contacted us. He said that his contacts knew that Sean was in a cabin up north and gave us the directions. We immediately drove there, only to discover that you guys got there first, and that Sean had left with you.

Matt's story of the plans for the attack on the lab matched Randy's descriptions exactly. Matt continued, "And yes, after entering the lab, I was told to secure Jennifer Sloan to ensure that Sean would either come with us or give us the formula. I was told that no bloodshed would take place," said Matt.

The questioning FBI agent replied with, "For seven guys not wanting to hurt anyone, you sure were armed to the teeth. You had enough firepower to take over the city of Boston. But it is confirmed by the agents there that, other than taking Jennifer Sloan at gunpoint, you did not engage the agents in the lab in the gunfight. This and your cooperation today should stand well for you in court."

Visibly relieved, Matt was escorted back to his jail cell.

Terrorists Never Sleep

In a world where billions of dollars float around the world in a moment's notice, news travels fast. Within the hour of the failed attempt on the lab, Amir, the Middle Eastern terrorist, was talking to one of his trusted operatives, Nybar, in America.

Nybar had been used to help acquire the military helicopter and was then sent to mingle with the crowd outside of Barns Lab and look like an innocent bystander.

Nybar immediately informed Amir that the attack on the lab had failed and, to the best, he could see most of the American operatives had been killed. He did not know if Sean Little was still alive. Amir thanked Nybar for his loyalty and told him to wait for further instructions. While Amir was planning his next move, his phone rang. It was his master, the crown prince of his oil-rich kingdom.

"Amir, I heard about the disaster at the lab in Boston. You failed. I will have that formula on my desk, or I will have your head in my trophy room. Get it and get it now." Then he hung up.

Amir, visibly shaken, started thinking about how to proceed next. He used American operatives, all of whom had worked for him in the past. Now these people were either dead or in prison. He had to go to his next set of operatives, who, being his countrymen, were not able to pass for innocent Americans as well as Donovan and his crew. But he had to act fast and use people who he could trust. They would just have to do it.

He picked up his phone and called Nybar back. "Assemble your men and wait for my instructions." That was all that Amir said, and he hung up.

Chapter 16
After the Attack on the Barns Laboratories

After the attack, work in the lab was impossible. The equipment had to be replaced, and the walls needed to be patched up. Plus, the entire lab had to be completely sterilized. Ralph gave the assistants the week off. The ones that did leave the building were accosted by the reporters and spectators outside.

Ralph, Sean, Jennifer, and Bill, still "guests of the FBI" in the lab, were forbidden to leave.

"We will bring you anything you need," was the often-heard statement from the FBI agents. Sean knew that the boredom of staying in their apartments was starting to wear on Jennifer and Bill.

Bill would constantly argue with Monica, "I know nothing and no longer want to be a part of this. If anyone asks, I'll just tell them that I let Sean use my cabin and that Jennifer came to my office, and I agreed to help her find Sean. That's it. Then I'm under house arrest by you, FBI agents, and forced to live in a small apartment in this lab." Bill kept on arguing every day, and finally, Monica relented and let him go home.

"You may be hunted down and killed by the same fellows who attacked us here," reasoned Sean.

"Killed for what? Giving Jennifer a ride to my cabin?" exclaimed Bill. "Regardless, I'm not spending another day in this awful place. Goodbye."

And with that, Bill was escorted out of the lab by the awaiting FBI agents. He was taken directly to an awaiting plane and flown back to Detroit, Michigan. The FBI retrieved his Yukon from the cabin and had it waiting in the parking lot for him. A few days later, some reporters showed up, and he gave them a complete explanation of the last number of days. After that, he was left alone. *I guess my story is just not that exciting, thank heavens,* mused Bill.

The rebuilding of the lab was taking longer than planned. The FBI had security on every floor, and dozens of agents kept watch over the building and roof night and day. They blocked off the entire street, and no reporters or onlookers were allowed near Barns Labs.

Somehow, the approval came through to continue testing on live human subjects.

Ralph couldn't believe it. Soon as he found out, he said, "I could have gone to jail for allowing you to ingest the fluid and then asking my uncle to take the formula. I violated every law in the book concerning the proper procedure for testing a new drug. If anything had happened to you or my uncle, I would be sitting in a jail cell right now."

In talking to Monica later that day, she was aware that the approval to resume live human testing had been approved by the highest levels of the US government. She said, "The media has ridden this story for all its worth. This has obviously forced the hand of the government to pressure those who grant such procedures to give you the green light. As they are all government employees themselves, they would have caved in. So there you have it. Conduct your experiments on live volunteers. You have the official go-ahead."

Ralph laid out his plans for conducting the experiments on live human subjects.

He knew there would be hundreds, if not thousands, of people wanting to be five years younger. He laid out his plans.

"As we have six observation rooms, we can do experiments on six people at a time. These test subjects must be both men and women of various ages and various nationalities. We need a complete cross-section of society," said Ralph.

He acquired three male and three female volunteers, all between the ages of forty to sixty years old, who had already passed their physical checkups and been pre-screened by associated testing laboratories. All six were totally aware of the risks involved and were being paid ten thousand dollars each to participate.

Once the repairs to the lab were finished, the application of the formula went smoothly, and as before, in the middle of the next day, all of their hair fell out, but the people all stated that they felt wonderful. Even though aware of this side effect, the women seemed to have the most difficulty with being bald. Two of the three women started crying when it happened and couldn't stop. They were kept for another week of observation, and eventually, all were released back into society.

The media pounced on them, interviewed them, and then immediately claimed that the "Barns Labs Has Discovered the Fountain of Youth." Everyone thought the media frenzy couldn't get more intense, but after the first test subjects started talking about how good they felt, there was no holding any stories back. Every news agency in the world was running these stories, and major governments around the world were accusing the US of withholding this important medical discovery from the rest of the world.

Ralph selected the next six test subjects. He again picked three males and three females, but this time one man and woman were of Chinese descent, another man and woman were of Middle Eastern descent, and the last were two of Native American Indian descent. *This should give us a good cross-section,* Ralph thought.

The procedure and tests ran exactly as before. Other than their hair falling out, the test subjects were in perfect health, likely in better health than before they started the procedure. Likewise, they were kept for one week of observation and then released back into society.

The media pounced on them, and news agencies in China and the Middle East made these people in their home countries "superstars". The American-native Indian couple was likewise celebrated in their societies. All reported good health and were happy with the procedure. They hoped that they would be accepted for further testing, as they all wanted to be even younger.

By this time, the crowds around the Barns Labs area just kept getting bigger and bigger. It would appear that every news agency in the world was outside their doors. Sean stated that he read about the media frenzy when Howard Carter unearthed King Tut's tomb in the 1920s but this was one thousand times worse. The news agencies kept up their relentless call to release this drug into society "so that everyone can benefit, not just a chosen few."

Going to Nevada

Sean, Jennifer, and Ralph were getting nervous. They mentioned their concerns to Monica, and she agreed, "The media can't stop speculating that you've found the fountain of youth. With the crowd growing larger every day, it won't be too long before they're bashing down the doors. I know that if the crowd wanted to, they would overpower the police we have surrounding the building. I agree that this situation is getting dangerous. Let me see what I can do." Monica then left and closed the door to her makeshift office.

The next morning, Monica called a meeting that everyone was to attend.

"Here it is. My superiors agree that the crowd outside is growing every day, egged on by the relentless media reporting. They also agree that at some point, the crowd will attack the building, and none of us will be safe. It has been approved by the highest levels of our government that all of us, Ralph, Sean, Jennifer, and all of the lab assistants, are to be moved immediately to an abandoned but still operational lab in the Nevada desert. Ralph, all of your equipment will be removed and relocated there, or you can order new equipment. All of your requests for equipment and materials are to be fulfilled without question. Any questions?"

One lab assistant yelled out, "Are you nuts? You want us to walk outside into that? They almost ripped our heads off the last time we went out!"

"No problem," assured Monica. "As soon as I send the word, military helicopters will be using the landing pad on the roof to ferry us to awaiting planes at the nearby military airstrip. Those of you who want to go, you have one hour to pack your bags and anything else you can carry." They all quickly agreed, as the Nevada desert sounded a lot nicer than being prisoners in this lab.

Ever since Ralph's wife had died, and he had no children, he was totally dedicated to his work. This amazing discovery was the most exciting thing that has happened to him in years. He was eager to go, and the rest of the lab assistants shared his enthusiasm.

Jennifer packed her clothes, and Sean stuffed his aluminum case with his ingredients and made sure he had the instructions. He and Ralph instructed which computers had to go to Nevada, and the agents assured him that they would be brought along on later flights.

The helicopter arrived on time and flew them off to the military landing strip. Awaiting them were forty armed guards and military passenger jets ready to take off. Without fanfare, once Sean, Jennifer, Ralph, and all the assistants were assembled, they boarded the first jet and took off for Nevada. All sighed a sigh of relief. Being cooped up in the lab and watching the crowd was starting to scare them.

Landing at the Nevada Compound

It was over a six-hour flight to the military airstrip in the Nevada desert. Once disembarked, they were motioned to the awaiting SUVs to take them to the abandoned military compound. Once there, Monica introduced them to Colonel Fred Wayne, who would give them a tour of the facility. Colonel Wayne was your typical career soldier. He was short and muscular, serious, and never cracked a smile. You knew that with him, everything was "by the book". Sean instantly knew that they would never become friends.

They were escorted to the awaiting SUVs. They entered the labs first. The rooms, as expected, were empty, and you could tell that they had recently been swept clean.

The Colonel spoke, "Ralph and Sean, this is your laboratory. All of your equipment from your labs in Boston will be arriving in the next few days. I have been given direct orders that all equipment you want is to be ordered and acquired immediately. Anything you want, no exceptions. You are to draw up plans on how you want your testing and observation rooms laid out, and the builders will be working on this facility twenty-four hours per day to get you up and running."

Next, the Colonel led them to their apartments and placed their bags in them. All were obviously quickly equipped with new beds, dressers, and bathroom supplies. Likewise, these rooms looked like they had just been cleaned.

The Colonel spoke again. "Dinner will be served at 1700 hours or five p.m. in the mess down that hallway. I expect after supper everyone will want to go to sleep, and we will meet tomorrow morning at eight a.m. Ralph and Sean, the sooner you let us know how you would like the lab laid out, the sooner my men can get working and have it ready for you. See you at dinner." With that, everyone retired to their selected rooms for a nap before dinner.

Dinner was an uneventful affair, with Ralph and Sean discussing how they would like the lab laid out. Sean would always defer to Ralph, saying, "You're the lab guy. Draw up the plans any way you like."

"But you're an architect," replied Ralph.

"Yeah," replied Sean, "I'm your guy if you want plants climbing out of the walls and reflecting natural light coming in through the skylights. I design office buildings, not testing labs. Ralph, do whatever you want. They'll build it. You can have thirty observation rooms if you want, I think they'll give it to you."

Ralph said that the existing ten rooms could become our observation rooms for now, and Sean agreed. With that, Ralph and Sean joined in on the conversations about the media frenzy and how the world was reacting to the news, the real news, and the speculated fake news. At the end of the meal, Colonel Fred Wayne appeared.

"Ladies and gentlemen, In Boston, you had to stay indoors for your own protection. Here, you are free to wander outside anytime, day or night. This is a military base and is now heavily protected on the ground and from the air. Please do not be alarmed by my men outside. Their sole job is to protect you. If you decide to go wandering off into the desert, they have been instructed to follow you at a safe distance. Go anywhere you want near the compound, and I can assure you of your safety. Any questions?"

One young lab assistant spoke up, "Is there a town I can go to and maybe a bar?" Everyone laughed.

"Good question," answered the Colonel. "You are in the middle of a 5000-acre compound surrounded by a desert, and the closest town, Myerstown, if you can call it a town, is fifteen miles away. Once news gets out that you are here, every news agency and the curious will flock to this area. For that reason, we cannot allow you to leave the compound. As for the bar idea, I like it. We will set aside one of the smaller buildings as a bar, TV, games room, and music hall for yourselves to relax in. I really like your suggestion of having a beer. I'm sure my superiors will go for it."

Everyone in the room clapped. With that, the Colonel smiled, saluted, and left the room. Everyone likewise retired to their rooms for a much-needed night's sleep.

Chapter 17
Prisoners in Nevada

Within two months, the lab had been laid out with everything that Ralph and his assistants requested. They had ten apartment/observation rooms set up for their test subjects. Anything they wanted, from the bar/games room to updating the buildings, was done to their specifications.

Jennifer, who loves to cook, started to help out in the kitchen. She always liked to joke.

"I guess I'm not going anywhere, so I might as well cook."

The evening meals became quite a treat, with everyone pitching in to make their dinner the highlight of the day. Anything they asked for was granted, except leaving the compound. But still, they could not shake off the feeling that they were prisoners, even if it was for their own safety.

Colonel Fred Wayne was right. News travels fast in America, and the nearby towns quickly filled up with reporters, cameramen, and the curious. Even in the middle of nowhere, the people still came. With the compound buildings being so far from its perimeter, nobody inside the compound noticed the crowds of people mingling about. For fun, they would have the guards take them for rides in the Jeeps to look at the people standing out in the hot sun. Many had signs asking to be a volunteer, help me, and just about anything else you could ask.

As this is a military compound, the perimeter was patrolled 24/7 and the entrance points had enough guards to outfit a small army. With the large crowd gathered at the main gate, other than large bulky items, everything was brought in by helicopter, test subjects, food, and equipment. The government was taking no chances that another attempt would be made to kidnap Sean and his formula.

After months of testing on more animals and various healthy human test subjects, all the results came back positive. It would appear that the test subjects from forty to sixty years old fared the best, with no adverse side effects.

When they did tests on various subjects over sixty years old, the results were positive as before, but the subjects took longer to start feeling good again. Therefore, for the last month, all tests were conducted on people aged 60–80 years old. As before, their hair would fall out about midway through the second day, but they would complain of being lethargic for days afterward. Then they would feel better, and their tests all came back positive. It would appear that the subjects seventy years and older tended to sleep more and took longer to return to normal than the sixty year olds.

Tests on the Sick and Terminally Ill

It was decided to begin testing on healthy human subjects eighty years and older. After the application, these test subjects took weeks to return to normal. They all reported that they felt lethargic and just wanted to sleep. Two weeks later, they all reported that they were feeling years younger and requested that they would like to volunteer for another application.

The positive test results were just too encouraging to ignore. Results were sent off to other government laboratories, and some of the test subjects were taken to these other labs for further testing. The test subjects were all being paid ten thousand dollars but said they would do it for nothing, given the chance to be years younger. Ralph was convinced that the procedure had curative powers and wanted to test it on sick subjects.

"We all know how well it works on perfectly healthy subjects, but we must find out what it can do for unhealthy ones," stated Ralph.

Sean protested, "I feel the shock to a sick person's body will be too much for them to bear, and they will die."

"Yes, I agree, but we won't know until we try," Ralph replied.

It was decided that they would begin testing subjects based on their illnesses. They decided that they would start with the scourge of mankind, cancer. Ten terminally ill cancer patients were then recruited with their families' full consent. These were people who were on death's doorway so they felt they had nothing to lose. Likewise, they were all paid ten thousand dollars. The families of these people approved of the testing but did not like that they could not be with them during the testing. The FBI and Ralph were adamant that no visitors would be allowed.

The test subjects were helicoptered in and prepared for the application.

Some even arrived in their hospital beds. They fasted for the required two days, and once prepared, Sean administered the formula. Everything was fine for the next day, but midway through the second day, horror-struck. While the subject's hair was falling out, their cancer took hold and spread all through their bodies, consuming them in hours. Sadly, all the test subjects with cancer died this way horribly. Sean, seeing this, was sick to his stomach. One body was selected for an autopsy, and the rest were all removed and cremated.

Ralph and the doctors decided that cancer seemed to be the only disease that reacted negatively to the application. Later, test subjects with respiratory problems, internal organ issues, and every other disease known to man were tested. The individuals remained healthy but still retained their illness, though most were in remission. It was the cancer that remained a puzzle. Sadly, it would appear that the procedure opened a doorway for the cancerous cells to spread, killing the test subject in hours.

Sean Wants Out

After months of testing on hundreds of test subjects, they were getting a clear picture of what this application could and could not do. Sean, burned out from the workload and stress of watching the cancer patients die, wanted out. He contacted Monica and said, "I want to go home. This place is driving me nuts. I work ten-twelve hours per day every day, and I'm leaving. Shoot me if you want, I'm going home."

"But we need you here, and my orders are to keep you here, alive," exclaimed Monica.

Sean said, "Look, you have the ingredients, you know the procedure. You videotape my every move and record me mixing the ingredients. You have copies of my notes. You don't need me any more. I want to go back to my old life and be an architect in Michigan."

Sean and Ralph were unaware that the other testing laboratories had been trying for months in vain to copy their results. They used the same ingredients and followed the same procedures to the letter. It's just that after everything, the test subjects didn't change. They came out of the observation rooms with their hair intact and feeling exactly how they went in. No changes. These other labs continued to test and retest on hundreds of subjects, but with no results, none.

"Do the tests yourself. You have everything you need, you don't need me any more," Sean told Monica.

With that, he retired to his room, and for the next four weeks, he and Jennifer just wandered around the compound. They were especially fond of having picnics in the open air of the desert. They were given an SUV to use, but as they expected, they were shadowed by six other SUVs full of military personnel wherever they went. But their guards kept their distance, so it wasn't so bad. Sean, viewing his constant escorts, would mutter to himself, *Little chance of some nooky in the desert. Oh well.*

Monica had other medical experts brought in to assume Sean's role. Seemed simple enough. But the only problem was that they could not duplicate the results. They tested and retested.

They would ask Sean, and he would politely tell them, "You hold me and Jennifer prisoner here, and now you want my help? Go to hell." He refused to discuss it with them or enter the lab.

"It's your problem now, not mine. I want to go home."

Ralph Plans to Escape

The isolation was wearing Ralph down. Over dinner, they concluded that they would be kept here forever, prisoners of their own government. They both knew that everything they said or did was being recorded. There was no getting away with anything. When they finished their dinner, Ralph winked at Sean, and Sean thought nothing of it. Even with Ralph's urging, Sean would not discuss the application or come back into the lab.

"They can kill me if they want. I'm done," Sean would always answer with.

Ralph convinced Monica that he needed some additional, very expensive high-tech equipment installed. When Ralph tried to explain what the new equipment was needed for, she protested, "I have no idea what you are talking about. Write out what you need, and I'll get it for you."

The next day, Ralph typed out exactly what he needed and then handed the list to Monica. Without looking at it, she passed it on to another FBI agent and told him to get this equipment brought in ASAP.

Ralph then called in some helpers to make room for the new

equipment. Two days went by, and Monica informed Ralph that his new testing equipment would be arriving by helicopter tomorrow morning.

"Just too risky bringing it in by truck. Too many people around the main gates. Someone will likely get hurt," Monica said and then exited the lab.

The equipment arrived and was brought in. The equipment was accompanied by two technicians, Dan and Oliver, who were prescreened by the government. Ralph liked Dan, the head installer, immediately. Dan was a serious, "I take no nonsense" tall intellectual type of person who looked like he carved his own path in life. Oliver was the more quiet type and obviously took his instructions from Dan. Ralph stood around and watched as the two highly qualified technicians hooked up the new equipment. Oliver was more of the "I take orders and do as I'm told" type of person.

They said that it would take them four hours for set up and two hours of testing and they would be done. Ralph stayed with them the whole time, and the guards mingled about. Once in a while, the guards would get too close to the equipment, and either Dan or Oliver would yell,

"Get away from that. Don't touch anything. This equipment costs three million dollars, and you can ruin it. Now go get a coffee or something and leave us alone."

As there wasn't much going on, the bored guards would often leave to get a coffee and a sandwich. Life in the compound was starting to get to them too, Ralph thought. There was little to guard here, just Ralph and the two installers. Just as the installers were finishing their final test, the two guards left to go to the lunch room.

Ralph went over to the wall where the installers had hung their coats, and Ralph, hiding his actions from the overhead cameras, slipped a note into the inside pocket of Dan's jacket. This is my only chance, he thought. Everything checked out okay, and Ralph was familiar with the testing equipment. He shook both Dan and Oliver's hands when they left, all the while looking them straight in the eye.

"Thank you very much. I am glad you could help me out," Ralph said to Dan as they were shaking hands.

They thanked him, and after making sure that he was familiar with the new equipment, they left for the awaiting helicopter. After a long day, Ralph got some dinner and went to bed.

Ralph's Note Hits the Airways

Back at home after a busy day, Dan, the one technician, started looking for his glasses and reached into the inside pocket of his jacket. He pulled out a slip of paper and, as he was throwing it into the trash, noticed that it was not his writing. The note read, "Help me. I am Ralph Barns, the fellow who watched you work. I, Sean Little, his girlfriend, and my assistants are being help prisoners here. We are not allowed to leave. The military is planning on developing Sean's age-reversing formula as a military weapon to blackmail the other world leaders. Please inform the news media. Please help us get out of here. Ralph Barns."

Dan, knowing of the security at the compound and having heard about Sean's miracle drug, knew exactly what to do. He looked up the email addresses of the major news outlets, took a photo of the note on his cell phone, wrote out the location of the compound and a brief note, and started sending it off. He even put it on his Facebook page and told everyone who read it to copy it and pass it on.

It was after ten p.m. so he didn't think anything would come of it until the morning. By eight o'clock the next morning, every single morning news program in America was showing photos of Ralph's note. The news media was in an uproar. The demands to release the prisoners were deafening. Other world leaders got wind of it and started calling the President of the United States to protest.

In the compound, the next morning at eight-thirty a.m. all hell broke loose. There were guards running around everywhere, and Monica came bursting into the lab and started screaming, "What have you done? You've ruined everything. The news is full of the note you slipped those installers, and the news media is calling for our heads. The world is saying that you are being held prisoners here and that the government is developing this formula into an instrument of warfare. What have you done?"

Ralph calmly looked at Monica and said, "We are tired of being your prisoner and tired of your government bullshit. We are finished helping you. Go to hell."

Just then Sean, hearing all the noise, came into the lab, and Ralph told him what he had done and that the installer informed the media, and it was all over the news. Sean was so shocked, he just stood and stared, then hugged Ralph.

"Thank you, thank you. You are a life-saver."

The news outlets reported on nothing else. The crowds outside the gates of the compound kept growing bigger and bigger. The news stations had their own helicopters flying overhead, and even after being told that this was a no-fly zone, they still kept flying. There must have been thirty camera trucks outside of the compound. The world-wide call for their release was deafening.

The President Makes a Statement

The President of the United States, an older, gray-haired, portly career politician, ordered his press secretary to make an announcement at twelve noon. Every news agency in the world was running the program of the government announcement. Associated Press, Reuters, and the other world-wide news media were live streaming this broadcast around the world.

The President called his press secretary, Mrs. Shannon Wilson. She was a tall pretty intellectual who had a comfortable way of speaking to the press that the President lacked. Mrs. Wilson, smartly dressed, entered the press briefing room of the White House, was introduced, and then spoke, "Early this morning, at approximately six p.m., the President of the United States of America was made aware that innocent American citizens, Ralph Barns of Barns Laboratories, Sean Little, an architect, his girlfriend Jennifer Sloan, and seven laboratory assistants were being held against their will in a government compound in the Nevada desert.

"He has ordered their immediate release and an investigation into the actions of persons and government organizations that have imprisoned these individuals. This investigation will be headed up by a special Senate committee, whose members will be selected in the coming days. That is all I know at this time. Thank you."

Then she exited the stage. While walking the newspaper, people started yelling questions at once, but Mrs. Shannon Wilson just kept on walking.

True to their word, helicopters arrived to escort them from the compound. Monica and the other FBI agents were being informed of their rights and that they would be held in custody until the Senate hearing was arranged. This is serious business, thought Sean. He did not bother to try to say goodbye to Monica. She was just doing what she was ordered to do. It was her superiors that would be starting to sweat right about now.

Though technically free, Ralph, Sean, and Jennifer all knew that their lives were still in danger. Whoever killed Jack would be regrouping and going after them. Sean's secret was just too big.

They were then introduced to their new FBI supervisor, Jeff Woods. Jeff Woods was a tall, slim career FBI agent who stood erect and took all his duties seriously.

"I am sorry for your troubles. I am sure that Monica and her people were just following orders. You all realize that your lives are still in danger, and there will be groups of people trying to get to you and your formula. You can go wherever you want, whenever you want. But please, we must guard you 24/7 or you'll be dead or kidnapped by the weekend. The people who killed your friend Jack will likely be coming after you again. Plus, on the bright side, I have been informed that you will be paid handsomely for the time you were under custody. How much that is, I do not know."

Sean spoke first, "Yes, we agree. Though we hated being held prisoners in the compound, we all know that our lives are not worth ten cents without your protection.

"As long as Jennifer and I can go back to Crystal Falls and resume our lives, you will get no complaints from me. Surround the property with your men. I don't care. Just leave us alone."

Ralph and Jennifer nodded in agreement. Everyone knew that it was Sean they were after. Everyone else was a secondary player in this drama.

Chapter 18
Sean and Jennifer in Crystal Falls

Everyone wanted to leave. Once they arrived at the government airfield, they all said their good-byes and went their own separate ways. Ralph and his assistants returned to their homes in Boston. Sean and Jennifer were flying back to Michigan and then being driven to Sean's home in Crystal Falls. They arrived at the local military airfield closest to Crystal Falls and were driven by an armed escort for the final forty-five minutes to Sean's home. Upon reaching his home, the guards kept Sean and Jennifer from exiting their vehicles while their men searched the house.

"We have made keys to your home while you were away. It had been broken into through the back door, but nothing seems to be missing. Heaven knows what they were looking for," reported Jeff Woods, their FBI supervisor. Mr. Woods was a tall, slim, no-nonsense individual who seemed very serious about his position with the FBI.

Fifteen minutes later, the armed FBI agents emerged and stated that the house was clear. Sean and Jennifer were then allowed to exit their vehicles.

Jeff Woods spoke again, "You are safe here. We will be guarding you 24/7. Anything you want, we will get for you—food, clothes, anything." Sean entered the house and saw his drawings scattered about.

"I doubt anyone was interested in my office building drawings," he said.

Sean, Jennifer, and Jeff entered the kitchen, and Jennifer opened the fridge. The food had been in there for months now and had all gone bad. Sean immediately grabbed some big garbage bags, and they both emptied the fridge and Sean took the spoiled food outside. When Sean returned, Jennifer said, "I'm starving. What about two extra-large meat-lovers pizzas, two bottles of white wine, and a case of Bud Light? Do you guys think you can handle that?"

Jeff Woods wrote his list out on a piece of paper, took it outside, and handed it to one of his men. You could hear him say, "This is what Sean and Jennifer want. Get enough food and soft drinks for the rest of the men. Now get going. The rest of you men set up a perimeter around the house with your vehicles and stay there. You will be relieved in the morning."

After a long wait, the food arrived. The pizzas were cold, but Jennifer heated them up in the oven, and Sean opened up a bottle of wine.

"Ah, my first taste of freedom." And then he hugged Jennifer. They ate and finally went up the stairs to bed. As they fell asleep, they could hear the men talking outside.

After a good night's sleep, they both showered and came downstairs. Jennifer, being the cook, started making out a grocery list of everything she needed. From milk and eggs down to chicken, pork chops, and steaks.

"Hey, it's on Uncle Sam's tab. We're going to at least eat well." She laughed. They ate the rest of last night's pizza and had only water to drink.

Sean said, "I might as well go out and meet with our protectors." Sean ventured outside, only to find that instead of twelve men, there were more like forty. He asked, "I am Sean Little and want to speak to whoever is in charge here."

"I'm in charge. I am Jeff Woods' partner, and my name is Harold Smith. What can I do for you?"

FBI Supervisor Smith was like his associate, Mr. Wood, as they were both tall and slim career FBI agents, determined to fulfill their duties. Even while Sean was talking to him, Agent Smith was always looking around for signs of any problems.

"First, this is the grocery list my girlfriend has made up plus, take my BBQ tank and fill it up, please. I like to cook outside," replied Sean.

"Second, we have been your prisoners in that Nevada compound for the last few months. We have just spent the last several months with the FBI breathing down our necks, and I don't want you and your men so close that we can hear you talking. This is a large property, so set up your perimeter along the fences.

"Third, order some portable toilets, as I don't want your men coming into my house at all hours. I am on a septic system, and it can only accept so much.

"Fourth, I want you to leave us alone and have no intention of going anywhere. If we want to talk to you, we will come out to see you.

"And fifth, we do not want to see anyone—none of your people, no reporters, nobody. Just leave us alone. Is that clear? And last, can you have some of your men go over to the Watts farm over there and ask for my pets? Jennifer and I would love to have them back."

"Yes, that is clear. I will get you your supplies and your pets and position my men along the fence lines away from the house, replied Harold Smith. He nodded, turned, and walked toward his men.

Within the hour, the FBI agents brought up all their pets. Sean's pets immediately surrounded Sean and almost knocked him over, jumping on him. They were so excited to see him and he them. He picked up each pet in turn, hugged them, and then introduced them each in turn to Jennifer. What a relief to have pets to play with again!

For the next six days, Sean, Jennifer, and their guards settled into a somewhat normal routine. Sean cleaned up his drawings off the floor and started working on the office towers he had been working on. Jennifer, meanwhile, busied herself with tidying up the house. *Surprising how dirty a house can get if it's not been lived in for months,* she thought.

The FBI left them alone and were quick to get their groceries and pet food. Sean BBQ'd every night whatever Jennifer prepared for them. Like in the compound, the evening dinner was the height of their day, and Jennifer went out of her way to make it special. Sean knew this house and knew it had been tampered with. His opinion was that the FBI had likely installed miniature cameras throughout, and everything that he and Jennifer said or did was being recorded. He made sure that he had music playing whenever he wanted to talk to Jennifer, just in case. Sean knew the government had not been able to duplicate his test results, and so they were determined to find out what Sean did that made the formula a success.

Sean set up a table for two in the main room near the fireplace. This was the nicest room in the house and far nicer to eat in that than the plain farmhouse kitchen. Sean especially liked the main room because this is where his parents liked to sit and talk to him. His habit every night was to BBQ outside and then retire to the main room to sit in front of a roaring fire to eat and drink.

On the second night of this routine, Jennifer, facing in the window, screamed as she saw the face of an FBI agent looking in. Sean was furious. He marched right outside and demanded to speak to the agent in charge. Jeff Woods came out. Sean started yelling, "What's going on here? I'm sitting down for a meal with Jennifer, and your pervert agents are looking in the window. What do you want next—to see us screwing? Get those assholes away from my house." And then he marched away. He went to the barn and came out with two tarps, a hammer, and some nails.

"This will keep you assholes from spying on me," he yelled out to the agents down the driveway.

Sean went into the main room and hammered the tarps up to the windows. Jennifer was still upset, but after a few glasses of wine, she settled down. They hardly talked for the rest of the night and then went off to bed.

With her next-day order, she ordered curtains for all the windows. The windows still had the old curtain rods on them, and Sean and Jennifer had no problem putting them up.

"This should keep those creeps from looking in," she said.

The following night passed, and the agents stayed away from the house. When Sean was out BBQing, he had the chance to see where the guards were.

Every night, Sean would start a fire in the main room and burn the drawings he was finished with. One night, while the fire was going, he took an old newspaper to see how long it would take to become ashes. The next night, he made sure that his pile of papers included a handful of plastic page protectors. These he also placed on the fire to see how long before they were consumed.

The next night, he was ready. He first started a fire in the main room and then went outside and BBQ'd as always. He looked around the house and saw no one. He knew that his fire inside would be going well, and then his chance came. Looking over his shoulder, he could see the takeout food delivery guy show up with boxes and boxes of Chinese food. Naturally, the guards from all over went over to eat. He casually turned off his BBQ and went inside.

Knowing fully well that they were always being watched, he casually locked the front door as he walked by. Then he entered the main room and placed the more easy burning pine kindling on the already roaring fire. Jennifer entered the room with the food, and they sat down. Sean got up, stoked the fire, and put more wood on it. Just as Jennifer was about to say the fire was hot enough, Sean reached around to the back of the fireplace and grabbed the plastic page protectors with the papyrus and his notes. These he scattered on the large fire and placed the extra pine kindling over them to help them burn. The roaring fire did its work. First, the plastic caught fire, and then the papyrus. Within what felt like seconds, everything was on fire.

He then grabbed Francois Lebelle's writing desk, emptied his dad's stuff onto the floor, and placed the box upside down on the roaring flames. Being over two-hundred years old, the wood was dry, and it was quickly caught by the flames and consumed. Sean stood there transfixed, watching the five-thousand years old papyrus and the writing desk burn.

Then, moments later, he could hear the agents wasting valuable seconds trying to open the locked front door. Once opened, in a flurry, the FBI agents came barging into the main room. Jennifer started screaming, and this delayed the men for a few seconds more.

"What's going on here?" demanded Sean.

"What are you burning?" yelled Jeff Woods.

"Just my old notes and a broken writing desk that I didn't need any more. What's all the trouble? Do you guys have nothing better to do that to frighten my girlfriend? Now get out."

FBI Agent Jeff Wood went to the fire and could tell that whatever was there was now gone. Did the fellow manning the cameras just see Sean burning his old drawings as he did every night, or did he really burn something of value? The flames were at their peak, the papers were gone, and the writing desk was a pure ball of flame.

The FBI agents now knew that Sean was aware that the house had been wired for sound and video. Sean thought, *I can never trust them again, and I will never will.* The agents apologized and left. Sean and Jennifer sat in silence, and Jennifer never asked what Sean pulled out of the back of the fireplace. After everything that had gone on, she didn't want to know.

Chapter 19
Sean Gains Control

For the next two weeks, life fell into a pleasant routine. The FBI agents promised to stop snooping on them, and Sean accepted their word but didn't believe them. Sean was infuriated that they had installed surveillance cameras in his house without his knowledge. Regardless, Sean thought, *we are still prisoners here, and there is nothing I can do about it.*

He then started thinking about his murdered cousin, Jack. Who really killed him? Was it the government or someone else? It was Monica who said that outsiders had tortured and killed Jack, and he had taken her word on it. He started to think that the attack on the lab could have been staged and that maybe the guys they shot were not really dead. He never got close enough to see what had happened, and the cleanup crews were there pretty quickly to cart the bodies away. As before, he took Monica's word for everything. Monica, the same FBI agent who held them prisoner in Boston and then arranged for the new prison compound in Nevada. *Am I being dubbed?* The more he thought about it, the angrier he got.

Due to the fact that Sean and Jennifer never left the farm, Sean later discovered that all the roads around their farm were cordoned off and admittance was restricted to only authorized FBI agents, military personnel, and the locals who lived nearby. They've turned the little town of Crystal Falls into an armed encampment.

Sean continued to send off his drawings to Hillsborough and Smith via FedEx.

Sean gave the FBI a list of phone numbers to allow through, and when Roger Hillsborough, his boss, called, Sean immediately cut him off and told him that this and all of his conversations were being recorded. Roger just wanted to say that he was glad he was okay and that everyone in the office wished him well. They spoke a bit about the media attention his discovery has made and Roger told him that "you're now world-famous."

"That would be okay except this nagging feeling that there are people out there trying to kill me," replied Sean.

After their short conversation, they bid each other goodbye and hung up.

As Jennifer and Sean hated being interrupted, they made a deal with the FBI agents. If they wanted to talk to them, they could come up to the house between the hours of ten a.m. to four p.m. No sooner and no later. So they fell into an easy routine of an agent coming about eleven and getting Jennifer's grocery list and anything else they wanted. For the time being, this system was working out well.

Then one day Jim Woods, the chief FBI agent assigned to protect Sean and Jennifer, arrives. Opening the door, Jennifer said, "Well, well, we have the head cheese here today. What brings you up to see the shut-ins? Here to fix the cameras?"

"I would like to see Sean," said Jim.

"No problem. Come in and sit down in the kitchen. Would you like a coffee?" asked Jennifer.

"Yes, please, just black," replied Jim. Jennifer got him a coffee and went to get Sean.

Sean sat down. After discovering that the house had been wired with miniature CCTV cameras, Sean made no attempt to be friends with or to be nice to Jim.

"You have some very important people coming out to see you today. As far as I can tell, it will be an FBI supervisor and a couple of scientists. Why they want to see you, I do not know, but I'm pretty sure to say it's important. I said that you would see them when they arrive, likely about three p.m.," said Jim.

Sean replied, "Well, seeing that I'm not going anywhere, I guess it's okay. Just bring them up to the house when they arrive. I'll be waiting."

"Thank you," stated Jim, who got up and then left. While opening the door, he said, "Thank you for the coffee, Jennifer." And then she walked outside.

More Government Intruders, More Threats

FBI Visit #1:Stan Walls, District Supervisor of the FBI

Around three o'clock, you could hear the FBI helicopter landing in their field by the FBI's encampment. Soon afterward, a black SUV arrived. Out stepped three individuals in dark suits. Sean greeted them at the door. He ushered them to the dining room table and offered them something to drink. All refused.

"Allow me to introduce myself. My name is Stan Walls, District Supervisor of the FBI. These two gentlemen are both scientists, Mr. Ambrose and Mr. Smyth. We have come here to discuss your discovery."

Mr. Walls was a tall, dark, and handsome FBI official with a full head of dark hair. He easily stood at 6'3" tall and had an air of authority around him. Mr. Ambrose to his left was obviously the senior of the two scientists, and both he and Mr. Smyth looked like the type of people who spent their lives looking into microscopes.

"Well, I didn't think you drove all the way to Crystal Falls to discuss the soybean crop," said Sean, who was growing more and more to dislike the people keeping him captive.

Mr. Ambrose, obviously the senior of the two scientists, started, "Sean, we have duplicated your formula and application down to the finest detail. But even after hundreds of trials on animals and humans, we cannot duplicate your results. We have even collected your successful human test subjects and have tested them on everything we can think of and yes, they appear to be years younger and with renewed energy. But we cannot determine why you are successful and we are not. What are we missing?"

"Wow! Isn't this a switch? You bastards keep me, my girlfriend, and the lab staff prisoners in Boston and then in the Nevada compound. You let us out only after Ralph slips an equipment installer a note, and the media clamor for our release is so great that the President of the United States has to order our release. Then you bring me back to my parent's farmhouse, where you bastards have installed video cameras everywhere to watch me and my girlfriend have sex. And now you want me to help you? Go to hell," Sean said, as angry as hell.

"But Sean, this is a matter of national security. What if another country got a hold of this secret? They could blackmail the world," explained Stan Walls, the FBI District Supervisor.

"Bullshit," replied Sean. "I don't give a shit about your problems. You would have kept us in that compound until we died or killed us all like you killed my friend Jack. And why the hell is it my problem that your people are so stupid that they can't figure it out? Now all of you get out and don't come back."

"Sean, you are being unreasonable," replied the FBI District Supervisor.

"Unreasonable, damn right. I'm unreasonable," yelled Sean. "You can kill me or torture me, but I won't help or assist you bastards ever again. Those agents outside right now are laughing and watching videos of me screwing my girlfriend, and you want me to help you? All you people have done is imprison me, Jennifer, and my friends, and you just keep lying to us. I'm still in the middle of that desert, except for Ralph. Now get out and don't come back." Without saying a word, the three got up and left.

Sean was so mad that he thought he was going to explode. He has had enough. *Wow, now they want my help, well it's not coming.* And he went back to his office and continued his work on some new office designs.

FBI Visit #2: Lewis Smith with the FBI

Three days later, four uniformed officers showed up at his door. Sean met them at the door and greeted them. Opening the door, he said, "Oh, just like the mafia, here comes the muscle. Are you going to tie me to a chair and torture me like you did to my cousin, Jack? Maybe you should electrocute me first before punching me in the face. It leaves less bruises, and I'll look better at my funeral."

"We are here to talk to you," said the obvious leader of the group.

"But if you want to talk, why do you need the extra three goons with you? Are they here to tie me down?" asked Sean.

"No, we just want to talk," continued the leader. "Okay, then have the three goons stay outside, and you come in and talk," said Sean.

The leader introduced himself as Lewis Smith with the FBI. Mr. Smith was a tall, blond, arrogant individual whom Sean disliked as soon as he started talking.

"You are making it very difficult on yourself by not cooperating," Mr. Smith said to Sean in a very direct and menacing way.

At this, Sean exploded. "Difficult. You bastards imprison me and my friends in Boston and then in the desert. We get out because Ralph slipped an installer a note, and the President himself has to order our release. If it wasn't for Ralph, you would have kept us there for the rest of our lives or just killed us like you killed my cousin Jack. Now we come here, and your bastard pervert agents have my house rigged with cameras and watch the videos of my girlfriend and me screwing while they eat their lunch. And now you tell me I'm making it difficult on myself?"

"You have to trust us," said Lewis. "We in the government will keep this a secret."

"Bullshit!" Sean yelled back with, "first, trust you. The only thing I trust you for is to imprison me and then kill me like you did Jack. I'll die before I ever trust you bastards again.

"And second, you idiots couldn't keep this a secret for two months. As soon as some lab technician wanted to help out his mother or his wife, he'd steal the secret.

"Or better yet, he'd sell it to the Chinese or Russians for a few hundred million, and where would you be? So your closely guarded secret would become common knowledge to the point where Walmart would be having it on sale for $299.00 or free with a washer and dryer. You people make me sick. I don't like you, and I don't trust you. Now get out."

Agent Lewis, knowing further discussions were futile, got up and left the room.

FBI Visit #3: Tyler Miles, Associate Director of the FBI, and Agent Monica Forsyth

Two weeks later, Jeff Woods, their FBI guardian, informed Sean that he would be having another visitor later that day.

"Why not? I'm sure I'll be here. But this guy won't be any more successful than the last," said Sean.

Sean took no notice as another helicopter landed. These landings were now a regular occurrence. About thirty minutes later, a dark SUV drove up. Out stepped Monica Forsyth, his original FBI guardian. She was accompanied by one guy in a suit and two obviously well-armed FBI agents. Sean, looking out the window, thinks to himself, *Okay, here comes the big one.*

The four FBI agents arrived at the back door just as Sean opened it.

"Well, hello Monica. The person who imprisoned me and the others against our will. And stupid me, I actually thought we had laws in this country. Did they just spring you out of jail to talk to me? What's this old home week? Sean sarcastically asked.

Monica said hello and ignored Sean's comments. She then introduced her boss, "This is Mr. Tyler Miles, the Associate Director of the FBI. We have come to speak to you."

Tyler Miles was an older gentleman with a short stature of about two-fifty pounds and well-toned muscle. He looked like the type of person who was comfortable ordering others around and getting his own way.

"Well, isn't that nice?" replied Sean. "You bring the big cheese and two heavies to soften me up. I guess they thought bringing you, Monica, would make me see the reason. But remember, you are the one who took us prisoner and had to be forced to release us. Now you expect me to like you? Are you all nuts?" But after a pause, "You are here anyway. Come in." But Sean could barely contain his anger.

Motioning for them to sit in the living room, Monica and Tyler sat while their two henchmen stood at their sides.

"Well, I'm glad to see you brought in the muscle today. Monica, I trusted you, and you repeatedly lied to me and held me prisoner. I now suspect that it was you or your henchmen that killed my friend Jack and maybe even staged the attack on the lab. All to force me into hiding until you discover the secret," stated Sean.

Monica responded, "No, Sean, we did not kill Jack, and the attack on the lab was not our doing. I give you my word on that."

Sean spat out, "Your word, your word, isn't worth shit. If it wasn't for Ralph slipping that installer a note, I would still be in that desert prison until I died or until you put a bullet in my head."

"Sean, we don't do that," replied Monica.

"What don't you do? You don't kill people, or you don't imprison them against their will. Which is it, Monica?" Sean yelled out, visibly upset.

Monica again ignored Sean's question. Then she said, "The Associate Director and myself have come to ask you to help us. Our best people cannot determine what you do to make the formula successful. We are at a loss without you,"

"Well, isn't that too bad? You kill my friend, Jack. You imprison us in Boston. You stage a fake attack on the lab, and then imprison us in a deserted compound in Nevada. You never had any intention of letting us go, you lying piece of shit.

"And now, after Ralph slips that installer a note and it hits the airways, the President himself has to order our release. I come home and your agents all smiles and with their "we are all here to help you" bullshit, I find out that they installed video cameras throughout the house and sit back and watch the videos of Jennifer and me screwing, and now you want my help? You people make me sick."

Tyler Miles, the Associate Director, gets upset himself and starts in on the conversation. "You will tell us what we want to know, whether you like it or not."

Sean yelled back, "Listen to me, you big fat lying piece of shit. I will not help you, and I will never help you. I will kill myself before I ever cooperate with you bastards again. Torture me like you did Jack, and then put a bullet in my head. I don't care. But I will not help you."

"You don't understand the situation you are in. We need your help, and we intend to get it," yelled back the Associate Director.

Sean yelled back, "Tell one of those morons you brought with you to give you their gun."

The director motioned for a handgun.

Sean said, "Great, now cock the hammer." The director cocked the hammer.

Now Sean, with his face right up to the directors, said, "Now put that gun up to my forehead and pull the trigger, you big fat lying piece of shit." By this time, Sean was seething with anger and put his nose one inch away from the director's face, and Sean wouldn't back down.

Sean, with his nose still up to the director's face, said, "Now pull the trigger or screw off, you lying pieces of shit. As I told you before not to come back, and I'm saying it again. Don't come back. Now get out, all of you."

Sean knew that they would not stop, but he didn't care. He would take the secret to his grave if need be. He wasn't going to let those bastards win, never, he promised.

As always, the TV was filled with stories and speculation about Sean and his age-reversing formula. Ever since Ralph's note appeared on the news and the President ordered their release, you would think that there was nothing else on the news.

The local TV reporters reported that this story was the main news topic around the world. Every news agency wanted to know and would do anything to get stories for their readers. Ralph Barns appeared on TV numerous times always to explain the attack on their lab, their move to Nevada, and their captivity there. He explained the successful test results and that, even after a few months, all of the test subjects were healthy and active. He always mentioned that it was Sean and Sean alone who knew the secret and administered the formula. No one else

The news agencies hunted down and interviewed all of the Barns Lab assistants, interviewing each in turn. They stated exactly what Ralph said— no more, no less. And they confirmed that it was only Sean Little who administered the formula.

Chapter 20
The Proposal

A week went by with little action. Unknown to Sean, there were constant meetings at the highest level of the federal government about Sean and his decision to not cooperate. During one of these Security Council meetings, it was the President of the United States, who addressed the group, "When you look at it, you can't blame the guy for not trusting us. We imprison him in the lab in Boston and then imprison him in Nevada. I am now told that he believes we killed his friend Jack and staged the attack on the lab. And to set everything off, the FBI screws up and orders surveillance cameras installed throughout his house, and he finds out. If someone did that to me, I'd hate their guts too."

The Associate Director of the FBI, Tyler Miles, then spoke. "I spoke to Sean, and yes, he hates our guts. He will not cooperate, and after what we have put him through, I can't blame him, but we must get that secret out of him."

The President replied in obvious anger, "Yeah, your attempts to talk to him really worked out well. You send the FBI out three times to threaten him, and he even gets you to put a gun to his head, and he tells you to pull the trigger. Great! That must have been a real bonding moment for you both. He probably thinks of you as his brother now. No wonder the guy hates the FBI's guts, and I can't blame him." The President continued, "Next, what do you want us to do—capture and torture him? Boy, that would look good on CNN. "Sean Little Tortured and Killed by the American Government". Great storyline, isn't it? Every news group is up our ass, telling me to stop his imprisonment in his house in Crystal Falls. Plus, every world leader thinks we are developing a new chemical weapon to use against them. My phone never stops ringing. This is driving me nuts."

"What do you propose we do?" asked Vice President John Harper.

Mr. Harper was the President's loyal friend and secretly had his eye on the top job. He was a 60-ish career politician who was accustomed to getting his own way. Getting up in years was bothering him, and he constantly thought of how he could try to gain Sean's secret. He and his wife both believed they deserved to be younger, just like everyone else.

The President spoke again, "It is obvious that threatening this guy won't work. First, he hates the FBI for good reason, so the FBI is off the case. The FBI agents surrounding his farmhouse will be replaced with regular military troops ASAP. Second, I will have John Harper, my vice President go and talk to Sean to ask for his forgiveness and to ask Sean to outline the conditions under which he would resume his work. Sean is the only person who can make this process successful, and he's no good to us if somebody kills him or, out of frustration, he takes his own life. I wouldn't doubt that this is an option that he's been thinking about. We need him."

Every person in the room could tell that the President had come to this conclusion long before entering it. They all nodded in agreement. Vice President, John Harper then said, "Tyler, inform your people in Michigan that I will be arriving today and that over the next few days they will be replaced by military personnel. Mr. President, I will leave as soon as I am able."

"Thank you, John," replied the President.

The President knew there was no other option. Only with Sean back in the lab could they eventually find out the final piece to the puzzle of why Sean and only Sean could make these ingredients work. At seventy-two years of age and almost totally bald, the President and his wife desperately wanted the application for themselves.

The President also realized that any nation that controlled this "age-reversing" formula could dictate terms to the world. Regardless of who you were or how powerful you were, who could resist the urge to be younger and live longer? They had to have Sean back in the lab now.

Monica Forsyth, on orders from FBI Associate Director Tyler Miles, her boss, contacted Jim Woods, the FBI supervisor, in front of Sean's farmhouse and informed him of the upcoming Vice President's visit. The Vice President was leaving shortly by jet to the closest air force base and arriving by helicopter shortly afterward. On orders from Tyler Miles, she was told not to inform Jim Woods that the FBI had been taken off the case and that the military was assuming control. She was told to tell him after the Vice President's visit.

Jim Woods immediately, after talking to Monica, ordered additional security around the makeshift landing pad and had an SUV ready for the Vice President's arrival. Jim Woods went up to tell Sean and Jennifer that the Vice President himself was coming up for a chat.

"This should be interesting," said Sean. "I told you I won't help you, and that's exactly what I'm going to tell him." And Sean slammed the door.

Visit from the Vice President, John Harper

The helicopter carrying the Vice President and his assistant arrived at about seven p.m. Sean could hear them land. Sean thought better of it and decided that he would at least be civil and listen to what he had to say. When the Vice President and his assistant arrived, it was Jennifer who greeted them. She ushered them into the living room, and after they were seated, she offered them tea or coffee. Both asked for coffee, so Jennifer left to get Sean and get the coffee.

After a few minutes, Sean arrived, introduced himself, and shook hands with the Vice President, who then introduced his assistant, Kevin Sanders. Kevin looked like the perfect assistant. He was about 5'8" inches tall with combed-back brown hair. He took his directions from the Vice President and never spoke unless spoken to. Sean liked him immediately.

As Sean took a seat, he said, "And what can I do for you today, gentlemen?"

The Vice President spoke, "Sean, I am here on behalf of the President of the United States. We wish to formally apologize for the way that you and your friends have been treated. We ask for your forgiveness."

"Mr. Vice President," Sean replied, "I appreciate your visit and your apology, but I am not in a forgiving mood. Had Ralph not slipped that note to the equipment installer in the lab in Boston, I would still be your prisoner. I also believe that it may have been my own government that tortured and killed my friend Jack and maybe staged the attack on the lab in Boston to frighten me. Then, to really piss me off, the FBI wires my house with video cameras so they can record my girlfriend and me in bed. Somehow, I don't think forgiveness is in the picture."

"Yes," calmly replied the Vice President, fully aware of Sean's explosive temper.

"The President and I understand your feelings. And personally, I can't

146

blame you. Whether you believe me or not, we were not responsible for Jack's death or the attack on the lab. By questioning the two survivors of the attack, we learned that it was they who tortured and killed your friend. The two survivors couldn't tell us who was behind the attempt to kidnap you. Their leader, an ex-military commander turned killer for hire, Donovan Kamps, was the one who was contacted and paid a lot of money to put together this operation.

"The two survivors said that each person involved was paid twenty thousand dollars in cash the first day they met and was sent an additional $100,000 that evening. Plus, they were promised ten million dollars each once they had successfully captured you. Whoever is behind this has lots of connections and very, very deep pockets. They even purchased an ex-military helicopter for cash a few days before the attack on the lab."

"How in hell did they get their hands on an ex-military helicopter? You don't see these for sale at the corner used car lot, do you?" exclaimed Sean.

"This is America, and everything is for sale," the Vice President replied.

"The helicopter was purchased by a fake film company from a New York movie supply house as a movie prop. They paid by e-transfer of funds from an account set up just for that purpose. We hit a dead end after that. We also suspect that Donovan Kamps has been involved in this type of operation before. We are still searching his phone and bank records, and it would appear that the money he received was wired from an untraceable offshore account. So far, that's all we know."

"Mr. Vice President, for the time being, I will accept that what you are saying is true. Other than to threaten me to come to work for you like the others, why are you here? You know I will not cooperate," stated Sean.

The Vice President Outlines the President's Proposal.

"First, let me say again that we are sorry for the problems we have caused you and your friends. The FBI has been taken off your case, so you need not worry about them any longer. The people assigned to protect you from now on are all American military personnel.

"Second, the President himself has asked for you to set down your conditions to start using your formula again. You can set up anywhere in the US you want, hire anyone you want, and be free to go wherever you want. The full power of the American government will be at your disposal to assist you.

"Third, to get you started, the President has agreed to a payment of hundred million dollars to use for your setup, and if you need more, just ask.

"And fourth, please allow us to protect you both. We firmly believe that without our around-the-clock protection, the people who killed your friend and attacked the lab will be coming after you again. These people won't quit, and likely there will be others. Your formula is that important."

"Wow, that's a switch. You mean that I will no longer be your prisoner? asked Sean.

"Yes, that is correct," replied the Vice President. "But please appreciate that if you leave the United States, we can't protect you properly, and those who want to capture or kill you would have an easier chance of doing it outside of the United States."

"That's not an issue. I don't like to travel anyway, so it's unlikely that I would get the urge to leave the USA," Sean replied.

Not wanting to overstay his welcome, the Vice President said, "Before I go, let me repeat myself. The President himself is guaranteeing your personal freedom and to set up a lab anywhere you want under any conditions you want. He has authorized a sum of hundred million dollars to be placed in a separate bank account for you to use however, you see fit, no questions asked. You will have complete control over your lab, its location, who you hire, and who you do your applications to."

Sean, standing up to shake the Vice President's hand, said, "I appreciate your visit. You have given me plenty to think about. Over the next few days, I will write out a list of my conditions for you and the President to discuss. And I ask again: I will be allowed my personal freedom to go live freely and go where I want."

"Yes," replied the Vice President. "You will have your freedom, but please allow our people to escort you for your own protection. When you are done with your list, put it in an envelope addressed to me and give it to the commanding officer at the outpost at the end of your driveway. I will tell him to expect it, and he will forward it to me."

"Thank you. That's fair enough," replied Sean.

At that, the Vice President and Sean shook hands, and the Vice President and Kevin Sanders left. There was a lot to think about.

Chapter 21
Sean's Conditions

Sean and Jennifer couldn't believe it! *Freedom to go wherever we want!*

Plus, Sean having hundred million dollars to equip a new lab that he controls. A dream come true. They both agreed that the media frenzy and public opinion to this process on must be huge. Sean told Jennifer that the Vice President admitted that they were getting heat from other world leaders, thinking that they were developing a new chemical weapon.

"But let me write out my conditions and let's see if this will really happen," said Sean. Sean then sat down and started writing. Over the next several days, he and Jennifer worked out a list of demands.

List of Conditions for Sean Little to Resume His Age Reversing Formula Work

Personal Conditions

I, Sean Little, and Jennifer Sloan, my girlfriend, are free to go whenever and wherever we want. We agree for our own protection that we will be escorted by security personnel.

—We will no longer be spied on. There will be no video cameras inside any buildings where we live or work.

—I would like diplomatic immunity for myself. Jennifer Sloan and Ralph Barns, who I hope will consent to work with me. I don't plan on doing anything illegal, but maybe this will deter any government agencies from harassing us.

—Concerning my difficulties with the FBI, I don't want them near me or Jennifer again. They are to have no part in any of our activities and to have no part in our protection. They are not to be allowed on or near the grounds where the new testing lab will be. I will accept the protection of the military personnel and the local police, but not the FBI.

The Laboratory

I would like to rent the abandoned Nevada desert compound from the US government for one dollar per year for the next twenty years. We will be allowed to fix up the compound in any way we see fit.

–This compound will remain a military facility, but within the confines of the compound, I am the boss.

–I would like another colonel sent in to replace Colonel Fred Wayne as head of the compound

Example: –The military personnel stationed within the compound will obey my instructions. My rules cannot be overruled by any military official, whoever they assign.

–I and I alone will decide who has access to the compound. For my own protection, I will place severe restrictions on who can enter.

No one except the President of the United States, the Vice President, or their single designated representative will have access to the compound and myself.

–Obviously, for security purposes, surveillance cameras are necessary to guard the compound outside, and I will have access to the control rooms using those cameras.

Applications and Tests

–I and I alone will decide on who receives the applications.

–I and I alone will hire the assistants to help me.

–This lab will be run as a privately owned corporation owned solely by myself, and I will charge for its services. The cost of an application will be my decision, and my decision alone.

–I will not be forced to perform applications on anyone I don't wish to.

Any attempt to force me to conduct applications on those I don't wish to will find me quitting this enterprise.

–There will be no free applications. Regardless of the national emergency, I will not do free applications.

–The government may not consider these applications as their own

150

property and offer these services to others, regardless of the situation. In short, my applications are not "National Policy" and cannot be used as bargaining chips in international negotiations.

–I will not do an application on a sitting member of the United States Federal or State governments or any active member of any American government organization.

–No government agency can criticize or attempt to stop me from performing, an application on someone friendly or unfriendly to the United States.

–I will continue to do testing as I see fit, without interference from any government organization or agency.

–Your FBI has made me fully aware that your scientists have not been able to duplicate my success. Once you are successful at duplicating my process, myself, Jennifer, Ralph, and his assistants are free to leave to resume our normal lives.

The Company's Revenues

–I am aware of the worldwide demand for this process and will be charging for this service. As the world presently has over three thousand billionaires, I am confident that whatever I wish to charge, they will pay. With this money, I will attempt to help the world and especially Americans in ways that I see fit.

–I am an environmentalist. Cleaning up America and the planet will not only help mankind but will create thousands of American jobs. Jobs are to be funded solely from the proceeds of these applications. I am especially concerned with cleaning up the American waterways and the world's oceans.

–I will under no circumstances give money to or purchase for the American military or any other government or military agency any items used as weapons of war. I will assist where I can in worthy causes, but will not purchase weapons designed to kill other human beings.

–For example, as my father was a disabled Vietnam War veteran. It has always been my desire to help out physically disabled American war veterans.

Later, I will consider your suggestions on how best to accomplish this.

–For worthy causes and charities, I will not give direct funding but instead will purchase items they need to continue their work. For example, food, educational materials, and medical supplies, etc.

–I am not a political person, so therefore I will not play favorites. I will not endorse a political party or electoral candidate, nor will I contribute to political campaigns or any political action committees.

–As a privately owned corporation, there will be no restrictions on where I deposit my money or on how it is spent.

–I will accept your offer of hundred million dollars to start up. This money is not to be considered ownership but merely as a personal loan. It is also my intention to pay this money back once I begin charging for my applications.

–Once per month, I will give a full and honest report of the people I have done the application to, the revenues received, and where the money has been spent, delivered directly to the President of the United States.

Acceptance

Jennifer and Sean thought about the conditions list over the next couple of days. *Seemed everything was there, especially the part where Sean is in control of the activities and people inside the compound.* Jennifer especially liked the part about the FBI being out of the picture.

"Those people give me the creeps," Jennifer said.

They both knew that they were only important as long as Sean was the only person who could successfully do the procedure. They also realized the other government labs were working day and night to replicate the procedure, and once they did, Sean and Jennifer would be evicted from the compound and thrown away like yesterday's garbage.

"Best to go along with it for as long as we can," said Jennifer.

While contemplating the list, Sean called Ralph and told him about the FBI's heavy tactics and the visit from the Vice President. He told him about the list of conditions that he and Jennifer had worked out, but knowing that their conversations were being recorded, he declined to further discuss the list with him. Ralph seemed eager to get involved and liked the idea of working out of Nevada.

"Being able to come and go as you please is obviously a relief to you, and Jennifer, I bet," replied Ralph.

"Sure, Ralph," replied Sean. "I will send this list off to the Vice President and if they agree, I'll contact you, and you can bring along your assistants. Please recruit everyone you need, as I don't want to rely on any government personnel helping us in the lab. We will pay them generously, and we can discuss that later.

"And I'll order in a bunch of RVs to live in for those of us who don't like living inside the buildings. I know that Jennifer and I would prefer an RV over those small apartments. I would think that your equipment is still in Nevada and has not been touched. Regardless, you will be able to order any equipment you need. It's all on Uncle Sam's tab."

"Sounds pretty exciting," replied Ralph. "I'll call my assistants to see which ones would like to join us. For those that don't, I'll just scout out some replacements. Thanks for calling and saying hello to Jennifer for me. Let me know as soon as you hear anything." And Ralph hung up.

Sean and Jennifer mulled over the list for the next couple of days. Finally, it seemed complete, so Sean made four copies, placed two in a large envelope, and addressed it to "John Harper, Vice President of the United States." His return address simply said, "Sean Little, Crystal Falls, Michigan."

With his pets in tow, he walked down the driveway and delivered the envelope to the commanding officer. The commanding officer was obviously expecting the package and immediately ordered that it be delivered to the nearby air force base to be delivered to Washington immediately.

The President's Acceptance of Sean's Conditions

Three days went by. Sean kept wondering how his list of conditions would be received. *They want to know what I need to get back to work, and they got it,* he thought. Early the morning of the third day, Jeff Woods arrived to pick up Jennifer's want list and to say that the Vice President would be arriving at about two p.m.

"Great," said Sean, "this should be exciting."

Close to one p.m. Sean could hear the arrival of a large military helicopter, so he was ready when the Vice President arrived. Sean greeted them at the back door and shook hands with Vice President John Harper and his assistant, Kevin Sanders. He ushered them into the room. After a brief chat, Jennifer entered the room with a tray of coffee, then she left.

"Okay, let's have it," Sean asked. "Where do we go from here?"

The Vice President noticed the stress in Sean's voice, so he spoke calmly, "Sean, I presented your conditions to the President. The President himself called a national security meeting to outline your conditions. As you can appreciate, there were a number of objections raised and heated opinions. But I have to say that the President did not put it to a vote, and he has agreed to hundred percent of your conditions. Plus, all the government agencies have been told not to bother you."

"You mean the President agreed?" Sean said in shock.

"Yes, Sean, the President agreed to everything," stated the Vice President. Then the Vice President outlined the President's comments, – First, to assure you of his intentions, he has signed each page of your conditions and stamped them with the seal of the President of the United States. This is now an official US government document. Here is your copy.

–Second, here are your banking documents, checks, and two credit cards on the Bank of America account set up in your name for the tune of hundred million dollars US. The money has already been deposited. Here is the bank's contact information in Washington, and all you have to do is call them, give them a copy of your signature and answer some security questions. The money is all yours. They are expecting your call.

–Third, the Nevada compound is yours. You are the boss. You are to conduct your work without interference. It is being cleaned and prepared for your arrival as we speak. Here is the contact information for the new commanding officer of the compound, Colonel John Williams. Call him and let him know when you and any others are arriving. The President of the United States personally contacted the Colonel, and he has been given direct orders to follow your instructions.

–Fourth, you, Jennifer, and Ralph have been granted diplomatic immunity.

This should help keep people off your back. But please don't kill anyone, it gets really messy, he laughed.

–Fifth, as everyone in the room wants a free application, including myself and the President, you not doing an application to a sitting member of the government or any of its agencies, caused quite an uproar. The

President says that he can understand your reasoning, and so he has agreed.

–Sixth, your statement that there will be no free applications and that the government cannot use these applications as an instrument of National Policy also caused an uproar. Again, the President understands and has agreed.

In short, Sean, you are the boss. Whatever you say goes. You are to run the compound however you see fit. As for revenue purposes, I believe that your friend Jack Alair set up a company for you both, "Little and Alair Inc., that you are now the sole owner of. That should work out fine.

And last, my trusted assistant here, Kevin Sanders, will be your contact for me and the President. You can contact him day or night. If you have any problems—any problems at all—with any persons or members of our government or agencies, you are to contact him directly. Kevin has direct access to myself and the President." The Vice President then sat back and waited for Sean's response.

Sean sat there, speechless. Shock would be a polite word for the feelings of relief he felt. The Vice President and his assistant Kevin got up to leave, and the Vice President said, "Let the commanding officer know when you want to leave and where you want to go. There is a government jet waiting for you at the airbase. But please, you are free to go anywhere you want, but please appreciate that we have to shadow you in order to keep you safe."

"No problem," said Sean. "Jennifer and I both agree that we need protection. Thank you both for coming out." With that, they shook hands, and the Vice President and his assistant departed.

Sean called Jennifer down from upstairs and told her the good news. They hugged and danced around in excitement.

"We get to go. We get to go anywhere." screamed Jennifer. "First, I want to go see my parents in Los Angeles. They'll be so shocked. When can we leave?"

"Let's leave tomorrow morning. We still have to pack, and I have to call the bank and let Ralph know. Plus, I'll contact the Watts and let them have the run of the place and look after the pets until we call for them. Later, all the pets will be joining us in our new home in Nevada," said Sean.

Jennifer ran upstairs to start packing and to call her parents and her sister. Sean called the bank. As expected, he had to send them a copy of his signature, select a pin number for the credit cards, and answer some security questions. With that finalized and a confirmation that hundred million dollars was in his account, he felt relieved.

This is really going to happen!

Sean Calls Ralph

Next, he called Ralph. Sean explained the meeting with the vice President and that the money was actually his. Ralph was elated at the news.

"I'm sending you five million dollars today to help with expenses and to have some money to pay your staff. I would think that everyone who was held prisoner in your lab should get at least $100,000 upfront, considering the grief they were put through. Plus, anyone that wants to come with you to Las Vegas will be getting the standard thousand dollars per week over and above their regular salary," stated Sean.

"I'll get the staff together right away. When do you want us there?" Ralph was so excited.

"Jennifer and I should be there in a few days. She wants to see her folks in Los Angeles before going to Nevada, and I can't blame her," replied Sean.

Later that night, over a steak and some wine, they could not believe the new turn of events. They talked of the changes they could make to the compound, and Jennifer should start shopping for new RVs as soon as they arrive. They were so excited! Both realized that without Sean, the government could not duplicate his process. Only by him continuing to do these applications might they finally be able to figure out why and start doing the applications themselves.

Once the government and military had the formula, Sean and Jennifer knew they would no longer be needed. They could then start using the formula as an instrument of National Policy and ultimately, economic blackmail. Sean had no doubt that the government, once they had the secret, would start bribing world leaders with the prospect of being younger—an offer no one could refuse. A frightening idea.

Chapter 22
Back in Nevada

The next morning, Jennifer and Sean flew to Los Angeles on a government jet.

They were accompanied by six well-dressed and well-armed members of the US military. These were their escorts, and Sean and Jennifer were getting accustomed to being shadowed. At the airport, three large black SUVs were waiting for them on the tarmac.

They arrived at Jennifer's parent's home about an hour later.

Jennifer was so happy to see her parents and her sister Emily again that she couldn't stop crying. They heard all about it on the news, and Jennifer explained everything that went on, from the FBI taking them from the cabin in northern Michigan to the President's release.

Sean really enjoyed the visit. He had met Jennifer's parents, Mr. and Mrs. Sloan, before and found them to be kind-hearted, honest people. They were very friendly, easy-going people who loved the outdoors. *If I'm ever going to start doing free applications, these two people will be on the top of my list,* he thought.

Emily, Jennifer's sister, was not at all like Jennifer. Emily was shorter and stout, with a round face and a big smile. But just like Jennifer, she had loads of energy and loved to go shopping. She was so nice to talk to, anyone who met Emily liked her.

They explained the need for their security, and Jennifer's family accepted it.

For the next two days, they had their military escorts drive them around the city.

While on route, their motorcade would be joined up with patrol cars from the LA police department.

"Standard operating procedure whenever a dignitary is being driven around. We contact them, and they escort us," said one of the drivers.

Jennifer went clothes shopping with her mom and her sister, Emily.

Their escorts called in members of the LA police department to guard Sean and Mr. Sloan in the house while they escorted the women out shopping.

"It must be quite a sight seeing all those big guys hanging around in a woman's clothing store." Laughed Mr. Sloan.

After three days and two nights, Jennifer and Sean left for Nevada. Jennifer assured her parents and Emily that they would all be allowed to visit and stay as long as they wanted in the compound. She said that she was going to buy the biggest and most expensive RV for them to live in when they visit.

"That's the President's orders. Sean is the boss in the compound, and we can have anything we want," Jennifer was fond of saying.

Back at the Compound

They were flown to the compound the next morning. They were greeted at the gate by Colonel John Williams, the new commander of the military instructed to protect the compound, Sean and Jennifer. He assured them that he had been told by "the highest authority" that within the confines of this compound, Sean's orders were to be obeyed, no questions asked. Sean immediately liked him more than Colonel Fred Wayne, whom he had to deal with last time.

"Do I have to salute you?" Colonel John asked Sean.

"No, you don't, but I appreciate you asking. But my late father, who fought in Vietnam, would appreciate the gesture," Sean said with a smile.

Colonel John was a trim, polite, good-looking career soldier with a big smile.

He liked to jog or bike around the compound to keep himself in shape. Sean liked Colonel John immediately and believed he could trust him. He knew they would both be getting along well.

Colonel John drove them around and gave them a welcome tour of the compound. He also mentioned that whenever they wished to leave the compound, to simply call the main gate, and they would assemble the team to accompany them.

"You can have us drive you, or you can go in your own vehicles and we can follow, but I think it's best we take you," said John.

John then pointed to the row of fifteen blacked-out military GMC

Yukon SUVs for the use of the guards here and stated, "These are the vehicles we have been provided with to take you off the compound. Anytime you want to go, just call us, and we will be ready."

Sean then thanked Colonel John for his concern.

"Yes, John, I think it's best you take us whenever we leave the compound. Could you make arrangements to have my new Lexus brought down from my house in Crystal Falls, Michigan? Here are the keys. Plus, could you please make arrangements to have my pets picked up at my neighbors in Crystal Falls, the Watts, and brought here?" asked Sean.

"No problem. We have transport planes flying from Michigan to Las Vegas all the time. I'll send up your keys, and they'll bring them down along with your pets," replied Colonel John.

"Great, I really appreciate it. And Colonel John, I expect my associate Ralph Barns and his team of assistants to be arriving at any time. Once I know when he is expected to land, could you pick them up at the airport?" Sean asked.

"No problem, just let us know, and we'll leave immediately to get them," he replied.

Sean thought, *What a switch from the last time we were here. Last time we were prisoners, and now we can have whatever we want and can go wherever we want. Fabulous.*

For the rest of the day, Jennifer cleaned up the apartment they had last time. She then proceeded to the kitchen area, and discovering none of the food to her liking, ordered Chinese food. She ordered fifty individual Chinese dinners and told the clerk to add an extra two hundred dollars to the bill to cover their delivery costs. The delivery service dropped off their food at the main gate. The guards brought their food in and expressed their appreciation for the good meal.

Later, after their warmed-up Chinese food, Sean and Jennifer started talking about the changes they would make. Sean suggested that Jennifer go out and buy a dozen or so really nice RVs for people to stay in and two really big ones, one for themselves and one for her parents.

Jennifer Goes Appliance Shopping

After relentless days of cleaning up, Jennifer decided to go shopping.

"First, I'm going to get some new appliances for the kitchen, and then I'll start looking at RVs," Jennifer said.

Sean gave her one of the credit cards the Vice President had given him. Might as well start using these. He pulled them out of the folder, and they were cards he had never seen before—Black American Express cards. *I hope these work.* Laughed Sean.

Never get in the way of a woman who wants to go shopping, Sean would say to himself. Sean was not a shopper, and so he simply said, "Go and enjoy yourself. You deserve it."

Jennifer arranged with the guards to take her shopping, and the three vehicles were ready for her when she walked over. She had researched a Las Vegas upscale appliance store over an hour's drive away.

She was really enjoying her new-found freedom and talked easily with the guards.

They drove up to the store, which Jennifer wanted to go into by herself. Colonel John refused. She agreed but told him to be quiet in the store. The other guards in the car laughed at seeing their colonel taking orders from a civilian and a woman at that. Once they arrived, he ordered his men out of the vehicles and to walk around.

Jennifer and John walked in. Jennifer went directly to the ultra-luxury forty-eight inch gas ranges with the electric convection ovens. A very nice strawberry-blonde saleslady, Cheryl McDonald, approached her and introduced herself. After a brief conversation and demonstration, Jennifer ordered two of the expensive stoves. She then ordered six microwaves and four very large and very expensive fridges. Naturally, Cheryl was shocked as the total came to well over $100,000 with taxes in. Jennifer pulled out her new Black American Express credit card, and to the saleslady's surprise, it cleared. Jennifer then asked that her purchases be delivered to the compound and gave her the directions.

Jennifer Goes RV Shopping

On the way to Las Vegas, Jennifer saw a large RV dealership on the outskirts of town. This time, she asked that she and John go in alone and the others stay across the road. She just wanted to see how they would be treated.

So John and Jennifer drove up and looked like the typical military couple looking at RVs. A number of the older, more experienced salespeople ignored them, and one even walked right by them. After about twenty minutes or so of opening RV doors and looking inside, this nice young gentleman approaches them and said, "Hello, my name is Jesse O'Rourke. Welcome to the Las Vegas RV Warehouse. What may I show you today?

Jennifer introduced herself and John and said they were looking for an RV to accommodate some guests. Jennifer liked Jesse right away. He was a polite young man of about thirty years of age, with curly dark hair and a big smile.

"Well," Jesse said, "the units you are looking at here are our Jayco line of trailers made right here in the United States. These are our best sellers, and everyone who buys one is happy with it. As you can see, all the models in the 24-28 foot range come fully equipped with two bedrooms, air conditioning, a full counter top range, a propane stove, and a full bathroom with a shower. Plus, with every unit purchased this month, the boss is including a full awning with each trailer."

"Very nice," said Jennifer as she was walking through a number of the 24 and 28 foot trailers. John kept his mouth shut and acted the "bored husband" part beautifully.

"How many of the twenty-four footers and how many of the twenty-eight footers do you have in stock?" asked Jennifer.

"Well, I can say for certain that we just got our new shipment in earlier this week, so we have at least eight of the twenty-four footers and ten of the twenty-eight footers," replied Jesse.

"Great, you've made a sale. Jesse, let's go write it up," said Jennifer. Now in the showroom and at his desk, Jesse asked, "Now which did you want, a twenty-four foot or a twenty-eight foot Jayco trailer?"

"I want them all," Jennifer, matter of fact, stated. Jesse sat there, shocked.

"Did you just say you wanted them all?"

"You said you had eight to twenty-four footers and ten to twenty-eight footers in stock. Is that correct?" asked Jennifer.

"Sure, but let me call my manager first," said Jesse.

He made a quick call, and the manager informed him that these trailers were in stock.

"Yes, my manager said that we have eight of the twenty-four footers and ten of the twenty-eight footers on the ground and for sale," stated Jesse.

"Great," said Jennifer, "and as I said, I want them all. Now take your time and work out the numbers as I walk around and look at the motorhomes in the showroom."

After about five minutes, Jesse and the manager approached Jennifer, and Jesse stated, "I have your numbers for you. The total comes to $1,220,000 including all setup fees, administration, and all taxes."

"Great," said Jennifer. "I'll pay for them now, and you can deliver them."

At his desk, she hands over her Black American Express card, and Jesse just looks at it.

"Go ahead, run it. It's okay," stated Jennifer.

Jesse comes back from his manager's office and said, "Please excuse my surprise. I have never even seen a Black American Express card before, and your total amount went through."

"Here is the address to the compound and contact John here at this number when you will be delivering them," said Jennifer.

Jennifer and John left to return to the compound. Jennifer was so excited to tell Sean about her day's shopping experience.

Chapter 23
Ralph Arrives in Nevada

Ralph Barnes arrived three days later with eight assistants in tow. After being shown their accommodations in the bunkhouses, they went to work immediately, cleaning up the lab and testing the equipment. Each of the ten clean rooms was cleaned and disinfected, and new furniture was brought in. Everyone agreed that they would be up and running within the next two weeks.

Ralph and Sean met and had a meeting. They discussed salaries for their staff, and Sean said, "Pay them thousand dollars per week up and above their regular salary of what they were making with you in Boston. There are isolated people here, and I want them to be happy," Ralph agreed.

To start, they agreed that, with the ten observation rooms they already had, they would start their first tests on five dogs and five pigs. Once prepared, the animals were secured, and the tests began. Just like before, in the middle of the second day after the application, all the animal's hair fell out. The dogs immediately started acting like pups.

"Boy, I felt great after my treatment, but I didn't have that much energy," said Sean.

"That's because you're not a dog," said Ralph, and they both laughed.

After testing the pets and finding them in perfect health, both Sean and Ralph agreed that they should look again at those who have already had treatment.

"First, I would like to start by inviting my loud-mouthed Uncle George. I'd like to see how he's feeling after all of these months," said Ralph.

"Good idea," replied Sean. "And then we can test any of those others who are willing to come to Nevada. I think we should pay them for their troubles. How does ten thousand for each test subject sound to you?"

"Sounds great, Sean. I think they'll all jump at the chance," said Ralph.

Over the next few days, they contacted those people whom they had already done applications to. From forty to eighty years old, perfectly healthy and not so healthy, they were all invited. All agreed, especially since they would be paid ten thousand dollars to show up. There were a number of test subjects who would not come unless they could bring their wives and families along.

At first, Sean and Ralph said no, we do not have the accommodation facilities for forty or so families, and then Ralph said, "Hey, wait a minute," Ralph said. "We're one hour from Las Vegas with thousands of hotel rooms. Let's cut a deal with one of the big hotels and have the families stay there." Sean thought it was an excellent idea and asked Jennifer to start looking for one to use.

After repeated shopping trips to Las Vegas, Jennifer settled on a thirty-year-old hotel, the Parkway Hotel, which was a little off the main strip and didn't have the advertising budget of big hotels like the MGM Grand to stay close to capacity. The Parkway Hotel was a beautiful older hotel with a grand foyer and beautiful rooms with large windows. Jennifer, after a brief tour, enjoyed meeting the owners and staff and loved the hotel. She told Sean all about it and said it would be perfect.

"Then that's settled," stated Sean. "Take an entire floor just for us, and the hotel can still rent out any suites we're not using."

"Do you really think you need to reserve an entire floor of fifty rooms?" asked Jennifer.

"Yes, I do. We will need those rooms for the test subject's families, the families of some of our staff, and rooms for the construction people who will be working on the compound," replied Sean. Jennifer hugged Sean, saying that he was right. Sean continued, "Contact these people at the Parkway Hotel and make the arrangement. Give them a fifty thousand dollars deposit on your credit card, and that should get their attention."

The new appliances for the compound came and were installed quickly. Sean ordered that all the appliance installers were to be escorted to their work area and guarded every minute they were there. Likewise with the new trailers. They were delivered but not installed. The delivery drivers said that the installers would be out in two days to set up and properly install the trailers. They were likewise escorted to the trailer area and guarded every minute they were in the compound.

No one complained about the security when Jennifer explained that they would be paying each installer a thousand dollars cash bonus once they were finished. She also had food brought in everyday for the trailer installers, so the work progressed efficiently.

Jennifer had three trailers placed in a U shape for herself, Sean, her parents, and her sister. She called her parents to give them the good news that they could move in. Upon their arrival, Jennifer's parents and her sister Emily loved it. *Great, problem solved,* smiled Sean. *This will keep Jennifer happy and give her someone to go shopping with.*

New Construction Plans Made

Sean then told Ralph of his plans to eventually do twenty human subjects per week and start charging for the services.

"Anything you want, Sean. You have the money, and you're the boss, so why not?" replied Ralph.

Sean then said we need a ten-story medical tower with twenty observation rooms per floor and staff offices and supply rooms on each floor. The main floor would house a new medical center, and the second floor would house the new application lab and lab offices. "Until we are prepared to go into full production with twenty subjects per week, we will just have to work with the ten rooms we have," Sean said.

Later that week, Ralph and Sean had a meeting about the plans for a medical tower to house the test subjects. Sean laid out all of his fancy plans, especially the circular tower with the observation rooms in the center overlooking the open space and the staff rooms on the outside.

"So you tell me that these subjects will be looking out of their windows only to see other test subjects looking back at them? I think you forgot that their rooms are totally enclosed with no windows, so why do we need a fancy building with an open space on each floor when they can't see it?" Ralph asked.

Sean was amazed. "Ralph, you're right. In my excitement, I totally forgot the subject's rooms having enclosed walls with no windows. How stupid of me."

"We need a plain and simple building ten stories high," replied Ralph. "The two basement levels could house our supplies. The first floor could be our new medical center, and the second floor could be our new application area and lab offices. The other floors 3–10 should be twenty observation rooms on one side of the corridor and, across from them, twenty staff rooms to house the staff looking after each subject. The two elevators would be in the center of the building, with every floor's supply room and staff common area across the hallway.

"The staff looking after each test subject will stay with them from the time they arrive to the time they leave, and with all of them living across from them in their own rooms. The staff could have rotating shifts of five days on and a couple of days off. If these staff have families, we can build a place for them here, or they can stay at the Parkway Hotel in town."

Sean was impressed.

"This is an excellent idea. My designs were just too fancy, while yours are straightforward and practical. I'll start working on those plans immediately and send them off to Hillsborough and Smith, my old company. I can't believe that I forgot that the observation rooms had no windows or doors to the outside."

Sean had completed plans he had drawn up in a couple of days. He showed them to Ralph, and he approved. Sean had the plans sent off to Roger Hillsborough in Dearborn, Michigan, to work out the final details. Roger suggested using Leibowitz and Co. out of Las Vegas to do the work. Sean said that he remembered talking to them about some office towers they designed in Las Vegas and promised to get a hold of him.

The next day, Sean called the offices of Leibowitz and Co. and talked to Barry Leibowitz. Barry said that Roger had called, and they discussed getting together. Knowing that a big project was on the hook and the celebrity status of Sean, Barry quickly agreed to meet with Sean the next day for lunch. Barry mentioned he would be bringing two of his top designers with him, and Sean agreed. Upon hanging up, Sean called the main gate to tell them that Barry and two assistants were arriving tomorrow for lunch.

They arrived the next day as scheduled. Barry was about 50-ish with a tanned face and muscular build. He showed up wearing a baseball cap, tee shirt, blue jeans, and work boots. Barry was a straight-to-the-point, no-nonsense type of guy. Sean liked Barry immediately. The four sat down in the makeshift boardroom and chatted easily. *Architects and designers are my people,* Sean thought, and he enjoyed every minute of the conversations. The two assistants introduced themselves, but basically just sat and listened as Sean outlined his plans.

Plans for the New Medical Building

"From what I can see, the medical building seems straight-forward enough," said Barry. "A lot of stainless steel that can easily be cleaned, tile floors and no carpeting, and the observation rooms having their outside walls completely sealed off. Supplies in the two basement levels, with a medical center on the main floor and your application center and lab offices on the second. The remaining eight floors are the subject observation rooms, with the staff quarters across the hallway. Dual elevators, with each floor having a supply room and a common room for the staff across from the elevators. Is that right?"

"Yeah, you've got it," Sean replied. "And one other thing: everything you build here is to be wheelchair accessible, no exceptions. That means ramps beside the stairs out front, larger doorways and hallways, and larger elevators. I will eventually be hiring ex-military personnel who are confined to wheelchairs, and I want this entire compound to be as comfortable as possible for them. And one other thing, please make sure that the observation rooms all have shatterproof glass in them. I don't want to hear about an applicant getting upset and smashing the glass with his chair and injuring the staff. And last, please make sure that all the observation rooms and application rooms have video cameras installed, just in case someone gets out of hand and we need proof of their actions."

"Both the wheelchair accessibility, the shatterproof glass, and the applicant's video monitoring are good ideas, Sean. I'll be sure to include them," replied Barry.

Sean continued, "The final plans will be coming to you from my former company, Hillsborough and Smith. I want the building to be located about thousand yards from the compound in the corner. I will arrange with the front gate to allow your people in to start the construction immediately. When can you start?"

"Well, with this being a federal military compound, we do not have to obtain any state or municipal approval of the plans or construction, so I can get started on it right away," replied Barry.

"Great," said Sean. "Here is a check for five million dollars to get you started. Invoice me however you want, and you'll be paid immediately. I will have a financial person in soon to handle all this money. Plus, please don't question me about the details. If you have questions, ask my associate Ralph; he's the lab guy.

"One other thing, this is a military compound, so expect to see armed military personnel guarding your people and the job site 24/7 and that everyone working in the compound will be having a background check."

They all nodded in agreement. At that, they all stood up and shook hands. Sean accompanied them to the main gate, introduced Barry to Colonel John, and asked to arrange for the construction workers to get through. *Great thought,* Sean, *once the new medical building is completed, I can get the ball rolling here.*

Testing Again

Those subjects who had previously undergone the process began to arrive. All took rooms at the Parkway Hotel, and the subjects themselves were picked up and brought to the lab. Ralph and the doctors conducted every test they could, and all the results came back positive. Each person was questioned about how they felt and if there were any side effects. The only issue stated was about their hair falling out, but they all reported that it was growing back in quite nicely. They were told that the new hair follicles were pushing out the old dead hair follicles, and that is why their hair fell out. Everyone accepted this explanation.

Surprisingly, the vast majority of the people wanted the application done again and asked if their partners could be included. The concept of a second application to an individual had not yet been fully discussed. Ralph had a meeting with Sean to discuss these requests. They both agreed that the ideal test subject would be Ralph's Uncle George. If there were complications, he was willing to accept them, Ralph believed.

Uncle George arrived and went through the standard testing. George was given his own trailer to live in, and he liked it. Everything seemed to be working out fine. Once the other test subjects were finished and went home, Ralph and Sean started doing the reapplications on Sean's pet dogs. *So far, so good,* thought Sean. *They are happy and as lively as before.*

Uncle George Gets a Second Application

Ralph approached his Uncle George and mentioned the possibility of redoing the application on him.

"Are you kidding me? You're asking me if I would like to be another five years younger? Sign me up and let's get rolling," pleaded George.

"We don't know the outcome of a second procedure on a human, but on the test animals, it seems to be working out with no complications. You've seen Sean's pets. They have all been given a second application, and they are as playful and healthy as ever," Ralph explained.

"Yeah," said George, "those dogs are all over the place, and they all act like pups, even the big ones."

"Uncle George, all this is medically uncharted territory. As we couldn't predict the results of the first applications on a human subject, we have no way of telling the results of a second application. You may have terrible side effects, or it may kill you," explained Ralph.

"You think I don't know that? Your aunts gone, so what have I got to lose? Plus, I like all the pretty reporters talking to me, and I love seeing myself on TV. I know the drill, so get off your ass and let's get the ball rolling," argued Uncle George.

Ralph prepared the standard human testing disclaimer forms for his Uncle George to sign. Once signed, Uncle George went into a clean room and fasted for two days.

Then he was totally washed and dried, and his body was rubbed down with olive oil and brought for the application. He lay on the table, and Sean poured the formula down his throat. He was escorted back into his observation room. Everything went as scheduled. In the middle of the second day, all his new hair fell out, and he reported that he felt great. Once released, Ralph did a number of tests, all positive.

"Uncle George, how do you feel?" Ralph kept asking.

"I feel great, and as soon as you let me out of here, I'm getting the biggest, fattest T-bone steak I can lay my hands on," Uncle George exclaimed.

Prearranged, Ralph already had the cook BBQing up some T-bone steaks and hot potatoes, Uncle George's favorite meal.

Once the tests were done, they led Uncle George into their dining area, and everyone there stood up and clapped. Sean even had the proceedings filmed for the website. They sat Uncle George down, and the cook laid the biggest T-bone steak he'd ever seen in front of him. The smile on his face was two feet wide.

"After five days with nothing to eat, this is all I've dreamed about," George said, and then he put his head down and started eating.

With Uncle George now living in one of the trailers, he was available for testing at any time. He loved having the military guys take him on tours of Las Vegas. And yes, the guards were always happy to accompany him, as he always stopped off at an expensive steak house for all of them to eat. The military guys liked taking George so much to Las Vegas that Colonel John had to set up a schedule to rotate the men going out with George.

Ralph reported to Sean, "The best we can tell is that my sixty-eight years old uncle, after the first procedure, had the metabolism and body of a sixty-three years old. Now, after this second application, everything tells me that he has the metabolism and body of a fifty-eight years old. There seem to be no adverse side effects. I've had the other doctors look like him, and they all agreed. The surprising thing is the guards who accompany him to Las Vegas tell me that he wants to start going drinking in strip bars. Who would have guessed?"

Sean and Ralph both discussed the idea of doing second applications.

"We seem to be pretty busy with our testing and have plenty of money, so let's leave the issue of the second application for a while," said Sean. Ralph agreed.

"Makes you wonder what some of these super rich people will pay for a first or second application, doesn't it?" mused Ralph. Sean didn't answer.

Over the next few weeks, Ralph and his team of doctors tested Uncle George time and time again. *Always the same result, positive.*

"Maybe if we work hard enough, we can get him to be forty years old again," joked one of the lab assistants.

That may be closer to the truth than you think, thought Ralph. *No one knows how far this will go.*

Chapter 24
Paying for Services

Ralph and Sean would meet regularly to discuss issues.

"Any problem with doing an application to Jennifer's parents?" asked Sean.

"Funny, you should mention that," Ralph said. "I had them both in for complete physicals the other day and the doctor's report that both of them are perfectly healthy. Let's ask them."

They agreed. For reasons unknown, both Jennifer, her sister and both their parents declined. the applications went smoothly, and in five days, both of Jennifer's parents came out of their rooms with no hair and as happy as could be.

Seems to be no problems here, thought Sean. Their refusals shocked Sean but he let it be and he did not press the issue.

Then Sean called Ralph in to lay the "bombshell" on him.

"Ralph, we have done our tests, and all have turned out positive except for those persons with cancer," said Sean. "We are not restricted by either the Food and Drug Administration or any other government agency, so let's start charging for and doing applications for the general public. There are people all over the world asking for this procedure, so let's get going."

"But we haven't done enough tests yet," argued Ralph.

"But what's enough tests?" explained Sean. "We could be doing these tests for the next ten years and always be getting the same results. I was the first, and I feel great, and now your uncle has undergone a second procedure and feels so good that he wants to start going to strip clubs." And they both started laughing.

After another twenty minutes of discussion, Ralph agreed.

"How will you be selecting them?" he inquired.

"Leave that up to me," replied Sean.

The Auctions

Sean hired a local website company to set up a site for him. He asked them to announce that they would be starting to do applications for the general public, selected via an auction basis. There were ten observation rooms ready, so they could do ten procedures every two weeks. The successful bidders would first be given full physicals, and if proven to be in good health and cancer-free, their applications would continue. They would have to sign off on a disclaimer form that they volunteered for this procedure and absolved the lab if any complications arose in the future.

The website company placed the announcement and the bidding application form on the website on Monday, and then they waited. The bidding application form asked for the applicants to fill out their personal information, occupations, age, health history, and their bid in US dollars, being prominently displayed on the first page. The bidding would close at five p.m. that upcoming Thursday.

The website people logically showed the applicants and their offers from the highest bid down to the lowest. For privacy purposes, the general public could only see the bid amounts and nothing on the individuals bidding, just like a regular online auction.

It was clearly stated that only ten bidders would be successful, at the sole discretion of Sean and Ralph. Once an applicant was accepted, the financial conditions were that their money must be deposited into the company's account within twenty-four hours of being accepted.

Very little happened on Monday or Tuesday. Then, starting Wednesday morning, all hell broke loose. No one could have anticipated the response. Once the news networks got hold of the idea that these " age-reversing" applications were now available, that's all they reported on. With this type of response, who needs to advertise? Smiled Sean.

The bids started coming in at a million dollars at a time and just kept going. At the end of the auction on Thursday, there were multiple bids around the fifty million dollars mark. Sean and Ralph had the top fifty bidders' information runoff. They only selected those persons who were forty to sixty years old, in good health, and who seemed to fit the profile of the subjects they wanted. They requested they go to their own doctors for a full and complete medical checkup and send the results to Ralph and the staff doctors.

Out of the original fifty, twenty applicants were eliminated due to being too old or too young. Next, another ten were eliminated due to their poor health conditions. Sean told Ralph to contact the remaining twenty successful applicants and have them send in their money within the next twenty-four hours. As expected, ten never sent in any money, leaving the remaining ten ready to accept the treatment. Out of the ten left, their bids ranged from sixty-five million dollars to forty-five million dollars. With their money in the bank, all $510 million dollars, they were invited to take a room at the Parkway Hotel.

The First 10 Paid Subjects

Everyone was amazed. Who could believe that people would pay so much?

Of the ten successful and paid-in-full applicants, seven were male and three were female.

On the first day, they were picked up from the Parkway Hotel in the guards SUVs and brought into the compound. The ten were introduced and shown a short video on what to expect over the next five days. They all agreed excitingly, saying they knew what to expect as it had been reported in the news hundreds of times.

After they were tested physically and had showers, their personal clothes, jewellery, laptops, and cell phones were removed, and they were given only white gowns and slippers to wear. Many of the people wanted their own clothes, laptops, and cell phones back, but Ralph logically refused. *Who knows what trouble someone could cause if they started making phone calls here?* thought Ralph.

They were now escorted into their own private clean rooms, where they fasted for two days. This they also accepted. At the start of the third day, the day of the treatment, they were all individually washed and their bodies rubbed down with olive oil. Then the unexpected happened. They started with the males first, and they brought out the first subject, an oil tycoon from Texas.

As soon as he saw Sean, he jumped off the table and started yelling, "Sean, you and I can go far with your formula. I have the money and people in place to take this all over the world. We have to get together."

As he lunged at Sean, the lab assistants quickly grabbed him and strapped him down. *Thank heavens some of these lab guys are strong. The guy might have hurt me,* thought Sean.

After settling him down, they got him to stop yelling and to open his mouth to accept the formula. Once completed, they carted him back to his room.

"Wow, that was exciting," said Sean.

The next subject was brought in, and in an almost identical fashion, as soon as he saw Sean, he started screaming, "Sean, you and I have to get together because, without me, you'll never go anywhere with this discovery. I'm the guy to make this really happen. You need me." By this time, the lab assistants had a hold of him and forced him onto the gurney. They strapped the marketing guru down to the table, and Sean merely said, "I do not need you or anyone else's help. I'm just fine on my own. Thank you."

While this fellow kept talking, an assistant wedged a plastic spacer in the guy's mouth and held it there while Sean poured the formula down his throat.

All except for two, five of the male subjects caused a fuss when seeing Sean when he went to administer the formula. All were so excited and wanted to offer Sean their "You and I can conquer the world" sales pitch that they became unruly and had to be strapped down.

Oddly enough, they had no problems with the three female subjects. All three ladies calmly introduced themselves to Sean and stated that they were looking forward to being five years younger. And without fuss, they laid on the table and took the formula.

Rattled by the day's activities, Ralph, Sean, and the lab assistants decided to have a meeting the next morning at ten o'clock. Ralph started out the meeting, "We all witnessed yesterday's events. I would like to hear from you in turn about your impressions of what happened. The general consensus was that the women were more agreeable to the treatment as their desire to be younger overcame any issues that they had upon seeing Sean."

The general opinion on the male subjects was that anyone who could afford fifty million dollars for anything is accustomed to being obeyed, and everyone around them is cowering at their every word.

"While talking to them in their clean rooms," one lab assistant said, "They have egos the size of Alaska and expect everyone to jump every time they speak. Besides disliking being closeted in these rooms, they like throwing their weight around. Here they are not in control, and it bothers them." Everyone nodded in agreement.

Then it was Ralph who said, "The way I see it is that they are businessmen and have these grand ideas that they and Sean should be partners. Sitting in their rooms for two days with only a TV to watch and books to read, they dream that if they could only get to Sean, he'd agree to their ideas and they could get together."

Sean agreed. He asked for suggestions on how to proceed, and all agreed that each subject, after being washed and rubbed down with olive oil, should be placed on a gurney and securely strapped down before being brought into the lab for Sean to do the treatment. And not to show favoritism. This should be done to all the subjects, male and female.

"Yeah, it doesn't do us any good if some ex-football player jumps off the gurney and starts strangling Sean," said Ralph. "So it's agreed, then. The standard operating procedure from now on is that the four assistants will enter the subject's room, and then, after the subjects, has been washed, rubbed down with olive oil, and dressed in a white robe, they are to be strapped down to a gurney before being wheeled out to the application room. This new condition will be placed on our website and in the disclaimer documents the subject signs before proceeding."

Sean and Ralph thanked all those in attendance and stated that if anyone had any further ideas on how to make the administration of the formula easier, to please suggest their ideas to Ralph or himself. With that, everyone exited the makeshift boardroom and resumed their duties.

Everything was going according to plan. The subjects were in their observation rooms, monitored 24/7, with no problems. As expected, in the middle of the second day, their hair fell out, and they all said they felt fantastic.

The only glitch was that the women, once their hair started falling out, started crying. The shock of seeing their hair on the ground was just too much. All stated that they felt good but were upset over the loss of their hair. The staff explained that the new hair was pushing out the old dead hair, but this didn't seem to have much of an effect, and they were still upset.

Once released from their rooms, they were escorted to a table with an assortment of hats, baseball caps, wigs, and scarves. Everyone put on a hat, as suddenly being bald in public was a little discomforting for them.

Ralph and the assistants sat and spoke to them as a group. Sean was nowhere to be seen. Almost all the men immediately insisted on speaking to Sean.

"You would think when you're paying fifty million dollars for something, you at least get a chance to talk to the fellow in charge?" seemed to be the common request.

"No, you don't," Ralph sternly stated. "That was never agreed to and Sean does not want to talk to any of you, period."

This naturally did not sit well with these egotistical gentlemen, as they are accustomed to getting what they want whenever they want. But all the men did report feeling really good. When addressing the ladies, they said that they were upset about the loss of their hair.

"But this was fully explained to you," said Ralph.

"Yes, I know, but seeing my hair on the floor was too much for me," said one lady, and then she and the other two ladies started crying.

After the ladies settled down, the seven male and three female subjects were asked to stay for further tests before they were allowed to go to the lunch room for some real food. No one had to encourage them. As soon as someone said "lunch room," they all stood up and said "where" and then marched off to get something to eat.

All their tests returned positive, and they were told they could go back to the Parkway Hotel and that vehicles were waiting outside.

"We would appreciate seeing you back here in three days for some further testing," requested Ralph, and all agreed.

Upon arriving at the Parkway Hotel, a legion of reporters was waiting for them. Three of the women and two of the men covered their faces and pushed their way into the lobby, the elevators, and up to their rooms. The remaining five men relished the media attention and immediately started talking to the reporters.

Their stores were pretty much all the same. They described the auction, the physical exams, and sending in their money within twenty-four hours. They described the two days of fasting, the washing and being rubbed down with olive oil, and meeting Sean and having him pour a liquid down their throats. Then off again to their observation rooms for another two days, this time with only bread and water to eat, and their release two days later. All the men mentioned their hair falling out but reported that they felt great.

"Where are you going now?" asked one reporter.

All five of the men yelled out, "The dining room."

Once all the applicants had left, Sean and Ralph got together over a coffee.

"I totally agree that the subjects, after being washed and rubbed down, need to be strapped down to the gurney before being brought to me. When that first guy approached me, I didn't know what to do," said Sean.

"Me too, Sean, I was in shock," said Ralph. "Thank heavens. The lab guys grabbed him before he got to you. Who knows how that may have turned out?"

The Next 10 Paid Subjects, All Female

The conversation turned to the emotional response the women had to their hair falling out. Ralph commented, "They all knew that this was going to happen. It was explained to them; they saw it on the video, and they signed off, knowing that this was a side effect of the treatment. What else can we do?" questioned Ralph.

"Not much," said Sean. "The only option is that we shave their heads before they go in, but this is likewise disturbing."

"I've got an idea," said Ralph. "Let's let them decide. They can have their heads shaved before they arrive, or we can shave their heads here, or they can go through with the treatment and have their hair fall out in the observation room. It's their hair, It's their decision."

"Ralph, you are a genius. What a great idea. Their hair is coming off anyway, so why not let them decide? I'll have the website people add these options to the site, and I'll have the consent forms updated as well. Good idea."

For the next few weeks, they witnessed the media storm over the interviews of the ten paid test subjects. The media complained about how they were going about selecting candidates by auction and that people were paying millions of dollars for this service.

"Should be available to everyone," cried out the reporters.

Hearing this, Sean laughed.

"Yeah, it's available to everyone, everyone who has fifty million dollars!"

So, for the next batch of ten, they specified on the website that this auction was only open to females. The same conditions applied, with the

177

only difference being that they could have their heads shaved themselves before the application, have their heads shaved here, or opt to have it fall out in the observation room. As before, everyone was surprised that people were bidding millions of dollars, with the winning bids all in excess of fifty million dollars.

"Must be a lot of people with a lot of money out there," said Sean after seeing the bids.

Once the auction was concluded, Ralph and Sean selected twenty likely candidates.

As before, many were eliminated due to either being too young or too old. Then the rest were eliminated due to their present health conditions. And then finally, with the fifteen left, five dropped out due to the fact that their money never arrived within the twenty-four hour time period. *Good,* thought Sean, *ten female subjects.*

Of this group of ten females, six opted to be shaved before the application, and four decided against it. After their two days of fasting, washed and rubbed down with olive oil, none had a problem with being strapped down to the gurney and then wheeled out to the application room. No one made a fuss, and they all introduced themselves to Sean and said how excited they were to be young again. Every single one said that they had personally spoken to someone who had undergone the treatment and convinced them to go ahead.

The four women who did not have their heads shaved were the only ones visibly upset at the end of the treatment. Regardless of whether they knew about it, having their hair all fall out and land on the floor was too upsetting, thought Sean.

Sean again called a meeting about this. The female staff observing these women reported that the subject women, upon seeing their hair fall out, all went hysterical and started crying.

"I thought the lady I was assigned to watch was going to have a nervous breakdown when her hair started falling out. I had to have two others enter her room to hold her down to console her," said one of the assistants.

"Any suggestions?" asked Sean. One female lab assistant spoke up and said, "It's simple, you make having their heads shaved part of the mandatory procedure before entering into their clean rooms. They can have it done themselves, or we can do it for them. This way, everyone is treated the same, and we don't have any women freaking out halfway through the process."

"Good idea. How do the rest of you feel about this?" asked Sean. Everyone agreed.

"But if this is mandatory for females, shouldn't we be making it mandatory for the males also?" asked another lab assistant.

"I'm really happy that I have such smart people working with me. Great idea, and I agree. How do the rest of you feel about it?" Sean asked. Everyone agreed.

"Well, that's it. From today forward, the shaving of a subject's head is a mandatory requirement of the procedure. This will be mentioned on the website, included in the procedure videos, and written into their disclaimer agreement. Thank you all for your participation." And Sean concluded the meeting.

Chapter 25
The Compound

Sean and Ralph were amazed. The response to the process and the auctions was incredible. With over one billion dollars in the bank in one month, it would appear that they could do or buy anything they wanted.

Barry Leibowitz, the owner of Leibowitz and Co., the construction company, and Sean were becoming good friends. Sean told Barry that he would have all the work and that there would be lots of it.

Sean's new designs were for a medical tower, an office tower, and an apartment building, all of ten stories and the same size. All were to resemble the medical building, built in a row, facing the morning sun. Barry naturally loved the idea and had Hillsborough and Smith Inc., Sean's former company, finalize the designs. Naturally, Sean had final approval for the plans. His only major difference was that he wanted a very large and impressive entrance foyer built in the office and apartment tower. Plus, in the apartment tower, all the apartments were to be spacious and to have two bedrooms each.

A few days later, Sean changed his mind. Sean met with Barry and told him that he wanted an additional two apartment towers built, similar in appearance to the two-bedroom apartment building. The next two apartment buildings would be totally one-bedroom apartments, and the next one would be all bachelor apartments.

"We seem to be growing at an incredible rate and I will be needing a lot of full-time staff for my protection and future environmental efforts. Best to get the living accommodations in place first before starting my big projects," said Sean.

"Barry, I also think that the present fresh water holding tank will not be close to our needs once additional staff are hired. Please look at having a larger tank or a tower installed closer to the perimeter fence so that the supply trucks can fill it from the roadway without having to enter the compound. I'll let you decide which is best.

"Plus, I would like all the human waste from all the buildings to be stored in septic tanks and then pumped out and trucked to large holding tanks in the ground at the far end of the compound. I have plans for this waste to be used as fertilizer at a later date."

"Well, that solves the fresh water and septic bed issues," stated Barry. "I was thinking that the present fresh water tank you have now would start causing you problems. And with apartments of these sizes, the septic beds would have to be huge.

"I like your idea of having the sewage pumped out and stored at the far end of the property to be used as fertilizer. I'll even look at having all the septic tanks connected and having their own underground piping going to the holding tanks."

In the following months, the medical tower was progressing around the clock, especially after Sean, insisted that regardless of cost, he wanted the work to continue seven days a week. Sean, ever conscious of his security, had the excellent idea that the new tower construction sites should be cordoned off from the rest of the compound with a portable fence, the ones you usually see surrounding any major job site. He then ordered five miles of portable fencing brought in to surround the tower building sites and designated that a separate guarded entrance be made in the outside compound fencing for all the construction crews.

With the construction people having their own entrance away from the main gate, Sean no longer had to worry about some construction workers wandering off to where they shouldn't be. The construction main gate was manned by military personnel 24/7 and every person checked in and checked out. It worked out beautifully, and everyone appreciated the noise reduction now that their crews had their own entrance.

Sean Hires Wendy Rawlings

As this was a military compound, Sean eventually asked Colonel John to supply him with the accounting, medical, and any other staff they needed. His only requirement was that these people be military personnel with clean criminal records. The accounting staff would be taking over one building, and the medical staff would be taking over another. They all made do with what they had, knowing that new offices would eventually be provided for.

Sean reviewed the resumes of the accounting staff. One in particular caught his eye. That was of Miss Wendy Rawlings, a thirty-five years old unmarried lady who was the assistant to the chief accounting clerk for the nearby Nellis Air Force Base. Sean asked Colonel John to have Wendy drop in to see him, and she was there the next day. Colonel John brought Wendy up to Sean's office, made the introductions, and then left.

Both Sean and Wendy got along very well, and it was obvious that she was a very disciplined and organized lady. She was a tall, professional, and attractive lady. After talking to her, it was obvious that she was a down-to-earth, straight-to-the-point type of person. Sean thought that they could work together quite well. Besides, she's not hard on the eyes, she would do nicely.

He immediately hired her as his Secretary Treasurer likely to oversee a staff of 30–40 people. Wendy was delighted, especially since she was able to hire her own staff and everyone in the compound was being paid their normal rate of pay from the military, plus an additional thousand dollars per week from Sean.

Wendy mentioned that she would like to work here, but that her commanding officers at the Nellis Air Force Base may not want to give her up. Sean knew that this was still a military compound, and with his influence, getting her to come over from Nellis would not be a problem. Sean made the call to Colonel John and requested that he make the arrangements for having Wendy Rawlings assigned to the compound. Obviously, Colonel John was delighted to do so. One call from Colonel John and the commanding office of the Nellis Air force Base agreed to let Wendy go. Colonel John then picked up Wendy and escorted her back to the outside parking lot and her car.

Two weeks later, with Wendy and her accounting people settled in, Sean had Wendy make up the first monthly detailed financial report plus a check for hundred million dollars made out to the President of the United States. Sean then contacted Kevin Sanders, the Vice Presidents assistant, and invited him to come and view the compound.

"Are you kidding? I'm so glad you called," Kevin said excitedly. "The President and John wanted me to drop in to see you, but we also didn't want to bother you. I'll be there tomorrow morning. Thanks for calling."

Kevin arrived the next day, and Sean had the guards drive them around. Kevin was amazed at the progress taking place in the medical building and the layouts for the office and apartment towers.

"It looks like you are creating your own city here," said Kevin.

He stayed for lunch, and Sean handed over the monthly financial report and the check for hundred million dollars to pay back the loan.

"The President will be happy to see this. He got so much flack from others in Congress about giving you this money. I can't wait to see the smile on his face and the frown on his critics," said Kevin.

Sean liked Kevin and felt he could trust him. They finished their lunch and Kevin left for Washington, D.C.

Jennifer, the Purchasing Agent

So far, Sean thought the improvements to the compound were coming along nicely. With Jennifer's mom, dad, and sister Emily now living in the compound, she couldn't be happier. All four of them would go on their shopping trips to Las Vegas to pick up whatever they or the compound needed. They were accustomed to being accompanied by their military guards, and they would probably get lost without them.

Sean thought, *Jennifer was doing an excellent job of acquiring everything the compound needs, so I guess she's our official "purchasing agent."* He then had Wendy, his new Secretary Treasurer, set up Jennifer with her own bank account for expenses. His only stipulation was that whenever possible, the items she bought had to be of high quality and "Made in America," and Jennifer agreed.

This newfound freedom and the title of "Purchasing Agent" suited Jennifer just fine. Eventually, Jennifer started having her more regular purchases delivered directly to the compound. The groceries were delivered to the restaurant and the office supplies, computers, and furniture were ordered through the local business office stores. These large orders were delivered to the main gate, and then the guards would accompany the drivers to make their deliveries. For small deliveries, the drivers would leave them at the gate, and the guards would drive them in. Obviously, for security reasons, Sean wanted as few outsiders on the property as possible.

Jennifer and her sister Emily started to work on the mess hall. Along with the new expensive appliances she ordered, she had all new furniture brought in and the walls covered in pine planking. A new ceiling was installed, along with new lighting. The mess hall now looked like a northern cottage resort, and Sean and Jennifer loved it.

As everyone ate there—Jennifer, Sean, Ralph, the lab people, and the military personnel—decided that the daily meals had to be something to look forward to.

The cooking crew that Colonel John hired were very friendly and could they cook. Jennifer thought, *These people put my cooking to shame.* They were easy to get along with, and Jennifer made sure they had everything they needed.

"Nothing is too good for our men," Jennifer would always say.

As the existing walk-in freezers needed repair, she instead had them replaced with new ones. Jennifer immediately called Cheryl McDonald at the high-end appliance store and ordered the new walk-in freezers. Once installed, Jennifer made sure that the freezers were immediately stocked with the finest food they could buy—steaks, roasts, sides of pork, everything.

Breakfast was usually a large buffet with lots of bacon, eggs, hash browns, fresh fruit, lots of toast, and gallons of coffee. Everyone's favorite. Dinners were always a surprise treat, ranging from T-bone steaks to roast beef to pork side ribs to salmon. Everyone complained that they were eating so well, they were all going to get fat. Jennifer was always happy to tell Sean, "I haven't heard anyone complaining about being stationed here." And Sean laughed.

Jennifer Buys Electric Jeeps

Sean said that he wanted vehicles to be used exclusively within the compound and other vehicles to be parked outside for the staff to use on their trips away. His reasoning was that when a staff member returned from their outside trip, they had to park their vehicle in the outside parking area and transfer their purchases to one of the interior compound electric vehicles before entering the compound. For security purposes, Sean wanted as few outside vehicles entering the compound area as possible. Jennifer agreed.

Jennifer then started researching vehicles on the internet. She made her decision to start looking at all-electric Jeep 4x4s with automatic transmissions for use outside the compound. These would be for everyone to use, especially if they wanted to go to Las Vegas shopping.

She noticed a nice Chrysler Jeep dealership on the way into Las Vegas and decided on her next trip out to drop in. Colonel John did not go, so she got the new Secretary Treasurer, Wendy and her sister Emily to come along. She told Wendy what she was planning, and Wendy put some information in a file folder. They drove on their own, followed by their guards, who were instructed them to remain in the parking lot across the road. All three girls entered and were greeted by a very pleasant receptionist, who said, "I'll get a salesperson for you."

The receptionist then left and went to speak to a salesman who obviously was not in a good mood. The three girls overheard what he said,

"Three girls out car shopping—what a treat! Let somebody else waste their time with those tire kickers," said the experienced salesperson.

The receptionist then went to talk to Tara, a new saleswoman who had just started last week. Tara was a very friendly, outgoing, and stylish lady who was eager to help.

The receptionist told her about the three ladies out front, and Tara was happy to meet them. Tara immediately got up and introduced herself.

"Good morning. Welcome to our Chrysler Jeep dealership. My name is Tara, and I'm new here, and I will help you the best I can. What are you interested in?" she asked.

All three girls immediately liked Tara.

"We are looking at some Jeeps. I think they should all have removable hard tops and soft tops, have automatic transmissions, and all be 4x4 and be totally electric," said Jennifer.

So for the next two hours, all three girls test-drove the Jeep models and compared them. Now back at Tara's desk, when it was time to write up the order, "Wendy and Emily, which ones did you like?" asked Jennifer.

"I like the Jeep Wrangler four-door in dark blue that I drove," replied Wendy.

"I like the same in dark green," said Emily.

"Great," said Jennifer, "we'll take those two, and I want the same vehicle, but in the dark red color, please," said Jennifer.

"Fabulous," said Tara, "this is my first sale, so you'll have to give me some time to write up the order."

As Tara was writing, Jennifer interrupted her and asked, "How many other Jeep Wrangler 4x4s electrics do you have in stock with automatic transmissions?"

"Pretty sure we have twenty-five or so electric Jeeps in stock. They are usually one of our best sellers," Tara replied.

"Super, I would like you to select an additional ten Jeep Wranglers four-door electrics with 4x4 with automatic transmissions in mostly dark colors and send them to the compound. I will be taking those also," said Jennifer.

"You are kidding, aren't you?" said Tara in amazement.

"No, we are taking three electric Jeeps for ourselves and ten electric Jeeps for the compound. And we'll be paying for them today," said Jennifer.

"No problem, but it will take me at least two hours to write up all the orders," replied Tara. While handing her file folder to Tara, Wendy said,

"Here is all the ownership, insurance information, directions to the compound, and my card—everything you need. I have already written out a fifty thousand dollars deposit check. We can drop by after lunch and pay you the rest."

"Sure, I don't see why not," replied Tara.

After a fun-filled afternoon of shopping and lunch, they returned to the dealership accompanied by four SUVs full of armed military guards who parked in the lane in front of the dealership's showroom. The dealership's staff all came out to look at the parade of military guards and their very large automatic weapons.

"These girls must be important," you could hear some of the staff say.

Wendy went in and paid for the remainder of the bill, slightly over seven hundred thousand dollars. The manager, having confirmed who these ladies were, was more than happy to take Wendy's check. After finishing the paperwork, Wendy came out with Tara, and Jennifer and Emily both gave her a big hug. Tara, of course, was shocked at seeing all the military guards with their automatic rifles in full view.

"These guys look tough," she said.

After goodbye hugs all around, all three ladies said they enjoyed dealing with Tara and the dealership. They parted as friends.

Three days later, arriving at the main gate and being driven in by the guards, thirteen brand new shiny electric Jeep 4X4s, all in different colors. Wendy, Emily, and Jennifer selected their Jeep's first. It was Jennifer who thought up the idea of having their names on their own personal Jeeps. This way, no one else would be driving them. Then Jennifer led Sean out and showed him her purchases. Wendy and Emily were surrounded by twenty guards, all admiring the Jeeps. Sean just shook his head.

"I got three all-electric Jeeps, one for us, one for Emily, and one for Wendy, for us to use within the compound. I also got ten additional Jeeps to be parked outside for whenever a staff member wishes to leave the compound," exclaimed Jennifer, and Sean smiled and agreed. Jennifer then contacted Barry to have the Jeep charging station positioned in the outside parking lot.

Electric Golf Carts

Jennifer was on a roll. Having acquired electric Jeeps for the staff to use outside, she started looking at electric vehicles to be used within the compound. She concluded that some electric golf cart-type vehicles would be enjoyable. She investigated and decided on twenty electric golf cart-type vehicles from a new manufacturer in California.

Ten of the golf cart-type vehicles would be two-seater models with a box on the back for groceries, and another ten would be four-seater models. The company was also planning on introducing some small electric utility vehicles that she could look at purchasing later. She made sure that the Jeep and the new vehicle charging stations were compatible and had them installed near the main gate, the three apartment buildings, the office tower, and the guest trailers.

She went ahead and ordered them and had the charging stations installed. The new electric Jeeps and golf carts were an instant hit, as everyone enjoyed driving them. And because they were quiet and pollution-free, she knew she'd be ordering more.

She talked to Colonel John about using the electric vehicles, and he insisted that, for security purposes, his staff stick to the gas powered full-sized GMC Yukon's for use within and outside of the compound. He did agree that the electric vehicles would be useful for doing regular chores and deliveries.

Chapter 26
Sean's Parent's Church

Sean spoke to Colonel John and asked him to bring in a military chaplain. Two days later, Colonel John introduced Sean to Ray Collins, a military chaplain from the Nellis Air Force base. Ray was a 40-ish, short, soft-spoken chaplain. Sean and Ray spoke for about twenty minutes, and then Sean took Ray over to a building that could be used as a temporary chapel.

"Anything you need, you contact my girlfriend Jennifer, and she will get it for you, no problems. I think you'll need some chairs and pews," Sean added.

Then, unknown to anyone, Sean contacted Barry and told him about an abandoned brick Catholic church just north of Crystal Falls, Michigan, where he grew up. He described the church and its location and added, "My parents used to attend this church, and I remember going there as a young boy. I want you to buy the church, dismantle it, and place it on a foundation with a basement here at the compound. I don't care how much it costs or how you get it here. I want this done."

Barry was getting used to working with Sean, and he knew not to ask any questions. Plus, Sean had his financial people pay their invoices as soon as they were delivered, so Barry never had to wait for his money. *Great way to do business,* thought Barry.

After buying the church and property from the Catholic Church, Barry hired his friend Eric, who specialized in moving old buildings to new locations. Eric was a stocky, big guy who liked to work alongside his men on a project. Hearing who he would be working for, Eric agreed to send a crew out there immediately. Barry then confirmed with Sean where he would like the church placed, and Sean showed him and asked that the front door be facing toward the morning sun.

"No problem, consider it done," stated Barry.

For security purposes, the portable fencing was moved to include the area for the new church. This way, the people working on the church used the same gate as the rest of the construction crews. Barry made sure that the basement and foundation of the church were started immediately. The material for the Crystal Falls church started arriving.

It was decided that, with this church being so old, the walls of the church would be made of a concrete block interior structure, and then, when up, the exterior of the old church would be placed over it. The same went for the interior. The existing interior walls of the original church were then placed over the inner concrete wall structure. The roof, of course, could not be saved, so Eric had a new one constructed in the same style and color as the original roof tiles. Eric had all the existing pews refinished before they were delivered to the compound. He was also careful to number to ensure that they were installed in the exact order that they were removed. Sean was impressed.

Incredible to believe, but with an unlimited budget and a request for the workmen to work seven days a week, the church was dismantled in Crystal Falls, trucked to Nevada, and reconstructed all within six weeks. When they had to replace a piece of wood, they even salvaged the nails from the original rotten wood to be used on the new piece. *These guys are good,* thought Sean.

Sean, Jennifer, Barry, and Eric toured the finished church. Sean had a tear in his eye as he told them all about attending this church with his mom and dad. They had replicated the original church down to the finest detail. Sean was overwhelmed. Then they went to lunch. Sean asked Eric for the final invoice. Once handed to him, Sean did not look at it and called over Wendy Rawlings, his new Secretary Treasurer and handed the invoice to her.

"Here is Eric's final invoice for giving me the church my parents and I used to attend. I want you to make out the check for his services and add twenty thousand dollars to the amount. I now want you to contact his head office and include a check for two thousand dollars for everyone who works for him and for anyone else who assisted in bringing this church to me. That includes the trucking people, clean-up crews, and everyone. Am I clear on this?"

"Yes, Mr. Little, I will get on it right away," Wendy stated, and then left.

"That is very generous of you. Thank you," said Eric. Everyone else sat in amazement.

"Think nothing of it. You have brought me a gift that I will cherish forever," said Sean. "And besides, if I ever contact you again, I want you to drop what you're doing and work for me." Everyone laughed.

"No problem there. I'll get on any project you want right away," replied Eric.

"Stick around for a bit and maybe take a jeep out for a drive while my people get your checks ready. Shouldn't take too long," said Sean. Eric agreed.

The Sermon

Sean took Ray Collins over to the church for his formal tour. Ray was very impressed. Sean was proud to tell him that this was the original church that he and his parents attended when he was a young boy.

"Talk to Jennifer about purchasing a restored antique pipe organ installed—a good one. And please start recruiting some gospel singers for the church. My mother and father loved the gospel music here, and they will hear it again in heaven."

Sean could not be happier. With the pews in place and everything ready to go, they planned the first Sunday morning mass. Sean requested that he address the congregation last. He mentioned to the chaplain that the sermon and his announcement would be recorded and placed on their website for the whole world to see.

The first Sunday morning mass included almost everyone in the compound. So many people showed up there was only standing room for the late arrivals. After the chaplain spoke, it was Sean's turn to address the congregation.

"Ladies and gentlemen, my name is Sean Little, and I am proud to say that I attended this church with my mother and father as a young boy. I have had it reconstructed here in honor of their memory. In the upcoming weeks, I have asked for an antique church pipe organ to be found and brought here for us. Plus, any of you who love gospel music are asked to form a choir for us. My mom and dad loved gospel music, and they will be able to hear our singing in heaven." Then Sean put his head down, and tears rolled down his face.

Once he composed himself, he spoke again. "Ladies and gentlemen, I am aware that every single laboratory in every country in the world is working day and night to replicate my formula. So far, no one has succeeded. But I tell you before God that as long as I am the sole owner of this secret, I will use the money raised to help others and to clean up this planet.

And I tell you now, and I swear before God, I swear on the Bible, and I swear on the memory of my mother and father, that I will never let any government or anyone take this secret from me. I will never allow this secret to be used as an instrument of war or an international bargaining chip. As long as I and I alone know the secret, it will be used to help mankind. I have dedicated my life to this cause and will not be deterred, so help me, God."

With tears in their eyes, everyone in the congregation stood up and clapped.

They must have clapped for ten minutes solid. Sean came down from the makeshift podium and hugged Jennifer. Everyone surrounded Sean to thank him and clapped him on the back.

Sean Proposes to Jennifer

Sean had always dreamed of marrying Jennifer at his parent's church. When they were both living together in Crystal Falls, he thought of proposing to her and, if she accepted, having the church cleaned up to the point where the service could be held. This never came to pass, as Jennifer eventually left him to become an airline stewardess. But now, with the church restored and on the property, and her parents and sister here, now was his chance.

That night, over dinner in their trailer, Sean proposed to Jennifer on one knee and offered her a ring of his mother. Jennifer immediately started crying. She hugged Sean with all her might.

"Yes, yes, I accept," she said, still crying.

After she stopped crying and they finished their meal, Jennifer went running over to her parents and sister to give them the good news. They were all so excited.

"No need for a long-drawn-out engagement, said Sean. Let's get married in two weeks."

Jennifer agreed. So for the next two weeks, she decorated the church and went shopping for dresses for her and her bridesmaids, Emily and Wendy. They visited every single dress and wedding shop in Las Vegas. For the occasion, Colonel John had six of his guards wear suits when accompanying the girls' dress shopping. He thought six heavily armed military guards would look out of place in these fancy shops, and he was right. Jennifer was driving the guards nuts. Here are six well-dressed guards in beautiful high-end dress and wedding shops: two guards inside the shop and four guards out front. Days and days of shopping, and then finally, Jennifer makes her decision.

One guard even exclaimed, "How much time does it take to select a dress? I feel like I've spent my whole life inside a dress store."

For her special day, Jennifer had the finest seafood and steaks brought in from San Francisco. *Oh well, why not? Let's make it a big deal. Hopefully, this only happens once,* thought Sean.

The day arrived, and the church was full. Sean waited patiently at the altar with his best man, Ralph Barns. Jennifer arrived in an absolutely stunning wedding gown that had a trail at least twelve feet long. The service by Chaplain Collins was beautiful, extolling the virtues of true love and happiness. Sean kissed his bride, and they went for a driving tour around the compound in a stunning 1936 Rolls-Royce Phantom three Saloon that Sean had brought in for the day.

Colonel John, ever conscious of security, had the church surrounded by thirty well-armed guards and the wedding coach, followed by six SUVs loaded with armed guards.

"You can never be too safe," said Colonel John.

At the end of their wedding tour, everyone went back to the restaurant for a fabulous seafood and steak meal. Sean had a small band brought in for the occasion, and everyone danced and had a wonderful time. Mr. and Mrs. Sloan were so happy to see their eldest daughter happily married off, they both just sat there crying. Everyone was happy, especially Jennifer. *What a wonderful day!*

Chapter 27
Women Only Applications

"Hire all the female staff you need," said Sean to Ralph. "At an additional thousand dollars per week, it should be no problem getting employees. Talk to Colonel John and Wendy about hiring ex-military ladies, and let's start doing the applications for just females. Jennifer can bring in more trailers to house the staff, no problem. When we run out of females to do, we can switch over to doing just the men."

Ralph laughed. "No problem. You're the boss. Besides, women are easier to handle and don't want to attack you when they see you."

So Ralph and his team set about hiring the lady lab assistants to start doing the applications on just the female subjects.

Jennifer later visited Jesse at the trailer dealership and ordered another twenty of the twenty-eight foot Jayco trailers, as these seemed to be everyone's favorites. She later laughed, telling Sean that Jesse at the dealership almost had a heart attack when she placed her order. They were becoming great friends.

Sean contacted the website people and explained that they were to announce that the age-reversing application is now available to any female subject under the following conditions.

Conditions for the Applications

Before the Application

–The next applications are for female candidates only.

  –Our applications seem to work best with those persons from 40–60 years of age.

  We will base our selection process favoring those years.

  –The cost of the procedure is fifty million in US dollars.

  There are no discounts, and there are no deals, so don't ask.

–Once notified of your successful placement, each candidate will have twenty-four hours to deposit their monies in full into our bank account. Partial payments are not allowed. Failure to have this money deposited in full within the required twenty-four hours disqualifies that candidate from the application.

–Once notified of your successful placement, your doctor must send us a statement of your present medical condition. We expect that this medical report will be honest and accurate.

–After being notified, you will reside at the Parkway Hotel in Las Vegas and await your instructions for pickup. You may not approach the compound for any reason. Failing pickup at the Parkway Hotel, your application will be refused and your money refunded.

–You may not be accompanied by an assistant or family member to the compound, nor will an assistant or family member be allowed in the compound while you are in our care.

–Regardless, you will be physically re-examined by our doctors when you arrive. Any evidence of your physician making a false report to us, for example, hiding an undisclosed medical condition, will render you unfit for the application, and you will be asked to leave. Your money will then be refunded.

–Your mass will not change. If you weigh two hundred pounds going into the procedure, you will weigh two hundred pounds coming out, minus the weight you lost while fasting.

–This process has proven quickly fatal to anyone with cancer. You will be tested for this disease. Once discovered, your application will not proceed.

–You will sign the mandatory disclaimer form, absolving "the company" of any wrongdoing before, during, or after the application. "The company" cannot be held liable in the event of your illness or death caused by the application. If you have an undisclosed illness or cancer that both your doctors and ours fail to uncover, you will die during this procedure, and "the company" cannot be held liable.

–It is accepted that all applicants have watched the introductory video and realize that they will be showered, that their clothes will be removed from them, and then they will be wearing only white robes and slippers for the remainder of their stay.

Application Procedure

–You are not allowed to bring anything with you. Nothing. All jewellery or religious artifacts will be taken from you. For example, if you have pierced earrings or other piercings, these will be removed before the application.

For the duration of the process, there can be nothing touching your skin except your white robe.

–You will be cut off from the outside world for the duration of your stay. You will not be permitted to take in or have access to a phone or a computer. While here, you will not be able to make a phone call or send an email, regardless of the reason. You will be refused all messages from the outside.

–You will be supplied with a TV, a movie channel, and any books or magazines you desire. You will also be supplied with pens and paper to write on.

–While here, you will be constantly under video surveillance for our protection and yours. All conversations you have with the staff and Sean Little will also be recorded.

–Your head must be shaven bare. This can be done before you arrive or our staff will do it for you. This is a mandatory condition of the procedure.

–All candidates agree that for their first two days (forty-eight hours), they will be locked in an observation room and be fasting with only water to drink. At the end of your first two days (forty-eight hours), you will be washed and your body coated with olive oil. You will then be strapped onto a gurney and wheeled down to the lab for the application.

–The application will be performed by Sean Little at the start of the third day.

This is the only time you will meet with Sean Little.

–Sean Little will not visit you in your observation rooms for any reason.

If he makes a visit to one applicant, he must visit them all, so he has decided not to visit anyone.

–After the applications, you will be brought back to your room, where you will be given only bread and water for the remaining two days (forty-eight hours). Halfway through the second day, the remainder of your hair

195

will fall out. You will be released at the end of the fifth day, examined by our medical people, and released. Releasing you sooner means that you will likely get an infection and die.

–After your treatment and for the following two weeks, you will notice that the outer layer of your skin is turning to fine dust. This is a natural process of the old skin being replaced with the newer, younger skin.

–Who is accepted and who is not is at the sole discretion of "the company."

Any candidate may be refused the application at any time for any reason and have their money refunded.

–These conditions apply to all persons and are designed with your safety in mind.

This is mandatory. There are no exceptions.

–Failure to abide by the above conditions renders you unfit for the application.

Sean read this over and had Ralph take a look. Ralph agreed, especially with the part where they could refuse an application to any individual for any reason.

"But Sean, I have to question your statement that you will not be visiting the applications while in their observation rooms. Not only will we be hosting international celebrities, but eventually world leaders and businessmen, people who would be fascinating to talk to," Sean replied. "And yes, I agree with you. But the problem is that if I visit one person, I have to visit them all. And with the egos that these men have, I will get nothing but grief if I visit one and not the other. So in my opinion, it's best that I do not visit anyone for any reason. Plus, to be honest with you, I really don't want to talk to them and hear about their crazy "you and I can conquer the world" fantasies or hear about their complaints about how they are being treated."

"Good point," replied Ralph. "Somehow, I can't blame you. You're the boss."

Sean sent this list of conditions off to the website people, and the site was updated within thirty minutes. He was hoping to have people ready for the application this coming Monday. As before, nothing happened until the news media got a hold of it. On the second day, the requests started coming in. Almost immediately, there were thirty female applicants. Sean and Ralph reviewed them and selected suitable candidates.

It was decided that they could do up to ten females at a time and to start doing a group of ten every two weeks. Sean thought this was a good idea. The first week would be for selecting the candidates, getting their medical reports, and getting their money. Then they could arrive, go for the two days of fasting, and continue with the procedure.

All candidates forwarded their doctors' physical reports almost immediately. They must have had these examinations done in advance. Sean thought. Sean had Wendy contact the suitable candidates and give them "the company's" account information. Within two hours, ten candidates had deposited fifty million dollars each. Even Sean and Ralph were surprised.

"This is slick," said Ralph, "just like having money growing on a tree."

As before, the women all followed the procedures to the letter and made no fuss.

When introduced after their two-day fast, Sean questioned them on their enthusiasm for the procedure. All reported that they had personally spoken to others who had undergone the procedure and were therefore convinced to do so themselves. They all mentioned that even with the expense of the procedure, most said, "What good is having all this money if you're too old to spend it?"

Obviously, their husbands approved of them getting the procedure done. A happy wife is a happy life, thought Sean. It also seemed unnecessary to have the women strapped down, but it's better to be safe than sorry. None of the women complained. To them, it was just part of the procedure.

Sean and Ralph were very happy with this all-female group. No problems, no troubles.

"Far nicer working with women than with men, isn't it, Ralph," said Sean.

Ralph agreed. They interviewed the lab assistants and observers, and all reported that these women were excited about being there and looking five years younger. Not one lab assistant reported a single problem.

The lab assistants also reported sitting outside the observation rooms and having wonderful conversations with their subjects. Many even reported the subjects inviting them to visit them at their homes. *The female subjects seem so much more relaxed than the male subjects. We'll never know. But it was certainly a welcome relief to hear the good reports from his coworkers. Makes for a better working environment,* thought Sean.

The lab assistants agreed that the women are more used to going to salons and ' spas so this is just another procedure. All the lab assistants agreed that having the subject's heads shaved before the application was the only way to go.

"No more hair falling out in their room and them crying" was the general conscientious.

The one-week-on, one-week-off program was very popular. The staff appreciated the first week off because this allowed them time off to see their families or just take a jeep and see the sights of Las Vegas. The administrative work could get done, and the candidates could be selected and have time for their money to be sent in.

Everything was now starting to fall into an orderly routine. More and more women were telling their other rich lady friends how great they felt. These women had their medical reports and money all ready to be sent in. Wendy told Sean, "We have at least thirty women all ready to go with their medical reports and money to send us. With this type of response, who needs to advertise?" And they both laughed.

The procedure was changed to once the previous group went into their last two days of observation, the next ten subjects were selected. These people were asked to send in their money, which usually arrived within an hour. They still waited a week to allow the staff time off, and everything was working like clockwork. Even Ralph was fond of saying, "You're pulling in five hundred million dollars every two weeks. Pretty tough to beat, and it certainly pays the bills."

Over supper one night with Jennifer, Sean told Ralph that he wanted him happy and content.

"Are you nuts? This is the greatest medical discovery of all time. The mere fact that I am involved is the greatest adventure of my life. We make a good team," said Ralph.

"And I appreciate that," said Sean. "Ralph, I am having Wendy place fifty million dollars in your bank account tomorrow. That should keep you from looking at any other job offers." Sean laughed. "And whenever you want an application for yourself, let's get it done. I need you and want you to be happy."

"I'm pretty happy doing what I'm doing, and I appreciate the money and the offer. Certainly beats testing out a new face cream, that's for sure."

Everyone laughed.

A New Chaplain

Sean, Jennifer, and her parents enjoyed going to church on Sunday mornings.

This was a family outing for them, and they enjoyed a good breakfast afterward. However, Chaplain Collins' sermons, and this morning's sermon in particular, had been rubbing Sean the wrong way. Sean felt the military Chaplain Ray Collins was allowing his political views to creep into his sermons.

Sean felt that the chaplain mentioning, "That the work done here would allow the United States to retake its prominence in the world and to restore the world to Christian values", did not sit well with Sean. Sean never intended his secret to become an instrument of US foreign policy or force American values on the rest of the world. He was well aware of what the US or any other government would do if they possessed the secret, and that is why he knew that every government lab in the world was working on duplicating his success.

The chaplain's statements really bothered Sean to the point where he called Colonel John in and asked him to replace Chaplain Ray Collins.

"Get me another Chaplain. This one has worn out his welcome. I didn't like him telling the congregation that my secret should be used to restore the power of the US or to force our religious values onto others. That goes against everything I believe in. This secret, as long as I have it, will be for the betterment of mankind, not one group or country. And please have him escorted off the property. I don't want to see him again," said Sean.

"No problem, Sean. I will inform Chaplain Collins of your decision and have his replacement within a few days," replied Colonel John. Then he left.

Sean met with the new chaplain. Chaplain Harry Furlong was a small, soft-spoken man with obvious sharp intelligence and wit. Sean liked his warm personality and knew he would make a good fit.

Sean outlined why the last chaplain was let go and Harry understood. Sean talked about the power that any government would have and how they could dictate their demands to the rest of the world and Harry agreed.

Harry then said, "I was in Afghanistan and while I believe in why we were there, I personally have seen enough of war. Reading the last rites to a dying soldier, it gets to you."

Sean felt comfortable with Harry and knew that they would get along. Sean said that at the end of the upcoming sermon, he would like to make an announcement.

Chapter 28
The First Helicopter Incident

Sean Moves Away from the Lab

Sean had been thinking for some time about distancing himself from the lab.

That's Ralph's department and other than administering the formula, I'm probably getting in the way, he thought.

Sean met with Ralph to discuss Sean's involvement.

"Ralph, I want you to take over all of the lab duties. Other than me coming in to administer the formula, the place is all yours. You select the candidates and we'll go from there. As you said, we're pulling in five hundred million dollars every two weeks and with well over two billion dollars in the bank already. I want to start doing my philanthropy."

"What do you want to do?" asked Ralph.

"You know it's always pissed me off how we have practically destroyed this planet and I want to start cleaning up the place. With the type of money we have, I can tackle those projects that are just too expensive for any one country to handle. The world governments turn a blind eye to our environmental issues. Oh sure, they talk a good story and make big promises, but when it comes right down to it, they do nothing," said Sean.

"Couldn't agree with you more," said Ralph. "Your ideas fit. The money is coming in like a river with no end in sight. As long as you're nearby, I can look after bringing in the money and you can look after spending it. Good deal."

"Yeah, if we don't start spending this money Uncle Sam is going to take it all away in taxes anyway." They both laughed.

"No kidding, I bet the tax department is licking their lips right now, looking at your bank account," said Ralph.

"So it's settled then. I'm going to take over the empty building attached to where the financial people are and get going on saving the world. Every second Monday, I'll come over and administer the formula and the rest is up to you," concluded Sean. Ralph smiled and agreed.

Sean asked Jennifer to renovate the empty building off the back of the financial offices with new furniture and computers, and he moved in almost immediately.

He had a meeting with Wendy Rawlings, the military appointed Secretary Treasurer and asked, "Wendy, I really think I made a smart move hiring you. From this day on, all checks under $500,000 you can sign and I'll sign all checks in excess of half a million dollars. Plus, I would like a one-page financial report on my desk every morning outlining cash on hand, outstanding liabilities, etc. And as always, I want all invoices to be paid and mailed out on the date they hit your desk. When I was an architect, I hated having to wait for my money and so I want all our contractors paid immediately."

"No problem, Sean. With the rate the money is coming in you don't have to be paying for overdraft protection," said Wendy and they both laughed.

Sean liked and trusted Wendy. Jennifer and Wendy were becoming close friends and enjoyed shopping together, so it was a good fit.

The First Helicopter

Everything seemed to be going smoothly. Ralph was looking after the lab, Wendy was handling the money, Jennifer looked after ordering supplies and Colonel John looked after security. The local police were looking after the curious onlookers when they showed up and ushering them along. Everything was going as planned.

Then early one morning, an uninvited CBX news helicopter arrived. This was a direct violation of their security. Colonel John had the helicopter immediately surrounded with armed guards. He quickly called Sean and informed him.

Sean's immediate response was, "I don't care who's in that helicopter. If we don't arrest them right now, we'll have ten lands tomorrow and twenty every day after that. We have to set a strong example that we take our privacy and security seriously. They are trespassing on restricted government property. Arrest them now and put them in jail or send them off to the local police. I want that helicopter impounded. We have no choice. And please have someone video the events. We'll need this as evidence later on."

When Colonel John got out to the CBX news helicopter, he knew that the people inside were scared. They were surrounded by military personnel pointing very big automatic weapons at them. Sean arrived and after consulting with him, Colonel John took out a bullhorn and addressed the occupants of the helicopter.

"I am Colonel John Williams of the United States military. You are under arrest for trespassing on a restricted Federal Government installation. You will exit the craft with your hands in the air and then, once out, you will kneel on the ground. Once you are on the ground, you will be handcuffed by my men."

Almost at once, the pilot emerged, put his hands in the air, and kneeled on the ground.

The rest of the passengers did likewise. They naturally protested that they were CBX news reporters, and this was a violation of their civil rights. Colonel John replied on the bull horn, "You gave up you civil rights the moment you decided to trespass on restricted Federal Government property. You will all be handcuffed by my men. It will do you no good to resist."

Seeing the automatic rifles pointing at them, the intruders made no fuss. Now with these people handcuffed, Colonel John consulted with Sean to see what he should do.

"Sean, we don't have anywhere to put these people," said Colonel John.

"Yes, I know," said Sean, "but if they stay here or meet with me, they will be getting what they want and we'll just be inviting every single news agency in the world to invade our privacy. Contact the local police and ask them to use their jail cells. Tell the police that I will be paying them $100,000 for helping us out. I want these intruders guarded by your men while they are there. I take full responsibility for this action."

Colonel John contacted the local police department, and they readily agreed to house the Federal prisoners. Colonel John had the intruders loaded into a large truck and were escorted by three other military vehicles to the main police compound in Las Vegas. Sean called Wendy and asked that a check for $100,000 be made up and delivered to the Las Vegas Police Department.

Once these intruders were gone and Wendy called, Sean and Colonel John were now standing in front of the helicopter and Sean asked that the helicopter tanks be drained of fuel. Colonel John had a technical crew handle this. While this was being done, Sean asked that the interior of the helicopter be checked and any personal items be removed. Once this was completed, he asked that a guard go to the office tower job site and ask Barry to bring one of those really big Caterpillar bulldozers over. A short time later, you could see the bulldozer coming through an opening in the portable fencing heading toward the helicopter.

Everyone stood in amazement. Sean asked that anyone with a cell phone put it on video and then ordered the equipment driver to crush the helicopter.

"Yes, I said drive over that helicopter," said Sean.

The driver refused and throwing up his hands, got out of the bulldozer and walked away, with the bulldozer still running. Sean then grabbed the bullhorn and said, "Does anyone here know how to drive this bulldozer?"

"Yes, I do, sir," said one of the guards.

"Great," Sean ordered. "Get in that bulldozer and run over that helicopter now." Colonel John seeing how mad Sean was, then ordered the guard to enter the bulldozer and do as Sean asked.

The heavy Caterpillar bulldozer crushed the Bell 206 helicopter like it was a tin can. There must have been twelve people taking videos.

Sean then said, "I want everyone who has taken a video of this to send it off to our website company. I want these videos to be a lesson to everyone that we take our privacy and security very seriously here."

Colonel John agreed and asked his men to do as Sean asked. Colonel John and Sean talked on the drive back to Sean's office.

"Sir, with all due respect, don't you think that was a little harsh?' asked Colonel John.

"No, I don't," Sean replied. "If we allow those reporters in, tomorrow there will be helicopters from every news agency in the world landing here looking for a story. Then we'll have to contend with the husbands of the wives having the application done, wanting to see how their wives are doing. Then we'll start getting those persons who insist that they have the application done to them immediately. In other words, the whole world would be landing here. And to assure you, I take full responsibility for all the actions today, so you are off the hook."

"But what about the reporters? They are going to create quite a fuss," said Colonel John.

"Let them, let them tell the world. Once those videos are loaded onto our website, I suspect that it will be on the five p.m. news around the world. Please order your men to videotape the reporters getting off the truck and being herded into the police compound. I also want videos of them in their jail cells."

Colonel John just looked at Sean and then picked up his phone and asked for these videos to be made.

"When they come back, have your men forward their videos to the website company. I will notify them of the videos and send off an explanation," said Sean

Once Sean entered his office, he gave the website people a call and told them of the incoming videos. Sean then gave a description of the day's events.

"Early today, at the Federal Government restricted access compound in the Nevada desert, an uninvited CBX news helicopter carrying new reporters landed. This is a Federal Government restricted military compound housing myself, Sean Little and my age-reversing laboratory. The persons who landed here today were in direct violation of Federal law and were immediately handcuffed and arrested on their arrival. They were sent off to the Las Vegas police departments holding cells for sentencing. They were arrested and their helicopter was destroyed on direct orders of myself, Sean Little."

"That's great, Sean," said the owner of the website company.

Sean was by far their biggest account, and whatever Sean wants, Sean gets, thought the owner.

"I recorded what you said, and I will play it over top of the videos my people are putting together right now. Should be up and running in about thirty minutes."

"Good. Once you're done, send it off to all the major news agencies, Associated Press, Reuters, CBS, CNN, the Washington Post, and anyone else you can think of, especially where those reporters came from. I want the entire world to know about this," stated Sean.

"No problem, will do, Sean," said the owner, and then he and Sean hung up.

The website company did a fabulous job. They made the video so that any news agency could run it directly on their news programs. It hit the five p.m. news, and the networks played it up beautifully.

Sean watched the five p.m. CBS news. The announcer couldn't help laughing at seeing his fellow reporters in handcuffs and being led into the truck and put in jail.

He howled with laughter when showing the clip of the Caterpillar bulldozer crushing the news reporter's Bell 206 helicopter. He even showed the bulldozer clip twice. He signed off with "Well, I don't think they'll be doing that again."

The next morning, the news agencies went nuts. Half wanted Sean arrested, and half supported Sean's actions. Sean, as always, did not answer them or grant an interview. Sean had already instructed Colonel John that he wanted the occupants of the helicopter formally charged with trespassing on a restricted federal compound. Colonel John agreed.

Kevin Sanders, the assistant to the Vice President, called.

"Sean, what's going on?" he asked.

"Exactly as you see it on the news. We were trespassed by a helicopter full of CBX news reporters, so I ordered Colonel John to arrest them and take them to jail in Las Vegas. Then, on my orders, I had a bulldozer drive over the helicopter. This was all my own doing, and Colonel John was merely following my instructions," Sean replied.

"Well, you really know how to make a statement," said Kevin.

"If I don't deter people from trespassing now, I'll have a hundred helicopters landing here in a day. Everything from more reporters to husbands wanting to talk to their wives to people who want an application to people wanting to put a bullet in my head," added Sean.

"Sean off the record," Kevin said, "myself, the Vice President and the President, know exactly why you did it. We all agree that if you don't deter trespassers now, you'll have the whole world on your doorstep. Do whatever you need to do and keep yourself safe. You are far too important to have someone harm you. And between you and me, we all couldn't stop laughing when we saw the bulldozer drive over that helicopter."

"Thanks, Kevin," replied Sean. "And express my appreciation for the support to the President and Vice President." And at that, they hung up.

The CBX news reporters were formally charged with trespassing on restricted federal government property, released, and arranged for sentencing at a later date.

All were furious at how they e were "manhandled" and stated that their company would be formerly suing the US Military and Sean Little. Sean laughed. Self-entitled misfits, he thought.

A few days later, Wendy walked into his office with an invoice from the CBX news agency for $1.5 million for the replacement of their Bell 206 helicopter. Sean calmly took the invoice and wrote on it in black magic marker, "Kiss my ass, Sean Little". He then took a photo of it on his cell phone and handed the invoice back to Wendy, saying, "Please forward this back to them." Wendy looked at the invoice and started laughing.

"Boy, they'll think twice before ever coming here again." She walked out. Sean sent the photo off to the website company to have it placed alongside the videos of the helicopter being crushed. *This should look pretty cool.* He smiled.

With Sean not answering questions or granting interviews, the media excitement over the news reporters and the destruction of their helicopter died down. Colonel John had to agree that they were not being bothered by any more intruders, especially anyone in a helicopter.

Sean Buys More Property

Ever conscious of his security, he started out drawing up more plans for the compound. He invited the Nevada State Governor, Dana Burroughs, to come down and have lunch with him. The governor arrived the next day. Dana was a tall, well-dressed, personable fellow, and it was obvious that he was passionate about helping out the State of Nevada and its citizens. After a brief tour of the compound, back in Sean's office, Sean asked, "Regardless of the cost, I would like to purchase an additional twenty thousand acres of desert. Is this possible?"

"Are you kidding?" replied the governor. "You want to buy twenty thousand acres of worthless sand and bush, absolutely, and the State of Nevada could certainly use the money."

"Whatever you want, it's fine with me," said Sean. "I just want more room. Please send all the documentation addressed here to my lawyer, Bill Fryer, and he will make all the arrangements."

After he left, Dana Burroughs had the state land surveyors meet with Sean to discuss which property surrounding the compound he wanted. The compound was surrounded on all sides by Nevada State property, so it was up to Sean to decide on the borders. Dana Burroughs called Sean and stated that hundred million dollars should do it for "this large plot of sand and bushes." Sean agreed, even though he felt that it was a high price to pay, *but best to keep peace with the State of Nevada,* he thought. He asked the governor to just send through the invoice, saying that it would be paid immediately.

Ralph and Sean met for lunch. As everything was going along so well, Ralph and he rarely spoke business any more.

"Doing the applications on the women is no sweat. All the ladies have spoken to others who have had the process done and are eager to proceed. We have not had a single problem with any woman, thank heavens. Plus, the staff report the female subjects are a pleasure to talk to. Seems that everyone is happy," said Ralph.

Sean then told Ralph about purchasing some extra property.

"The more property we have around us, the more privacy we have, I agree," stated Ralph.

Sean had a meeting with Barry Leibowitz, the owner of the construction company. Sean told Barry that he was pleased with the progress on the new medical tower and with the start of the new office tower and the three additional apartment towers.

Barry had hundreds of trailers rented for accommodation for the construction crews and his office staff. The construction area was starting to look like a small city. As the construction areas were separated from the rest of the compound, there was little interference from the crews.

"Next, along the south perimeter, I want a row of twenty 20-foot-wide by 60-foot-long metal huts built on concrete pads. All are to have complete hydro and washroom facilities. Each is to have a small reception area and office at the front. And please remember to make all these building wheelchair accessible. Here are the designs I like with the large lift door and the front entrance door. Have a similar lift door on the back with another entrance door. Naturally, all the buildings will be the same. Have at least twenty feet separating the huts from one another just in case we need to move a transport truck or other equipment down between them," requested Sean.

"Sure," said Barry. "I know the people who make these, and they are great to deal with. What do you need them for? he asked.

Sean laughed. "I don't know yet. I just want them." And both of them laughed.

Barry was amazed. "Sean, you really think big. I'll contact my friend and get the ball rolling on the metal buildings. Sean, myself, and the subcontractors really appreciate being paid on time. These are really big projects."

"Don't mention it," said Sean, "you and your people are doing great work and I appreciate it. I told you you'd have work for years." And with that, they shook hands, and Barry left.

Chapter 29
Sean Decides to Save the World

Project #1: The Fresh Water Initiative

With Sean now distancing himself from the lab and the helicopter incident behind him, Sean put his mind toward spending his money for the betterment of mankind. Now with ten applications being done every two weeks at fifty million dollars per application, Sean felt that with roughly one billion dollars coming in per month, he could set his mind toward his dream of cleaning up the world.

He had David Kim, a South Korean internationally renowned scientist and environmentalist in mind, to head up his first major project. David was a devoted environmentalist, dedicated to saving the world's oceans.

David presently had his own laboratory set up, looking for ways to clean up the oceans and remove the harmful microscopic plastic particles ever-present in sea water. His vision was to set up centers around the world that could be placed in the ocean currents where such particles could be removed. Sean knew of David's work and liked what he saw.

Sean put a call into David Kim, and he arrived in three days. After the customary tour of the compound, Sean and David had lunch. Even during lunch, Sean felt that he and David Kim were on the same page on their mutual goals of cleaning up the world's oceans. Later, in Sean's office, Sean and David Kim quickly came to an agreement. Both David and Sean remained tight-lipped as to its contents. Sean paid David Kim ten million dollars immediately and he would continue to receive a program director's salary of fifty thousand dollars per month. The only person aware of this agreement was Wendy Rawlings, his Secretary Treasurer. No one else knew.

Sean asked David Kim to attend the upcoming Sunday morning service, and David, not being Catholic, very respectfully sat and enjoyed the service. After a very good sermon by the new minister, Chaplain

Furlong, talking about the virtues of being true to oneself and to God, he asked Sean to come up for his announcement.

As the church services were recorded and placed on the company's website, Sean thought that this would be an excellent way for him to start making company-wide announcements. News agencies wanting to report on one of his announcements could simply record the video clip and place it directly on their news broadcast.

Sean thanked the new chaplain for his valuable sermon today. Then Sean stated, "Ladies and gentlemen, from now on, I will be making my important announcements before you and in this the church of my parents. These announcements are being recorded and can be viewed on our website.

"First, I would like to introduce to you Mr. David Kim, an internationally respected scientist, environmentalist, and friend. Please stand up, David." David stood up, and the congregation clapped.

"David Kim is here to assist me on what will be the greatest legacy to my work. After careful consideration, David and I have concluded that if I were to promote a world-wide effort to unlock the secret of how to economically remove the salt from salt water and the microscopic plastic particles, the benefits to mankind would be enormous. Previously useless land would now become arable, and people would have enough water to drink, enough water for their crops, and enough water for their animals. The benefits to the world would be enormous.

"We have harnessed the power of the atom. We have placed people on the moon, but we sit frustrated on a planet covered seventy-one percent with water we cannot use or drink because it contains salt. I now quote from the poet Samuel Taylor Coleridge, in The Rime of the Ancient Mariner, 'Water, water everywhere, but not a drop to drink'.

"David and I both hold the opinion that we have not looked hard enough for the solution. But this has all changed. The ability to separate salt from salt water is already known. The only trouble is that these systems are expensive to set up and maintain. I dream of having a device that could be shipped out to every village and every town in the world that would allow those people to take salt water and then turn it into fresh, clean drinking water. Fresh, clean water for themselves, their crops, and their farm animals.

So to start, with David Kim at the forefront of this initiative, I am offering to the citizens of the world a payment of two-fifty million dollars in US dollars to any individual, group, university, or government that can produce an inexpensive method for separating salt from salt water. Legally, with the two-fifty million dollars payment, I will be buying the rights to this discovery, which I will then be releasing to the world free of charge.

All processes presented will be reviewed by the foremost university in the world dedicated to removing the salt from salt water. I am speaking of the King Abdullah University of Science and Technology located in Saudi Arabia.

After they have released their findings, it will be David Kim and myself who will make the final decision.

By the grace of God, I pray that he will be successful, and one day we will be.

The world needs a quick and easy method for turning salt water into fresh, clean drinking water, and I stand before you, before God, and in my parent's church and promise that this will take place, so help me, God."

The congregation all stood up and erupted in applause. How could anyone argue with such an unselfish act? News networks from around the world showed the video clips of Sean's speech, applauded Sean and David Kim's efforts, and hoped that, for the benefit of mankind, they would be successful.

One reporter stated in Sean's video, "You've got to like a guy who puts his money where his mouth is. I have changed my opinion of Sean Little, and I hope a lot of others have to. I applaud his and David Kim's efforts and wish them success. Their success here is success for the entire world."

The world was elated that someone was finally going to create a world-wide initiative to solve this problem, which has plagued mankind since the beginning of time. Sean was a hero to the world.

Later, at their final meeting, "David, you have enough money to continue with your lab research and monthly payments to allow you to administer this initiative. You are in complete control. You do not have to consult with me, as I have already cut myself off from all incoming phone calls and emails. If I need to talk to you, I'll call. All I ask is that you FedEx me a written report of your progress once a month to land on my desk around the 20th of every month. Any questions?"

"No questions, Sean. I appreciate your confidence in me and my work on this issue. I will administer this effort and coordinate different universities to work on different aspects of the problem. Somehow someone will come up with the answer," replied David. They both stood up, shook hands and parted ways as friends.

Over the coming months, David Kim had a few universities working on this issue. Naturally, the countries in the more water-starved areas of the world were most eager for this solution. Universities in Europe and North America, where water is plentiful, were less enthusiastic. Its very difficult trying to convince North Americans that there is a world- wide freshwater shortage when most of them live by rivers and lakes and they themselves have never experienced a drought.

David Kim, overseeing Sean's Fresh Water Initiative, was dedicated to his job. Sean emailed David and asked him for a list of universities that had set up specific labs for attempting to remove the salt from salt water. David replied with the list of eight universities.

Sean then called David, "I am sending you checks made out to those universities for ten million dollars each. I would like you to go and make a big presentation on my behalf and present them with these checks. Make it a big media event. I want the world to know that I am serious about this project and willing to pay. Understood?"

"Sean, whenever someone gives a university money, it's a big deal, and ten million dollars is a big deal. I'll start making the presentations as soon as the checks arrive. Thank you."

Project #2:The "Sean Little Veterans Benefit Bill" Chapter #30

After the dust settled after David Kim's visit, Sean contacted Kevin Sanders, assistant to the Vice President John Harper, and Kevin was happy to hear from him.

"John Harper and the President are very impressed with your Fresh Water Initiative," said Kevin.

"Thanks, I had to start somewhere, and cleaning up the oceans is a good place to start. Kevin, I need a favor from you."

"No problem, Sean; what do you need," answered Kevin.

Sean outlined his request, "First, I want you to please contact Veterans Affairs and have them email us a list of all physically disabled American war veterans and a brief description of their disability.

Second, I want a list of the surviving family members of our veterans who lost their lives serving their country and

Third, I would like a list of the families of those veterans who have either died at their own hands or have died since returning to the US.

Have you got this?"

"Yes, every word," said Kevin.

"Next, Kevin, this is the hard part," said Sean. "I wish to start sending our physically disabled war veterans checks for five hundred dollars per month. But I will only send these checks out as long as they are an obvious tax deduction for myself and received by the veterans free of all federal, state, and income tax. Free and clear, do you understand?

I will have my people prepare the checks the moment I have written confirmation from you that the federal government and all the individual state governments will allow the veterans to receive this money tax-free. I have not mentioned my intentions to anyone else. Any questions?" asked Sean. "No questions, seems pretty clear to me. Let me get you those Veterans Affairs lists of names and addresses first, and then I will talk to John, the VP, about this," said Kevin.

"Okay, when you get confirmation that the veterans can receive this money tax-free, send the documentation to me, and I will start sending out the checks. Thank you." And Sean hung up.

Sean then called Wendy, his Secretary Treasurer into his office. Sean explained, "Likely later today, you'll be receiving lists of the American physically disabled veterans from the Veterans Affairs office. I am going to start sending monthly checks of five hundred dollars to physically disabled war veterans and to the families of the deceased war veterans."

Wendy was elated. Being in the military, she knew of the economic hardship faced by physically disabled veterans when they returned home to their families.

"My father fought in Vietnam and was slightly disabled," explained Sean.

"When I was a young boy, we were on our way to church, and he once said to me 'If you ever get a chance to help out physically disabled war veterans, please help them, Sean.' Well, I'm in a position to help them now, and I'm keeping my promise to my dad."

Wendy could see the tears swelling up in Sean's eyes as he talked about his dad. The more she worked for Sean, the more she liked him.

"I have asked Kevin Sanders, the VP's assistant, to arrange that these checks be received by the veterans free of all federal and state taxes. I'm not sure what hoops he has to go through, but these checks will not be sent out until I get written confirmation of that. Maybe this needs the Senate or House of Representatives" approval. I don't know, but that's Kevin's problem.

But please keep this to yourself for the time being, okay? And I think you should order in about 100,000 checks—you know, the ones with the tear-off letter portion on the bottom. Plus, you will need a computerized check-writing program and a paper folding machine that stuffs the checks in the envelopes."

"My lips are sealed, and those items will be ordered today. But Sean, don't you think that e-transfering them this money would be easier? That's how veterans presently get their disability checks."

"Yes, you are right, Wendy," Sean replied. "But by sending checks, I get more public exposure, and I like the ability to include a message on the bottom of the checks. So checks it will be."

"No problem, Sean, and thank you, Sean this means a lot to us in the military," Wendy said, leaving her with a tear of happiness in her eye.

The Veterans Affairs lists arrived early the next morning. Sean then set to work on the letter portion of the checks.

On the bottom of every check, Sean included this note.

To Honor Those Who Have Served Our Country

My name is Sean Little, and my father was a physically disabled Vietnam War veteran. When I was a young boy, he asked me, "If you ever get a chance to help out physically disabled war veterans, please help them." Today I am honoring my pledge to my father.

Starting this month and every month afterward, you will be receiving a check from me.

These are the following conditions:

–These checks are being sent to you from myself, Seal Little, free of all federal, state and all income taxes. We will not e-transfer you this money.

–I have received written confirmation that these checks are free of all federal, state and income taxes. If this ever changes, I will cancel this

215

program and stop sending out these checks.

–These checks were sent to you by myself, Sean Little. Other than using their lists, these payments have nothing to do with the US Government or the Veterans Affairs Offices.

–The day I find that any payments to you from the US government or the Veterans Affairs offices have been altered or diminished because of your receiving this money. I will cancel this program and stop sending out these checks.

–These checks will be sent to you directly. I will not be handing over this money to any government agency or the Veterans Affairs Office to distribute.

–I reserve the right to stop payments to any individual without penalty to myself or my organization.

–I reserve the right to cancel this program at any time without reason, without warning and without penalty.

Thank you for your service,

Sean Little

"The Sean Little Veterans Benefit Bill" Gets Approved

Both the President and VP knew that once it hit the news that Sean Little wanted to start sending physically disabled war veterans' money every month tax-free, it was impossible for any member of the Senate or the House of Representatives to object.

The President knew that any government representative that voiced an objection to this unselfish act would live to regret it at election time.

But the week before it came to a vote, CBW News interviewed one member of the House of Representatives, Clive Sills, who was outspoken in his opposition to the physically disabled veterans receiving Sean Little's money tax-free. Rep. Sills was an 80-ish career politician who had spent most of his life in Washington, D.C. Now he was just a cranky old man who hated the world and criticized everyone who tried to improve it. Out of touch with the modern world, he looked and acted like his best days were behind him.

CBW Reporter: Representative Sills, on what grounds do you oppose our physically disabled American war veterans from receiving five hundred dollars per month tax-free from Sean Little?"

Rep. Sills: "We are setting a dangerous precedent here with people handing out money to others and avoiding paying the tax. It's just like it's part of the underground economy, and now we want to sanction it?"

Reporter: "But don't you think that Mr. Little, in wanting to pay these disabled war veterans out of his own pocket, should be encouraged? I, for one, herald Mr. Little's actions."

Rep. Sills: "Can't you see the position this is putting us in, where anyone can now decide whether they pay their taxes or not? We need that money, and the government needs that money. And if it's up to me, the war veterans will have to pay tax on any money coming from Sean Little."

Reporter: "But Representative Sills, I personally know physically disabled war veterans, and here is a chance to let them live better lives.

These are American men and women who have been permanently injured fighting for our country and our freedom, and you don't think they should have this money? Money going to our disabled veterans that is not costing the American government one red cent."

Rep. Sills: "You're not listening to me. We can't allow people to not pay their taxes. This money is income and must be taxed. I think it's selfish of the war veterans to expect this money without tax. We in the government need this money."

Reporter: "So what you are saying is that it's okay for a disabled war veteran who fought and was injured for our country that they cannot accept this money from Sean Little? Money that will help them live better and feed their families?"

Rep. Sills: "Yes, this is a free handout to them, and they shouldn't be allowed to accept money without paying tax on it."

Reporter: (getting upset) "Well, okay, you say these undeserving disabled war veterans should not be able to accept money without paying tax on it. So let's look at what you make. As a member of the House of Representatives, you make $174,000 dollars per year with $900,000 per year in a tax-free staff allowance plus $250,000 per year in a tax-free travel allowance plus a dozen other tax-free perks of office. So you yourself get an annual tax-free allowance of $1,150,000 per year or over $95,000 per month, and you're complaining about a war veteran who has had both his legs shot off from getting $500 a month tax-free?"

Rep. Sills: "But I work for that money. I am an elected representative of the US government."

Reporter: "And you don't think that the brave men and women of our armed forces are not representing us? They risk their lives so that you and I can enjoy our great nation and our freedoms. And when they return home, people like you spit on them. You should be ashamed of yourself. I'm disgusted even having to talk to you."

At this point, everyone in the audience stood up, cheered, and started heckling Rep. Clive Sills. He was so upset and embarrassed that he got up and stormed off the stage. That night, this CBW interview was replayed on every major news program in the United States. The storm of protest was deafening. Every Veterans Association, every veteran, disabled or not, was up in arms and contacted their elected representatives, madder than hell.

The President watching this said, "Representative Sills couldn't run for dogcatcher after this. Plus, it's going to take his party months to remove the embarrassment of being associated with Representative Sills. Glad he's not on our side."

Representative Clive Sills' own party denounced him for his statements and immediately voiced their support for all war veterans and their support for the passage of the "Sean Little Veterans Benefit Bill". Especially since Representative Clive Sills' statements, everyone knew that if anyone voiced an objection to the bill, their faces would appear on the evening news as being "anti-American" and against those who fought for their country. During the next election, their quotes would be brought up to haunt them. Now anyone who opposed the "Sean Little Veterans Benefit Bill" wisely kept their mouth shut.

Later that week, the bill passed both the Senate and the House of Representatives with unanimous support. Surprisingly, Representative Sills was nowhere to be seen anywhere near the House of Representatives, and the evening CBW news reporter stated, "With the firestorm and emotional backlash from Representative Sills outright denial of the worthiness of our disabled war veterans and his refusal to allow them to accept Sean Little's money tax-free, I don't think you'll be seeing him around here anytime soon. His own political party has pushed him aside and wants him gone.

His presence in the House is an embarrassment to all Americans and an insult to all our war veterans, our' heroes. I for one, hope we never see him on Capital Hill again."

The President and VP made a big announcement about the passage of the bill over a news broadcast and made as much political benefit out of it as they could. Sean said to Jennifer, "Hearing them speak, you would think that it was their idea and that they convinced me to go along. Oh well, who cares? That's politics, I guess."

Kevin Sanders contacted Sean and said that he had the necessary government approvals for the veterans to receive this money from Sean, all tax-free. Sean and Kevin talked about the media event caused by the CBW interview and the President's announcement, and Sean voiced his approval.

Sean then called Wendy and told her, "Send out the first batch of checks today. I will have Colonel John drop by to pick them up and take them to the post office. Plus, the next batch is to start going out the first of every month. I leave it in your capable hands to make this happen, Wendy," Sean said.

"With pleasure, Sean, this is a great thing you have done for America and I am proud to be involved. Thank you," said Wendy.

Sean called Kevin Sanders and told him that the checks were being made up and would be sent out later today. Kevin was generous in his praise of Sean's environmental efforts and helping the war veterans.

"Anything else I can do, just ask," said Kevin.

Sean then contacted Colonel John and asked him to personally pickup the checks and deliver them to the main post in Las Vegas and to take a video photographer along to record the delivery.

"Make a media event out of this, please. I'll be placing this delivery on the website," stated Sean.

"With pleasure," replied Colonel John.

Colonel John returned and told Sean about the big scene they made at the main Post Office. He said that all the military personnel and postal workers formed a line and emptied the trucks.

"I even had them all stand together for a photo shoot. It will look great on the website," said Colonel John. "And thank you again for helping our veterans. You are a good man, Sean."

Sean then contacted the website company and had them place the video of the checks being delivered to the Post Office on the website. The public reaction was immense. News networks around the US copied the video of the checks being unloaded and placed it along with the photos of the President and the Vice President signing "The Sean Little Veterans Benefit Bill" into law. All the news agencies expressed appreciation for Sean's efforts. The President and Vice President even contacted Sean to thank him. *Good to have connections,* thought Sean.

Later that night, Sean looked up to heaven and said, "I did it, Dad. Just like you wanted." Then Sean put his head down and, thinking about his dad, started to cry.

Chapter 30
Additional Environmental Projects

With David Kim looking after his Fresh Water Initiative and Wendy looking after the payments to the disabled war veterans, Sean looked to other environmental issues he could become involved in. He first sat down and drew up a list of guidelines that he would want his Project Directors to adhere to. *Might as well have everything I expect from them right out front and on the table when they are hired.*

Project Director's Guidelines:

—Project Directors have a standard pay of fifty thousand dollars per month.

—Your project offices and all your administrative and accounting staff will be located here in the compounds office tower. All checks will be processed and sent out from here.

—Wendy Rawlings, my Secretary Treasurer overseas, all the finances of the compound and all the projects. She will help you select your staff here and oversee your activities.

—Bill Fryer of Todd and Todd Lawyers Inc. handles all our legal affairs. He will establish a corporation for you to conduct your activities under.

—In the field, you are to hire your own staff of retired ex-military personnel at the standard pay of thousand dollars per week. Where possible, I would like to see that physically disabled war veterans have top priority for any and all jobs.

—Where possible, please make your purchases of products made in America.

—I will not support or be associated with any environmental group or individuals that advocates violence or the destruction of property.

—Except in the case of really worthy environmental initiatives, I do not

simply hand out checks to environmental groups or charities. I prefer to

be proactively involved in cleaning up these environmental issues myself.

—I do not micromanage my people. If you are given a project to complete, you are left to your own devices. My attitude is that if I hire someone and they have to keep calling me to get my approval, I don't need them. If I need to talk to you, I'll call you. You do not call me.

—You will supply me with a complete hard copy progress report on every program under your control, and this per-program report will be on my desk by the 20th of every month.

—Outside of a close family member, you do not have the authority to bring anyone to the compound. Never bring anyone here to meet me. If you wish me to meet someone, hand in a written request to Wendy, and we will decide later. You will be swamped with requests from people wanting to meet me. Regardless of who they are, you will refuse.

—You will inform Wendy of your arrival at the compound at least forty-eight hours in advance.

—I dislike publicity and having my picture taken. As my Project Director you are my public representative on this issue and in the media. You, therefore, will be attending all award presentations and gala dinners on my behalf. Never ask me to attend any function, as I will not go.

On important issues, you may ask Jennifer or Wendy to attend, but not me.

—I and I alone decide if I am to give out a free application. Regardless of the reason, do not ever ask or imply to someone that I will do so.

—And none of my efforts will go toward helping any government use my formula as an instrument of public policy or as an instrument of war.

You will be automatically relieved of your position if you…

—Lie to me or withhold important information from me. I expect honesty in my dealings with all my employees.

—You are forbidden to use a helicopter to come to the compound. If I allow one helicopter in today, I will have a hundred helicopters landing here tomorrow.

—I and I alone decide which initiatives will be undertaken. You may not

222

support or give money to any other organization without my expressed written permission.

—You may not become involved in any project where we are expected to pay any government official or person, a payout, graft money, or a kickback.

Any project that is dependent on giving out a cash payment for an individual's compliance is automatically canceled.

—Regardless of your personal opinions, you may not endorse or contribute to any political candidate, campaign, or political action committee. As my representative, you will be flooded with endorsement requests, all of which you must refuse. You must remain politically impartial.

—At any time that I feel that your position has been compromised by you wanting to interfere with my activities, steal the formula, or do me harm.

<u>*And always remember…*</u>

—I do not answer questions, and I do not grant interviews.
—Never forget, I make the rules, and Wendy signs the checks.

_____

Program Director's Signature

Sean told Wendy that he had written up a standard list of conditions for all of his future Project Directors to adhere to and she agreed.

"Please give this a read-over and let me know tomorrow if you would like any changes," said Sean.

"Looks like you have all the bases covered, but let me think about it, and I'll get back to you. Plus, I'll run it by Bill Fryer to see if he has anything else to add," stated Wendy.

<u>Project #3: Subsidizing the Telephone Pole and Railway Tie Manufactures</u>

One evening over dinner with Jennifer, her family, and Wendy, Sean asked,

"With today's technology, why are we still cutting down live trees to make them into telephone poles and railway ties? They soak the poles and ties in harmful chemicals that leech into the surrounding soil. In the countries where trees are scarce, they manufacture their own poles and ties, so why can't we? The problem really only exists in North and South America and Europe."

Mr. Sloan replied with, "I know that the reason we still use wood here is that the manufactured poles and ties are more expensive."

Sean then said to Wendy, "I want you to call Bill at Todd & Todd and have him draw up an agreement that we will give to the North and South American and European telephone pole and railway tie manufacturers that for every single unit they sell, we will pay them five hundred US dollars per pole or railway tie, payable once per month. That should put the price of a manufactured pole or tie well below the cost of a wood one."

"Hard to argue with that. I'll contact Bill and get him working on the contract right away," said Wendy.

Sean then contacted the website company and asked them to put up an announcement about subsidizing the telephone pole and railway tie manufacturers to the tune of five hundred dollars per *unit. That should get people talking, especially the purchasing agents,* thought Sean. *I have to do something to stop these people from destroying our forests, and this is as good a place as any to start.*

Later, Sean talked to Jennifer and Ralph about his environmental efforts.

"I think this solving an environmental problem with a check seems to be working out pretty well. Bill at Todd & Todd in Detroit handles the legal work, and Wendy handles the money. I'll try to tackle one project at a time and see how far it goes."

Both Jennifer and Ralph agreed.

"The work you have done so far with the Fresh Water Initiative, the payments to the veterans and now subsidizing the telephone pole and railway tie manufactures, I think, is really making a difference. I'm proud of you," said Jennifer. Ralph agreed.

Project #4: The Incinerator

Sean had been reading about the Chinese efforts to build huge garbage incinerators to not only burn their garbage but also produce electricity. He liked what he read and wanted to take it one step further. He contacted the head of the Koris Corporation out of New York and invited Pete Johnson, the CEO, down to see him.

Pete arrived two days later. He was a well-dressed, technical fellow who was passionate about saving the environment. Sean and Pete had an enjoyable lunch where they discussed Sean's efforts to date. Pete applauded Sean's efforts, and they both agreed that the one thing the environmental movement was lacking was money.

"Impossible to get the politicians to carry through on their promises when there are no votes there. Saving the world never becomes a priority because it never becomes an election issue," said Pete. Sean agreed.

Sean then laid out his plans. "Pete, I want you to design and install an incinerator in the compound here that will not only burn our garbage and old car tires, but I want it to have an automatic feed to push used railway ties into it. There must be millions of old car tires lying around and millions of used railway ties sitting in rail yards across America.

I want an incinerator large enough to produce enough electricity to power this entire compound. Also, the incinerator must have a system for capturing the harmful exhaust gases given off when the tires and ties are being burned so it must have zero impact on the environment.

Plus, I want to start having salt water trucked or pumped in that could go into the incinerator and be evaporated off, and then having the fresh water pumped over to the compounds fresh water holding tank. The salt could be removed and stored elsewhere."

"I'll get my people right on it," replied Pete. "What will you be doing with the ashes?"

"Good question," answered Sean. "The tire belts, railway spikes, and other metal objects could fall onto a metal conveyor belt and then be removed and trucked away. The ashes themselves could fall down through the conveyor belt system to a holding pit below. This pit could have its own conveyor system, bringing the ashes out and into awaiting dump trucks. Once the ashes are removed, they are trucked to the septic holding tanks that have been installed at the far end of the property.

"These ashes mixed in with our human waste, once broken down, I plan on using to fertilize my new field crops. Any questions about the holding tanks, please ask Barry Leibowitz of Leibowitz and Company. You'll usually find him in one of his construction site trailers, I think he lives there." Sean laughed.

Sean continued, "Should be easy to put in a railway spur line nearby where we can unload the car tires and railway ties. I think the scrap yards and rail companies would be thrilled to finally be getting rid of their tires and ties. I'll work out the exact location later, but I would like it far from our living quarters. There is an old but usable rail line on the additional property I just bought from the Nevada government, so the new incinerator could be placed down there."

"Let me go back and talk to my people and put some ideas together," Pete said.

"Should have the finished plans in my hand within the month."

Sean also said that if this new design was successful, he thought Pete could market these car tire and railway tie-burning incinerators elsewhere. Pete agreed. Sean gave Pete a deposit check for five million dollars to get everything started. Pete thanked Sean and then left to catch his flight back to New York. Sean liked Pete and was looking forward to seeing the plans.

Six Months Later, the Incinerator is Completed

Once the plans were made for the new garbage, car tire, and railway tie incinerator, it took almost six months for the massive structure to be completed. And as Sean expected, the scrap yards and railway companies were happy to send Sean their used car tires and railway ties.

The incinerator was so huge that half of it was buried underground. The mechanics of the machine were above ground, and the combustion chamber was below. To feed the machine, the railway ties were placed on a conveyor system and automatically fed into the incinerator. The car tires and compound garbage were collected in a large bin, and when the bin was full, the entire pile was then automatically forced into the incinerator.

Emptying the incinerator was completed exactly as Sean wanted. The metal was removed by its own conveyor system to a large bin, and the ashes had their own conveyor system that emptied directly into the dump trucks.

The ashes were then trucked off and mixed in with the compounds human waste for later use.

The immense heat from the incinerator was then used to operate the steam generators to produce all the electricity the compound needed. The water used for the steam generators was in a closed-loop system where the steam itself powered the generators, and then the steam was cooled back to water and returned to a holding tank to be turned into steam again. Even with this source of electricity, Sean still insisted that large generators be placed beside the medical building, the office tower, and the three apartment towers, just in case.

True to his word, Pete Johnson made the incinerator environmentally friendly. The smoke from the burning tires and ties was recycled through the incinerator and eventually filtered through water to remove its harmful chemicals. This water was then evaporated, leaving just the ash behind.

As requested, Sean wanted to have salt water brought in and evaporated. Outside of the cost of having the salt water trucked in, the system worked beautifully. They trucked in the salt water to a pipe located outside of the compound. It was evaporated off and cooled in large tubes, and at the end, clean water emerged. This fresh water was then piped to their filtration plant and constantly tested for purity. The salt they recovered was stored in a holding tank far out in the desert. Sean loved the new process, and seeing the large, exposed condensation tubes made him remark, "I own the world's largest still."

The designer and manufacturer of the incinerator, Pete Johnson, the CEO of the Koris Corporation, was so proud of his work that, with Sean's permission, he had a day for reporters and municipal representatives to come and see the incinerator. Sean made sure that for that one day, the portable fencing was moved to allow their guests to be driven by the guards to the incinerator without any of them venturing off into the compound. Seeing the heavily armed guards standing nearby and knowing of Sean's compulsive need for security, no one dared wander off.

The presentation lasted four hours, with speeches and video presentations. Everyone watched in awe as they were shown the garbage, car tires, and railway ties being pushed into the incinerator for burning. Then they were shown the salt water being pumped in and the fresh water coming out the other side. Pete had a cup of water removed and stood proudly as he drank the glass of water. Everyone cheered. Then the railway representatives stood up and outlined that there were millions and millions of these railway ties available free of charge to any municipality that would build one of these incinerators.

Pete Johnson of Koris was happy with the day's events. He told Sean, "Everyone is impressed with your ideas and plans. They want to wait for a few months and then revisit the incinerator before placing their orders. Your idea of burning the discarded car tires and railway ties is pure genius. Thank you for everything you have done for us."

They parted company as friends, happy with the day's presentation.

Chapter 31
The New Office Tower

With the present system of having ten applications done every two weeks working out well, Sean asked Barry to concentrate on getting the office tower done first. His reasoning was that if they were going to be eventually doing applications every week, plus his environmental projects, he needed the administrative staff in place to handle everything. Best to get that in place first before completing the medical building.

Once the office tower was complete, Sean asked Barry to get the three apartment towers completed next.

"Got to have a place for all these staff to live," said Sean.

The office tower was complete, and after a brief ribbon-cutting ceremony, the building was prepared for its new occupants. Jennifer and her sister Emily had been busy buying office furniture, blinds, supplies, and just about everything a ten-story office tower needs. The staff simply gave Jennifer their lists, and she saw that it was ordered and delivered.

When the supplies arrived, the guards escorted the trucks to the front of the office tower and unloaded its contents into the lobby. There were piles of office desks, chairs, filing cabinets, computers, and boxes and boxes of office supplies. Jennifer and Emily were delighted to help distribute the office supplies and take additional orders. Everyone pitched in to make deliveries to the offices. Somehow, the lady office staff never had any problems asking the handsome guards to carry some office supplies upstairs for them.

Office Tower Layout

Sean and Wendy divided up the office tower as such.

Basement Supplies and storage

Left Wing Right Wing

First Floor: Security Cameras and a Bank
Personnel (Reception and Post Office in Foyer)
Second Floor: Compound Administration and Military Offices
Third Floor: Restaurant Area-Major Board Room
Fourth Floor: Ralph's Office and Lab Administrative Staff (temporary)
Fifth Floor: Todd & Todd Lawyers, Inc. Offices: Government Offices
Sixth Floor: Sean's Office, Wendy's, and Financial Offices
Seventy Floor: Environmental Projects Offices
Eighth Floor: Empty
Ninth Floor: Empty
Tenth Floor: Empty

Sean immediately took his office on the sixth-floor left wing, and Jennifer ordered in his furniture. He asked for separate desks along one wall to store his notes for the major projects he was involved in. Once settled, he left the furnishing of the other offices to Jennifer, her sister Emily, and Wendy.

Invoices and Incoming Mail

Wendy and the accounting staff immediately moved into the right wing of the sixth floor, across from Sean. They set it up very quickly. Sean was then concerned with people running up to the sixth floor to get a check from the accounting office.

Except for Barry Leibowitz, Sean's general contractor, who had his invoices paid immediately, all regular invoices would be delivered to the reception desk in the main lobby and then delivered upstairs. Once delivered, the invoices were to be paid that day and mailed the next.

Wendy had all the compound's incoming mail and courier packages delivered directly to the front gate, and then the guards would deliver them to the office tower. Wendy arranged for a small postal office to be set up beside the reception area for the guards to sort the mail. Various departments had their own large mail slots, and for individuals, the slots were arranged in alphabetical order. If you wanted your mail, you simply went to the "Post Office" in the office tower reception area, found the slot for the first letter of your last name, and took your mail. Perfect.

Unfortunately, most of the incoming mail to Sean Little was nuisance mail. With the volume of mail going to Sean ever increasing, Sean asked Wendy to have someone open his mail and only send it to him if it was important. The FedEx packages from the Program Directors were to be sent to Sean unopened.

As for the outgoing mail, there was a large supply of stamps on hand and a large table with a wooden box on it labeled "Outgoing Mail". Every day, the guards took the outgoing mail to the postal box just outside of the main gate for the postal people to pick up. Everyone was happy with the new postal setup, including Sean.

The Bank of America Branch

Sean liked Wendy's idea of having a bank branch on the main floor, as she did not want staff coming upstairs to the financial offices. So the bank branch was placed on the main floor, to the right of the main reception area and post office.

Wendy oversaw the installation of the new bank branch. Sean insisted that she also have an office in the bank for when she was doing her work down there. The staff were delighted when the new bank branch opened. They could come in, set up an account, deposit their checks, get cash, get a loan if needed, and get a Bank of America Visa credit card all in one location. Sean was very impressed with how well Wendy organized this all within a space of four weeks.

This left the previous financial office building empty, so Sean had the pub and games room building moved into these empty buildings. Everyone needs a place to relax and watch the football and baseball games, and this building would do the trick.

Jennifer had the place redecorated to again look like an Adirondack lodge with pine walls and pine furniture. She had four massive flat-screen TVs installed and ordered from all the movie and sports channels. She set up a bar area and a small cafeteria for sandwiches. The staff enjoyed having a place to get a beer and a sandwich and watch their favorite movies or sports. Good move.

Ralph was then invited to take over his offices on the fourth floor, but he declined.

His objection was that moving himself or any of his laboratory staff into the fourth floor of the office tower meant that in a few months he'd have to move all over again into the new medical building, so why bother? Plus, it doesn't make sense to have the lab administration offices so far from the lab. He said he was okay where they were until the new medical building was up and running.

Sean agreed. Sean also had the idea that a major environmental project would likely take up the entire fourth floor.

Colonel John was shown the first and second floors and liked what he saw.

The first floor, left wing, was for the security cameras and personnel. The second floor was strictly for his compound administrative people and his military offices. "Everything you need is here for you to look after us, Colonel John," said Sean. Colonel John smiled with a courtesy salute to Sean.

Sean felt that the rest of the floor's offices would not be filled with staff until after the apartment towers were complete. Sean asked that these empty floors have furniture in them so that they are ready to go when needed. Especially, the environmental projects would require a considerable staff, and to start any projects before having the staff in place would only create confusion.

The present system of housing people in the trailers was working out well.

Sean and Jennifer, her parents and sister, each loved having their own trailers. If they needed more living trailers, Jennifer simply made a phone call to Jesse O'Rourke and had more brought in. At present, they had 40 trailers, some 24 foot and the most popular being the more popular 28 footers. It was decided that once the apartment tower was complete, that staff could move into the apartments, and the trailers would be used for housing any visitors.

Sean Stops Receiving Phone Calls and Emails

Once settled into his new offices, Sean's mind went to his security concerns.

He felt that Colonel John was doing an excellent job, and the local police were being a great help.

Sean really liked the new system of Wendy screening his mail. No more reading stupid letters from people who want something. What was really annoying to Sean was that no matter how often he changed his phone number, it quickly became common knowledge, and the number of nuisance calls he got every day kept growing. The same with his emails. He had one of the girls in the financial department assigned to reviewing all of his emails, but she was getting over a thousand emails per day, and it was driving the poor girl crazy. This was turning into a full-time job.

Other than Kevin Sanders, the assistant to the Vice President, all outside calls and emails were just "I want money, I need your help, or I want an interview" nuisance calls. Sean then decided that people only contacted him for three reasons:

#1: They want money for themselves or their pet projects.

#2: They want a free application for themselves or someone else.

#3: They wanted Sean to change or alter one of his projects.

Nobody calls me because they like how I look. Everybody wants something. As he already had ninety-nine percent of his incoming mail stopped, he then decided that he would totally stop receiving incoming phone calls or emails. As he was already in the habit of turning his cell phone off, this should not be a problem. He had Wendy arrange that his cell phone could only make outgoing calls, and all incoming calls were to go to a voicemail that was erased every six hours. The only exceptions were for calls from the President of the United States, the Vice President, Kevin Sanders, Wendy Rawlings, Colonel John Williams, or Jennifer. The same went for his personal emails. He contacted the website company, who arranged that he could still send out emails, but all his incoming emails were automatically erased every six hours. What a relief!

Like his cell phone, he asked Wendy to arrange that his office landline could not take incoming calls except from those people already allowed to call his cell phone. *Except for those six, if I want to talk to someone, I'll call them,* thought Sean.

Sean also started to think that as the staff grew larger, the demands on his time were getting greater. It seemed that whenever he ventured outside, the constant interruptions from staff members wanting to talk to him were becoming annoying.

When the staff and military personnel numbers were small and everyone knew one another, everything was fine. But as the staff numbers started to grow, problems started to surface.

Sean was getting annoyed that every time he ventured outside, a staff member would want to stop and talk to him. The conversation invariably turned around to that individual's sick relative or friend who would benefit from an application. Jennifer and Wendy were also being constantly questioned, especially by the newer staff. Everyone thought that this being a military compound meant that Sean would not be disturbed, but as the numbers grew, so did the problems.

Then the inevitable happened. One of Wendy's newer accounting staff, Marlene Forbes, a girl of about thirty years of age, barged into Sean's office one day, sat down, and started telling Sean about her sick mother-in-law. Marlene was a good-looking accountant type who liked to dress well. It was also evident that she was a little hot-headed and opinionated and was causing some problems with the other staff members.

Sean, trying to be polite, tried to explain to her that his procedure did not cure illnesses, it just made them younger. Any illnesses a person had going into the procedure, they still had when they came out. This explanation did not sit well with Marlene, who insisted that Sean could cure her mother-in-law. Sean, in frustration, had to call Wendy in and usher her out.

A week later, Marlene again barged into Sean's office. She pleaded with Sean to help her sick mother-in-law. Sean politely explained again that the process did not cure illnesses, just made people younger. She started crying, saying that Sean was cruel and ' wouldn't help anybody else, just his friends. Sean was sympathetic to her problems and again had Wendy usher her out.

Two weeks went by, and Marlene came storming into Sean's office again, yelling,

"Sean Little, you're a horrible person. Your uncaring attitude has killed my mother-in-law and you should be ashamed of yourself. You could have saved her, but you didn't."

She was so hysterical that Sean had to call security, who escorted her out of the building.

Sean talked to Wendy, and she said that Marlene's attitude toward her work and the other staff was becoming intolerable. Marlene would come to work crying and complaining about Sean's refusal to help her mother-in-law which was constantly upsetting the other staff. Both Wendy and Sean concluded that they had no choice but to remove Marlene and have her residency rights terminated.

Wendy contacted Colonel John, and he had Marlene immediately posted to the accounting department at the nearby Nellis Air Force Base. Female members of Colonel John's staff helped pack her things and drove her out of the compound to her new accommodations at the base at Nellis.

This incident really upset Sean, and he talked to Jennifer that night. They both concluded that they needed a "Compound Rules of Conduct" list written up with the do's and don'ts of the compound. This list must state clearly under which grounds a person would be disciplined, dismissed, and denied access to the compound.

Sean didn't think he would have any problems with the staff under Colonel John's command, as he ran a tight ship, and all his people were well disciplined. That night, Sean sat down and came up with his list.

Compound Rules of Conduct

This is a military compound ruled under the code of conduct as specified by the US Military. Colonel John Williams is the commander-in-chief of the compound and head of security.

When you see Sean Little, Jennifer Little, or Wendy Rawlings, please be respectful and do not engage them in a conversation about your personal concerns. If you have an important issue to discuss, please ask your direct supervisor.

Anyone asking Sean Little for a free application for themselves, a relative, or a friend will have their employment and residency rights terminated immediately and will be assigned to a posting outside of the compound.

For obvious security reasons, you are not allowed to bring outsiders into the compound. If you have visiting friends or relatives, it's best to meet them in Las Vegas and not at the compound.

We have reserved and paid for an entire floor of rooms at the Parkway Hotel in Las Vegas. Call ahead and reserve a room for yourself and your guests.

The use of these rooms is free of charge. If you wish to use a room for more than two weeks, you must get Wendy Rawlings or Colonel John's approval.

Only Sean Little, Jennifer Little, Wendy Rawlings, Ralph Barns, and Colonel John Walker have the right to allow outsiders onto the property. I suggest that you do not ask them.

Threats of violence, physical violence, domestic violence, sexual harassment, or racial discrimination will not be tolerated and will be dealt with swiftly and harshly.

Whisky and hard liquor will be served at the bar as long as there is no fighting. At the first sign of violence, where one or both of the participants have been drinking hard liquor, the bar will stop serving hard liquor and serve only beer and wine from then on.

The driving of any vehicles while intoxicated or in a dangerous manner will not be tolerated.

Theft willful damage, or graffiti to compound property or to the vehicles will not be tolerated.

If you have a pet, you are responsible for cleaning up after your pet.

You may only drive a vehicle if you have a valid driver's license.

Electric Jeeps and golf carts have been provided for everyone to use within the compound. When parked for a long duration, please leave the keys in the ignition for others to use.

Certain individuals and security have been assigned their own vehicles, and these are identified with their names along the driver's side door. You are not allowed to drive these vehicles.

If you wish to leave the compound, vehicles are provided for you and parked outside at the main gate. These outside vehicles are used only for going outside, and you may not bring one of these outside vehicles back into the compound. Likewise, the vehicles provided for you inside the compound may not be taken outside of the compound.

If you plan on staying away for more than one day, you must give the *main gate guards your expected date of return.*

When off the compound grounds, you will be approached by members of the press. You are free to talk to them. But please understand that your employment and residency rights will be terminated if you make a false or misleading statement to them. So if interviewed, I suggest that you be very careful in what you say, or for your own benefit, maybe avoid talking to the press altogether.

The next day, Sean handed this list to Wendy, and she liked what she read, "This should clear up a lot of confusion, especially with the newer staff. I'll have Bill look it over just in case and then put it on the website," she said.

Chapter 32
Evil People Never Sleep

Sean was pleased. The improvements to the compound were proceeding, and his environmental projects were progressing. Sean constantly told his environmental Project Directors, "I am placing you in complete control. You have the money to make this happen. If you need to call me constantly, asking for my opinion means that you are incapable of handling the job, and I will replace you. When I want to talk to you, I will call you. You will not be able to call me. I do expect a hard copy monthly report of your progress on my desk on the 20th of each month."

Not being bothered by his Project Directors and nuisance phone calls and emails, he felt that a burden had been lifted off his shoulders. He felt relieved that he had more time to concentrate on his "save the world" projects.

Ralph was looking after the lab, Wendy was looking after the money, Colonel John looked after the security, Barry looked after all the construction projects, and Jennifer looked after purchasing. Good people doing a good job. Staff were happy and seemed to be enjoying their lives here.

What still bothered Sean is that he felt that angry, resentful people were still planning on his demise and to steal the secret that, until now, only he possessed. Every government and private lab in the world knew the ingredients of Sean's formula, but no matter how much they tried, they could not achieve any results. Angry, evil people knew this and became even more and more determined to have the secret.

Amir's master, the king of his oil-rich Middle Eastern country, was still enraged by Amir's failure to kidnap Sean in Boston.

"Anyone who controls this secret can dictate their terms to the world. Every world leader would be forced to bend to my will if I alone knew the secrets of restoring youth. Who could resist? The idea of having this secret is driving me crazy. I must have it, and I must have it now."

The ruler contacted Amir and gave him his orders. Amir had already hired new operatives in America, ready to do his work. The only problem was that, with Donovan gone, Amir did not know of any other ex-US military personnel he could trust. I have to rely on my most trusted operative, Nybar, and his countrymen.

Amir told his master of his plans to kidnap either Sean Little or Ralph Barns, Sean's partner. His reasoning was that by now Ralph must be privy to the secret, and they would force it out of whichever one they could kidnap. Amir's master then said, "Once you have the secret, you must immediately send me the secret and then kill your hostage. Then you must immediately attack the compound and kill the other. This you will do, for only I must possess the secret. Tell your men they will receive Five million dollars each at the end of this mission and a hero's welcome when they come home."

"Yes, master, I will do as you ask," replied Amir.

Amir explained that he had purchased a small, out-of-the way mechanic's shop near the desert compound where his eight operatives worked on cars. They would buy used cars, fix them up, and then send them to the local auto auction. This kept their involvement with local people to a minimum, but still looked like a legitimate business. No one questions people coming and going at all hours from an auto repair shop.

Amir's master questioned, "Can these people be trusted?"

"Yes, my master," replied Amir. "These are our countrymen who have been in America for years, and I trust them with my life." His master angrily replied with, "Good, because if you fail again, that is exactly what you will be giving up!" Then he hung up. Amir knew that this was his last chance. He must succeed or die.

Amir's operatives kept up the facade of the mechanical shop beautifully. The shop was at the end of an old industrial area where most of the buildings sat vacant. No one questioned their activities, and once there for a few months, no one even noticed them coming or going.

Nybar was a small, thick man with beady eyes and oily black hair. His assault team was all from his same desert village back home and grew up together. This operation is going to work, and then we can all retire back to our homeland as rich ' heroes. The millions Amir was offering for securing the secret and then killing both Sean and Ralph's guaranteed the loyalty of his men.

"We cannot and will not fail," he said to his staff.

Nybar's shop was located in Myerstown, fifteen miles from the compound. He purchased another building with a large fenced-in area where they stored their vehicles waiting to be repaired. This new building was down the highway from the compound, and Nybar's men drove past the compound every day, picking up and delivering cars.

No one questioned the flatbed tow trucks from the auto shop driving by. A great way to keep an eye on the compound.

This went on for months. Nybar's men saw Jennifer and her family constantly leaving under heavy escort but knew that she did not know the secret.

"She is not even involved in the lab, so to capture her gives us nothing and reveals our plans. No, we must wait for either Sean Little or Ralph Barns to leave the compound, and then we can act. We have one chance and one chance only. We must succeed."

Then, after three months of waiting, their time finally came. They had their computer people stationed on the second floor of the auto shop, hacking into every computer system in the compound and their email network. The computer assistant, his nephew, came running down to meet Nybar.

"Master, I have just intercepted an email from Ralph Barns to his sister saying that he is going to Boston on American Airlines Flight #172 tomorrow at two p.m. She is sick, and he has promised to see her. I have also looked up his sister's home address and the hospital, Massachusetts General Hospital, where she is."

"Thank you, God shines on us today," said Nybar. "This is our chance."

Nybar considered his options. *Ralph would be heavily guarded right up to getting on the plane, so we would have little chance of getting him there. We must get him in Boston, where he will not be so heavily guarded.* He thought about taking his men on a commercial flight or chartering a private jet to take them there. *Both are too risky, as once Ralph is captured, the police would surely check all outgoing flights from Las Vegas to Boston. We have little choice but to drive the forty hours to Boston,* Nybar thought.

He ordered his men to pack the two large cargo vans with clothes, weapons, and the rest of their tactical gear. Nybar placed a notice on the door: "Closed for two weeks due to a family emergency." They left immediately and drove the forty hours to Boston, almost nonstop. Being professionals, they paid for everything with cash, leaving no paper trail.

Upon arriving in Boston, they rented two cheap hotel rooms on the outskirts of town. No one paid them any notice. After a good meal and much-needed sleep, Nybar's men drove him to Ralph's sister's home and the Massachusetts General Hospital where she was staying. Calling from a pay phone, Nybar was easily told the floor and room number of Ralph's sister and the visiting hours.

Sitting in a parking lot across from the hospital, they could see Ralph entering the hospital and then, a few hours later, leaving to return to his sister's home. Nybar was pleased to see that Ralph was guarded by only two men. *An easy job,* he thought.

Later that day, Nybar using, his phony ID, purchased for cash a used van with a sliding side door from a used car lot and then waited for his chance.

As scheduled, Ralph left the next day with his guards to visit his sister. Nybar had his men split up into two groups. One was the attack group in the small van located near Ralph's sister's home, and the other was under surveillance at the hospital.

After visiting his sister, Ralph came out of the hospital and was met by his two guards. On their way home, the surveillance team followed at a safe distance and reported that Ralph and his guards had stopped at a burger place to pick up some food.

They reported that they were again on their way. The attack team lay in wait.

Ralph and the guards arrived at Ralph's sister's home and entered. Nybar's men had already broken in through the back door and were waiting in the house. When Ralph and the guards entered, once they closed the door, Nybar's men came out of hiding and, with silencers on their guns, immediately shot the two guards in the head. Ralph stood there speechless.

The one kidnapper placed a gun to Ralph's head and said, "If you speak or yell, you will be joining your dead friends here. We will be calmly walking outside and getting into a van. Any attempt on your part to alarm anyone or to yell out, and I will kill you. Do you understand?" Ralph nodded his head in agreement.

The van was waiting for them in the driveway with the sliding side door open. Ralph was escorted out at gunpoint and got in the van. In the van, they zip-tied his hands together. They left and went to a deserted area, where they were met by one of the original vans. They exited the van with Ralph and got into the big cargo van. Leaving the van here would make it look like some kids had stolen it and then abandoned it.

And as Nybar had used his phony identification to purchase it, it could not be traced back to him.

They returned to the old hotel and easily got Ralph into one of the rooms. Nybar's men immediately strapped Ralph to a chair. Then one assailant set up a video camera with a tripod in front of Ralph. The kidnappers then put on face masks to avoid being identified in the film. Once the video camera was turned on, Nybar wasted no time in questioning Ralph.

"Ralph Barns, you are going to tell us the secret to Sean Little's age-reversing formula, or we will be making life very difficult for you."

"I do not know the secret," Ralph protested. "Only Sean Little knows the secret. I get the people ready, and he comes over with the formula and administers it. That's all."

Nybar continued to slap Ralph, but Ralph would not tell him what he wanted to know. With the camera still running, Nybar ordered Ralph's mouth duct taped shut, and then Nybar, with a large knife, cut off two of Ralph's fingers. Ralph was screaming in pain and then passed out. Showing the severed fingers to the camera, Nybar said, "This message is for Sean Little in Nevada. We have killed the two guards protecting your friend, Ralph Barns. He is now our prisoner, and we will kill him if you do not forward the secret of your age-reversing formula to the following email address."

Nybar held up a piece of paper with an email address on it.

"Mr. Little, you have two hours to respond, or your friend's death will be on your hands."

The camera showed another shot of Ralph's face and his two severed fingers.

This video arrived at the compound slightly after five p.m. Wendy came running into the restaurant to tell Sean. She showed him the video on her phone, and Jennifer was in tears. Everyone was in total shock. Sean immediately asked for Colonel John. He burst into the dining room moments later. He said that Wendy had sent him the video and stated his opinion was that Ralph was already dead, as these people would not be letting him leave alive.

"What do I do now?" asked Sean.

Colonel John said, "I have already contacted the FBI in Boston. On our end, there is nothing you can do. Even if you give them the formula, they will kill Ralph and blackmail the rest of the world. We know that Ralph was visiting his sister in Boston, so he is being held captive there. From a neighbor, we got an approximate time of his capture at his sister's house of twelve-thirty p.m. Boston time. Allowing for the switchover of the vehicles and a drive, the video reached us at two p.m. Boston time. So, in one and a half hours, they switched vehicles, then drove to where they are staying, and then set up their cameras. We can tell from their accents that they are from the Middle East.

"I have been in contact with the FBI and local authorities in Boston, and they are doing a sweep of all the hotels in the area looking for a number of Middle Eastern men who have checked in the last 24–48 hours. If they are staying in an associate's house, we won't find them, but we hope they settled for a hotel, knowing that Ralph's visit was on a last-minute basis.

The President and Vice President were made aware of the events, and the President called the FBI in Boston and said that every effort must be made to find these kidnappers and Ralph Barns. The local FBI and police had every single agent and officer out looking at the local hotels."

The FBI immediately had their people call every single hotel in and around Boston. Quickly, they hit pay dirt. A small hotel on the outskirts of town reported renting rooms to some Middle Eastern men in two cargo vans. Plus, they insisted on paying in cash.

The FBI and the local police took no chances. They flew in an FBI special agent, Ron Newland, to be charge of the rescue. Ron Newland was a tall, physically fit African American ex-military Navy Seal who didn't consider failure in anything he did as an option. He created a reputation for himself in the service of rescuing hostages in the most difficult situations and never failed to achieve his mission. The FBI couldn't fail here, so they called in Ron Newland, their best. He was the right man for the job.

Ron arrived within the hour with three additional men. He immediately ordered that the local roads near the hotel be blocked off and that two officers, one male, and one female, posing as a couple on holiday, go in to rent rooms beside the suspect's hotel rooms, the room with all the lights on.

Once in the room, they could hear the occupants in the next room arguing in Farsi, a Middle Eastern language. Once they heard the words

"Ralph Barns," they reported, and FBI agent Ron Newland and his three other agents arrived in a large van and calmly walked up to their room. Each man knew his position and his job. These were trained Navy Seals who had worked with Ron Newland before, and they never failed. Without a moment's hesitation, they immediately attacked by using a battering ram and breaking into the front door of the kidnapper's hotel room.

As soon as the front door exploded under the pressure of the battering ram, the two men behind them burst into the room, followed by the agents previously using the battering ram. Within seconds, the four FBI agents were in the room, firing.

Two of the kidnappers closest to the door reached for their guns and opened fire.

Ron, being the first to enter, saw the kidnappers reach for their guns and cut them down. The six other kidnappers, reaching for their weapons, were cut down in turn by the three other FBI agents. Within ten seconds, eight kidnappers lay dead on the floor. Ralph witnessed this all while being bound to his chair.

After ensuring that all the kidnappers were dead, they removed the duct tape covering Ralph's mouth, cut the zip ties binding him to the chair, and further tried to bandage his bleeding hand. FBI supervisor and commander Ron Newland of the attack team yelled, "Get this man to the hospital, and do not let him out of your sight. He is to be guarded 24/7. The guys who did this likely have friends nearby that will try to capture him again. Now get moving."

Ron Newland called in the success of the mission and reported, "This is Special Agent Ron Newland reporting. Mr. Barns is now safe and on his way to the Massachusetts General Hospital. He must be protected around the clock by the FBI and Boston's Finest. The kidnappers, all eight of them, lay on the floor in front of me dead."

The Assistant Director of the FBI, Tyler Myles, the same one who had the argument with Sean Little months ago, said, "Congratulations, Special Agent Newland. Fine work. The President of the United States will be happy to hear of your success. I would have to mention that a commendation and a promotion will likely be coming your way for you and your men."

"Thank you, sir, only doing my job," replied Special Agent Newland.

Within minutes, the entire hotel parking lot was covered with FBI and

Boston police vehicles. Before the bodies were taken away, the entire scene was video recorded. Special Agent Ron Newland ordered that all the kidnapper's wallets and personal effects be removed from their bodies and placed in a box for their inspection. Once acquired, the dead kidnappers were placed in body bags, put in a van, and delivered to the local morgue. Agent Ron, after finding the keys, ordered that the kidnappers' vans be driven to the police compound for inspection.

The Assistant Director, Tyler Miles, called Colonel John to tell him Ralph Barns was safe and was likely in an operating room getting his hand looked after. Sean took the phone, and Tyler Miles introduced himself and repeated his message to Sean. Sean was overcome with emotion, telling him how happy he was to hear that Ralph was safe. Sean and Tyler Miles hung up, and Sean and Jennifer just hugged each other. Everyone was still in shock but relieved that Ralph was alive.

For the funeral of the two guards, Sean needed someone to represent himself and Ralph. Obviously, he couldn't go, and Ralph was still in the hospital, so he asked Wendy and Colonel John to go and represent them. It was obvious that Wendy and John had eyes for each other. So Sean mentioned that Boston was a beautiful city and they should spend some time together there.

"You and John have been working a lot lately, and I believe you need to take two weeks off. Why don't you stay in Boston and enjoy the sights? You both deserve it. And to make it official, I order you to take two-weeks holiday. Please contact Colonel John and ask him to accompany you."

Wendy, trying to hide her smile, simply said, "I'll let him know. I'm sure he'll be happy to accompany me."

At the funeral in Boston, Wendy made a brief speech thanking the men and their families for their bravery. Later, after the service, Wendy and Colonel John approached the two families and expressed their appreciation for the dedication of the two deceased agents. Wendy handed each family a check for $250,000 tax-free. Wendy had already contacted the tax department and paid any taxes owed. Plus, Wendy included their names in their Veterans' monthly check system to ensure that they would be receiving five hundred dollars per month from now on.

After the funeral, Tyler Miles, the Assistant Director of the FBI, himself came to see Sean. Sean had obviously forgotten all about his argument with Assistant Director and Sean welcomed him with open arms.

Tyler Miles said, "Sean, this is what we know. The people who kidnapped Ralph were likely the same bunch that tortured and killed your friend, Jack. From the evidence that we found on their bodies, they had been using a small auto repair shop in Myerstown, Nevada, as their base of operations. They rented a building down the road from the compound to allow themselves to drive in front of the compound and not arouse suspicion.

"My people entered their auto shop and found that upstairs they had sophisticated eavesdropping and computer surveillance equipment installed, hacking into the phones and emails at the compound. We arrested the lone individual we found there, but all we can make out is that he is from a small, middle eastern country, and the people we killed were all from the same village. We expect to gain very little from questioning him.

"Whoever these people are, they are very well-financed and dedicated. We are now presently searching their phone records and bank statements, but they appear to be coming up empty-handed. These guys were pros. Everything they used in the kidnapping of Ralph they paid with cash and we discovered fifty thousand dollars in cash hidden in their hotel rooms and another $300,000 in a hidden safe in the auto shop. So far, that is all we know. One other thing: these people are not the type to give up easily. We believe they will continue to try to either kidnap you or Ralph to gain the secret to your formula in any way possible. They obviously don't have any problems killing anyone who gets in their way." Sean agreed.

Two days later, and not reported in America, the Middle Eastern newspapers reported that Amir, an international businessman and diplomat, was found dead in his bed with a bullet in his head. In an area where business and political assassination is a way of life, few people even took notice.

Chapter 33
Additional Security

Everyone in the compound was shocked at the news of Ralph's capture. They were also surprised to hear that the persons responsible were just down the road in a mechanical shop in Myerstown and had been there for months. Once Ralph was able to speak, Sean called, and Ralph told him the whole story.

"They were waiting for us back at my sister's house. Just as we walked in, they immediately killed the two agents. Thank heavens my sister's husband was away on business, or I'm sure they would have killed him too. They took me to where I was transferred to a white van and taken to a hotel room just outside of Boston. After videotaping me and cutting off two of my fingers, the hotel door gets kicked in, and everyone starts firing. All of those bastards were killed, and none of our guys were hurt. I am sure that they would have killed me regardless of what I told them.

"The doctors did a wonderful job of sewing my two fingers back on, and they say I'll be here for another two weeks to make sure that no infection sets in. I've got four really big guards with really big guns outside of my room 24/7 so I think I'm okay.

"The only bright spot is that every day they wheel my sister in to see me."

Sean listened to Ralph's story and knew that others would also be after the secret. *These people certainly don't seem too bothered about killing people,* he thought. He explained to Ralph that even though he would like to visit him, for everyone's safety, it would be best if he stayed in the compound. Ralph agreed.

Compound Security

Sean's first move was to call in Colonel John and have the guards around the compound doubled. They did not have to patrol the entire area just outside the original five thousand acre compound perimeter, especially the living quarters. And as Sean was paying everyone working at the compound, military or otherwise, an additional thousand dollars up and over, their weekly salary, John quickly agreed.

"If we need more living quarters, contact Jennifer, and she'll order in more trailers," said Sean.

"Every single off-site worker who comes into the compound is to be escorted by armed guards at all times, no exceptions. I want background checks on each and every worker who is working on the existing buildings and the new fence being installed. Next, I want every outside delivery vehicle to drop their deliveries at the main gate and have the guards drive them in. Where this is not possible, for example, with the grocery delivery vehicle, I want at least two guards to accompany each delivery vehicle while inside the compound. Hire extra guards if you have to. I don't care, but I want the security of the compound to be watertight. Do you understand?

"And I want you to look into having the security on our computer and phone systems improved. Keep the website public, because if we make it private, it will look like we're trying to hide something. Besides, we have no secrets here."

"No problem, and I agree," replied Colonel John Williams.

Sean had leased the entire five thousand acre military compound from the government for twenty years, plus recently purchased twenty thousand additional acres around the compound for additional security. As this compound had been abandoned for years, he, Jennifer, and some guards took some Jeeps out for a perimeter inspection. Sean saw what he needed to see. Contacting Barry, he ordered new security fencing for all of the original five thousand acres military site.

"Are you sure you want it for the entire five thousand acres?" asked Barry.

"Yes, I want eight-foot-tall military-grade, quality fencing installed," Sean replied.

"No problem, you're the boss, Sean. And thank you for all the work, my men, and I really appreciate it," said Barry.

Sean replied with, "With the plans, I have for this place you and your men won't be going anywhere for about five years. I have so many projects

I want done."

"Great," said Barry, and they both hung up.

Meeting with the Local Police

Fortunately, being fifteen miles from the closest small town and a one-hour drive from Las Vegas, they did not have the large crowds of spectators outside like they did in Boston. The hot sun also played a factor in keeping people away. Naturally, curious onlookers would drive by.

A few people in RVs started showing up and parking on the roadway. Sean saw this and mentioned it to Colonel John. John made a couple of phone calls, and then the next day, "No Parking" signs appeared all along the roadways, and the local police would constantly show up and clear the illegally parked RVs out.

The local Las Vegas police and the smaller police departments were doing a great job keeping the roadways clear of stopped vehicles and ushering people along.

Sean called a meeting with the Chief of Police for Las Vegas, heads of the smaller municipal police departments near the compound, Colonel John, and Wendy, his Secretary Treasurer. They all knew of Ralph's kidnapping and that the kidnappers were right down the road all the time.

They met for lunch, and after Sean introduced Wendy and Colonel John, the Chief of Police for Las Vegas, Fred Matthews gave a brief description of what they knew about the kidnappers and how they were able to hideout as operators of a small mechanical shop. Chief of Police Fred Matthews was a tall, no-nonsense, African-American ex-military officer who inspired confidence in anyone he spoke to. Sean liked him the moment they met and knew that his concerns would be taken care of.

After Fred's description of the events, all the police officers present expressed their appreciation for Sean's work on the environment and helping the disabled war veterans.

"No, I thank you. You are keeping us safe here and have been doing an excellent job. The people after us are obviously very well-financed and determined. I just want to make sure you were aware," said Sean.

The Las Vegas Chief of Police, Fred Matthews, spoke again, "Well, to be quite honest with you, we do appreciate what you are doing, but I would like to add that since Ralph's kidnapping, we have been contacted by every government agency in the US, telling us that you and your compound are to be protected at all costs. Wow, they must think of you as a national treasure." Everyone laughed.

"Thank you again," said Sean. "And to express my appreciation, first, I am going to pay for any and all renovations you need for your police departments. Anything you need—renovations, furniture, new computers—just drop the invoices off to Colonel John at the main gate or mail them to Wendy, and she'll see to it that the bills are paid."

Everyone looked at Wendy because, as soon as Sean started talking, she began writing in her notebook. She looked up and smiled.

"He doesn't often tell me what he's up to, so my notes become my authorization. If I don't take notes, I can't keep up with him." And everyone laughed, especially Sean.

Sean continued, "Second, as you all know, Colonel John, I want you to inform him about how many of your police vehicles need to be replaced, and we will provide you with new ones. Anything you want. Nothing is too good for those who protect me and my people."

The police officers just sat there stunned. One of the police officers asked, "What do you want us to do with the old vehicles?

Sean quickly replied with, "What do I care? Just don't bring them here!" And everyone laughed.

"Third," Sean continued. "I would like to see a new modern police department building in Myerstown, closest to us. The old police department just can't handle anything if things get exciting around here. So a new, larger police department staffed with more officers. And make sure to include plenty of jail cells in the basement. Never know when they might come in handy.

"And fourth, I am formally asking a favor of Fred Matthews, the Chief of Police for Las Vegas."

"No problem, Sean, what do you need?" answered Fred.

"I want you to supply Wendy here with an emailed list of all police officers across America who are now physically disabled and a brief description of their disability.

"Plus, a list of those officers who have died regardless of cause and who have left families behind. We will start sending out checks to them, along with our veterans' checks, as soon as your lists arrive."

Again, the officers sat there in amazement.

"Thank you, thank you very much, Sean," said Fred while shaking Sean's hand. "I will acquire those lists ASAP and get them off to Wendy."

Sean ended with, "Your police officers protect us just as much as our fighting men do, so they deserve to be treated as such. You deserve our respect."

With that, everyone finished their lunch, shook hands with Sean, and went back to their duties.

A Better Main Gate

Sean asked Colonel John to stay back. "Colonel, you and your men are doing a fine job keeping the onlookers out. Is there anything else you need from me to help you at the main gate, anything at all?" asked Sean.

"Yes, now that you ask, there is," said Colonel John. "I would like to have your permission to make a three-stage entrance, just like our military outposts have overseas.

"We should have the road directly in front of the main gate blocked off to all outside traffic. This could be easily accomplished by blocking off the road on both the east and west ends and installing the first guard posts there.

"Then, to proceed in, you have to pass by the first set of guards and a gate, then proceed to the main gate, where you are further questioned by the guards at the second gate, and then you are still questioned by the guards at the third gate. As always, the visitors leave their vehicles in the parking lot and proceed into the compound on foot.

"Plus, the entrance we have on the south end for staff to leave to go joyriding in the desert should be closed. Anyone wanting to go for a ride can simply come to the front gate and take out a vehicle from us. Easier for us to guard one gate than two.

"The present system we have of you emailing us who you are expecting that day is working out well. And when a visitor shows up and claims 'I have to see Sean Little. It's important', isn't on your list, they don't get in, period. I have your days list posted at the first gate, and then their attendance is confirmed at the second and third gate. I would also like a proper guard building, two machine gun guard towers, and better lighting."

"I'm impressed," said Sean. "You have my authorization for any improvements you want. I will inform Wendy of your requests. Talk to Barry, the main contractor, about it and get whatever you need."

Colonel John continued, "With so many people coming and going around here, I would like to see a photo ID card system made up that we can scan every time someone enters or leaves the compound."

"John, these are great ideas. I can see Wendy talking to someone outside. Let me get her back in to let her know what's going on." Sean got up and called Wendy out the window.

Wendy walks back in and laughingly said, "Spending more money again, hey Sean." And all three laughed.

Colonel John then talked about his ideas for a new security three-gate system, new guard buildings, a guard tower, and better lighting. Then he explained his ideas about compound personnel and frequent visitors having their own photo ID cards that could be scanned when people came into or left the compound.

Wendy looked at him and, touching his arm calmly, said, "And I just thought you were a pretty face that carried a big gun." And both Sean and John started laughing. It was obvious that Wendy and John were becoming a couple ever since their trip to Boston.

"I like the ideas. What can I say? I've always felt that as this place grows, we need more security, and now, with what happened to Ralph, I'm convinced of it," said Wendy. They all agreed, Wendy made her notes, and then everyone went off to their own duties.

Additional Fencing

A couple of days later, Sean asked Colonel John to meet with him. When he arrived, Sean outlined his ideas.

"What do you think of having additional security fencing installed just around the compound buildings and living quarters? This way, the guards with their dogs can patrol the areas close to our work buildings and living quarters day and night. You can have guards with dogs patrolling the outside of this fence or set it up with motion sensors, whichever you think is best."

"That's a good idea, Sean," replied Colonel John. "The problem with the motion sensors is that they go off every time a bird or a coyote passes by. Let me think about it. Maybe having the inner fence area patrolled by guards and their dogs and sensors placed outward from that fence facing into the desert."

Sean answered with, "Whatever you think is best, inform Barry and Wendy and get it done ASAP."

Additional security was on everyone's mind. Sean had the website people place an announcement that if any staff had an idea for improved security, please send an email to Colonel John and let him know. The website stated, "Any and all additional security ideas will be considered. The protection of my people is my top concern. Sean Little."

Colonel John and Wendy arranged for the security ID people to arrive in the next few days to start taking the staff pictures. They set up the photo booth area in the boardroom with only Sean, Wendy, Colonel John, or Ralph Barns being able to authorize a visitor to the compound or to issue a photo ID.

Everyone quickly got accustomed to showing their ID cards every time they left or entered the compound. The three-gate security system was well received. Staff who were known to the guards were waved through, but any visitors were quickly questioned, and those without prior authorization were turned around. A few unauthorized people complained after seeing the automatic weapons the guards were carrying.

The guards loved exchanging stories of the "I've got to see Sean Little now. It's a matter of life or death", or "I'm Sean Little's best friend from Grade four and I've got to see him" or "I'm the reporter for the Big Swamp City news and I have to see Sean Little right away" ploys. No one was allowed past the front gate unless you were on staff or had prior authorization from Sean Little, Wendy, Colonel John, or Ralph Barns.

As a visitor, you parked your car in the parking lot outside of the compound, and then the guards drove you in. Any staff members who wanted to meet with their family members or friends usually just met off the compound in Las Vegas. As you had to get direct permission from the top four to have a visitor in, few staff members ever bothered asking.

New Website Notification

Sean decided to update his policy statement on the website. He emailed the website people these notes:

From this date forward, I, Sean Little

Will not answer phone calls or answer emails.

I do not answer questions, and I do not grant interviews.

Other than administering the formula, I will not meet with or speak to any of our clients while they are undergoing treatment here.

Other than test applications or for a select few of my staff, I will not do free applications of the treatment.

Only myself, Wendy Rawlings, Colonel John Williams, or Ralph Barns may have visitors to the compound. To have a visitor, you must get one of these individuals' permission. I suggest you do not ask them.

I suggest that if you have family or friends visiting, you meet them in Las Vegas. You and your guests are welcome to stay at the Parkway Hotel.

The new security measures are designed to improve the security of all of us in the compound.

After what has happened to my associate, Ralph, it is unlikely that I will ever be leaving the protection of the compound.

Trespassers on this compound will be handled harshly and arrested. Any and all vehicles or aircraft used to trespass on the compound property will be automatically destroyed.

I will not become involved in any government or military actions.

I will not contribute to any political campaigns or political action committees.

Sean Little

Chapter 34
Ralph Returns to Work

Ralph returned to work with much fanfare. It was almost like a parade at the front gate when he arrived. Everyone lined the roadway, clapping and cheering.

Jennifer and Emily had the dining room all decked out with large banners saying, "Welcome Home, Ralph." Jennifer ordered plenty of steaks and lobster tails for Ralph's favorite meal. Ralph appreciated the fanfare and the welcome-home dinner. Before the meal, Ralph stood up and said, "While in Boston, I thought my time was up. And when they cut my fingers off, I really knew I would not be leaving that hotel room alive. Then somehow I woke up to everyone firing around me and the kidnappers dropping like flies. I'm really glad our guys are good shots, or I wouldn't be here today. Thank you to everyone here today and to those brave men who rescued me. I now would like to call on Chaplain Furlong to say a special prayer for those two FBI agents who gave their lives protecting me and then to say grace." Anyone close to him could see that he had a tear in his eye.

The next day, he gave a moving speech about his ordeal. Sean had it recorded and placed on the website. With Ralph back and eventually clearing up the backlog of applications, the world returned to normal.

Surprisingly, there were no complaints from the female applicants resulting from the delays. Ralph's kidnapping was all over the news, so everyone was aware of the problems. Plus, there is plenty to do in Las Vegas, and the ladies were even bragging about how much of their husband's money they were spending. All were in good humor and anxious about being years younger.

The money for the applications was flowing into the compound's bank account like a river. There just didn't seem to be any end in sight. As more and more ladies had the application, they in turn told more and more of their rich friends, and they couldn't wait to have the treatment done themselves.

Most candidates had their physical exams, information, and money ready to be sent in. *Too bad we can only do ten people every two weeks, but this will soon change,* thought Sean.

Ralph had the lab work back under control.

"The female subjects were so appreciative of being years younger" was the staff's often heard comment. Ralph and Sean did agree that once they ran out of female subjects from 40–60 years of age, they would simply up the age limit to seventy years.

"That should keep you going for a while, hey, Ralph," said Sean.

Project #5: Save the Whales

Sean was now able to turn his attention to his next project. He called Bill Fryer, he and Jennifer's friend, who lent Sean his cabin to hide out in and who drove Jennifer up to the cabin to see him. Bill was now a top lawyer for Todd & Todd Lawyers Inc., out of Detroit, Michigan. Sean called Bill, explained that he had a project for him and invited him to come down and view the compound.

"Are you kidding? I'd love to come down," said Bill. "That's all everyone talks about up here, and I'm a celebrity because I drove Jennifer up to see you. Your Fresh Water Initiative caught everyone by surprise and helping out the veterans, you're a national hero. Let me tidy things up here, and I'll be there in two days."

"Great," said Sean, "I'll have my plans all laid out for you by then. Goodbye."

Bill arrived in the early morning two days later. After getting settled in one of the guest trailers, Sean and Jennifer gave him the royal tour, which included some empty offices on the left wing of the fifth floor. After the tour, they had lunch, and then Sean and Bill went into Sean's office.

Sean started out, "Bill, as you can tell, the money is flowing in here like a river. I now have the means to clean up this planet without asking for donations or any government assistance." Bill agreed.

"Besides my Fresh Water Initiative, my next project relies on you secretly buying up every company and ship in the world that harpoons whales. If you do it out in the open, a few will not sell, hoping to be the last ones left harvesting these defenseless animals. I want you to work

256

exclusively on this for me. Those empty offices you saw on the fifth floor are all yours to use as you see fit. Wendy can set you up with anything you need, including staff. It's your call," said Sean.

"Incredible, buying up every company and ship that harpoons whales. Well, I couldn't agree more. Asking these people to stop hunting whales has fallen on deaf ears. At present, the only way they'll stop is after they've killed every single whale. You have my total support, and I know staff who would jump at the chance to get involved," said Bill.

"Good," said Sean. "But for the start, I want you to do this out of your offices in Detroit. Please do not mention my involvement in this. Maybe set up an offshore corporation to buy these companies. Once purchased, immediately stop their harvesting, have them return to their home ports and pay the men for their time off. I have an idea for using the ships and crews later on. Heaven knows we have the money."

Sean then called Wendy Rawlings, his Secretary Treasurer and introduced Bill Fryer to her as his friend and new lawyer. He also explained that Todd & Todd Lawyers Inc. would be their exclusive lawyers firm. He will be occupying the empty offices on the fifth floor in the office tower. Sean explained his latest project to Wendy, and she couldn't agree more.

"Sean, you never cease to amaze me."

"When Bill returns to Detroit, he will be contacting you with how much he needs to buy these companies. I expect it will likely be well over one billion dollars. I don't want anyone to know about this. If word gets out, these companies won't sell and will just keep on killing these defenseless animals," said Sean.

"As always, my lips are sealed," said Wendy.

Bill spent the next day touring the compound, then left with Jennifer and her parents on a sight-seeing tour of Las Vegas. Sean had a problem letting Jennifer out of the compound but settled on doubling the number of guards accompanying them.

Bill was amazed as Jennifer calmly notified the main gate they were going out. When they drove up, eight large black SUVs full of well-armed military personnel accompanied them. Jennifer and her parents took no notice, so Bill thought, *When in Rome, do as the Romans do.*

The next morning, before Bill left, Sean handed him a check for ten million dollars made out to Todd & Todd Lawyers Inc. to "get the ball rolling" on this project.

"My boss will be glad to see this," said Bill.

He was then driven by a military escort to the airport.

Good, that should get them started on saving those whales. Why in the 21st century, we have to continue killing whales to extinction? I'll never know, but I'm going to put a stop to it, thought Sean.

For the next three months, Bill set up an offshore dummy corporation and started buying up all the whaling companies. In some instances, he had to buy out the entire corporation, keeping the whaling portion itself and reselling the head office and other businesses.

Sean kept encouraging him, saying, "I don't care how you do it or what you have to pay. Buy up those companies and stop them killing those whales."

With the new office tower complete, the whaling companies bought and the ships brought back to port, Bill could start moving into his new offices. Some of his staff moved with him from Detroit. When asked, many replied with, "Are you kidding? There's no snow in Nevada, and it's down the road from Las Vegas. Plus, you're paying thousand dollars per week over and above our regular salary, and everything's free on the compound. I can't wait to go!"

Sean waited until the dust cleared over Bill buying up the whaling companies and their ships. He then asked Bill to buy up the two companies that made the powerful harpoons used for killing these defenseless creatures. Once purchased, he had the company's inventories of harpooning equipment immediately sold for scrap. When the whaling ships finally made port, their harpoons and equipment were likewise removed from the boats and sold for scrap. Everything was video recorded. *You never know when such videos can come in handy later on,* Sean said to himself. With the ships in port, he had them sit idle and pay the crews their full salaries while they sat at home with their families. No complaints there.

Chapter 35
Project # 6 – The Great Pacific Garbage Patch

With Bill Fryer and his staff settling comfortably into their new offices and living quarters, Sean could now introduce his largest environmental project. Bill did a superb job of secretly buying up all the world's whaling companies and having their ships return to their home port. This was done with little fanfare, and the news agencies hardly took any notice of it.

Sean called Wendy and Bill Fryer and stated that he wanted a meeting when Kevin Sanders, the assistant to John Harper, the Vice President, arrived. Kevin arrived in two days, and the meeting was held later that afternoon. After introducing Kevin to the others, Sean addressed the meeting in his new fancy boardroom.

"Ladies and gentlemen, I am going to introduce to you our most aggressive environmental project. It will likely take a year to organize and five years to complete. Here it is.

"With the efforts of Mr. Bill Fryer, I now own every single factory whaling ship in the world, along with their support vessels. All these whaling ships are now sitting in their home ports and have had their whaling equipment removed and sold for scrap. To start, six of these factory whaling ships will eventually be outfitted with collector fins off the sides, incinerators, and holding areas. Plus, I have asked Bill to buy twelve abandoned but still seaworthy ocean-going oil tankers. These other twelve oil tankers will be for offloading the goods from the original collector ships and transporting them to port."

Everyone but Wendy and Bill looked at Sean like he was going out of his mind. Kevin spoke first, "Sean, you are the boss here, and heaven knows you have the money, but why do you want to buy twelve used oil tankers? What do you need them for?" Everyone else nodded their heads in agreement.

"I am going to clean up the most disgusting mess that we have infected our world with. I am going to clean up the "Great Pacific Garbage Patch" replied Sean.

"Sean," replied Kevin Sanders, "you know that Garbage Patch is now the size of Texas and growing?"

"Yes, I do, Kevin. But no government will take responsibility for it, and the United Nations will not even discuss cleaning it up, but I will. This will be accomplished with my money, my ships, and my crews. It can be done and will be done. Let me explain."

Sean then went to his prepared drawings and outlined the procedure.

"The six collector ships will be made out of the six whaling factory ships that Bill Fryer purchased from Japan and Norway. They will have 20-30-foot-wide stainless steel collector conveyors sticking out front on each side to scoop up the garbage as the ship moves slowly forward.

"On deck, this garbage will fall onto another conveyor belt, where large fans will assist in drying it out. The garbage will then be fed into a large incinerator in front of the ship, where it will be burned to a fine ash. The ashes will be stored in the hold of the ship to be offloaded onto the transport ships. The fumes from the plastic burning will be recycled back into the ship, with zero pollution being emitted."

"But can't you transport the garbage without burning it?" asked Wendy.

"Good question, Wendy," replied Sean. "We could, but the volume of garbage is just too great. By burning it aboard ship allows us to collect the harmful fumes and clean them up before they get into the environment. By burning the garbage in place, we reduce its mass down to less than thirty percent of what we started with. This we are more able to transport."

The group sat in amazement.

"I think it will work," said Wendy. She knew about Bill buying up the ships but did not know what Sean wanted them for. "If anyone in the world can do this, it will be you. I'm all for it."

"Thank you, Wendy," said Sean. "Needless to say, once again, this is top secret while we work the logistics out. To start, I am asking Bill and his team to ascertain buying up twelve used but seaworthy oil tankers through the off-shore dummy company. Next, Bill will be setting up meetings with America's largest nautical shipbuilders and getting them to progress on the plans for outfitting the collector ships.

"My intention is that this will be a world-wide effort with various countries involved. To start, the countries I want to see involved are:

-The USA

-China

-India

-Pakistan

-Japan and

-Norway

"Obviously, the crews from Japan and Norway will be composed of the now-idle whaling ship crews. If any of the above countries do not have the facilities for modifying these ships, Bill can make arrangements for another country to outfit the ships. Everything I leave up to Bill.

"Once the plans for the collector ships are finalized, I want one collector ship and two transport ships to be outfitted in each of the above countries. I will fund hundred percent of these ships' modifications. Each country will crew its own ships at my expense.

"Knowing fully well that this is in a sensitive area of the world, I am asking Kevin Sanders here to discuss with the appropriate government agencies and each country's ambassadors how I should proceed. I do know that this attempt will fail if it is seen as only an American initiative. I think that it will likely take five years to clean up the Garbage Patch and likely cost several billions of dollars. That is why no one else will attempt it or even bother to discuss it.

"The fourth floor of the office tower, originally set aside for Ralph and his lab assistants, will now be exclusively occupied with the staff necessary for cleaning up the Garbage Patch. I will personally head up this project, assisted by Wendy and Bill. We will clean this up, I promise." The small group clapped and expressed their approval.

Sean continued, "And my last request of Kevin is to ask which countries would like to make use of these tons and tons of fine ash. I suspect that either China or India would like to use it for landfill or something else. As this is my most aggressive project, I will remain its Director until I find a suitable replacement."

Then Kevin broke the silence and said, "Sean, you really know how to make a statement."

Sean asked Kevin to stay back and have lunch with him. Kevin, being with the government, naturally wanted to use this initiative to boost the President's and Vice President's status at home and abroad.

Sean objected, "The minute that any other country sees this as an American project, it is doomed. They will have their warships all around the patch, and no one will be able to get near it. No, this must appear as my project, with my funding, but with the cooperation of the entire world. If you, the President and VP, want to pay for this and take this project over, go ahead."

Kevin, with a laugh, replied with, "Well, we don't have the money for this project, and I agree with you. Especially if China and India see this as an American intrusion into their area of the world, they won't allow anything to happen. Best to go along with your plan of getting everyone involved."

"Glad you agree, Kevin? Now, when you return to Washington, start asking the ambassadors of those countries and see if they are interested. You get them talking, and I'll work on my end. Let's get together when you have something to report," stated Sean.

After Three Months

Bill Fryer found twelve unused ocean-going oil tankers that would work. The shipping companies were happy to sell them for far more than their scrap value and leave them in their ports until needed.

Three large American nautical engineering companies supplied plans for the stainless-steel collector systems to be installed in the front of the collector ships. Sean favored the one from the San Francisco company Hurne and Co. that allowed for the outside conveyor systems to lay flat against the hull when in transit and then to be moved into position when they reached the Garbage Patch. Hurne and Co. also included plans for the above deck conveyor systems and the incinerator itself. Once the garbage was burned, the fine ash would be conveyed to the holding area, waiting to be offloaded onto the transport ships.

Kevin Sanders met with the ambassadors of each of the five countries involved and explained the plans. In the world of international politics, nothing moves quickly. Kevin was faced with the delicate task of getting all five countries to agree. It was only after the ambassadors of each of the five countries visited Sean at the compound that things finally started to happen.

Sean eventually reached an agreement with all five countries that each would outfit one collector ship and two transport ships. These ships would be crewed with their own countrymen, and Sean would pay for everything.

Sean asked Kevin to get all countries, especially Japan and Norway, to agree to never allow the whaling industry to start up again. They only agreed to this after their ambassadors met with Sean, and he stated that he would refuse to do age-reversing applications for anyone from any country that allowed the whaling industry to start up again. The ambassadors took this message back to their home countries, and all countries enacted legislation ensuring that the whaling industry would never return.

A stipulation that Sean insisted on was that there would be no military presence anywhere near the Garbage Patch. No planes, no warships. If any government decided to get silly and start patrolling the area, the project would be abandoned, and the vessels would be returned to the US and sold for scrap.

His biggest holdout was China, but they did eventually agree. Sean told the Chinese Ambassador, "No problem, it's your mess, you clean it up. I can't wait to start seeing the Garbage Patch grow so large that it starts washing up on your shores. Drown in your own garbage, I don't care."

After a while, the Chinese warmed up to Sean and respected the sincerity of his efforts. As expected, each ambassador in turn tried to make their commitment to cleaning up the Garbage Patch conditional on Sean giving their rulers free applications.

Sean just laughed. "There are no free applications, not now, not ever, and please don't ask again."

The ambassadors were satisfied with this, knowing that Sean was constantly refusing to give free applications to his own government officials.

With everyone in agreement, Sean had one factory whaling ship and two oil tankers sent to each of the six participating countries ports to be refitted. Norway was the only country that did not have the large facilities to outfit the ships, so Bill made arrangements for the ships to go to France for their modifications.

As for the disposal of the ash, both India and China wanted it to be used in their land fill operations. It was agreed that one southern port in each country would be designated as an unloading port for the transport ships and that this ash would be supplied free of charge. Both India and

China also agreed to take any metal salvaged from the burned ashes.

Announcement to the World

Sean wanted to make a splash. He decided that Bill Fryer would attend the upcoming World Environmental Forum taking place in Brussels in the next two months. Using his influence and a check for ten million dollars, he arranged for Bill to be the opening speaker and to do a video presentation to the audience. That day, with every single environmental organization in attendance and with world-wide news coverage of the proceedings, Bill took the stage.

"Ladies and gentlemen, my name is Bill Fryer. I stand before you on behalf of Sean Little. Sean has asked me to make these announcements. First, I direct your attention to the large screen behind me. Here you see every single whaling ship in the world now sitting in their home port. Each ship has been stripped of all whaling equipment, and their equipment has been sold for scrap and melted down. Sean has purchased both of the companies that make whale harpooning equipment and has likewise had their inventories sold for scrap. The employees of these companies have been adequately compensated.

"Ladies and gentlemen, let me tell you with pride that the world-wide hunting and harvesting of the defenseless whaling population is now at an end. Sean has also personally arranged that the previous whaling nations will not resume their whaling operations and will be enacting laws to guarantee such."

The audience of normally quiet people went crazy. They stood up, clapped, and cheered. There had been rumors of Sean's efforts, but no one knew for sure. Some of the audience members were so happy they were in tears. Bill stood there and soaked up the applause. When the audience finally quietened down, he spoke again. "Ladies and gentlemen, on behalf of Sean Little, we appreciate your support. The ending of the world-wide whaling hunt is long overdue. Sean Little has answered all of our prayers." The crowd again stood up, clapped, and cheered.

"Ladies and gentlemen, Sean wishes me to address you on one other concern. A project that will likely take five years and billions of dollars to complete. I now again direct your attention to the large screen behind me.

Here you see photos of the largest and most disgusting environmental catastrophe known to man. I am showing you pictures of the Great Pacific Garbage Patch, where the world's plastic garbage now floats in an area almost the size of the State of Texas.

"I now direct you to the pictures of the whaling factory ships that are presently being outfitted with collector systems for picking up the garbage, incinerating it, and turning it into fine ash. Ladies and gentlemen, I stand before you to announce that, on Sean's instructions and at his sole expense, a fleet of six collector ships supported by twelve transport ships will eliminate this Garbage Patch. This is a worldwide effort involving the countries of the US, China, India, Pakistan, Japan, and Norway, who have all agreed to assist in this effort.

"Sean has put every available resource at his disposal to rid the world of this environmental disaster, and it will be done. The Great Pacific Garbage Patch will one day be nothing but a distant memory."

People now stood up, and half of them were crying. They clapped, cheered, and wouldn't stop. Rumors abounded about Sean's efforts, but there had never been a formal announcement. The world press carried these announcements on the afternoon news, and by the end of the day, Sean Little's name and efforts were on everyone's lips.

Sean was now more than a hero. He was becoming the environmental savior of the world.

One Year Later

With the collector and transport ships ready to go, all that was needed were crews. Japan and Norway were asked to pick their crews from the original whaling crews. In the US, Sean asked that ex-armed forces and navy personnel be given first priority. In all countries, it quickly became a "badge of honor" among the environmentalists when they signed up to become a crew member. Sean made sure of having enough crew members after announcing that the standard rate of pay was thousand dollars per week and a bonus of $100,000 in US funds at the end of their six-month contract. Needless to say, upon hearing of the pay plan, every country had tens of thousands of applicants.

The roar of world-wide support made Sean a hero. Sean, ever

conscious of public opinion, had a luxury ocean liner chartered and invited two members from each of the world's largest newspapers and TV networks to go to the Garbage Patch to see for themselves. Representing himself, he insisted that Bill Fryer, Wendy, Colonel John, Jennifer, Mr. and Mrs. Sloan, her parents, and her sister Emily go along. Bill Fryer, Wendy, and Colonel John also included some of their staff.

Sean asked Ralph if he wanted to go, and he declined.

"But," Ralph said, "I'll talk to my Uncle George. I'm sure he'd like to go. Plus, he loves talking to reporters." Sean agreed.

Sean had been told before that if you want the news media to like you, you have to feed them well and give them plenty to drink. He made sure that the ocean liner was fully stocked with liquor and the finest food. The guests were flown at Sean's expense to the port in India for boarding.

On board, it was quite a festive atmosphere. There was plenty to eat and drink, and everyone took full advantage. Every evening, the dance hall was opened up, and everyone ate, drank, and danced to the excellent band playing. Everyone was enjoying themselves, especially the staff who had been cooped up in the compound. Jennifer couldn't help but notice that Colonel John and Wendy were sitting alone by themselves and dancing together a lot. *I think I hear wedding bells,* she thought with a smile.

To assist the news reporters, Sean had a floating helicopter landing pad installed five miles inside the Garbage Patch. Once the ocean liner arrived at the patch, the reporters were offered helicopter rides inside the Garbage Patch to see for themselves. The photo ops were too great to ignore. With the two helicopters on board, they were able to ferry four reporters to the center of the Garbage Patch per trip and land on the floating pad. They would stay for approximately twenty minutes as the reporters and camera people got out and took pictures. Once in the air to return to the ship, they would radio ahead, and the next helicopter would leave with their passengers.

After three days, everyone who wanted to go went. They returned to the port in India for a few days of rest and relaxation, and then back to their respective countries.

Sean believed this would solidify world-wide support for his environmental efforts, and he was right. The world now became aware of the Garbage Patch and was outraged that no one to date had done anything about it. Sean's efforts were discussed at the United Nations, with every country voicing their approval.

National Geographic Films the Cleanup

Now fully operational, the collector ships arrived and started collecting the garbage, burning it, and offloading the ash to the awaiting transport ships and onto the ports in India or China. Sean had Wendy arrange for National Geographic to do a program on their efforts. The film crews filmed on each collector ship, making sure to show the country of origin of the crew members. Sean insisted that this cleanup be shown as a worldwide effort and the program produced by National Geographic did just that.

The program they produced was incredible. During the opening credits, they had a helicopter fly over the Garbage Patch to show how vast it was. The next shots were from the floating platform in the middle of the patch, showing the garbage up close.

In France, they filmed a Norwegian whaling ship being refitted into a collector ship and underway toward the Garbage Patch. The inside of the ship was shown with the conveyors, incinerator, and ash storage area. In China, an abandoned oil tanker was shown being refitted into a transport ship.

On the Indian-crewed collector ship, National Geographic did an excellent job of showing the ship collecting up the garbage, it being brought on board, air-dried and incinerated, and the ashes stored in the massive hold. The film switched to the Pakistani-crewed collector ship, where it showed the ashes unloaded onto the transport ship. Now the film switched to a Japanese-crewed transport ship docking and unloading its ashes at the Chinese dock. They filmed an American-crewed transport ship delivering and unloading its ashes at the dock in India.

Sean and Wendy reviewed the film before it was released and were very excited about what they saw. The National Geographic film crews did an excellent job of showing this cleanup as a world-wide effort with full cooperation between all six of the countries involved. They especially liked the fact that there was a film clip of every collector ship showing the crew's country of origin.

The film also explained that India and China were to receive fifty percent of the ashes each and that the transport ships would unload at whichever dock was available to them.

One especially funny episode is when the reporter asked a Chinese crew member if he felt good about cleaning up this garbage. In broken English, he said, "Garbage, who cares about the garbage? Mr. Little, the crazy American, is paying me thousand dollars a week and promises me $100,000 in US dollars at the end of six months. When I go home, I will be rich!"

National Geographic had this program translated into several languages and shown around the world. World leaders heralded Sean's actions. Sean Little was quickly becoming the environmental savior of the world.

Chapter 36
The Compound Grows

With the office tower complete, Sean had Barry's people working seven days a week on the medical and apartment towers. It's amazing how much work can get done if you put enough money behind it. After a year, the medical building and three apartment towers were finally finished.

The administration of the apartments was all handled by Colonel John's administrative people in the office tower. The single people moved into the bachelor apartments, and the others moved into the building with one- or two-bedroom apartments. Obviously, people with children were given priority over the two-bedroom apartments.

All apartments were fully furnished with new appliances, furniture, and 50' flat-screen TVs. Sean asked that the appliances, where possible be "Made in the US" and Jennifer agreed. She did have to source the TVs, microwaves, toasters, and other electronics from outside the US, as these simply are not manufactured in the US.

To accommodate the children, the main floor of the one-bedroom apartment building was converted into a school, with each room representing a classroom. Teachers were hired, and Jennifer made sure they had everything they needed.

The administrative staff for his environmental projects seemed to get larger and larger. Thank heavens I had those extra apartment buildings built, or we wouldn't have any place for the staff to stay, he would constantly tell himself.

Sean called Barry one day. Sean offered him the use of one of the office tower floors, and Barry declined, saying that it's best that they continue working out of their site trailers "to be close to where the action is." Fair enough.

The Medical Center

The main floor of the medical building now a clinic Sean asked Wendy, "Please staff the medical offices with ex-military doctors and nurses where possible and ensure they have everything they need. Please make sure there is a dental office on the main floor. Naturally, all services are free of charge to compound residents. If any of our people need any medical services of the compound, this will also be paid for."

"Great idea. I'll get on it right away," replied Wendy. "I have a lady doctor friend who I will ask, and I don't think that we need a dentist right away, as the clinic in Myerstown can handle it."

A few days later, Wendy introduced her friend, Dr. Cindy Marshall, a beautiful Chinese female military doctor. Cindy was a small, petite firecracker of a lady, and Sean liked her immediately. Sean and Cindy briefly spoke, and she seemed qualified and responsible. Being a lady doctor and having done a tour of duty in Afghanistan, Sean was assured that she was able to handle the men in the compound. Sean liked her and approved of Wendy's hiring her. As Cindy was leaving his office, Sean mumbled under his breath, "Just another friend for Jennifer to go shopping with."

A Grocery Store

Sean was concerned about the constant flow of people coming and going at the compound. As he didn't wish to put restrictions on people's movements, he started thinking of how to make his staff content and want to stay at the compound.

His first idea was concerning the people having to leave the compound to do their grocery shopping. *Pretty silly having to go through the guarded main gate just to get milk, eggs, and bread. Why not just have our own grocery store here? We can easily outfit one of our metal-out buildings to be a grocery store stocked with life's basic necessities. Milk, eggs, bread, soap, toothpaste, etc.* He contacted Jennifer to determine what everyone needed on a regular basis and to contact a grocery supply company and have it delivered. He also mentioned that she should start looking at ordering some commercial freezers and coolers.

He then requested that the store be stocked with beer and wine, but not hard liquor. His personal experience is that whiskey can make some people mean and argumentative, so he thought it was best to avoid the hard liquor altogether. He also decided to exclude stocking cigarettes and cigars. If people want hard liquor or cigarettes, they can go to town and get it themselves.

Over lunch, he discussed this with Jennifer and Wendy. Both were totally in favor of the idea.

"Having our own grocery store would make everyone's life so much easier. No more running into town and carting your groceries back," said Wendy.

"I also think the store should be free. Having people pay is too complicated and not necessary, and I'm really not too worried about people hoarding toilet paper." Both Wendy and Jennifer laughed.

So it was finalized that Jennifer would contact a grocery supply company to make deliveries once per week. Sean insisted that when the truck arrived, it would be accompanied by the guards to the store; they would help unload it and then escort the truck back to the main gate. He also asked that he would prefer to see fewer items but more of them.

"I don't want it to be a stampede of people every time the delivery truck arrives. I don't want this to turn into a competition for food and supplies. If we have to get milk and eggs delivered more often, that's okay," said Sean.

A metal-out building was selected and stocked with freezers, coolers, and shelves. Jennifer and Wendy then decided on the first order, and Colonel John selected the staff. The first delivery arrived the next week, full of life's necessities: milk, eggs, bread, butter, cereal, canned meat plus bathroom supplies, liquid soap, toothpaste, etc. The new grocery store was a hit. All staff and military personnel had access to the store, and everyone expressed their appreciation.

Jennifer placed a notice on the website asking for suggestions on what else to order for the store and any ideas to make life at the compound easier. People in the compound appreciated being able to offer their suggestions for items to be included in the store, and somehow potato chips and ice cream kept coming up.

A good suggestion was for office and school supplies—paper, pens, and notebooks—to be available for everyone to use, especially the children.

This was quickly included in a large shelving unit just for these supplies.

Someone suggested BBQs, and Jennifer ordered in fifty American-made BBQs and had the guards put them together. All the trailers had their own BBQ, and there were plenty stationed around the apartments and in the guard areas. They were an instant hit.

Then someone suggested an automatic ice-making machine that dispensed ice cubes into your own container. Jennifer thought this was a fabulous idea and had a large commercial one ordered immediately. Now it seems that everyone has a small, insulated cooler bag to carry their ice in. In the hot desert climate, it was used around the clock, especially by the front gate guards.

Sean then contacted the website company and had this added to the Compound Rules of Conduct:

The store supplies are available to all free of charge. Any problems created by these supplies will result in the closing of the store.

The store does not and cannot supply all your needs. It is for general supplies only. You will likely still have to visit the local off-site stores to get particular items.

If you feel something should be included in the store, please send your suggestions to Jennifer Little. She handles all purchases for the compound and the store.

The Wood Shed

One really good suggestion appeared, asking if one of the metal-out buildings could become a woodworking shop. Sean loved this idea. It would be used by the staff on their off hours, plus students could use it for their tech classes.

Jennifer, not knowing anything about woodworking, asked Colonel John for his help, and he introduced her to a guard who was a woodworking hobbyist. He suggested the layout of the shop and helped her order the supplies. The layout was efficient, with the larger tools along one wall and the woodworking benches along the other. Screws, nails, and small supplies were located on industrial racks along the back. They ordered lots of wood, and the woodworking shed was an instant hit.

Sean insisted that the shed be manned by experienced woodworkers at all times.

It was decided that four qualified wood hobbyist guards would now man the woodshed from eight a.m. to eight p.m. Amazing projects were being made, and the instructors were always available to help and offer suggestions.

Electric and Appliance Repair Shed

A few days later, Sean decided that next to the wood shed, they needed a "Electric and Appliance Repair Shed. *This is where everyone could take their broken electronics for repair without having to go off the compound. Plus, any electronics or appliances beyond repair could be dismantled here and their components recycled.*

Maintenance Building

Sean also asked that one of the building be designated as a compound's maintenance building. Besides the regular maintenance equipment, he asked that there be at least one or two Jeeps with experienced handymen and tools available that the compound residents could call upon to fix the small things, like unclogging a drain, fixing a lamp, unlocking a door, etc.

Recycling Center

Sean insisted that there should be a recycling depot. *Here, people could drop off their glass bottles and aluminum cans for recycling.* He also planned on having posts stationed on the property with garbage cans hanging off them, one for glass, one for aluminum, and one for garbage for the incinerator.

Behind the main buildings and apartment buildings, there could be large bins for recycling and household garbage. He asked Colonel John to put someone in charge of the recycling depot and the recycling pickup. Colonel John took care of it immediately.

Movie, Music, and Book Library

Sean asked Wendy to allocate one metal building as a lending library for DVD movies, music CDs, and books. Sean's idea was to have the movies and music along one wall and the other wall with books. Sean suggested that Jennifer could visit the second-hand stores and buy up their movies, music, and books to get the store started. And as Sean loved old black-and-white horror movies, he asked Jennifer to include lots of those too.

When the lending library opened up, it was an instant hit. Everyone was excited to have access to movies, music, and books. People exchanged and donated their own collections. Jennifer made sure that every apartment was stocked with 50" TVs, a DVD player, and a small CD music player.

The Bowling Alley

It was Wendy who came up with the suggestion of a bowling alley. Everyone loved the idea of getting an old five-lane bowling alley brought in. Sean contacted Eric, the contractor who brought in Sean's parents' church and made his request. Eric knew of an old Brunswick bowling alley for sale and would bring Sean in for some photos.

A few days later, Eric arrived with the photos. Sean and Wendy loved it and ordered it right away. Wendy gave Eric a check to buy the bowling alley along with a fifty thousand dollars check to start with bringing the bowling alley here. They could determine its final location later on. Sean then contacted Barry and told him what he was up to and how to assist Eric with his new bowling alley.

The location was selected and within the month the bowling alley was up and running. Bowling leagues and tournaments were soon set into motion. The bowling alley instantly became a favorite spot to go, especially for the staff with families.

The Movie Cinema

Another popular suggestion was for a movie cinema. Sean and Jennifer loved the idea and set about making plans. They both shared the idea of having an old movie cinema to go along with their old bowling alley. Sean again contacted Eric, Barry's friend, and asked him to come down to meet him.

The next day Eric arrived and after Sean expressed his gratitude for Eric bringing him his parents' church and his new bowling alley, he outlined his next request.

"Eric, I want you to find me an old movie cinema. You know, the ones from the 1950s where the girl sits in the front wicket and takes your money and hands you your ticket. You then proceed down a hallway and into the lobby that sells pop, popcorn, and candy bars. The seats in the cinema are all sloping down in front of the large screen with the projector room above the seating. You know what I mean?"

"I know exactly what you mean," Eric replied. "My parents used to take me to one when I was a kid and I loved it. Why don't I start looking and when I find one, I'll fly out and look at it and then send you pictures for your approval."

"Yeah, that sounds great," said Sean. "Send the pictures to Wendy and I'll check them over. I don't care where it comes from or how much it costs. I want you to give me an authentic 1950s movie cinema right down to the upholstery seats. When you find one and we approve, contact Wendy and she'll make sure the people will get their money for the cinema and for you to move it here. Then we'll figure out where to put it. Here is a check for fifty thousand dollars to get you started."

"I'm on it, Sean and I'll let Wendy know how I make out and thank you again." Eric got up and left.

Two weeks later, Eric found the perfect 1950s movie cinema. Developers were in the process of tearing down a block of old downtown Chicago and put the entire cinema up for sale. Eric called and showed up the next day. It was exactly what Sean wanted. It was abandoned. It was dirty, and a movie hadn't been played there for likely twenty years, fabulous.

Eric forwarded the pictures to Wendy, and she showed Sean, and he was in love.

"I want that cinema!" Sean explained.

Sean was so excited that he even called the head of the corporation Miles Maxwell doing the development to tell him he was taking the cinema.

Miles was happy to hear from Sean and promised him the cinema was his. He even said that his men would help dismantle it along with Eric's men.

"My Secretary Treasurer Wendy will send you the full amount for the cinema this afternoon and please send through your invoice for the payments for your men dismantling it," said Sean.

"Sean, take my word the cinema is yours. Thank you for everything you are doing for our disabled vets and police officers. Myself and many of my employees are war veterans ourselves and we all respect what you have done. I will make sure that special care is taken. And thank you for your call," said Miles.

A site was selected for the stand-alone vintage cinema, and everyone in the compound was excited. The portable fencing was moved to allow the construction workers in, and the work on the basement and foundation started immediately. A week later, trucks started arriving with everything from the cinema: chairs, curtains, carpeting, snack bar, ticket booths, etc. Then two weeks later the big stuff started appearing, walls, roof, and stage. There just didn't seem to be any end to the trucks hauling the old building in.

Eric and Barry must have had thirty workers on the building seven days a week. Sean was so excited that he went out and promised every workman a two thousand dollars bonus when the work was completed. Two months of seven days a week, the two shifts working six hour shifts per day had the cinema up and ready to go.

Sean arranged for a copy of the not yet released MGM's new super spy thriller to be delivered to him. The only restriction placed by MGM was that the movie was not to be played until its official opening night throughout the US. Sean agreed and had movie posters made up to advertise the event.

"This way, our people won't have to go to Las Vegas to see the movie opening night," said Sean.

Opening night was a hit. You reserved your ticket online and then had to go see the girl in the wicket to get your ticket. Then, walking down the hallway, you handed your ticket to the porter, who allowed you in. Then off to the snack bar to get your pop and popcorn! You then entered the dark cinema and took your seat. As seating was limited, only an exact number of people were allowed in. After the opening night, the spy thriller played every day for one week to ensure that everyone who wanted to see it did. It was a smashing success!

Sean put his mind to work on the weekly playlist for the cinema. He decided that there would be a weekly schedule:

Sunday: Family movies, mostly Disney movies

Monday: Police movies, action

Tuesday: Romance, boy meets girl movies

Wednesday: Comedy

Thursday: Old black-and-white horror, science fiction movies

Friday: Modern horror-science fiction movies

Saturday: Action, spy, or new releases

This list, he thought, should cover just about everything. The play times would be two p.m. and seven p.m., during the week, with an additional ten p.m. feature on Friday and Saturday nights.

Sean loved the old black-and-white Dracula, Frankenstein, and Werewolf movies and couldn't wait to see them in the cinema again. His request for the first Thursday night horror film was to be his favorite horror movie, *The Wolfman* made in 1941 and starring Lon Chaney Jr.

For the first modern horror movie for Friday night, he requested the first *Alien* movie starring Sigourney Weaver—the one movie that, when he first saw it, scared him to death. The other nights, he left it up to the cinema manager and suggestions from the staff.

He did ask that a sign be placed in the cinema:

Patrons, this movie cinema has been brought in for all to enjoy.

If there is a movie that you do not like or object to, please be kind and do not attend the movie.

Likewise, any yelling or disrupting the enjoyment of the other patrons will not be tolerated.

Persons rejected by staff for their unruly behavior will have their movie privileges revoked. Basically, during any movie, keep your mouth shut and your opinions to yourself.

Everyone loved going to the movies in their own cinema. The managers placed the week's playlist on the website, and everyone planned ahead and reserved their seats online. Jennifer got together with the girls, and they made a night of dinner and went to the movies on Tuesday nights. Worked out pretty well, thought Sean.

Everyone seemed happy living in the compound. Being in a secured, guarded community, there was no crime or trouble. When Sean and Jennifer would go out for their late-night walks, they could smell the BBQs cooking and the people talking. No matter where you went, you could hear the children running around and playing games. People walked around and mingled with others with no regard for one-upmanship or who had the better of this or that. Most of the trailer sites had their own little campfires going, and Sean and Jennifer would sit down and have a drink with the people around the campfires. Always a pleasant evening walk.

The compound was turning into its own community. And everyone expressed their appreciation to Sean. Sean would say to Jennifer, "I'm happy. I've done something good here. It makes me feel good that the compound has now developed into a family community."

Chapter 37
The Sports Complex

Suggestions to improve life at the compound kept coming in. As always, it was the simple ideas that were usually the best. like suggestions for tennis and basketball courts. Sean couldn't believe that he had not thought of this himself. He called Barry to have the courts installed outside, but it was Jennifer who asked, "With the hot Nevada sun, don't you think we should have indoor and outdoor courts?"

"Yes, you are absolutely right," said Sean. "Barry could easily make us a major sports complex, and as we added more sports, he could just add on additional buildings."

So the next day, Sean set his mind toward designing a sports complex that everyone could enjoy. He decided that inside the sports complex would have:

three tennis courts
three basketball courts
three squash courts
two Olympic-sized swimming pools and one half-sized
two whirlpool spas
two large saunas, one for the women and one for the men
an Olympic-sized hockey rink (in its own separate building)
large fully equipped weight and exercise rooms
spacious lockers and showers
a soda, hot dog, and hamburger stand
administration and offices on the second floor
and a jogging track around the second level
all accessed by a center courtyard

The tennis, basketball, and squash courts were easy to explain, but he had other ideas for the pools.

Pool #1: The first pool would be for the children. One third of this pool would be two feet deep, the next third would be three feet deep, and the last third would be four feet deep. The shallow end would be closest to the entrance to the pool. There would be three permanent chairs for the lifeguards to sit in.

A Splash Pad: Beside the children's pool would be a children's splash pad, complete with the colorful climbing structures.

Pool #2: The second pool would be more for older children and adults. One third of this pool would be four feet deep, and another third would be six feet deep, and the last third would be fifteen feet deep, along with two diving boards. Likewise, there would be three permanent chairs for the lifeguards to sit in.

Pool #3: The third pool, a half Olympic-size pool, would be for wheelchair-restricted individuals. Half of the pool would be two feet deep, and the other half would be three feet deep. He would ask Barry to design a wheel chair ramp where the helpers could walk the person in the wheel chair down in the shallow end of the pool.

Two Whirlpool Spas

Sean wanted a large regular whirlpool spa over by Pool #2. Beside Pool #3, Sean wanted a three-foot-deep whirlpool spa designed just for wheelchair-restricted individuals with the same wheelchair ramp as in Pool #3. Being close together, the lifeguards could monitor both Pool #3 and the spa at the same time. This way, wheelchair-restricted individuals could have their own bathing area.

The Sports Store

Sean asked for a "Sports Store" to be fully stocked with all sporting equipment, free of charge. Sean also wanted it to be a sports lending store where people were encouraged to return their sporting goods after they had outgrown them, recycling them for the next user.

After Colonel John selected staff to man the store, Jennifer and her sister had a great time ordering supplies. "Nothing but the best and American-made" was her favorite saying.

A Hockey Rink

Being from Michigan, Sean was a huge Detroit Red Wings hockey fan. As a special treat, his dad would take him to Detroit to watch a game. Sean loved to skate himself, so a hockey arena was a natural addition. He talked to Barry about having an Olympic-sized hockey arena built in its own building for everyone to enjoy. And he wanted proper bleachers for the spectators. And with the ice pad being so large, Sean had foam dividers brought in so that the pad could be divided into three, allowing three children's hockey games to go on at once.

Outside Field Sports

Sean asked Barry to construct some outside field sports areas.

Baseball: Two baseball diamonds, one major league size for adults and a smaller one for children.

Football: Two professional-sized football fields. All the football Sean decided would be "flag" football and not "tackle" football. In "flag" football, you grab the flag hanging off the belt of the person carrying the ball instead of tackling them. Sean's reasoning was that if a military guy were to tackle a pencil pusher like himself, he'd be in the hospital. Plus, the girls could have their own teams or join the men's teams. Somehow, none of the men objected to the women playing on their teams.

Basketball: Four outside basketball courts. Sean asked that the basketball hoops extend out from their posts at least four feet so that no one would be injured by hitting the post when dunking a basket. These four courts would have two road hockey nets each to use for road hockey.

Soccer: Two professional-sized soccer fields.

Tennis. Four outside tennis courts

The fields were to have bleachers set up between the fields for the spectators, with overhead lights installed. Sean also asked for washroom facilities to be installed nearby.

The staff and guards were elated about the sports fields. They were in use immediately. Flag football teams were set up for friendly games, and everyone got involved. Teams were formed sporting colorful names like the "Desert Rats, Sand Snakes, Wandering Coyotes, and the Fierce Prairie Dogs!"

A Shooting Range

A good suggestion came from one of the guards. He suggested that the military people on their time off would enjoy a shooting range. Upon hearing the suggestion, Sean immediately said, "Of course, we have the room, and the range can be made totally out of our railway ties. What a fabulous idea!"

So with the thousands of railway ties available, Sean designed four shooting ranges fifty yards long, lined completely with railway ties. The area where the shooters stood, except the doorway, was to be completely enclosed in railway ties. Sean, who had done some clay pigeon shooting back in Crystal Falls, Michigan, asked for two outside skeet shooting areas to be set up.

Attached to these ranges was the concrete block supply shed, where the guns and ammo were stored and dispersed. Once established, eight guards were selected to man the gun range from eight a.m. to eight p.m., every day.

Sean insisted that all civilians wanting to shoot had to go through four hours of hands-on gun handling and safety instruction before being allowed to use the shooting range. Not one person complained. Sean also insisted on a strict set of rules.

You must sign into the shooting range with your compound ID card.

No card, no entrance. Only Sean Little, Ralph Barns, or Colonel John Williams may be accompanied by outside guests.

All non-military personnel must complete the four-hour gun handling and safety instruction course before using the shooting range.

No person who has consumed alcohol may be allowed to use the range.

The managers of the gun range have breathalyzers on hand, and if asked, you must comply and give them a breath sample.

Anyone attempting to use the gun range twice while intoxicated bars themselves from the gun range for life.

Any person who recklessly uses a firearm or points a firearm at another individual will be barred from the gun range for life.

The managers of the gun range may refuse entrance to or remove any person from the range without notice or reason. Their word is final.

Jennifer Visits "Desert Firearms"

Jennifer knew nothing about guns but was really excited about buying the guns and ammo for the range. She then decided that she wanted to select one gun store to supply all their needs. She asked Colonel John to accompany her to their first stop was a small country gun store called "Desert Firearms" halfway between Myerstown and Las Vegas.

Upon entering, they were met by and immediately liked Stan Rodrigues, the Mexican American owner. He was obviously an ex-military vet, short, muscular, and tattooed. Jennifer stated that she was in to buy a firearm, and Stan was very patient and helpful in showing Jennifer different firearms. He even allowed her to shoot in the gun range he had at the back of the store. When Jennifer was finished and standing at the counter, ready to make her purchase, she nodded to Colonel John. Colonel John handed Stan his list of firearms and ammunition he needed.

She later told Sean, "Here is this nice guy thinking I'm finally going to buy a gun.

Stan almost faints when Colonel John places his order in front of him. I don't know if it was the eighty rifles, the ten shotguns, the twenty handguns, the twenty large gun lockers, or the 100,000 rounds of ammunition he ordered, but the poor guy couldn't catch his breath.

He was so nervous that he couldn't write up the order. I told him to relax, and I gave him a twenty thousand dollars deposit and to bring the equipment and the rest of the bill to the guardhouse. He was so grateful, he almost kissed me. What a great guy."

A week later, Stan had to borrow his friend's farm truck to make the delivery. As it was his first trip to the compound, Colonel John hopped in the truck with him and gave him a tour of the compound before going to the gun range. He called Wendy to get a check for the remainder of Stan's bill. Once they delivered everything to the rifle range, Colonel John had Stan drive over to the office tower and take Stan up to meet Wendy to get paid.

"This is the lady that signs the checks. Be nice to her," said Colonel John with a smile.

Wendy also smiled, knowing that Colonel John used any excuse to come and visit her during working hours. When they left, Colonel John told Stan that whenever they placed an order, deliver it along with your invoice and ask for me, and I'll see to it that you are paid immediately. Stan agreed and shook Colonel John's hand vigorously.

On the website, the manager of the gun range would schedule which guns would be available to shoot on which days. For example, this coming Monday might be a single shot .22, Tuesday might be .308 Winchester, Wednesday might be 12-gauge shotgun, and the days rotated. This way, the staff only had to handle one type of gun and one type of ammo per day, reducing the chance of mix-ups.

Colonel John did request that two days per month be set aside for his men to use their own weapons on the range. This way, his men remained familiar with their own weapons and remained in practice. The 10th and 20th days of every month were set aside for military personnel to use the range exclusively.

On the tenth day of the next month, Colonel John presented Sean with his own Smith and Wesson pistol saying, "One day, you may need this."

Colonel John then insisted that Sean accompany him to the firing range to "get comfortable with your new gun."

Sean went along, and Colonel John instructed Sean on its use and made him fire off over fifty rounds. Colonel John showed Sean how to clean his handgun and how to properly store it. Sean thanked Colonel John for the gift and promised to keep it in his office drawer.

"You are right, I may need this one day," said Sean.

Chapter 38
A Rock Concert

Up until this time, they had frequent requests to do husband-and-wife applications at the same time, and they refused. It just seemed more logical to do women for a month and men the next month. But the requests kept coming in, and Ralph simply ignored them.

One day, Sean was reviewing the list of paid-in applicants. One caught his eye.

That was for the four members of "Glider" their wives, backup musicians, and managers. They paid for twenty applications in advance. *Incredible, one group has sent in one billion dollars to have their treatments. Who would have guessed?* thought Sean. But along with their payments was the request that they have the treatment done the same week as their wives. So the first week was ten applications for the musicians and their wives, and two weeks later, ten applications for their managers and backup musicians.

Sean had an idea and ran it across Colonel John, Wendy, and Ralph. His idea was that, as the three basketball courts and three tennis courts all had removable walls between them, these could be opened up to make room for a rock concert. He then asked Wendy if she could contact "Glider" to see if they would put on a free concert on Sunday evening before getting their applications. He wanted this to be a surprise for Jennifer and the entire compound, so secrecy was a must. Colonel John and Wendy went to work and arranged everything. Wendy was surprised when she called the manager of the group, who instantly agreed to put on the concert for them, saying, "For Sean Little and for what he's doing to clean up the world, I'm sure they would be more than happy to play."

Colonel John arranged for the sports complex to be "closed for repairs" for two days. They set up a makeshift stage in one basketball court and opened all the partitions between the basketball and tennis courts.

The band's equipment crews came in and were escorted to the sports complex the morning of the concert. Colonel John was at the main gate to usher them through. This was a small venue, so their massive equipment was not needed—just the band's instruments themselves. Everything else would be supplied at the compound. They were allowed to stay for the concert, and it was agreed that they would be escorted back to the Parkway Hotel with their equipment at the end of the show.

That day, Sean placed a special announcement on the website requesting that everyone not on duty attend the sports complex for a special event at seven p.m. that evening. The announcement worked, and everyone not on duty showed up.

One hour before the concert, three blacked-out SUVs arrived at the front gate, with the first SUV being driven by Colonel John himself. At the gate, he did not allow any of the guards to look into the vehicles and the guards waved the three vehicles through.

He parked at the back of the sports complex and ushered the members of "Glider" and their wives into a private room off to one side.

Realizing the hundreds of construction personnel would like to attend the concert but, for safety reasons, could not, Sean got Barry two large 90" flat-screen TVs for their mess hall and hooked up the video feeds of the concert. The staff enjoyed the concert and used the TVs for watching sports and playing movies later on. A sure-win situation.

Rumors abounded, but obviously, everyone knew that a rock concert was going to take place. *Tough keeping a secret in this place,* thought Sean. People started showing up two hours in advance in order to get close to the front, just like a real rock concert. There were those in blue jeans and shirts and those women in fancy evening gowns like Wendy and Jennifer. There was excitement in the air, and everyone was talking.

The Rock Group "Glider"

When the time came, Wendy walked over and took center stage. "Ladies and gentlemen, we have all been asked to attend this special event held for Jennifer Little's birthday. This is a once-in-a lifetime opportunity. Ladies and gentlemen, may I introduce to you the greatest rock and roll band of all time?

"Glider."

Everyone went wild. The band members wives then came out, and Holly Dobson, the wife of the lead singer, introduced herself to Jennifer, and she and the rest of the band members wives stood with Jennifer and danced. Holly was a beautiful lady, tall, slim, with wavy dark hair, and truly excited to be here and get the application.

Nathan Dobson and the band came out, and with just a wave to the crowd, started in with their early hits, and the crowd went crazy. Nathan was a slender, short fellow with a long gray beard and a ponytail. But boy, can he sing? Jennifer had tears in her eyes. She was so happy. She couldn't stop jumping up and down. They played their early hits and then broke for an intermission.

Keith Davidson then took the mike. "Ladies and gentlemen, Sean Little and Jennifer Little. We are playing for you tonight not only because we are here for an application of Sean's wonder drug but also because of the world-wide benefit that all of you are doing. I am speaking for the world right now, and the world appreciates the environmental actions taken by Sean Little and everyone in this compound. We are playing to thank you and are proud to be here before you." The crowd couldn't stop cheering.

And being in a small venue, the four band members came off the makeshift stage and mingled with the crowd. There must have been thousand selfies taken with the band members. At Sean's request, the band members crowded around Jennifer for a group photo. Jennifer was crying. She was so happy!

Back on stage, "Glider" played hits from their more recent albums. The wives of the band and Jennifer kept dancing together. At the end of the performance, the band again mingled with the crowd and made their way to the restaurant.

With the limited seating, Colonel John had the tables reserved. The staff in the restaurant could leisurely talk to the band members and their wives. Keith Davidson asked Ralph what he could eat and drink, and Ralph replied with, "Eat and drink anything you want because you won't be for the next four days." And everyone laughed.

After an evening of good music and food, the band members were escorted to their guest trailers for a good night's sleep. Colonel John had guards posted outside of the guest trailer area with strict instructions that they were not to be disturbed for any reason.

The next morning, the band members and their wives entered into

Ralph's care.

They all agreed to have their heads shaved and then entered their observation rooms. The lab assistants were so excited about meeting the members of "Glider" in person. The band members requested, and Ralph made the exception and allowed them to bring in some guitars to play while they were there. Ralph also supplied them with tape recorders in case they were working on a song. The band members appreciated being able to use their instruments and were looking forward to being five years younger. Ralph and Sean knew that they would be telling all their musical friends about the procedure. And as Sean always says, "With responses like this, who needs to advertise?"

New Stage

After the "Glider" concert, naturally, everyone wanted more. *Oh, well, why not?* thought Sean. He contacted Barry and requested that the basketball and tennis court buildings be extended to include a permanent stage. Ralph assured him that it would be an easy thing to open up one wall and build an additional building with a music and performing arts stage, complete with curtains and sound equipment. Barry assured Sean that he would put a rush on this new building, and it would likely be up and running in 4–6 weeks.

The Rock Group, "The Ancient Minstrels"

A month went by, and another husband-and-wife request came in from the "Ancient Minstrels," a British rock group headed up by their lead singer, Brenden Knowles. Their modern rock adaptations of old English ballads had taken the world by storm. It seemed that every song they wrote became an instant worldwide hit. Jennifer loved their music, as did most of the people in the compound.

They paid for ten applications up front and, like "Glider" wanted their wives to have the application at the same time. With the new stage area almost complete, Sean asked Wendy to contact them for a free concert on Sunday night before their applications on Monday. Wendy said it was a "go" and made the arrangements with Ralph to have the husbands and wives come in together.

As before, Colonel John escorted the primary band technicians the day before to set up the equipment. They only needed to bring in the guitars, keyboards, and drum kit as the new stage was outfitted with the latest and best American-made sound equipment.

A few hours before the concert, Colonel John escorted the group and their wives in, and the performance was amazing. Sean ordered five-hundred stacking chairs, but nobody could sit and watch the "Ancient Minstrels" play just before their eyes. Jennifer, of course, was jumping up and down. She was so happy. Sean thought to himself, *Well, these concerts are certainly becoming a regular event.*

Being a small venue of less than five-hundred well-behaved people, the band members and their wives easily mingled with the crowd. Again, there must have been thousand selfies taken. At the end of the concert, Brenden expressed his admiration for Sean's work toward cleaning up the planet, and everyone gave a round of applause for Sean. They made their way to the restaurant area, and as before, it was reserved seating only.

Before ordering the dinner, Ralph stood up and said, "You had all better eat well because you won't be getting any real food for the next four days." And everyone laughed.

After the dinner, Brenden came over and sat by Sean, and they easily fell into a conversation. Brenden was a guy who had been in a struggling rock group for twenty years. He was mid-40ish with long hair and looked like he had seen one too many bars in his day.

"How did you guys get started?" asked Sean. "You exploded onto the world stage like a tidal wave. One day I didn't even know your name, and in one day, that's all that's playing on the radio. I even heard that they can't keep up with the demand for your records, CDs, and internet downloads. Is that true?"

"Yes, Sean, it's true. The guys and I have been together for over twenty years now, playing in local bars, and then one day a record producer guy comes in with his friends and goes nuts over us. We think he's drunk, so don't think much about it. Then two days later, the same guy comes up and gives us twenty thousand dollars cash and wants us to play a gig in a hall in London. We, of course, accept. We play the hall, and they ask us to stay in our hotel rooms the next day, and they'll see us at two p.m.

"At two p.m., we walk all these suits and their lawyers and have contracts all printed out, and all we have to do is sign, and they'll make us stars. They gave us $100,000 each on signing. So here we are, a down-and-out rock band playing our versions of old English ballads, and in two weeks we will be the headliners for our own European and American rock concert tours.

"That's pretty amazing," replied Sean. "Well, Jennifer and I really love your music, and I guess so do a few million more." Then the conversation moved on to more current matters.

Sean Explains His Reasons for Only Doing Environmental Projects

"Sean, thank you," said Brenden. "I must also compliment you on your world-wide environment efforts. I wish there were more persons like you in positions of power. The world would certainly be a better place. But Sean, if you don't mind me asking, I notice that you are handling only environmental issues and not political ones. Why is that?"

"Good question," replied Sean. "With the environmental issues, I have a set start and a finish date, and these are issues that everyone else is afraid to touch or even talk about. I am not a political person. I am an architect. So I understand this start-and-finish process and can direct the money and resources to see it through. Plus, by doing only environmental issues, I try to distance myself as far as possible from the politicians who want to get involved for their own personal gain."

"Yes, I know what you mean, replied Brenden. "My work in Africa, trying to establish schools and hospitals and feed the poor, has met with not only government interference but also government corruption. Everybody there wants a kickback to approve building a hospital, a school, or supplying food or water for the poor. It's sickening. But still, Sean, they need your help."

"Yes, Brenden, and one day they'll get it," replied Sean. "But for right now, my intention is to clean up the planet. I want to prove that we can have an industrial society that cleans up its own waste at the same time. Right now, we have an industrial society that discards its waste and does nothing to eliminate it. In the Pacific Ocean, for example, there are billions of tons of garbage floating in the sea, and nobody even talks about it except me."

"But some of your efforts could be put toward helping the poor around the world," replied Brenden.

"Yes, you're right, and I admire your humanitarian efforts in Africa," replied Sean. "But for right now, I am tackling a few major projects and seeing them through to their completion. I feel that no matter how I try to help people directly, there is someone else saying that I'm a terrible person and that I'm not helping them either. Where do I start?"

"Yes, Sean, I agree," replied Brenden. "In Africa, for example, if you help build a school in one country, the politicians in the neighboring countries start screaming "favoritism". It always seems that while you're trying to help one group, the others around them are always mad at you. Sean, I understand your frustration."

"Brenden," replied Sean. "I appreciate your input, and your points are well taken. What I would like you to do is write out how you think I could help the world once my environmental efforts are finished. Especially your thoughts on improving the world's food supply and then improving health care and education in the less developed areas of the world."

"Yes, Sean, I'll write out my ideas when I'm in your observation rooms. Heaven knows I'll have enough time to think about them." And they both laughed. At this point, both Jennifer and Brenden's wives came and broke them both up and got them up to dance.

New Forms in the Observation Rooms

Sean kept thinking about his conversation with Brenden. *Maybe my focus is too narrow? Maybe there are other areas to help the world I should be considering? Best way to accept new ideas is to have the people getting treatments write out their ideas on how I can help the world.* He then designed forms on his computer for the applicants to fill out while they were in their rooms.

Help Me Help the World Forms

The forms Sean designed had spaces for the applicant's name, their position in their home country, contact information, and most importantly, their application number.

I, Sean Little, welcome your ideas on how I can further work toward helping our world and its people. I am especially interested in ideas on cleaning up the environment, improving the world food supply, and improving health and education. I will personally read each and every suggestion. I will only contact you back if I have a question.

Form #1: Cleaning Up the World

Please use this form to write out your ideas on how I, Sean Little, could use my resources to help clean up our world.

Form #2: Cleaning Up Your Country

Please use this form to write out your ideas on how I, Sean Little, could use my resources to help clean up an environment problem in your country.

Form #3: Helping Out Your People

Please use this form to write out your ideas on how I, Sean Little, could use my resources to help out your fellow countrymen. For example, improving agriculture, building hospitals, building schools, etc.

Everyone he showed the forms thought they were a great idea.

"Maybe these forms should be put on the website for people to print off and email in," Jennifer mentioned.

"Email is too easy, and everyone would be sending us nuisance emails. By having them mailed in, maybe the replies would be a little more serious," replied Sean.

So from that point on, each observation room had a quantity of forms for people to fill out, and the website had the same forms for people to print off and mail in.

Sean made a point of reading all the suggestions from the people getting the applications. As for the forms that were being mailed in, he had these read by Wendy's staff to eliminate the nuisance mail and only allow the more serious suggestions through. This system was working out well, and he filed those suggestions he liked for future consideration.

Chapter 39
Doing Applications to Males

After a year of doing mostly applications to females, Sean figured they had done around 260 applications so far. Wendy had informed him that he had received about thirteen billion dollars in the last year, minus expenses and taxes, and still had four billion dollars left in the bank.

The requests to start doing male subjects kept coming in, and Ralph and Sean simply ignored them. *Maybe if I make them wait, they won't be such egotistical idiots when they get here,* hoped Sean. But he did have to admit that doing the musical groups worked very well.

News reporters kept saying that a discovery of this magnitude should be shared with the world. Sean would always say his favorite joke, "I am sharing it with the world, but only with those people who have fifty million dollars to spend."

The world-wide clamor for Sean to start doing male subjects grew louder. Even the President of the United States and his VP, John Harper, had been asking him, "Sean, please start doing male subjects. Whenever I meet a head of state, that's all they want to talk about is you. Please reconsider."

Sean and Ralph discussed this and made some updates to their list of conditions.

Additional Conditions for the Applications

We, "the company, Sean Little Inc." have decided to start doing the "age reversing" process on male subjects with the following conditions:

All applications are done at our secure federal military compound located in Nevada, USA.

We are now accepting male subjects between the ages of 40–70 years of age for our age-reversing applications. We will base our candidate selections on favoring those years.

Applicants who speak English will be given priority. If we decide to do an application to someone who does not speak English, we will supply our own interpreters to assist the staff attending to them.

Sports figures and athletes will only be approved after five years from the date they formally retired.

Who is and who is not accepted is at the sole discretion of "the company." Any candidate may be refused the application at any time for any reason and will have their money refunded.

The cost of the procedure is fifty million in US dollars. There are no discounts, and there are no deals, so don't ask.

Once notified of your successful placement, each successful candidate will have twenty-four hours to deposit their monies in full into our bank account. Partial payments are unacceptable. Failure to have this money deposited in full within the required twenty-four hours disqualifies that candidate from the application.

You are required to send us your doctor's medical report along with a list of any medicines you are taking. We expect that your medical report will be honest and accurate. Our doctors here will supply you with your medications.

You will be physically re-examined by our doctors upon your arrival. Any evidence of your physician making a false report to us, for example, hiding an undisclosed medical condition, will render you unfit for the application, and you will be asked to leave. Your money will then be refunded.

This process has proven quickly fatal to anyone with cancer. You will be tested for this disease. Once this disease is discovered, your application will not proceed, and your money will be refunded.

Upon arrival at the compound, you will sign the mandatory disclaimer form, absolving "the company" of any wrongdoing before, during, or after the application.

"The company" cannot be held liable in the event of your illness or death caused by this application. If you have an undisclosed illness that both your doctors and our doctors fail to uncover, you will die during this procedure, and "the company" cannot be held liable.

Once selected, you are expected to reside at the Parkway Hotel in Las Vegas until you are called. On your appointed day, you will be picked up by one of our vehicles and accompanied by armed guards to the compound, which is about an hour's drive away. No one else may accompany you on the ride to the compound.

Do not approach the compound in any other manner. If you attempt to arrive here in a helicopter, for example, you will be arrested and placed in jail, and your means of transportation will be destroyed.

We will not apply the application to any sitting member of the US Federal, State or any US government agencies. This is regardless of whether they meet the above qualifications or not.

The Procedure

Your body weight will not change. If you weigh two-fifty pounds going into the procedure, you will weigh two-fifty pounds coming out, minus the weight you lost while fasting.

You may not be accompanied by an assistant, nor will you be allowed to have an assistant or family member on the property while you are in our care. You are not allowed visitors for any reason.

You are not allowed to bring anything with you. Nothing.

Do not bring Sean Little a gift. All gifts will be refused, and if accepted, they will be donated to a local charity auction to help the needy.

All jewellery or religious artifacts will be taken from you. These and your clothes will be returned to you when you leave.

Your head will be shaven bare. This you can do before you arrive, or our staff will do this for you. This is a mandatory condition of the procedure.

For the duration of the process, there can be nothing touching your skin except your white robe.

You will be cut off from the outside world for the duration of your stay. You will not be permitted to take in or have access to a phone or a computer. While here, you will not be able to receive, make a phone call, or send an email, regardless of the reason. We will notify your family of your condition.

You will be supplied with a TV, a movie channel, and any books or magazines you desire. You will also be supplied with pens and paper to write with.

It is accepted that all applicants have watched the introductory video and realize upon arrival that their heads will be shaved, they will be *showered, their clothes will be removed, and they will be wearing only white robes and slippers for the remainder of their stay.*

You agree that for your first two days (forty-eight hours) here, you will be locked in an observation room and be fasting with only water to drink. At the end of your first two days (forty-eight hours), you will be washed and your body coated with olive oil. You will then be strapped onto a gurney and wheeled down to the lab for the application.

The application will be performed at the start of the third day. You will meet Sean Little during the brief time he is administering the formula to you. Other than a customary greeting, Sean Little will not talk to you. This is the only time that you will meet Sean Little.

After the application, you will be brought back to your room, where you will be given only bread and water for the remaining two days (forty-eight hours). You will be released at the end of the fifth day, examined by our medical people and returned to the Parkway Hotel. Releasing you sooner almost guarantees that you will get an infection and die.

After your treatment and for the following two weeks, you will notice that the outer layer of your skin is turning to fine dust. This is a natural process of the old skin being replaced with the newer, younger skin.

These conditions apply to all persons and are designed for your safety in mind. These conditions are mandatory. There are no exceptions.

Failure to abide by the above conditions renders you unfit for the application.

Ralph looked over the conditions and was satisfied.

"I like the part where we can refuse to treat anyone for any reason and that we cannot be held liable for any problems caused by the application," said Ralph.

"No kidding. I will forward this to the website company right away and ensure that the applicants print off a copy and forward a signed copy to us," said Sean.

"But Sean, why don't you only want to do sports figures and athletes only after they have been retired for five years?" asked Ralph.

"Look at it this way: if we start doing applications to athletes as they start getting older, there will be no room for younger, new athletes to advance and play on their team. Take football, for example. The teams would be full of players who we kept young, leaving no room for new players to advance. I think it would be bad for any sport and unfair to the new rising stars."

"Fair enough," replied Ralph. "Plus, knowing the problems we had before when doing men, I propose that in our new building we continue to do ten applicants every two weeks, like we have been doing with the females."

"I agree, let's go easy to start," said Sean.

The conditions were placed on the website, and the response was deafening.

There must have been five-hundred applicants immediately. Both Sean and Ralph had to decide on how to weed out the unlikely candidates. Naturally, the athlete's requests were ignored by those still active in their sport.

Applications to Movie Stars and Celebrities

Ralph then came up with the idea of, "We have so many applicants. Let's start accepting them via their occupation. I propose, with California so close, let's start doing applications to local media celebrities to start."

"Seems good to me. Our experience with doing businessmen is that they are always too aggressive," said Sean.

With the help of some lab assistants, the most likely media celebrities were selected. Once notified, their medical reports and monies came in within the hour. They took the top ten candidates and notified them to arrive at the Parkway Hotel. A few selected were at movie locations, so the staff simply went down the list to select alternative candidates. Now that the ten suitable candidates were comfortably lodged in the hotel, they were prepared to proceed.

The media celebrities were naturally swamped by onlookers and news reporters at the hotel. They were accustomed to it. They proceeded with their armed guards to the compound and were immediately disrobed, showered, and given white robes to wear. Then they were examined by the compound doctors and proven to be healthy and free of disease. The three that had not shaven their heads were brought into a room and had their heads shaved, whether they liked it or not. All ten candidates were then led into their observation rooms. A TV with all the sports and movie channels was provided, as were any books or magazines they requested. All asked for but were refused a laptop computer.

For the next two days, the patients got along with their staff quite well. The staff were so excited to be able to meet and talk to famous celebrities, and the two days passed quickly. At the start of the third day, the staff entered their observation rooms, insisted that their subjects have a good shower, and then applied olive oil to their bodies. Once applied, the subjects were asked to lie down on the gurney and were securely strapped down. They were led to the elevator.

Arriving at the lab, Sean Little and Ralph introduced themselves and had a brief chat. All subjects reported talking to others who had undergone the process and were excited about the idea of being five years younger. Sean administered the formula.

The subjects were wheeled back to their rooms. *No problems,* thought Sean.

Upon their release and return to the Parkway Hotel, they were mobbed by a crowd of onlookers and reporters. This is what they expected, and most gave a full account of the procedure. All seemed pleased with how they felt, and when questioned about their hair falling out, one movie star replied with, "Who cares? It will grow back. Besides, I like my new hat." And everyone laughed. Once this hit the celebrity news channels, Sean knew that every celebrity in the world would want the formula. And, as he was always fond of saying, "With media coverage like this, who needs to advertise?"

They continued down the list of celebrities. Doing ten subjects every two weeks didn't seem to diminish the list of people who requested an application. After a few months the number of celebrities dwindled, and Sean and Ralph thought they would open the applications to others.

Chapter 40
Applications to World Leaders

Sean and Ralph decided to start looking at candidates from all over the world.

The torrent of requests was incredible. At the request of the Vice President, they began accepting applications from other countries' businessmen and politicians.

The Vice President's requests for "free applications" for themselves and those world leaders friendly to the United States were simply ignored. Sean had to constantly remind the Vice President, "Once we start doing applications for free, they'll all be free. Everyone pays, no exceptions."

Unfortunately, whenever they did the applications to businessmen, they always insisted on talking to Sean about their "special deal." This was solved by one of the lab assistants placing a small wedge-shaped piece of plastic that would be lodged into the subject's mouths once the subjects started yelling at Sean. Being strapped down seemed to quieten most men, and the plastic wedge lodged in their mouths worked on those who became agitated. Ralph and Sean felt that these men getting upset was a natural reaction to them not being in control and being separated from their families and staff for days.

Other than Sean dropping in to administer the formula, Ralph and Sean would get together for lunch once per week, and Ralph would entertain Sean with the stories of the businessmen going nuts in their observation rooms, wanting to be let out or to see Sean for their great ideas.

"You'd think that when one of these businessmen start yelling at you, you'd swear they just scored a touchdown in the Super Bowl," said Ralph. Both of them laughed.

"Thank heavens. We strap everyone down and place the plastic wedges in the mouths of the unruly ones. I can't handle any more men jumping off their beds and grabbing me," said Sean.

"Yeah, no kidding, obviously, the guys with that type of money are accustomed to being in control, and being caged up must drive them nuts. I think it's incredibly important that we keep them cut off from the outside world while they are here. Heaven knows the trouble they would cause if they could call back home," said Ralph.

"You're right," said Sean. "Can you imagine us doing a world leader and he gets mad or depressed about three days in and orders his military to attack us? We'd make the evening news with that, I bet."

Sean and Ralph were to find out quickly that doing applications to foreign politicians was a whole different set of problems. The first group of politicians was selected, and their medical information and money were sent in.

Later, talking to Wendy, she said, "With the speed they sent their money and medical reports in, they've likely been waiting months, so have everything ready to go once they read your announcement. But Sean, why do you have them stay in the Parkway Hotel and then be driven one hour to the compound? Wouldn't it be easier to have them come here?"

"Good point, Wendy. But I feel we have to establish our authority at the start because these world leaders and businessmen are accustomed to being in control. By ordering them to stay at the Parkway Hotel and then driving them one hour to the compound establishes who is the boss. They are picked up where we say and when we say, no exceptions. Any closer to us, and we would have thousands of their staff and family members hanging around out front."

"You know, Sean, I think you're right. Anyone with fifty million dollars to spend is accustomed to being obeyed, so by establishing control early on, we eliminate their attitudes and excessive demands right at the start. And could you imagine the grief we would have if we let them and their entourage come here? It would be a nightmare."

"No kidding," replied Sean, and both of them laughed.

Sean then told Wendy that he asked Jennifer to purchase ten Lincoln Navigators, all in the same color, to be used for picking up people from the Parkway Hotel.

"Might as well treat these self-important businessmen and diplomats in the way that they are accustomed. Plus, it will likely make their drive to the compound a little nicer.

"Yes, I agree," said Wendy. "They're paying fifty million dollars for a treatment, and they're getting picked up in blacked-out military Yukon's. I think the Lincoln idea is a good one."

Jennifer Buys Lincoln Navigators

The next day, Jennifer and Emily got dressed up and visited a local Las Vegas Lincoln dealer. As Jennifer wanted to go into the dealership alone with her sister, she had the guards park down the road, and they walked in by themselves. Once in, they asked to be served by the newest member of the sales staff. They were then introduced to Judi Postar, a new sales lady who had just started two days prior. Obviously a little nervous, she immediately apologized, saying that she was new to the business and that she would do the best she could. Judi was short, with long, curly hair, and well-dressed. Jennifer and Emily liked her immediately.

Jennifer said that she was interested in a full-size Lincoln SUV. Judi showed them the Lincoln Navigator in the showroom. Jennifer and Emily both got in and liked what they saw. Judi offered to bring one up front for a test drive, and Jennifer declined, saying it was not necessary.

Now, with both Jennifer and Emily sitting at Judi's desk, Judi just sat there and looked at Jennifer, obviously too afraid to ask for the order. Jennifer, realizing this, just smiled and said that she would like to order not one but twelve Lincoln Navigators, all black with tan leather interiors. Jennifer felt she needed ten Lincolns to transport the dignitaries around and two as spares, for twelve in total.

Judi was so confused that she picked up the phone and told her manager. The manager came out and, seeing that Judi was getting flustered, introduced himself, then went and got Mark, his fleet manager. When he returned, he introduced Mark and informed Jennifer that Mark would be handling the transaction. Jennifer calmly looked at them both and said, "No, Judi is doing a fine job here, and I like her. I do not want to deal with either of you two gentlemen, and Judi can proceed with the order."

The manager, fearing he might lose this huge sale, protested, saying that Judi was new and would likely make a mistake. Jennifer then calmly replied with, "I guess you didn't hear me. I have the time for Judi to collect herself and write up the order. I will be dealing with her and her alone. Now you two gentlemen may leave us alone. I'm sure if Judi has a question, she can go and ask you. Thank you and goodbye."

The sales manager wisely bid Jennifer goodbye, and both he and Mark returned to their offices.

Jennifer already had Wendy write out a $500,000 dollar deposit check made out to the Lincoln dealership in advance and show the check to Judi. Judi was in such shock that she started crying. Both Jennifer and Emily went over and gave her a big hug, telling her that everything was okay.

"Let's do this. Why don't you come to lunch with us, and we can let your sales manager write up the orders? This way, you get a nice lunch, and the manager gets to feel important. When we return, I'll sign all the papers, and you'll have made your first sale."

So as Judi was composing herself, Jennifer went over to the manager's office and, while standing in the doorway, said, "Judi has just sold me twelve Lincoln Navigators, all black in color with tan leather interiors. This is her deal, and her deal alone. Here is a half-million-dollar deposit check. I am taking her for lunch, and when I return, I will sign the orders."

Jennifer then just turned around and got Judi by the hand, and all three left the showroom. While standing outside the showroom door, Judi was shocked when Jennifer simply pulled out her cell phone and made a call. Moments later, eight blacked-out military Yukon SUVs drove onto the lot, and four heavily armed guards got out and opened the doors of their vehicles for Jennifer, Emily, and Judi to get in. Emily got in first, and Jennifer motioned to Judi to get in, and in shock, she did. Seeing the surprise on Judi's face, Emily said, "Believe me, it's a shock at first, but you get used to it."

Jennifer then asked Judi what restaurant you always wanted to go to but never did. Judi mentioned a restaurant that only the very rich could go to, and Jennifer looked it up on her phone and made the reservation for three. The girls went in on their own, and the two guards, who were dressed in suits, also accompanied them but sat at their own tables. The guards took a table in the corner, where they could see the entire restaurant and the girls. The rest of the guards stayed outside and surrounded the building. All three girls had a wonderful time together, and then Jennifer took Emily and Judi to her favorite dress store. Likewise, the two guards in suits accompanied them inside the dress store.

"Can't go to Las Vegas without buying a new outfit," said Jennifer.

They all picked out two outfits each and had a great time. Jennifer asked Judi to spend the day with her at the compound when the Lincolns were delivered. Now, when returning to the dealership, Jennifer signed the purchase agreements and made sure that Judi signed herself on the agreements. Now completed, she gave the sales manager Colonel John's card, saying, "If you have any questions, contact Colonel John at this number." Then she got up, and after giving Judi a big hug, she and Emily left.

Upon finding out who the vehicles were for, the Ford Motor Company put a rush on the order, and they arrived in a month. All the Lincolns were driven by dealership employees to the main gate and driven in by the guards themselves.

Jennifer was waiting for Judi, who was escorted into the compound by Colonel John. Jennifer and Emily had a guard give them and Judi a tour of the compound in one of the new Lincolns. The three got along famously. Over lunch, Judi explained that her husband Nelio was a mechanic at the Nellis Air Force Base. Nelio did a tour in Afghanistan, but being a mechanic, he did not see any action. She said that she took the sales job at the Lincoln dealership to earn some extra money. She said she and Nelio were married as soon as he returned and were saving up to buy a house and have a baby. Jennifer's heart melted.

After spending a fabulous day together, Jennifer and Emily escorted Judi back home in one of the Lincolns. Judi lived in a modest rented apartment on the outskirts of Las Vegas. They all hugged each other and promised to get together again.

Upon arriving back at the base, Jennifer searched out Colonel John and asked him to investigate Nelio Postar, a mechanic now working at the Nellis Air Force base, and report back to her. Within two hours, Colonel John reported that Nelio Postar was a respected mechanic at the base and had a solid record of his tour of duty overseas.

Jennifer, hearing this, asked Colonel John to seek him out, take him for lunch, and report back on what he thought of him. Colonel John did not know why, but wisely complied.

Two days later, Colonel John reported that he had spent an enjoyable afternoon with Nelio Postar and felt that he was a fine individual and a quality mechanic. He said that his superiors spoke highly of him. She asked Colonel John, point blank, "Colonel John, do you believe that Nelio Postar would be a good addition to our staff here?"

"Yes, I do," replied Colonel John. "Everyone I spoke to said that if it was on four wheels, Nelio could fix it. We could sure use a top-level auto mechanic around here. We certainly have enough vehicles, and taking them off the compound for common repairs is becoming a nuisance. And besides, I like the guy."

"Great, I am going to invite Nelio and his wife, Judi, to come and spend the day with us. I'll let you know the date," replied Jennifer.

That was good enough for Jennifer. She contacted Judi and invited her and Nelio to come and spend the day at the compound. They arranged for the following Wednesday, and Jennifer let Colonel John know of their arrival. Jennifer and Emily met them at the main gate and gave them a tour of the compound. Nelio was short in stature but built like a pro football player. He had a big smile and a friendly manner, and Jennifer liked him immediately. Nelio, upon being introduced to Jennifer, said, "I've heard about the compound here but never thought I'd ever see inside. The whole world is talking about your husband's environmental projects, and the help he is giving disabled veterans and police officers is simply amazing."

Jennifer had the guard drive over to the office tower, and she went up and got Sean to come down for lunch. Jennifer simply barged into Sean's office and waited for Sean to get off the phone.

"Sean, put your work away. You're coming to lunch," Jennifer demanded.

"But Jennifer, I'm too busy," Sean protested.

"You're always too busy," Jennifer said in a commanding voice. "You're coming to lunch right now and meeting someone I invited to tour the compound. Now put your notes away and let's get going."

Things sure change after you get married. Sean smiled to himself. He calmly did as he was told and came downstairs, and after introductions to Judi and Nelio, they walked over to the restaurant for lunch. At the end of the meal, they parted company, and Jennifer escorted them back to their car at the main gate.

Later that night, Jennifer told Sean that she had Colonel John check out Nelio, take him to lunch, and give her his opinions.

"I want you to talk to Colonel John about having Nelio and Judi come to join us on the base. He says that Nelio is a top mechanic, and with him here, we would not have to be sending our vehicles off the compound for repairs."

Sean knew exactly where this was going, so he promised to talk to

304

Colonel John in the morning. After their meeting, Colonel John again contacted Nelio and requested that they meet for lunch that day. Colonel John simply told Nelio that he and Judi were being asked to become part of the compound community, and he would like their answer in forty-eight hours. Nelio would have his own mechanic shop, and Judi could take a job somewhere on the compound. Colonel John explained, "If you're looking to save money to buy a house, this is it. You get thousand dollars per week over and above your regular military salary. Judi can quit her job at the dealership and will get at least thousand dollars per week, regardless of how she helps out around here. You can live either in the apartments or in a trailer free of charge, and we have a free grocery store here. All the services of the compound are free.

"There are plenty of brand new vehicles to drive, some for inside the compound and some for outside, so you can even give up your car if you want. There are no restrictions on leaving the compound, but naturally, you do have to check in and out at the main gate. I can make a call and have you posted here, but we would prefer to let it be both of your decisions. Talk it over with Judi and get back to me."

The next morning, Nelio contacted Colonel John and said they would be delighted to become part of their community. Colonel John contacted Sean, and Sean approved. Colonel John made the call to the commander at the Nellis Air Force Base and arranged Nelio's transfer, which was put into effect immediately.

Sean called Jennifer and told her the good news. Jennifer was so excited that she immediately called Judi and told her she was taking her to lunch. Two hours later, Jennifer, Wendy, and Emily showed up at the dealership in one of the new Lincolns, flanked by eight military SUVs full of military guards. For dramatic effect, the three girls entered the showroom with two heavily armed guards with automatic weapons strapped to their chests. Jennifer went over to Judi, gave her a hug, and said we were going for lunch

"But I'm on shift. I can't go."

"No," replied Jennifer, "you're quitting and taking a job at the base. Now say goodbye and let's get out of here!"

Wendy then walked over to the sales manager's office and informed him that Judi was quitting and leaving immediately. If he had any questions, he was to contact herself, and she handed him her card. The manager wanted to protest, but when a lady who is talking to you is also standing in front of two very large and heavily armed guards sporting automatic rifles, you don't argue.

All four girls had a wonderful time over lunch describing life at the compound. Somehow, they couldn't stop laughing. They were having so much fun. Maybe it was the wine. Then off to a dress store to buy new outfits.

When they dropped off Judi at her apartment, Jennifer and Emily said they would be back tomorrow to help Judi pack. And true to their word, at nine a.m., Jennifer, Emily, and thirty plus guards showed up to help pack and move them both to the compound. Fifteen of the guards stood duty while another fifteen helped carry down the boxes. Nelio, being in the military, was comfortable being around these men, but Judi was still in shock at this unlikely turn of events.

Back at the base, they decided to stay in a trailer and settled in comfortably.

Judi took a job as a nurse's assistant in the clinic, and the four girls became close friends. Sean was shaking his head and thinking, *Just another friend for Jennifer to take shopping.*

Chapter 41
Problems with World Leaders

Parkway Hotel Problem #1

Everything was going smoothly until the day the world leaders were to be picked up from the Parkway Hotel. Each vehicle in turn waited with three guards, one driving, one in the front passenger seat, and one in the back beside the applicant. The first three vehicles picked up their assigned passengers without a problem and proceeded to the compound. The next vehicles drove up, and the guard in the back got out and announced the name of the passenger, Mr. Hans Falbersham, a German industrialist.

Mr. Falbersham approached, and the guard compared his picture to that of the individual, checked his ID, and then nodded his head in approval. But upon opening the rear door to let Mr. Falbersham enter the vehicle, Mr. Falbersham's young assistant, Paul, came running out and tried to enter the limo.

This took the guard by surprise. The guard in the front seat got out to assist, and both guards and Paul were in a scuffle. The pencil-pushing Paul was no match for the heavily armed and physically fit guards and was quickly subdued. One guard held Paul in a neck hold while the other guard asked, "What is going on here? You were told that no one may accompany you in your drive to the compound. This was clearly spelled out to you."

"What harm is there with him coming along? I don't go anywhere without my assistant," argued Mr. Falbersham.

Colonel John had witnessed the altercation, approached the group, and said, "Mr. Falbersham, you decide right now. Do you want to go with us to the compound for the application or do we leave you here right now and you forgo the application, and we refund you your money?"

"I want to speak to the man in charge," yelled Mr. Falbersham, accustomed to his word being obeyed.

"I am Colonel John Williams, Chief of Security for the compound, and

I am the man in charge. You have fifteen seconds to make up your mind. Do you go with my men now or stay here? You decide."

Seeing that his assistant Paul was still in a neck hold by the large, powerful guard, Mr. Falbersham finally mumbled, "I guess I have to do what you say. Paul, stay here, and I will contact you when I get out. Now please release him."

The guard was released. Paul, Mr. Falbersham, and the two guards entered the vehicle and left the parking lot. Wow, that was a little excitement for one morning, thought Colonel John. But his excitement was far from over.

Parkway Hotel Problem #2

The guards had no problems with the next four subjects. All four were quiet and respectful and entered their awaiting vehicles with no problem. The next subject, Mr. Chin Kang, a high-ranking Chinese businessman and politician, was hailed next to enter his vehicle. Then all hell broke loose. Mr. Kang approached with eight others and, in broken English, started demanding that his staff must accompany him to the compound.

"I am Mr. Chin Kang, Vice President of one of the largest electronics manufacturing firms in China, and I will not proceed without my trusted staff with me. I have direct authorization from the President of the United States that I will be allowed in with my associates. You will do what I say, or all of you will be in jail."

By this time, Colonel John had had enough.

"Mr. Kang, I wish to accommodate your concerns. May I see the document signed by the President of the United States granting you access to the compound with your staff?"

"But I do not have it. He told me himself that I would be allowed to proceed," protested Mr. Kang.

"Mr. Kang, allow me to consult with my superiors," at which point Colonel John called Sean on his secure line.

Colonel John explained the situation to Sean, and Sean replied, "He's lying. The President never gave him permission, and they know I won't allow it. Tell him for me that his application has now been rejected, and we will be forwarding his money back. I take hundred percent responsibility

308

for this. I do not want this man in the compound under any circumstances, do you understand?"

"Yes, Sean, I hear you loud and clear," said Colonel John.

Colonel John returned to the group and said, "Mr. Kang, I am sorry for the problems caused here. (He waited for Mr. Kang to smile.) To right this wrong, your admittance to the compound and your receiving the application have now been rejected. Your money will be returned to you later today."

Colonel John turned and directed the driver of the vehicle to return to the compound. Watching the vehicle leave without him, Mr. Kang, realizing that his bluff was being called and being refused the application, went into a fury. He and his eight assistants all started yelling in Chinese. The other guards came over and drew their weapons to assist their friends.

Mr. Kang was made to vacate the front of the Parkway Hotel entrance while yelling that he was going to contact the President himself immediately. Once Mr. Kang and his associates had left the area and gone back to their rooms, Colonel John said to his men, "Guys, some days are easy, and some days are hard. This is a hard day." They all agreed.

Witnessing the actions Mr. Kang caused, the next applicants entered their vehicles willingly and without fuss.

Additional Security for the Parkway Hotel

Colonel John met with Sean the next day and outlined the problems they experienced at the Parkway Hotel. Sean and Colonel John felt the politicians and businessmen shared the same problem of a heightened sense of their own importance.

Colonel John then said, "Sean, you had problems with the first group of businessmen you did applications on. Now I'm having problems picking these important people up at the Parkway Hotel. They seem to believe that their word is the law and everyone must do as they say. Somehow, they don't think rules apply to them. Maybe we should be having them arrive by helicopter."

"No, no more helicopters," explained Sean. "I have enough problems with the military people arriving by helicopter. If we start allowing more helicopters here, the applicants will be renting their own and arriving with their entire staff and assistants. Plus, every news agency in the world would be landing here, creating a real mess. We'd have to buy another bulldozer just to crush them," Sean said, laughing.

"Let's do this," Sean continued. "On the morning of the pickup, let's have a busload of forty additional armed guards arrive at the Parkway Hotel at five a.m. This way, you can enter the lobby with, let's say, four of them, select the next candidate, and have the four escort them out individually to their awaiting vehicle. The vehicles could have had eight more guards surrounding them. That should deter any troublemakers."

"Yes, Sean, I think adding the additional guards would do it. We could load the vehicles, park them, and when all of our passengers are in, we could all leave at once as a convoy. We could have two SUVs with guards leading the way and the other guards in the bus following in the rear," said Colonel John.

"Great, that settles it. You arrange for as much additional security as you need for the Parkway Hotel. Thank you," said Sean.

Problems with Drones

"And one other thing?" asked Colonel John. "We didn't have a problem with outside drones before, but now with these more modern drones capable of flying great distances and you doing applications to world leaders, we seem to be getting more and more of them every day. They were never a nuisance before and were silent, and they were likely just flown by people wanting to get a photo of their favorite celebrity. But once you started doing applications to world leaders, the drones we see are now larger and more sophisticated. I don't know if these new drones are from news networks, businesses, or governments, but they certainly are not the type you buy at the local electronics store. I would like your permission to shoot down any drones that enter the airspace above the compound."

"Absolutely, I want them all shot down and displayed on the website," Sean replied. "Because, just like the helicopters, we allow one drone over the property, and tomorrow we'll have one hundred. Shoot them all down and put a picture of the drone and the marksman who shot it down on the website and then nail the drone to either the fence or a wall in the shooting range. Even get trophies made up if you want, but I want them all shot down, no exceptions."

Within the week, Colonel John had every guard post and outside perimeter guard equipped with 12-gauge shotguns for the express purpose of shooting down the drones. A female guard, Lindsay Hunter, was the first to shoot down a drone, and everyone hearing the shot came running.

Everyone was amazed at its size. It was obviously remotely controlled and large enough to have two cameras on board. Colonel John disabled the cameras, and the staff took pictures of Lindsay with her prize. These were promptly displayed on the website, and the drone itself was nailed to the wall of the shooting range as a trophy.

But after investigation, it was impossible to determine where the drone came from or who owned it. The drone itself had no marking or serial numbers and was a model not available in the US. It was from a South Korean manufacturer that supplies military drones to the Middle East. Colonel John reported to Sean that this was likely from a foreign government wanting information on the compound.

Sean replied, "I want everyone to know that we take our security here very seriously. I want every single guard who shoots down a drone to get a check for ten thousand dollars along with their trophy photos on the website. Make a big splash about handing out the checks to those who have already shot down some drones. That should put an end to these flyovers."

Chapter 42
Attack at the Gate

Little did Colonel John realize that more troubles were brewing. Two weeks went by without a problem. The additional heavily armed guards deterred anyone from making a fuss or trying to jump into a vehicle to go to the compound.

The last vehicle to leave that day picked up Mr. Dimitri Lenkova, a Russian diplomat, without incident. Mr. Lenkova was a tall, arrogant diplomat who looked at the guards like they were garbage. The guard sitting next to him disliked him immediately.

Without knowing it, behind the end bus with the additional guards, the convoy was being followed by four of Mr. Lenkova's countrymen.

When the vehicle carrying Mr. Lenkova approached the main first gate and stopped, Mr. Lenkova's four countrymen burst forth from their parked SUV, surrounding the vehicle carrying Mr. Lenkova, demanding that they be allowed into the compound with him. They were screaming and yelling in Russian. Two of the men pulled out pistols and started waving them in the air, keeping the guards in the vehicle from getting out.

The guards at Gate #2 and #3 could hear these men screaming. The security guards near the vehicle backed off immediately, knowing full well that the silent alarms had been tripped by the guards in the towers. The attackers then ordered the bus with the additional guards to back up and leave. Everyone was on full alert, and guns were being drawn.

Then the worst happened. Obviously, the leader of the band of four forces the driver out, putting a gun to his head, and orders that they and Mr. Lenkova be allowed into the compound.

The military guard in the back of the vehicle with Mr. Lenkova reacted quickly. Seeing his friend in distress, he withdraws his pistol, switches off the safety, pulls back on the gun to load a shell in the chamber, and puts the gun on Mr. Lenkova's head. He motions for Mr. Lenkova to exit the vehicle, and his associate opens the door for him.

Now out of the vehicle, the guard puts his left arm around Mr. Lenkova's neck, and with his right hand, he has his 9mm Glock pressed so hard to Mr. Lenkova's head that he cries out in pain. Now it's his turn to talk, "You harm my friend, and I will blow his head off. Go ahead, shoot, and I'll splatter your boss's brains all over the desert."

From inside the compound, the military SUVs were starting to arrive, and the guards knew the snipers were getting in place. They couldn't see them, but they knew. The assailant holding the guard hostage kept yelling in Russian, and the other assailant was now pointing his gun toward the guard holding Mr. Lenkova. This was starting to get ugly.

Colonel John had been called and made aware of the situation. He was at the Parkway Hotel explaining the procedure to the families of the subjects there, so he was easily over an hour's drive away. He knew that it was futile to direct operations, if not on the scene. He ordered the commander of the post to make his own decisions and that he would take full responsibility for his actions.

The guards being held captive were all ex-military and had served in Afghanistan, so they knew exactly what to do. Slowly, the original driver being held hostage moved to the right, allowing for a clear shot from the snipers. The guard holding Mr. Lenkova also moved to give a sniper a clear shot at the assailant, pointing a gun at him.

Then, on the signal from their commander, two shots in unison rang out, and both the assailant's heads exploded when .50 caliber bullets from their Barrett M82 sniper rifles entered their brains. The assailant holding the driver hostage had a bullet enter just over the top of his left ear. The assailant, pointing his gun at the guard holding Mr. Lenkova, had a bullet enter his forehead just above his left eye. Clear shots, dead shots.

The guards raced toward the two unarmed assailants as they were running back to their SUV. Throwing them on the ground, they placed their hands behind their backs, and zip-tied their hands together. Mr. Lenkova had his hands placed behind his back and his hands were also zip-tied. Mr. Lenkova started yelling that he had diplomatic immunity, but nobody cared.

The guards held Mr. Lenkova and the two remaining assailants on the ground for forty minutes until Colonel John's arrived. When he arrived, he pulled back the tarps to take a look at the two dead assailants. Looking at where their heads used to be, he thought to himself, good shooting. When a.50-caliber bullet enters the soft brain tissue, there is not much left to

313

identify. He then went to inspect the prisoners. Mr. Lenkova continued to protest that he had diplomatic immunity and was to be released immediately.

"I'm not too sure about diplomatic immunity when four of your men, obviously on your orders, storm a US Federal compound and take two of my men hostage at gunpoint. But for now, the three of you are my prisoners and will be treated as such," stated Colonel John as his men pulled the assailants off the ground.

Colonel John contacted the Las Vegas police department, briefly described what had happened, and asked to store three prisoners in their cells and two dead ones in their morgue.

"Permission granted, bring them all down," replied the Staff Sergeant on duty. Colonel John had them loaded into the SUVs, and under heavily armed guard, the prisoners were taken to the Las Vegas Police Department's main branch and held in cells.

By this time, Sean and Ralph arrived but were wisely held back until Colonel John arrived. They were both told what happened, and Sean thanked all the men for their actions and bravery. Knowing that the main gate had its own security cameras recording 24/7 he ordered copies of the incident made up and one copy to be sent immediately to the website company.

"The film of what happened here will be up and running on our website before the accusations of us mishandling the situation come out. Once on our website, the news channels will pick it up, and the world can see for themselves what went on here," said Sean.

While Sean and Ralph were talking to Colonel John, an excited guard approached them and asked, "Colonel, you must come and see what we've found."

Colonel John, Sean, and Ralph followed him to the assailant's SUV. In it were four automatic rifles, four pistols, boxes of shells, and a box of hand grenades.

After seeing this, both Sean and Ralph were visibly shaken. They both personally thanked and shook hands with the guard commander and the two snipers who did their duty. Sean assured them they did the right thing, and their actions likely saved people's lives.

Sean stated in a loud voice so that everyone could hear, "These people were not here to accompany Mr. Lenkova. They were here to either kidnap me, kill me, or cause whatever damage they could to the compound and our people."

In the coming days, Sean's decision to put the attack film footage on the website turned out to be correct. Every news agency in the US picked it up and had it on their eight a.m. news the next morning.

The Russian Ambassador to the United States launched a formal protest against how Mr. Lenkova was treated. The Ambassador stated in a recorded interview that Mr. Lenkova was violently attacked. The news agencies played his interview alongside the film clip of the attack. Anyone seeing the footage could tell who the aggressors were. The ambassador, having made a fool of himself, was called back to Russia and replaced.

But as world politics goes, Mr. Lenkova and his two assistants had the charges against them dropped and were eventually allowed to leave the United States. Later, Sean Little was contacted by the Vice President, asking him to refund the Russians their fifty million dollars. Upon hearing this, Sean said, "I refuse to refund money to people who want to kill me. Besides, I'm using that money to update the security around the compound."

Even a personal request from the President himself had no effect. Sean refused to refund their money.

Chapter 43
Thank You for Saving Our Lives

Sean and Jennifer discussed how they could thank those brave individuals who saved both Ralph and Sean's lives. They discussed the carnage that could have taken place if the assailants had gained access to the compound. Secretly, without fanfare, Sean asked Wendy to arrange for the twelve FBI guards (but not Monica), who saved them in the attack on the lab in Boston. Families of the two FBI agents who were killed protecting Ralph and Ron Newland, the FBI commander of the assault team, and the seven other FBI agents who rescued Ralph (including the two posing as men and wives who rented the hotel room beside the kidnappers) were all flown in from Boston.

"By why not Monica? asked Wendy. "She led the team that killed the assailants in their attack on the lab in Boston?"

"Yes, I know," replied Sean, "but I have so much resentment toward her because she constantly lied to me and was the one that kept myself, Ralph, and Jennifer prisoners. If it wasn't for Ralph slipping that installer a note, I would still be her prisoner, hanging by my thumbs somewhere. I refuse to reward her for her actions."

Wendy, seeing how upset Sean was, let the issue rest.

Two weeks later, those twenty-two invited FBI agents and families, plus the commander at the gate and the two snipers involved in the attack on the gate, attended a ceremony and dinner in their honor.

To start, Sean gave a brief description of the attack on the lab in Boston and then called up each of the fourteen FBI agents involved by name. Sean then handed each FBI agent a check for $100,000 dollars. Attached with a rubber band to the check was a wad of ten thousand dollars cash in hundred dollar bills. Sean thanked each, in turn for saving his life.

Ralph spoke, and after a brief description of his capture and rescue in Boston, he asked the families of the two FBI agents who were killed protecting Ralph to come up. Ralph thanked them for their bravery, and Chaplain Furlong led the group in prayer for the two agents. He then asked

FBI Special Agent Ron Newland, the commander of the raid that saved him and his five agents, to come up to the front. Ralph then, in turn, thanked every agent and the two families and handed them a check for $100,000 attached to a stack of bills for $10,000 dollars.

It was Sean's turn again. He briefly described the attack at the gate and the carnage that could have taken place had these people gained access to the compound.

He called up the commander at the gate, the two guards, and the two snipers who killed the assailants. He thanked them and handed each a check for $100,000 along with a wad of cash for ten thousand dollars. He then announced that every single military guard on the compound, whether they were at the front gate or not, would be receiving their own check for ten thousand dollars.

Sean then said, "These checks are coming to you tax-free. Any problems with the tax department, you tell them to contact me directly." Everybody cheered.

Wendy, unknown to Sean, had already contacted the tax department and paid the tax. Sean continued, "And for those of you who just received ten thousand dollars in cash, it's just in case you want to enjoy the sights of Las Vegas while you're here. I'm sure the casinos will be happy to take your money." Everyone cheered.

"And if any of you would like to stay in Las Vegas, please call the Parkway Hotel and tell them who you are. I have an entire floor of rooms there permanently rented, so you are welcome to stay as long as you like. Wendy here has called ahead and given the hotel your names. "Now I have a special announcement," said Sean.

Ralph and Sean then called up the fourteen FBI agents involved in the attack on the lab in Boston two FBI agent's families of the agents killed during Ralph's kidnapping six FBI agents who rescued Ralph in Boston and the two guards, the commander, and the two snipers who killed the assailants at the attack on the gate.

"Ladies and gentlemen, we now have to step out back for a special presentation."

With Sean and Ralph leading the way and the twenty FBI agents, two families and five guards involved in the attack at the gate following behind, there were twenty-seven brand new Cadillac Escalade SUVs all in Pearl White sitting in the parking lot. Each one had a sign of it, and one of the twenty-seven individuals who now owned it

"Ladies and gentlemen, each one of these people who directly saved Ralph and myself, and to the two families of the agents that were killed protecting Ralph Barns and the five guards involved in the attack on the gate, you now have your own brand new, fully loaded Cadillac Escalade SUVs. They are already licensed in your names, plated, and the insurance paid for the first year. The keys are in the ignition, and the tanks are full. Thank you and thank you again to all of you for saving Ralph's and all our lives. Enjoy these. You deserve them." Everyone cheered.

FBI Special Agent Ron Newland, the commander of the assault team that rescued Ralph in Boston, raised his arm to talk.

"Ladies and gentlemen, on behalf of myself and my agents, I want to thank Sean and Ralph for today's presentation and generosity. I am sure we will all find homes for this money and our new vehicles. On behalf of all the disabled war veterans, disabled police officers, and everyone here today, I would formally like to thank Sean Little for his generosity. Sean, you deserve our respect and our praise. Let's all have a round of applause for Sean Little." Everyone cheered.

Later, after lunch, Ralph had a question for Special Agent Ron Newland.

"Again, Ron, I want to thank you. I owe you my life. Once they cut off two of my fingers, I knew I wouldn't be leaving that hotel room alive, regardless of what Sean did. But I have to ask, why did you only have yourself and three other agents break into the hotel room? Would not twenty or more agents have been better?"

"Good question, Ralph. Everyone thinks that there is strength in numbers, and in certain situations, there is. But in the confined quarters of a hotel room, too many agents would only complicate things, and the operation would get confused. Better to go in with a small group where everyone has a specific job and has room to move and fire. Plus, a large group would likely be noticed walking up to the hotel. Better to go with quality and not quantity in this situation."

"Thank you, that answers it. And thank you again for saving my life," said Ralph.

"You are welcome. All in a day's work," said Ron. And both he and Ralph shook hands as friends.

FBI Special Agent Ron Newland Questions Sean

After the presentations and during lunch, Colonel John, FBI Special Agent Ron Newland, Ralph Barns, and Sean fell into a casual conversation about Sean's involvement in cleaning up the world.

"Sean, do you mind if I ask you a question?" asked Special Agent Ron Newland.

"Sure," replied Sean. "We are all in your debt for rescuing Ralph here. Ask anything you want."

"As a former member of the American Armed Forces and now with the FBI, I appreciate all the work you are doing to help our disabled war veterans and police officers. I can fully appreciate your animosity toward the FBI for holding you up in the lab in Boston and then in Nevada. But does your dislike for the FBI also include our armed forces?"

"Excellent question, Ron," replied Sean. "I respect the FBI and its work on internal security and its good works. I also appreciate that those persons who held me and my friends hostage were merely acting on orders from those higher up. But what really makes me mad is that we were constantly being lied to and that those higher-ups only wanted my secret to use it as a method of imposing their will on the rest of the world. I have stated time and time again that as long as I hold this secret, it will never be used as an instrument of war or as an international bargaining chip."

"Yes, I understand and can appreciate your dislike for those who held you hostage," stated FBI Special Agent Ron. "But with your considerable influence at home here, I hope that any of your comments against those who held you hostage are not received as a condemnation of the men and women serving in our armed services."

Sean replied, "I have nothing but the greatest admiration for the members of our armed services, and I do not believe that I have ever said anything to make anyone believe that I do not support their efforts hundred percent. My father was proud to have served in Vietnam, and he himself was slightly disabled. While I do not support any war efforts and will not supply any organization with weapons, I do firmly believe that we need a strong military to protect our nation and our freedoms. The history of the world shows that despots and dictators will always strive to undermine and attack democratic and peaceful nations, so we must strive to protect ourselves from the evil forces around us.

"For example, look at the attempts to capture my secret. I highly doubt that those people, if successful, would be using my secret for the betterment of mankind but for increasing their own power and blackmailing the rest of the world. We must have a strong military for our own protection, or we, as a nation, will perish. My favorite quote is from the old 1940s black-and-white film, "Charlie Chan in Panama". While looking over the American fleet at the end of the film, he said to his son, "Intelligent defense of nation best guarantee for years of peace."

So, Ron, while I do not support war, I totally support the men and women of our armed forces and the defense and protection they provide. Without them, we would quickly be overrun, and the world would fall into anarchy."

"Yes, thank you, Sean," replied Special Agent Ron. "I see your position clearly now. And thank you again for all the good work you are doing for the environment and for helping our disabled war veterans and police officers."

"You're welcome," replied Sean, and Ralph broke up the serious conversation by starting to talk about football, and everyone else joined in.

Chapter 44
The Presidential Election

Regardless of the good work that Sean was doing, greedy eyes in America and abroad looked upon Sean's success and plotted against him. With the recent attack at the gate by the Russian businessman and diplomat Mr. Lenkova, Sean was convinced that others would also be planning on his demise or capture.

The foreign threats Sean felt were well understood, but the domestic ones were not. Powerful people in America were constantly plotting against Sean to force him to reveal his secret. From government agencies to major corporations, everyone wanted what Sean had. This was to rear its ugly head in the upcoming Presidential elections.

The President and Vice President John Harper were up for re-election in the coming months. Their stand on Sean Little and his age-reversing formula was officially, "We in the United States are working on duplicating the formula and will achieve a breakthrough soon."

But the President and Vice President were constantly attacked for protecting Sean and not forcing him to reveal his secret. His presidential opponent took a different stance. Whenever the discussion turned to Sean Little and his formula, Presidential Candidate Samuel Walker would say, "This formula is a benefit for all Americans, rich and poor. No one man should hold the power over life and death, whether young or old. If elected, I will ensure that his age- reversing formula is available to all."

Senator Samuel Walker was mid-70s, gray-haired, and a little thick around the middle. He was all fired up about his own importance and wanted the age-reversing application for himself and his wife at all costs.

Yes, there were other issues, such as foreign policy and the economy, which the existing President did well on. But the media and voters were obsessed with Sean Little, and during Presidential debates, Sean Little's name constantly came up. The existing President always backed himself into a corner, saying that they would soon be duplicating the formula, and until then, Sean Little had to be protected because of the good work he was doing.

Senator Samuel Walker would always attack back, saying, "We know where the formula is. It's with Sean Little. If we don't get it from him, some other foreign government will, and then we will be at their mercy. No single man should have total control of this age-reversing process. The people of America need this formula. America needs this formula. If elected, I will make this process available to all."

Sean and Jennifer nervously watched the election on TV. They knew that if the existing President and the VP lost, trouble would be brewing. They went to bed uneasy that night, only to discover that Samuel Walker and his group won the election by a landslide. Samuel Walker was elected President of the United States, with Vince Rogers as his Vice President.

"Our world as we know it is about to change," Sean said to Jennifer.

Even during the Presidential swearing-in ceremony, Samuel Walker mentioned Sean Little by name and stated that working with Sean was one of his highest domestic priorities.

Visit from Vice President Vince Rogers

Once in power, President Walker lost no time having his new Vice President, Vince Rogers flew off to meet with Sean. VP Vince Rogers, like the President, was all fired up with his new authority, and being in his early 70s, he was determined to obtain this application for himself and his wife.

The FBI called ahead to notify and order Colonel John to allow the three helicopters to land. He had no choice. Not to do so would result in Colonel John being court marshalled.

Colonel John informed Sean of his incoming guests. Colonel John said, "Sean, I'm sorry. I was given direct orders. I had to obey."

"No problem, John," said Sean. "I knew this was going to happen ever since my formula became an election issue. I've been expecting them."

Sean met with Vice President Vince Rogers. VP Rogers started out the conversation, "Sean, you have been privy to this secret for over two years now, and we all appreciate the fine work you are doing. You are aware that our labs and the labs all over the world are unable to duplicate your process. This is too powerful of a secret to be kept by one man. You must share this with us in the US government, and we will see that it is put to good use."

Then Sean, getting angry, spoke, "Because your lab people are stupid and cannot replicate my results, it is not my fault. I have stated hundreds of times that this secret will never be used as an instrument of war or an international bargaining chip. I will go to my grave protecting this secret."

The Vice President then replied with, "Sean, you don't know the position you're in. You feel you're safe here, but without our protection, others like those who killed your friend, Jack, kidnapped your associate Ralph, and attacked your main gate are still out there and will likely torture and kill you once you leave this federal compound. You must cooperate and reveal the secret of your formula to us."

Sean exploded, "Reveal the secret to you, reveal the secret to you! You're the bastards who lied to us and put me and my friends in prison. If it wasn't for Ralph slipping a note to that installer, I'd still be your prisoner now, hanging from my arms in a federal prison. I can't trust you for one second."

"Yes, how you were treated by the FBI was unfortunate, and I promise it won't happen again," stated the Vice President.

"Promise?" Sean shot back. "You actually expect me to accept your word? All you care about is getting elected. I am personally funding important projects around the world, and you want to use this secret, like you used the atom bomb, to kill people. I will not allow it, not now, not ever. I will take this secret to my grave if I have to, but I will not help you. Now get out. I've had enough of your bullshit."

The Vice President, Vince Rogers, got up to leave.

"Sean, this is not over, and you know it."

Sean came back with, "Wow, I'm getting threatened by the Vice President. I have broken no laws. I am funding important environment projects around the world and sending money to physically disabled American war veterans and police officers, and now you want to change that and use this secret as an instrument of war? You and your kind make me sick. Get out."

Sean got up, walked away, and refused to shake the vice President's hand.

The Vice President left to go to the awaiting helicopters.

Sean Little was furious. He contacted the website company and had this written on his website.

"Earlier today I, Sean Little, was visited by the Vice President of the United States, Vince Rogers. Vice President Rogers, in no uncertain terms, has threatened me to reveal my age-reversing formula to the US government. I have stated before and I will state again that, as long as I am the sole possessor of this formula, I will never allow it to be used as an instrument of war or as an international bargaining chip.

"I am using this formula and its benefits for the good of all mankind. Obviously, my world-wide environment efforts and my assistance to the physically disabled war veterans and police officers are not to their liking. I swear to you now that I will take this secret to my grave before I reveal it to any government determined to use it for harm."

The website people had this up on the site within thirty minutes. The news agency, constantly watching Sean's site, picked it up immediately. Any news about Sean Little received worldwide attention, and this statement was no different.

Quickly, it would appear that half of Americans thought that Sean Little should be forced to reveal his secret, and the other half felt that he should be left alone to continue with his environmental projects. Within the day, major worldwide environmental movements produced a joint statement to the press.

"We, the major world environment movements, are unanimous in our support for Sean Little. Mankind has been destroying this planet for centuries, and we are now drowning in our own filth. Sean Little, with his money, is finally tackling projects that every government in the world is too cowardly to act upon. Even the United Nations will not touch on these issues.

"After years of useless talk, it was finally Sean Little alone who stopped the worldwide whale hunt. He is successfully working on cleaning up the billions of tons of garbage in the South Pacific. Sean Little is right in his refusal to help the government. Sean Little is the environmental savior of our planet and deserves our support."

Sean Little's website statement and the environmentalists' position appeared in every news program and newspaper around the world. The worldwide condemnation of the US wanting to have sole access to this formula to use it for their own gain was deafening. The Republic of China was the most vocal. "We, the Republic of China, have sat back quietly to watch how the events surrounding Sean Little and his age-reversing formula would play out. To date, we totally agree with the efforts of Sean Little to use this formula and the monies received to clean up the planet. Our representatives have met with Mr. Little and have found him dedicated to this task.

"We, the Republic of China, herald Mr. Little's environmental efforts. We also warn that any government attempts to gain his formula and bribe the rest of the world will be viewed by the Republic of China as a hostile act, warranting military action."

When Sean saw this on the evening news, he was stunned.

"Wow, I didn't know that my efforts were so closely watched. Thank heavens for that," he said to Jennifer.

"But Sean, I'm scared," said Jennifer.

"Well, I don't think they can put us in prison again because that would stop all my environmental efforts and my checks to the physically disabled war veterans and police officers. And it looks like other nations are very sensitive about my secret being revealed to the US government. So I think we're safe as long as I stay in the limelight and stay visible. Nobody wants to kill me. They just want to kidnap me and make me reveal the secret," said Sean.

Sean knew that the efforts to obtain the formula's secret would never stop. A few days later, Colonel John and Wendy both reported that they had been positioned elsewhere. Sean asked them if they would like to stay here, and both agreed. Sean knew the games the VP was playing and decided to react.

He immediately called Vice President Vince Rogers, and his call was immediately put through. "Hello, Vince. This is Sean Little. If you want to play games, I will play games. You order your people to allow Colonel John Williams and Wendy Rawlings, my Secretary Treasurer to remain with me. If I don't have them both walking through my door within the next two hours saying they can stay, I will be placing on my website a statement outlining that I will be canceling the payments to all physically disabled war veterans and police officers and laying the blame for my actions directly on you. Do you understand?"

"Yes, Sean, I do," mumbled the Vice President.

"Good. Thank you," replied Sean, and he hung up.

The Vice President knew exactly the media firestorm that would be created if Sean Little even hinted at canceling the checks for the war veterans and police officers. He had no choice. He called the Head of the Armed Forces and requested that they see to it that Colonel John Williams and Wendy Rawlings remain with Sean Little at his compound.

He later explained to the President, Samuel Walker, that he had no choice, and the President agreed. The President replied with, "I think he's got us over a barrel on this one. You and I don't need every war vet and police association up our ass, and the bad press would sink us."

The Vice President had to agree.

Over the coming months, further attempts to talk to Sean were made, but all failed. As long as Sean was the only one with the formula and continued to do prominent work, no one could touch him. His threat to cancel the payments to the disabled war vets and police officers was a good one and kept the President and Vice President at bay. *But they would still keep coming,* thought Sean.

It would seem that every military helicopter in the US got into the habit of landing in the Nevada compound. Colonel John was helpless in stopping them, as he was simply ordered to let them land. Sean knew this and told Colonel John not to worry about it and just bring the uninvited guests in to see him.

The President and Vice President knew that Sean would continue to protect himself behind the threat to cancel the payments to the physically disabled war veterans and police officers. At present, his stature as an American was untouchable, and the members of the government knew it.

Visit from Mrs. Lorraine Smith, the President's National Adviser on the Environment

The next Presidential helicopter to arrive carried Mrs. Lorraine Smith, the President's National Adviser on the Environment. Sean had Colonel John bring her into his office as soon as she landed. Sean decided that it was useless to try to be nice to these people because they all wanted one thing: the secret.

When Mrs. Smith entered Sean's office, Sean started out the conversation, "Nice to meet you, Mrs. Smith, and why do I warrant this unauthorized intrusion into my privacy?"

Mrs. Smith was a petite, strong-willed, determined career diplomat who was accustomed to taking charge. She took a seat and stated sternly, "Sean, we in the environment movement herald your actions. But we in the government feel that your efforts would be better directed on a national level, by our top people."

"Well, isn't that great?" Sean yelled. "You want me to hand over my formula so that instead of helping the environment, you and your cronies can buy bigger and better weapons. The American governments actions to date on the environment have been dismal, and you know it. You're just a puppet with no money and no authority.

"Name one major environment project that your department has carried through to completion while you have been its head. None, not one single project. All you're good for is photo ops.

"You want to know why I just don't hand money over to national governments? Well, I'll tell you. When you give any national government any money, they don't spend it on health, education, food, or the well-being of their citizens. No, they spend it on weapons to wage war and kill people. Why, I'll never know.

"We have billions of dollars in unused military equipment rusting in fields, but you idiots just keep buying more. This money could be used to fund a national health care system or a breakfast program for disadvantaged children, but no, you morons just have to have your weapons. Now get out and don't come back."

Mrs. Smith knew that talking to Sean any more was useless. She was told of Sean's explosive temper, and she experienced it firsthand. She left, and Colonel John drove her back to the awaiting helicopter.

Visit from Scott Donaldson, Associate Director of the CIA

It would seem that every two weeks, a new intruder would arrive in a military helicopter to pester Sean. *This is becoming a nuisance,* thought Sean. He had the Associate Director of the CIA, Scott Donaldson, show up. Mr. Donaldson was a good-looking, tall career ex-military commander who was accustomed to people taking his orders and getting what he wanted.

Mr. Donaldson wanted Sean to give the new heads of state of a newly formed African nation free applications. Sean was not impressed.

"Wow, these guys, last weeks, terrorists and freedom fighters with your backing, overthrow a democratically elected government and kill hundreds of people during this takeover. And now that they have established themselves as the head of their country at gunpoint, you want me to reward them with free applications? Maybe I should give the free applications to the people they killed when they seized power. Maybe I could bring them all back to life."

"You need to do this for us. It's a matter of national interest," said the Associate Director.

"You're not listening. I have stated time and time again that my formula will never be used as an instrument of foreign policy. Because you want to reward these murderers, that is your problem, not mine. And in a year from now, someone will overthrow and kill them, and the cycle will start all over again. Can't you see how ridiculous you sound?

"Sean, your constant refusals to help out the US government is really starting to piss everyone off," yelled the Associate Director.

"I don't give a shit," Sean yelled back. "I will never let you bastards have this secret. If you could, you would have me arrested right now and have me tortured in some prison cell, and you know it. You just can't wait to get your hands on this secret so you can dictate your terms to the rest of the world. All you bastards think of is how to use this secret as a weapon. I will put a bullet in my head before I ever let you have it. You make me sick. Now get out."

A very angry Associate Director of the CIA stormed out and was driven back to the awaiting helicopter. Colonel John wisely stayed away from the conversation and sat outside in the vehicle. His opinion was that the less he knew, the better.

As Sean started to settle down, he thought to himself, *This will never stop. As long as I have the secret, they will continue trying. There is nothing they won't do. Heaven knows where I would be without the threat of canceling the war veterans' and police officers' payments. I'd probably be hanging up by my thumbs in some prison by now.*

Sean Updates the Conditions

Later that day, Sean and Ralph got together.

"I have asked the President and Vice President to stop contacting me for free applications or giving me advice on handling their "special friends. Once we start doing applications for free, they'll all be free. Everyone pays, no exceptions."

Sean then wrote out some ideas about the addition to the List of Conditions on his notepad and handed it to Ralph.

–We "the company," and I, Sean Little, are not part of the American government, and we do not answer to them. If you believe that you deserve special treatment because of your status in your home country, your religion, or because of your relationship with the US government, you will be disappointed.

–I. Sean Little and my staff at the Nevada compound take our security very seriously. We will defend ourselves without hesitation and use deadly force when necessary.

–Not only will trespassers be arrested and imprisoned, but their means of travel, especially a helicopter, will be destroyed.

–Any and all drones flying over or near the compound will be shot down.

–There are no exceptions to the above rules.

–Failure to comply means that you will be refused the treatment and your money refunded.

"I think you hit the nail on the head," said Ralph. "At least these big shots know what they are getting into before coming here. You and I both know they have talked to others who have had the treatment and seen the videos, so they know what to expect. I think you've done an excellent job."

Chapter 45
New President

Sean was concerned about the relentless government pressure to reveal his age-reversing formula, Ralph's kidnapping, and the recent attack at the gate. That evening, at dinner with Jennifer, her sister, and her parents, it was all they could talk about.

Jennifer started, "Sean, all of us here have decided that if we are kidnapped, we would prefer to die rather than have you reveal your secret. Ralph's kidnapping proves that even if you did try to save him by revealing the secret, they would have killed him anyway and then come after you to ensure that they alone had the secret. If kidnapped, we are already dead, and we all accept that. Your secret and its benefits to mankind must never fall into the hands of those who wish to control the world or to do others harm."

Everyone else nodded in agreement and expressed their approval.

Then the conversation turned to the recent Vice President's visit and his threats to Sean to reveal his secret. Everyone agreed that if it were not for Sean threatening to cancel the war vets' and police officers' checks, they would likely have him in jail on some "threat to national security" charge.

It was Jennifer's father, Mr. Sloan, who came up with the solution. "Well, the solution is simple, Sean," replied Mr. Sloan. "To even further increase your stature in America to the point where the government cannot touch you…" He paused for dramatic intent and to take another mouthful of food. "All you have to do is start funding major environmental projects in the US. Once you do, the media will pick up on it, and you're free and clear."

Sean thought about it for a minute. "Mr. Sloan, you are a genius. Of course. If I fund national projects, who can complain? I keep my money going toward projects to help the environment and create jobs, and I become so prominent that maybe, just maybe, my friends in the government will stop harassing me. I think it will work. Thank you. I'll start on it tomorrow."

The next day, Sean had Wendy investigate a number of the US environmental associations to determine who should head up his American efforts. Wendy came in and said, "Sean, you might as well start at the top. I've invited Curt Kurnes, the Head of Operations for the Sierra Club out of Oakland, California, to see you. Curt has been responsible for setting up branches of the Sierra Club throughout the US and has his hands in just about every environmental project going on in the US, government or private."

"Great," Sean replied, "I'm looking forward to meeting him."

Curt arrived the next day, and Sean took him for a quick tour of the compound and lunch. Curt was a friendly guy and as sharp as a whip. He could talk about every single environmental project now underway in the US without resorting to his notes. Sean was impressed.

Curt wanted to hear all about the Fresh Water Initiative, Saving the Whales, and the clean-up of the Great Pacific Garbage Patch. He was so enthusiastic that Sean felt comfortable with him and thought he could talk to him for hours.

They discussed the work of the Sierra Club, and Curt mentioned the difficulty of getting any government environmental initiatives off the ground. They both agreed that while politicians talk a good story about the environment at election time, their promises simply became hot air once they were elected.

"Seems no matter who gets elected, the industrial and business interests have more clout than any environmental issue. We're left out in the cold," said Curt.

Sean asked him about himself. Curt said, "Well, there is not much to tell you. I'm married to a wonderful gal, Sandra, who is a nurse at the local hospital in Oakland, California. No kids yet, but that's likely to change in the future. For myself, I studied business at Georgetown University in Washington, D.C. Right out of university, I got a job with IBM and quickly rose to become Washington, D.C's district manager. After ten years at IBM, I met Sandra, and we got married. Shortly after that, I felt this business was just not for me, and if I wanted to help the world, I must start using my organizational talents to help the environment.

"My contacts in Washington, D.C, quickly introduced me to an important position with the Sierra Club out of California. With Sandra's approval, I took a drastic cut in pay but now feel that my work means something to the world. After five years, I got promoted to be their Head of Operations. I coordinate all the state chapters and have my hand in just about every government environmental program there is. I must add that I would like to see the government more involved, but I have to be happy with any initiatives they have."

Project #7: Planting More Trees

Sean and Curt discussed the efforts to reforest the United States and other countries. Curt said that he has worked with three major environmental groups dedicated to planting trees and believed they were doing a great job.

"Is it true that you could get a single tree planted for one dollar?" Sean asked.

"Yes," Curt replied. "For every dollar they raise, they are able to plant one tree."

"I'm impressed," said Sean.

Sean then concluded the meeting by handing Curt a check for five million dollars made out to the Sierra Club and another check made out for ten million dollars to go toward planting more trees in the US and abroad.

"You said they will plant one tree for every dollar invested, so I guess I just bought ten million trees," said Sean. They both laughed. Curt left, totally convinced of Sean's sincerity toward helping the environment.

Sean immediately went across the hall to Wendy's office.

"Wendy, I want you to contact Curt Kurnes tomorrow and have him send you his resume. Here is his card. Then I want you to personally call and check out everything Curt has ever done. Educational, work background, and his status with the Sierra Club. I want to know everything this guy has ever done before I speak to him again."

The following day, Wendy contacted Curt, and he sent in his resume. Curt just thought asking for his resume was routine procedure whenever Sean handed over a big check. Wendy contacted Georgetown University, his supervisors at IBM, and the heads of the Sierra Club and inquired about Curt. All gave glowing reports of his work effort and dedication to completing the task at hand. The CEO of the Sierra Club also reported highly of Curt's efforts and organizational skills, plus he thanked Wendy for Sean's five million dollar generous contribution to their efforts. *This Curt seems to be a good guy,* thought Wendy.

She handed Curt's resume and her notes on her contacts to Sean.

"This guy checks out hundred percent," Wendy reported.

Sean reviewed the resume and Wendy's notes and sat on them for a few days. Two days later, Sean asked Wendy to invite Curt and his wife Sandra down to spend a couple of nights at the compound.

"When would you like them here?" asked Wendy.

"Who cares? said Sean. I'm always here. You and Jennifer can take Sandra to Las Vegas and view the sites and do a little shopping." Wendy just laughed.

"Jennifer has already bought me enough outfits to last me until I'm three-hundred years old." Wendy and Sean both laughed.

Curt's Offered a Job

Curt and Sandra arrived three days later. Both Curt and Sandra were met at the airport by military guards and escorted to the compound. Sandra was quite surprised, as she was not accustomed to being escorted by big men carrying even bigger guns. Nobody will mess with these guys, she thought.

Jennifer and Sean met them at the gate with a jeep to drive around in. Sandra was a tall, beautiful, friendly girl with long, curly brown hair. Sean instantly knew that she and Jennifer would become friends.

Followed by the guards, they proceeded to tour the compound, the new medical tower, the office tower, and the three apartment towers. Sean made a special point of showing Sandra the brand-new medical facilities and introduced her to the staff on hand. Sean showed off his new office tower, his office, and the vast available offices upstairs. They had a delicious meal and all retired to their trailers for the night.

The next day, Jennifer took Wendy and Sandra for a girl's day out to Las Vegas. Sean joked to Curt, "Never get in the way of a group of women hell-bent on shopping." And they both laughed.

Curt noticed that eight large SUVs full of armed guards accompanied the women as they drove out of the compound.

"Standard operating procedure," replied Sean.

"Curt, get to know your way around," said Sean. "You are welcome to go anywhere and talk to anyone you want. There are plenty of Jeeps around for you to use, but why don't you use mine? Here are the keys. I have a few hours of work left to do, so I'll see you in about four hours."

In Las Vegas, Jennifer insisted they check out the shows at the casinos. The rest of the day they spent in the spa, relaxing. The girls came back loaded with supplies and new outfits. That night for dinner, Sean invited Wendy, Colonel John, and Ralph to join them, and of course, the girls all showed up in their new outfits. Colonel John was obviously very pleased with how Wendy looked when she arrived in her new outfit.

The meal of steaks and prime rib was delicious, and the wine flowed a little too freely. Curt and Sandra were obviously a good fit.

The next morning, Sean suggested that Jennifer and Sandra go out and explore the desert together. Sandra was happy to see the sights, so off they went, with their guards following close behind. Sean invited Curt into his office.

Sean spoke. "Curt, I like what I see. Jennifer and Wendy adore Sandra. I am going to make you a job offer, and I would like you to hear my terms out and take some time to decide. I am in desperate need of someone to take over my environmental projects in the USA. To date, the only projects on American soil are my subsidies to the telephone pole and railway tie manufacturers, the large incinerator project for the compound, which has just recently been completed, and the check I gave you for ten million dollars to help plant trees in the US and overseas.

My other major projects, for example, are:

–the Fresh Water Initiative, headed up by David Kim,

–the physically disabled veterans and police officer's checks are handled by Wendy,

–the Save the Whales program is handled by my lawyer, Bill Fryer, and

–the Great Pacific Garbage Patch is unfortunately still being handled by myself.

I propose that you can come and go as you please. You can retain your home in Oakland or live anywhere you like. I will even build a house on the compound for you and Sandra, if you like. You will have all the office space and staff you need and a standard Project Director's salary of fifty thousand dollars per month."

Sean then handed Curt the standard list of Project Director's conditions and said, "Keep this and think it over. Do you have any questions?"

"Well, I'm overwhelmed," said Curt. "The salary you're offering me is five times what I'm making now, and the chance to work with you heading up your American projects is pretty exciting. Please, if you don't mind, this is a lifetime commitment, and I need a few days to think it over and talk to Sandra. I know that she's impressed with the work you're doing here, and she's as passionate about the environment as I am. But please give us some time to think it over."

"No problem," said Sean. "It is a big decision and a big responsibility. Give yourself a few days and please get back to Wendy. I've had so many people calling and emailing me that I have cut off all phone calls and emails from the outside. Basically, I can call you, but you can't call me."

Curt and Sean warmly shook hands, and Curt promised to get back to Wendy later that week.

"No problem, it's a big decision," said Sean. "But if you're in, you're in all the way. This is a total commitment."

Curt and Sandra Accept

Jennifer, Wendy, and Sean discussed having Curt and Sandra on board. Both were all for it.

"Seems like a perfect fit, and Curt's involved in many of the environmental projects going on in the US, so he'll make a good head for your US operations," said Wendy.

Curt contacted Wendy a couple of days later.

"Tell Sean we're in all the way. If it's all right with you, we'll be there in the middle of next week."

"Great Curt, Sean, and Jennifer will be so excited," Wendy said. "We all think you're the perfect person to head up Sean's US operations. Welcome aboard. When you arrive, we'll set up some offices for you and get you a guest trailer or apartment to stay in."

Sean was really happy with the news. He could now get started on his environmental projects in the USA. Curt and Sandra settled in quickly, and Sandra took a job helping out in the medical department. Curt quickly organized his office and Wendy helped him recruit his staff.

Project #8: The Mississippi River Pollution Map

Sean, in his first official meeting with Curt, asked, "Why can't I drink the water out of the Mississippi River? Why have we allowed it to become so polluted? What I want are water samples taken about five feet off the bottom every five miles from the start of the Mississippi, all the way down to the Gulf of Mexico.

"Next, I want water samples taken from every single river and stream entering the Mississippi. I want at least two samples, one five miles up and another at the mouth where the stream or river enters the Mississippi. These samples will be taken from about five feet off the bottom. I would think having a university tackle this problem is the way to go, but Curt, it's your call.

"Once this pollution map is completed, I want to clean up each river, starting from the source right down to its mouth. While others are cleaning up the garbage from the shorelines, we will be going one step further. I plan to take each tributary in turn and install pollution controls for every municipality and business on that river at my expense."

"Sean, that's a fabulous idea," said Curt in amazement. "Let me get organized here, and I'll get a university or two involved. I'm sure they'll jump at the chance."

Project #9: Individual State Environmental Cleanup

A few days later, Sean approached Curt with another project.

"My next project is that I want your staff to contact every governor in every state of the US and ask them for information on their worst dump or environmental spill sites.

"I think that old industrial job sites that no one wants to clean up would be the first place to start. Ask Bill Fryer to set up a separate corporation for you in which to conduct this business.

"One stipulation I have is that we must be able to purchase the entire dump or environmental spill site for one dollar before we start the cleanup. You or your staff would first have to visit the selected site, purchase it, and then hire the local cleanup contractors. Once the contractors are finished, I want an independent company to test the site to ensure it's safe to use. I would like to see these cleaned-up sites turned into parks or playgrounds and handing them back to the municipality would be a good idea."

"Sean, I couldn't be more impressed," replied Curt. "These are both valuable long-range projects that will have a major impact on the quality of life in the US. I'm proud to look after this for you. But can I ask you a question?

"Sure, Curt, go ahead," responded Sean.

"On numerous occasions, you have stated that you will not be writing any environmental organizations a check, preferring to do the work yourself, which I understand. But why, when we first met, did you give me a check for ten million dollars for planting more trees in the US and overseas and five million dollars to the Sierra Club?" asked Curt.

"Simply, with any donation, you assured me that I would be purchasing and planting one tree for every dollar spent. That seemed like a good deal to me. As for the five million dollars to the Sierra Club, I had to compensate them for stealing you away from them." Laughed Sean.

"But how did you know that I would sign on?" asked Curt.

"That's simple," said Sean. "I would just keep dangling my environmental projects in front of you and make working for me so attractive you couldn't refuse. Plus, I knew that you wouldn't be able to resist being in charge of such major projects."

"Well, I can't argue there. Being in charge and answering only to you is very attractive. Knowing that my work here will make a difference is just too good to pass up. You won me over, for sure. Happy to be aboard, and thank you," stated Curt.

Curt got to work on all the projects. And as promised, a hard copy report on each project was on Sean's desk by the 20th of every month. Sean had a separate table set up in his office for each major project. When investigating a project, he would sit at that desk and read his notes without being disturbed by any other distractions.

Chapter 46
American Projects

Project #10-The National Firearms Buy Back Program

Sean had a problem and called Colonel John in to see him.

"John, I want you to find me a retired general who could head up a national firearms buyback program. It would entail a lot of travel, and he would likely be overseeing a staff of about fifty people. See who you can come up with for me, please."

"I think I know just the guy," replied Colonel John. "He is a retired general and friend, Cameron Paul, and I think he'd love to be involved. Last time we talked, he said he was going crazy because he had nothing to do."

"Great, if he's interested, have him come over whenever he wants. Heaven knows I'm always here." And both Sean and John laughed.

Sean contacted Bill Fryer, his lawyer, and left a message.

"Bill, I am planning on setting up a firearms buyback program throughout the US. Would there be any restrictions on doing so? Do I buy these guns under my name, under the company name of Little and Alair Inc., or do we set up a new company? Please let me know. Thank you."

Bill got back to Sean within the hour.

"First, I think we should drop the Little and Alair Inc. company name and form a new holding company "Sean Little Inc." with you as the sole stockholder. Second, I will set up a separate company, "The National Firearms Buy Back Program", which will allow you to purchase guns in all states of the US."

"Wonderful," said Sean. "I'll get started on the program once I have a person in place to head it up."

Retired General Cameron Paul and Colonel John walked into Sean's office the next day. Colonel John made the introductions and left. Sean and Cameron exchanged some idle chitchat. Sean took him for a ride in a jeep to overlook the compound. General Cameron was a tall blonde gentleman, about sixty-seven years old. He was very personable, and Sean got a good feeling about him and that they could work together.

Cameron spoke, "Sean, everyone in the world, including myself, is impressed with your work. And I must say that I am in your debt for the payments you are making to our physically disabled war vets and police officers. It is a shame how these men who have fought so hard for their country have to struggle once they get home; it tears your heart out. You have my admiration."

"Thank you, Cameron. I'm trying to do the best I can with what I have," said Sean.

Over a relaxed lunch, Sean outlined his program for a national firearms buyback program.

"Cameron, I see it as teams of ex-military personnel traveling around the US and either setting up locations, say, in a Walmart parking lot; to buy the guns or maybe visiting every mom-and-pop gun store and buying their used guns. I think that fifty dollars per gun should do it and get some of these cheap guns off the streets. Any suggestions?"

Cameron stated, "First off, I think that fifty dollars is far too cheap for an effective gun buy back program. If you want any volume of guns to be turned in, you would have to at least be paying hundred dollars per gun. These would be used guns only, or we would be having some manufacturer build guns to sell to us with no end in sight. As to the location of the buybacks, managing the sites ourselves is not a good idea. People bringing their old guns to, say, an area in a Walmart parking lot would only cause problems. Someone is bound to get shot.

"My suggestion is to have the independent gun stores buy the guns and we show up and buy the guns from them. If the police want to first inspect the guns, they can do so while the guns are at the shops before we pick them up. We can simply contact the gun shops when we are in the area, and they can have the guns ready for us to pick up."

"Well, it looks like you've given it some thought," said Sean.

Cameron replied with, "Ever since I retired and my wife passed, I have nothing to do. I think I'm mentally okay, and the doctors tell me I'm in good health and would love the opportunity to become involved in this project with you."

"If I was to hire you, when could you start?" asked Sean.

Cameron laughed. "Right now or whenever you want."

"Well, that's settled then," said Sean. "The job is yours. Your main office is here, but I realize that ninety-nine percent of the time you'll be in the field. As I suspect that most of the guns are along the populated east coast, I would like you to begin your efforts there. You will have to acquire a warehouse for the guns to be stored and then sawed down for scrap. Maybe renting a building inside a military base would work.

"I want each gun to be destroyed either by being sawed apart or by being crushed in a hydraulic press. Under no circumstances, even if some of these guns are later stolen, could they ever be made operational again. You are to find a local steel factory that will take all the metal scrap. Your men are to video record the destroyed gun parts being loaded into the furnaces.

"All guns are to be destroyed except for any potentially historic weapons, for example, all antique black powder, flintlock or percussion cap rifles, and handguns. These guns will be transported here and stored in one of the metal huts. I will personally inspect these weapons and decide which to keep and which to discard. But if you are picking up the guns from the gun shops, I suspect the shop owners will simply keep and resell the valuable guns themselves.

"Let me introduce you to Wendy. She handles the money, and she'll set you up with a bank account and credit cards to start buying the guns and the ID you need to get in and out of this place. She'll also go over our list of Project Director's guidelines and explain what is expected of you. Wendy will help you in outfitting your office and selecting your staff. Please also select a guest trailer to stay in. Wendy will assign someone to show you the trailers and introduce you around."

Cameron was in shock.

"Sean, you sure work fast. I've only been here two hours, and I'm now the head of a national firearms buyback program. Amazing."

"Well, I'll be honest with you," said Sean. "Once Colonel John mentioned your name, I had Wendy find out everything about you. I probably even know your shoe size.

"What we saw we liked, and with Colonel John's recommendation, you were in even before we met. And now that you're here, you're perfect for the job.

"One other thing. I do not micromanage my people. You are in complete control. You do not need to be called to ask me questions. My opinion is that if I hire someone who has to keep asking me questions, it's obvious I hired the wrong person. I have made it so I don't receive incoming phone calls or emails. If you have a question, ask Wendy or Colonel John, but they will not hand the phone over to me. If I want to talk to you or have a question about your monthly report, I will contact you. Understood?"

Cameron responded with, "Exactly. I will build you a buy back program that will be the envy of the nation. If you've got the money, which I think you do, I'll clean up all the junk guns in the US from Maine to California."

Sean introduced Cameron to Wendy, and Sean outlined the firearms buy back program. Sean stated, "Wendy, for every billion dollars spent, I get to take ten million junk guns off the streets. To me, that's a good deal. Please set up Cameron here on a salary of fifty thousand dollars per month and be sure that he has everything he needs and the money to make this happen. Contact Bill Fryer and introduce Cameron, and Bill will decide on the legalities of this buy back program. Cameron, I leave you now in Wendy's capable hands. And the last thing, never piss Wendy off, she writes the checks." They all laughed, and Sean left.

Wendy knew all about the firearms buyback program in advance, so she told Cameron that he and his people would be using two different credit cards. The Bank of America Visa credit cards were to be used exclusively for gun purchases. Living expenses, hotel food, transportation expenses, etc. were all on their Mastercard credit cards.

This way, Wendy could easily keep track of their gun purchases separately from their living and overhead expenses.

Cameron settled into his new offices quickly. He sat down and started thinking about the most effective ways to go about buying up the millions of junk guns in America. *Buying the guns directly from the gun owners themselves puts us in competition with every gun store owner in America. Therefore, it's best that we buy the used guns from the gun shops themselves. This way, they become our collecting agents, and we merely pick up the guns from them.* Cameron then produced a policy statement:

National Firearms Buy Back Program

—We believe in the private individual's right to own firearms as guaranteed

by the Second Amendment of the United States Constitution

—We support the smaller independent gun shops. Therefore, we will be purchasing any and all used guns supplied to us by legitimate licensed gun shops.

—In order to further support the smaller, independent gun shops, we will not be purchasing our used guns from the national chains.

—Only under rare occasions will we be purchasing our guns directly from the gun owners themselves.

—We will be paying hundred dollars per used gun, in any condition. We will pay all tax applicable to our purchases. We will visit the gun shops ourselves and collect and purchase their used guns.

—All guns purchased will be sawed apart and/or crushed in a hydraulic press.

These gun parts will then be sold to a steel refinery for melting into scrap.

Cameron thought about it. Every small gun store in America can now offer up to hundred dollars per traded-in firearm, knowing they have a guaranteed sale for even non-working firearms. Cameron had friends who were gun shop owners who were always complaining about the money they had in used, unsaleable guns. He was confident his friends would be happy to turn their used guns into cash.

Cameron contacted Colonel John and showed him his policy statement. Colonel John approved and said that he would have Wendy contact the website company and tell them of our plans and to post the policy statement. Colonel John was happy to have his good friend on board and believed he would do an admirable job.

Cameron knew it would be a slow start. He immediately contacted the head office of US Steel, which has steel plants throughout the United States. The management team at US Steel stated all their existing facilities would be happy to take the high-quality scrap steel. Cameron decided that along the east coast, he wanted three locations to send the metal scrap to.

He selected:

—Fairfield Works in Fairfield, Alabama

—Mon Valley Works in Clairton, Pennsylvania

—Great Lakes Works in River Rouge, Michigan

The management agreed, saying they would inform the plants of their agreement to accept this gun scrap. His next issue was having a location to drop off the guns for dismantling. He contacted his friends in the US military and was able to rent abandoned warehouses close to these steel factories.

Fairfield Steel Works in Fairfield, Alabama

His first location would be Fairfield, Alabama. When he arrived, he immediately visited and introduced himself to the managers of the Fairfield Steel Works. And after a brief discussion, they were excited to assist Sean Little in this effort and accept the high-grade steel. Next, Cameron inspected an empty local US military warehouse that was perfect for his needs. A large steel building in good shape with large transport doors in the front and rear. He hired a plant manager, Jim Wills, an ex-military colonel who he knew could handle the job. They brought in ten cutting chop saws and had them mounted onto the existing steel worktables. They also ordered ten small hydraulic presses and changed the flat press plates with ones that were "V" shaped for crushing the guns.

Jim Wills went about hiring the staff, relying on ex-military personnel as requested by Sean Little. He placed the ad in the newspaper looking for ex-military personnel with a salary of thousand dollars per week, and they were swamped with applications. As mentioned in the ad, physically disabled war veterans would be given top priority for the positions as specified by Sean Little.

Cameron turned his attention to the truck and collection crews. He purchased five new one-ton trucks with large square cargo boxes on the back. He purchased a thousand used military equipment boxes, 60" long, 30" wide, 30" tall, with solid metal handles on the side, and had them delivered to the warehouse. He had a staff member call the small local gun shops to inform them they would be dropping by tomorrow to purchase any guns they had for hundred dollars. The next morning, the five trucks left with their own routes to follow.

The response was amazing. The gun shop owners had all their cheap guns laid out for the crews when they arrived. One gun shop owner said, "You guys are heaven-sent. I've had these junk guns hanging around here for years. Please take them all."

The crews brought in the boxes, rechecked the guns themselves to make sure they were not loaded and stored them in the boxes. One crew member had a company credit card with which to purchase the guns.

When the five trucks arrived back at the warehouse, they were full to the brim. Each crew said the lowest number of guns they picked up from a store was usually thirty with most gun stores having over hundred or more used guns to pick up. The five trucks picked up 5100 guns that day. Amazing!

Cameron Then Determined the Following Warehouse Procedure:

Rifles: *When each rifle is removed from the metal cases, they are to be rechecked to ensure they are unloaded and their magazines removed.*

—they are to be handed off to the first table, where the rifle barrels are to be cut down to the top of the wooden stock.

—At the second table, the rifles are to be dismantled and their wood stocks thrown into their own separate bin.

—At the hydraulic presses, the guns are individually placed inside and the operator crushes the guns across their firing mechanism.

—All metal parts are thrown into the dumpsters that are emptied by the large industrial tow motors and then dumped into the awaiting dump trucks, to be taken to the steel plant.

Handguns: *Likewise, when each pistol is removed from the metal cases, they are rechecked again to make sure they are unloaded and their magazines removed.*

—The handguns are placed on a table where their non-metal handles are removed.

—These guns are placed in a metal tote bin and

—taken directly to the hydraulic presses to be crushed.

—These guns are then placed in the dumpsters to be taken away to the dump trucks.

The next morning, Cameron contacted a local trucking company to haul the metal scrap to the steel plant. The trucking company was just down the road, and he saw no need to purchase his own dump trucks. They can be here in twenty minutes after we call them. The dump truck would show up, and the operators on the tow motors would empty the bins of metal scrap into the trucks.

Cameron accompanied the dump truck driver to the steel plant to record the gun scrap being deposited in the furnace. The driver entered the steel plant yard and dropped the metal scrap where he was motioned to do so. The plant foreman came out and ordered their scrap to be loaded next. A very large crane came over with a round electric magnet on the end and simply picked up the scrap and moved it over to the conveyor system leading to the blast furnace. Cameron took detailed pictures on his phone.

Everything was working out smoothly. After the first day, Cameron had a meeting with all the staff.

"Ladies and gentlemen, I am proud to say that we processed and took approximately 5100 junk guns off the streets today. The gun shop owners are happy, the local police are happy, and we are happy. Our efforts here in Fairfield, Alabama, will be the blueprint for the entire National Firearms Buy Back Program. I am proud of you all. Thank you." And everyone cheered.

Cameron had plastic signs made up for the gun shops to hang in their windows.

National Firearms Buy Back Program
Purchasing Center
We Pay Hundred Dollars For Your Used Guns
In Any Condition

The next day, the trucks went out again and returned, loaded with cheap guns.

By this time, the second day, the staff were falling into a routine. Being ex-military personnel, they knew their way around guns and treated them with respect.

They greatly appreciated the jobs and the high rate of pay. One very friendly fellow even said to Cameron, "With a thousand per week salary, I don't think you will see any of us quitting." Everyone laughed.

Cameron was encouraged by the progress to date. The trucks obviously had to travel farther and farther out to visit more gun shops. Cameron hoped that once the word got out, they would buy up the old used guns, which would encourage people to dig out their old guns and sell them to the gun shops. What was also happening was that the collectors with lots of guns were trading in their older guns and getting newer guns. Everybody wins, he thought.

The local CBW news outlets caught wind of this and arranged for a film crew to meet at a local gun shop to film the procedure. The cameramen filmed the entire process of the gun shop owner handing over their sixty junk guns and showed the guns being checked and loaded into the cases. Next, they showed the guns being paid for and the guns loaded onto the trucks. The film crews showed up at the warehouse and filmed the entire procedure of the guns being removed, checked, dismantled, cut up, and crushed.

The film crew then followed the dump truck to the steel plant to record the gun scrap being loaded into the furnace. This film clip was shown on CBW morning news across the country, and the response was very favorable. The news announcers were encouraging everyone to turn in their old junk guns for cash and let their guns be destroyed.

One news announcer even signed off with, "Ladies and gentlemen, if you have any spare or non-working guns lying around, take them to your local gun shop and turn them in for a quick hundred dollars. Easy money."

For the next three months, using the warehouse in Fairfield, Alabama, as a home base, Cameron went with his five crews and would stay overnight farther afield. He contracted with the local transport companies to have all five of his trucks meet the transport truck at their own transport compound and load their gun cases onto the awaiting truck for delivery back to Fairfield.

Cameron and his crews would move into an area, rent hotel rooms, and the next day start collecting up the guns. That afternoon, they would meet at the truck yard and load their guns into the awaiting transport truck. Now loaded with about eight thousand guns, the truck would make the delivery to the warehouse in Fairfield, Alabama. The truck would then unload its full cases, refill with empty cases, and then return the next day for more guns.

On the fifteenth of the month, Cameron produced a hard copy report for Sean outlining the areas covered, the guns purchased, and the monies spent. He also included a DVD copy of the newscast about the gun program, along with his monthly report.

The truck crews stationed out of Fairfield, Alabama, covered the southern states of Texas, Louisiana, Alabama, Georgia, Florida, North and South Carolina, and Tennessee. Once the process was up and running, Cameron hired a manager for the truck and collection crews, Fred Thompson. Both the Fairfield plant manager, Jim Wills, and the truck manager, Fred Thompson, were known to Keith from being in the service together and he felt he could trust them both.

Mon Valley Works in Clairton, Pennsylvania

Cameron left them in charge and visited the US Steel plant, Mon Valley Works, in Clairton, Pennsylvania. This plant would take the guns they would be collecting from the north eastern seaboard. The managers gave Cameron a warm welcome, and they were excited to take his high-grade steel.

He rented an abandoned military warehouse and had it laid out exactly like the warehouse in Fairfield. He hired a plant manager and ex-military staff and purchased five one-ton trucks with large boxes on the back. He hired the staff and a truck manager. Cameron himself would go out with each crew on their first day to ensure that everything worked smoothly. He supervised the delivery of the guns back to the warehouse and set up the procedure for their destruction and delivery to the local steel plant. Cameron stayed here for two months just to make sure. The staff appreciated the job and the money.

Great Lakes Works in River Rough, Michigan

His next location was the US Steel plant, Great Lakes Works, in River Rouge, Michigan. After visiting the plant, he found a warehouse and set up everything exactly like the Fairfield, Alabama, and Clairton, Pennsylvania, facilities. He again hired all ex-military personnel, along with a warehouse manager and a truck/collections manager. Hiring the ex-military personnel was working out great. They were disciplined, hard-working people who knew their way around guns. At all three locations, he was able to hire a considerable number of physically disabled war veterans to help dismantle the guns. Wonderful.

In his report to Sean, he stated that with warehouse locations in Alabama, Pennsylvania, and now Michigan, the eastern USA was covered. He mentioned that he would have more warehouses in the future, likely ones in Montana, California, and Nevada.

The truck and collection crews could revisit an area every three months

347

and pick up more guns. This way, with these vehicles covering all the continental US, they could eventually rid the USA of all its junk guns over the next few years. He also reported that the news of buying the guns was being broadcast. They were taking in about ten thousand guns per day. Cameron was pleased with his report and believed that Sean would be too. And Cameron said, "Somehow, I enjoy this a lot more than just helping out at the local bingo hall."

Chapter 47
American Infrastructure

Outside of his work on American environmental issues, Sean knew that any ideas he had for working on American infrastructure would require a separate Project Director. He asked Colonel John to contact the US Army Corps of Engineers and ask about any retired military engineers who might like to apply.

In the next couple of days, there were four resumes on his desk. Sean had Wendy check out each of them, and all the responses were favorable. He asked Wendy to invite them to the compound for an interview, arriving two hours apart. Before meeting them, he purposely let each wait for about twenty minutes in Wendy's office for her to make her own assessment. When they would ask if she had any authority, "No, sir, I don't. I just help out with the accounting." Then she would let them talk.

After Sean interviewed each one in turn, he had them go with Colonel John to take a tour of the compound. Later that day, Sean asked Wendy, "You had each one of these men sit with you for twenty minutes. I want you to give me your honest assessment of each individual."

Wendy liked one in particular, a retired General Braeden Gordon, who she felt would fit in well. The other three she wasn't too fussy about because they became upset when they had to wait and wanted to "throw their weight around." Two even ordered her to get them a coffee, which really annoyed her.

Sean talked to Colonel John, "John, I want your honest assessment on which one of those four retired officers would make the best fit for us heading up my American infrastructure projects."

"Well, to be honest," Colonel John replied. "I happen to like the retired General Braeden Gordon. The other three kept telling me what to do and bragging that if they were in control around here, things would be different. They also seemed to have their heads full of their own importance and, in my opinion, would likely cause you trouble later on."

"Good, thank you for your honesty," said Sean.

When Colonel John left, Sean went to Wendy's office and asked her to contact General Gordon and offer him the job. Wendy immediately called General Gordon.

When Wendy called General Gordon, he was so excited, "Take the job, take the job, are you kidding? Being retired is for the birds.

I hate it. I was doing big projects all around the world for forty years and now I help out at the seniors center. I'll start right now, anything you want."

When Sean heard that General Gordon would take the job, he asked Wendy to contact the others to tell them that the position had been filled. Wendy walked out of Sean's office smiling and said, "With pleasure."

General Gordon and his wife came in to see Sean. Mrs. Gordon was a fun-loving lady, and Sean introduced her to Jennifer, and they both left to take a tour of the compound and select some accommodations. Sean gave General Gordon the usual list of conditions and gave him back to Wendy to get him situated. Sean also said with a smile, "Be nice to Wendy. She writes the checks."

Once General Gordon and his wife were situated in an apartment with an office and a few staff, Sean met with him for his first assignment.

Project #11: Individual State Highway Overpasses

Sean stated, "Braeden, I want your staff to contact every governor in every state and select one highway overpass for us to either repair or tear down, and build a new one. At present, the municipalities are strapped for cash, and repairing the infrastructure is too much of a burden for them. I want to have your engineers select a number of quality overpass plans and stick with those. This way, we can keep track of our costs and make sure no one is skimping on the materials."

"Sounds like a good plan," Braeden replied. "I've heard about some highways they've had to close because the overpasses are falling down on the motorists. I would expect the municipalities to be excited at this news."

Then Sean said, "I want the municipality to contract for the new overpasses themselves. We will pay for the entire project, along with any interest, once the project is completed and after we have inspected it. This way, the municipality is on the hook for the project, and you don't have to be bothered on a daily basis with fifty or so bridges being built and driving Wendy nuts constantly asking for checks."

"I like that idea, Sean, because they would be driving me nuts too." Both he and Sean laughed.

General Gordon got onto the project right away. He immediately sent out letters to each of the state governors, asking them to select one highway overpass for him to consider. Shortly after, phone calls started coming in, and General Gordon was off inspecting the projects in question. Before he left, Sean did mention that General Gordon would have to hire a team of engineers, as he would likely be too busy to review every project.

"I agree, Sean, but I'm so excited to get busy that I'm going to inspect these overpasses myself," said General Gordon as he and Mrs. Gordon jumped into their car and off they went.

Project #12: Municipal Pollution Control in the Mississippi River Watershed

A month later, Sean placed his next project on General Gordon's desk. Sean wanted to pay for all the updates to the municipal and industrial pollution control systems on or near the Mississippi River Watershed. He informed him of the pollution map of the Mississippi River that Curt Kurnes was making up and asked him to use this as an outline. He asked him to please cooperate with Curt and start cleaning up the Mississippi River, starting from the source to downstream.

Wendy as Sean's Executive Secretary

Sean called Wendy into his office and asked her to sit down.

"Wendy, whether I like it or not, I don't seem to be able to handle my workload around here. I'm delegating everything I can. We've stopped all incoming emails and phone calls to lighten my load. What I'm trying to get around to is that Jennifer and I have been talking, and I would like you to quit the armed services and become my Executive Secretary," asked Sean.

You can retain your own office or have a new one outside of mine, whatever you want. I still want you to oversee the entire financial department and staff. Some of the projects that are handled with just a check, for example, Veterans and Police Officers pay, the subsidies to the telephone and railway tie manufacturers, and the Great Pacific Garbage Parch, you and I would still control. Like all my other Project Directors, your salary would be fifty thousand dollars per month plus expenses. What do you say?"

"I accept. I think the final straw was those arrogant generals sitting in my office talking down to me, and when the first one ordered me to go get him a coffee, I almost spit. I was busy approving the checks for the veterans and police officers for close to twenty-seven million dollars and he orders me to get him a coffee, an unemployed ex-general. The nerve. The other general did the same thing. When would you like me to start?"

"Ten minutes ago," Sean said with a smile.

"Thank you, Sean. I won't let you down. But Sean, can I ask you one favor? Colonel John and I have started seeing one another, and I would certainly appreciate him not being positioned elsewhere," she said.

"Well, I don't think he'll be going anywhere. I'll just make him my Chief of Security and give him an offer he can't refuse." And they both laughed.

"Thank you, Sean," then she turned around and walked out.

Over the next couple of months, Sean really liked Wendy as his Executive Secretary. She absolutely flourished after being put in control. Sean was amazed that she never got flustered or upset, just kept right on working. Her organizational skills were off the charts. He used to muse to himself that he could go missing for two months, and with Wendy in charge, nobody would notice.

He even started allowing her access to the Project Director's monthly reports and started listening to her opinions. Along with her new title, he gave her signing authority on checks up to one million dollars with himself signing anything over that. Sean's favorite joke for everyone else was, "Whatever you do, don't piss Wendy off. She writes the checks."

The only problem he had was that Jennifer would constantly show up unannounced and drag Wendy out for a girl's day in Las Vegas.

"Have fun" was all Sean could say while he shook his head. It really didn't matter as with Wendy and the staff living right in the compound, most staff visited their offices on Saturday and Sunday anyway.

"As long as the work gets done, I don't care what you do," he would say as Jennifer and Wendy waved to him as they headed to the elevator.

Chapter 48
Annual Projects General Meeting

Knowing that Sean was a reader and preferred written reports over oral reports, Wendy placed a large file folder on Sean's desk. It was her proposal for an annual general meeting where all the Project Directors would outline their projects and progress to date. Each Project Director would give a short speech followed by a media presentation, limited to twenty minutes each.

Sean liked the idea but requested that during the presentations no money be discussed or expenses outlined.

"The cost of each project is only for you and me to know," and Wendy agreed.

She felt that this annual meeting should be recorded and recommended that the National Geographic association will be allowed to film and produce the event. She felt that they had done an excellent job on their documentary about cleaning up the Great Pacific Garbage Patch, and Wendy said they were easy to deal with.

Sean read it and was impressed.

"Looks like you've really thought this through," Sean said approvingly. "Whatever you want, you arrange it. I really like the idea of the National Geographic being involved, as this guarantees its world-wide coverage.

But please, this is not to be a media event. Only the National Geographic cameramen will be allowed in. No other news agency will be allowed in or will anyone be allowed to ask questions.

And we will both preview the production before it goes to the airwaves. Agreed?"

"Agreed," replied Wendy, obviously happy to be able to arrange this production.

Wendy got right into organizing the general meeting.

Once the word got out about this meeting, she was bombarded with requests from news agencies and other environmental groups to attend.

They were all refused, in turn. She was also shocked at the number of politicians who wanted to see their name alongside these projects for no other reason than to bolster their image at home. Likewise, these requests were also turned down. She was fond of saying, "You let one in, and you have to let them all in."

She called the National Geographic Head Office and explained that they were welcome to record the meeting, but that no reporters would be allowed. They agreed to send two camera people and six technicians. They arrived a few days before the meeting, and Wendy issued them temporary ID cards. She outlined the conditions of their work here.

"Remember, if one of you can't make it, we will not allow a substitute into the compound. You are to photograph the events, but you are not allowed to talk to anyone or ask questions. Once finished, you are to supply me with the finished production for my approval before going to air." They all agreed.

They set up their cameras and equipment and left to spend their time enjoying the sights of Las Vegas.

On the date of the meeting, Wendy chaired it herself, along with doing her own project presentations. Each Project Director was allowed one assistant, who sat along with the others in the forty chairs along one side. Even though Sean's new boardroom took up one half of a floor of the office tower, it was full. Besides the Project Directors themselves, there were twelve project assistants, members of the Director's families, Jennifer and her family, and Ralph Barns. There were plenty of armed guards, and every door was guarded. Originally planned as a serious affair, but with all these friends together, it turned into a friendly gathering.

The camera people were let in at six a.m. and got accustomed to the heavily armed guards always standing by them. The media center was basically just a DVD player with a very large-screen TV behind the speaker podium. Coffee, muffins, and fruit were provided with a start time of ten a.m.

At ten a.m. sharp, Wendy introduced the meeting and thanked the participants.

She outlined that the camera people were from the National Geographic, who would be producing a program on today's proceedings. She then introduced David Kim, the Project Director for the Fresh Water Initiative.

Project #1: The Fresh Water Initiative, Directed by David Kim

David Kim outlined that his mission objective was to finally discover how to separate salt from salt water. He outlined the universities that were being funded to test every imaginable method. From filtration systems to evaporation systems to trying to figure out what the salt could be attracted to in order to be removed, With the generous incentive of two hundred and fifty million US dollars to any group or individual who could solve this problem, he hoped that someone somewhere would come through with a breakthrough. He then said, "Removing the salt from salt water would mean fresh water for the world to drink, fresh water for farmers' crops, and fresh water for their farm animals. Once discovered, this would be one of the greatest discoveries of mankind. I want to personally thank Sean Little for allowing me to be a part of this." Then, after a brief video of work being done in a lab, David Kim sat down.

Project #2: Disabled Veteran's and Police Officers Pay, Directed by Wendy Rawlings

Wendy introduced herself. She stated that sending out five hundred dollars monthly checks to the disabled veterans and police officers tax-free was well received. She then outlined that all physically disabled veterans and police officers would continue to receive the five hundred dollars checks. She then paused and pointed to Sean. Sean stood up and addressed the small group.

"Ladies and gentlemen, I propose that from now on,

–First, as well as those disabled veterans and police officers receiving five hundred dollars per month, I would like the list expanded to include physically disabled federal agents of the FBI, CIA, DEA, and Home Security.

–Second, those persons, veterans, police officers and federal agents who have lost one leg or one arm should start to receive checks for fifteen hundred dollars per month.

–Third, those others who have disabilities that have kept them from getting a job, for example, loss of both legs, loss of one arm and one leg, and for those of our veterans, police officers and federal agents who have passed away for whatever reason, leaving families behind, their families will now receive three thousand dollars per month, tax-free. What do you think?"

Everyone sat in amazement and then started clapping.

"Sean, this is wonderful. I'm all for it. You are doing great things, and this is wonderful. The number of people you will be helping is amazing," said Wendy.

Sean spoke again, "Well, it's decided. Wendy, I leave you in charge of contacting the FBI, CIA, DEA, and Home Security to acquire their disabled agent's lists. Plus, it's your call on who gets the new checks for fifteen hundred dollars and three thousand dollars." Sean then sat down as everyone else was standing and clapping.

Wendy was close to tears.

"Well, you've heard it from the man. Starting today war veterans, police officers, and federal agents who are severely disabled or who are no longer with us and have left families behind will be receiving new checks from fifteen hundred dollars to three thousand dollars tax-free."

The audience couldn't stop clapping. Somehow, Wendy composed herself and continued.

Project #3: Subsidizing the Telephone Pole and Railway Tie Manufactures, Directed by Wendy Rawlings

Wendy reported that the existing telephone pole and railway tie manufacturers were working at full capacity, and most were expanding their factories to handle the orders. She reported that the telephone and railway purchasing agents were delighted to hear that they could now start using factory-manufactured metal poles and ties instead of having to buy poles and ties made from real trees. While showing a video of inside a telephone pole manufacturing company, she said, "For every manufactured telephone pole or railway tie we subsidize means one less tree cut down." There was a roar of applause from the group.

Project #4: The Incinerator, CEO Pete Johnson of the Koris Corporation

Wendy then introduced Pete, "Ladies and gentlemen, I would like to introduce Pete Johnson of the Koris Corporation, the man responsible for having our lights working today."

Pete took the podium. "Ladies and gentlemen, about a year ago I got contacted by Sean Little to build an electricity-producing generator, a big one, powered mainly from the burning of discarded car tires, railway ties, and household garbage. The task looked impossible, but with Sean's urging and money, we saw it through. Ladies and gentlemen, I am proud to say that today this entire compound is run off of one generator powered by the environmentally friendly Koris's incinerator. I asked Sean if he wanted to name the incinerator, and he declined. He didn't think naming it the Little Generator was suitable." Everyone got a good laugh over that one.

"Today, this incinerator is the envy of the world. Sean also wanted to prove that if such an incinerator could be placed near the seashore, you could pipe in salt water, have it evaporate, and remove the fresh water. On his insistence, he has proven that this works, and along with electricity, this incinerator can also be a source of clean, fresh drinking water.

"We now have confirmed orders for fifteen more incinerators, with another thirty being discussed. I would like you to now give a round of applause for Sean Little, a true visionary." Once again, everyone stood, clapped, and cheered.

Project #5: Save the Whales, Directed by Bill Fryer

Then it was Bill Fryer's turn. Bill outlined how he was asked by Sean to quietly buy up all the world's whaling companies and ships and have their whaling equipment removed and sold for scrap. He then outlined that these large whaling factory ships had been refitted and used as collector ships to clean up the Great Pacific Garbage Patch. He outlined that some of the smaller whaling ships were now being used as support ships for the collector and transport ships, and the rest were sold off for scrap.

Bill mentioned that Sean personally made those countries, especially Japan and Norway, enact legislation to outlaw any future whale hunting.

Bill turned to the screen, where videos of the large harpooning guns were being cut up at a steel factory. Then the screen turned to beautiful videos of blue whales swimming in a deep blue ocean.

"Ladies and gentlemen, I would all like you to stand and give a round of applause to Sean Little, who has single-handedly stopped the world-wide hunting and killing of our beautiful whales." Everyone cheered.

Project #6: The Great Pacific Garbage Patch

Wendy then introduced Sean, and he said, "Somehow, I'm still doing this job." Everyone laughed.

"Ladies and gentlemen, In seriousness, my efforts would be for nothing except for the generous help of Bill Fryer, my lawyer, and Wendy Rawlings, my Executive Secretary, in cleaning up the Great Pacific Garbage Patch. Please give them a round of applause.

"The arrangements I have made with the US, China, India, Pakistan, Japan, and Norway are working out well. I supply the ships, and they supply the crews. With the crew members getting a salary of thousand dollars per week and a bonus of one hundred thousand dollars in American dollars at the end of their six-month work contract, there are thousands of people eager to go to work. In most countries, it is a badge of honor to have worked on the ships cleaning up this mess. Countless tons of ash are now being accepted by India and China and used in their landfill projects. So I must say so myself, it's proceeding along as planned." Everyone cheered!

Sean turned to the TV screen, and the audience watched some clips of the National Geographic program on cleaning up the Garbage Patch. At the end, he merely said, "Thank you" and sat down.

Wendy stood up and started yelling, "No, you don't. You don't get away that easily. Everybody stand up and give Sean Little the admiration he deserves. He is responsible for cleaning up the world."

The audience clapped and cheered for minutes. Wendy could see that Sean had a tear in his eye.

Project #7: Planting More Trees, Directed by Curt Kurnes

When the clapping finally subsided, Wendy introduced Curt Kurnes, who will be outlining the next three projects.

"Ladies and gentlemen, I am Curt Kurnes, and up until Sean hired me, I was the Head of Operations for the Sierra Club out of Oakland, California. Sean caught my attention when he handed me a check for five million dollars for the Sierra Club and then a check for ten million dollars to go toward those organizations dedicated to planting more trees in the US and overseas. He said he hoped this bought him ten million trees, and let me tell you, it did. And from that and every year since Sean has donated ten million dollars sponsoring ten million trees being planted throughout the world."

Curt pointed to the screen showing people planting trees in different countries around the world.

Project #8-Mississippi River Pollution Map, Directed by Curt Kurnes

Curt outlined the plans for a detailed pollution map of the Mississippi River and its tributaries. This has been completed with the help of four universities. This map will now be our template for cleaning up the river. In conjunction with our other projects, we will start cleaning up the Mississippi River, starting from the mouth down to the Gulf of Mexico.

Project #9-Individual State Dump Site Cleanup

Curt continued, "Sean, not wanting me to be idle, gave me the agenda to contact every state governor and request that they select one dump or spill site that we could clean up. Needless to say, they were enthusiastic. Under Sean's direction, we have purchased one dump or environmental spill site in each of our fifty-two American states, and the contractors are cleaning them up as we speak. Making jobs for Americans and cleaning up environmental problems, one mess at a time!"

Curt then pointed to the screen with a short video of a large dump site being cleaned up, and to a round of applause, he sat down.

Project #10-The National Firearms Buy Back Program

Wendy thanked Curt for his dedicated work on the three projects. She introduced retired General Cameron Paul.

"Ladies and gentlemen, Sean, thinking I wasn't too busy working on my afternoon bingo hall steering committee, asked me to head up a project for him. I am proud to say that under Sean's direction, we have created a National Firearms Buy Back Program. With firearm collection facilities now in Alabama, Pennsylvania, and Michigan, and with three more planned in Montana, Nevada, and California. Since its start, I am proud to say that we have purchased 2.5 million guns. That's 2.5 million guns being dismantled and melted down for scrap, never to be fired again."

He then pointed to the screen with a scene of people cutting up rifles and the metal scrap being poured into a furnace.

"As long as Sean keeps supplying the money, I'll keep getting those guns off the streets and right into the furnaces. Let's have a round of applause for Sean." Everyone stood and cheered.

Project #11-Individual State Highway Overpasses

Wendy then introduced retired General Braeden Gordon. Sean asked me to contact every state governor and have them select one highway overpass that we could either repair or replace. I am proud to say that Sean is now responsible for fifty-two highway overpasses being repaired or replaced throughout the USA."

He then pointed to the screen behind him, showing the repairs being done to an overpass in Georgia.

Project #12-Mississippi Municipal Pollution Control Updates

"And to be coordinated with Curt Kurnes with his Mississippi River Pollution Map, I am to oversee that every municipality and business presently polluting the Mississippi River gets the pollution control systems they need and installed. Under Sean's guidance, one day you will be able to drink the water out of the Mississippi River."

General Gordon then pointed to the screen behind him, showing the installation of a very large pollution control device being installed at a steel factory.

Wendy then thanked all the Project Directors and turned the meeting over to Sean.

"Ladies and gentlemen, my Project Directors here, David Kim and Wendy Rawlings, Bill Fryer, Curt Kurnes, General Cameron Paul, and General Braeden Gordon, are putting together my dreams of a cleaner, safer planet. Our work will continue, and more projects will be added over time. I am proud to be associated with you all. Thank you and keep up the good work. And ladies and gentlemen, I am very proud to announce that the bar is now open." The room exploded in laughter.

Sean had hoped for a laid-back, pleasant event, and this was exactly what he got.

He loved the jokes told by the retired generals and the festive atmosphere of the gathering. He encouraged the directors to get to know one another and wanted them to become friends. He reminded the cameramen that they could take pictures but could not talk to the participants.

"There are no interviews taking place here today," Sean said.

Sean was pleased with the day's events, and after a large banquet with all the participants in attendance, he left and slept well that night.

Later that week, Wendy and Sean reviewed the National Geographic film production of the meeting and approved of what they saw. It would be aired in the coming two weeks. As expected, the world raved about the important works that Sean was funding. At the time, it seemed not much could go wrong. They were wrong.

Chapter 49
The World Turns Against Sean

Sean was satisfied that his dreams of cleaning up the world were coming true. The President, the Vice President, the CIA, and the FBI were off his back, the guards and the police kept the onlookers out, and the operations inside the compound were going smoothly. Everyone left him alone as long as he continued the payments to the war vets and police officers. And the FBI and CIA all expressed their appreciation for including their physically disabled agents in his monthly check program.

The publicity created by doing his environmental projects made him a hero around the world. The news agencies did the best they could to get an interview, but with Sean's personal policy of "no incoming calls, no emails, and no interviews," they were kept at a distance.

Everything he wished to tell the world he either stated at church on Sunday or had an announcement made on the website. The website was monitored by every news agency around the world, and any announcement there guaranteed that it was on the news channels within the hour.

Sean always felt that there were evil forces waiting for him just outside the gates. Others could leave, but he could not. He and he alone possessed the secret, and everyone wanted it. From his own government and businesses to foreign governments and their business interests. Sean felt that everyone had a use for this secret, but few wanted to do any good with it. Most wanted it for the control it would give them over others.

He viewed it like the four years from the end of World War II in 1945 to 1949 (when Russia detonated its own atomic bomb) when the US had sole ownership of the atomic bomb. For that brief time, they could do what they wanted, whenever they wanted. They had the secret, and they were in control. Similar to this secret. Any government could use it to blackmail other world leaders and control the world.

The National Geographic aired the program of their Annual General Meeting, and it was viewed by millions around the world. Of course, there were news agencies that criticized Sean for not doing more for their country or for not getting involved in their own pet projects, but that was to be expected.

"News reporters are always complaining. No matter how much you try to help, there are always those who complain that you're not doing enough. Well, I don't see them doing anything about it, but boy, they sure like to tell others what to do," Sean told his friends at dinner one night. Everyone agreed.

The demand of the news agencies for interviews was relentless. The news agencies had reporters permanently stationed in Las Vegas, ready to interview everyone they could, from clients and lab assistants to Jennifer and her family and even the construction workers. But these interviews all told the same story. It was only Sean who knew the secret, and nobody could get to him. Sean knew something would break, and it did.

Another Helicopter

Another unauthorized helicopter arrived. Instead of being filled with news reporters like the last one, this one housed the executives of the "Friends of the Planet and All Its Creatures Foundation." Environmental foundations and charities around the world were frustrated that Sean would not just write them a "blank check" to allow them to carry on their activities.

"When you just hand out money," Sean would say, "that doesn't mean the people will use the money the way they said they would. I prefer to be proactive myself, fund my own projects, and see them through to completion. For this reason, I have given orders to all my Project Directors that they cannot fund or support any outside organizations without my direct permission."

The procedure for accepting an unauthorized helicopter had already been decided upon by Sean and Colonel John. The Bell 407 GX helicopter, upon landing, was surrounded by heavily armed guards who ordered the occupants of the helicopter to remain inside. To ensure this, two Caterpillar backhoes were brought over and placed their buckets up to the helicopter doors, not allowing the helicopter to leave or the occupants to get out. With the occupants still inside, Colonel John ordered that the helicopter be drained of fuel. Colonel John even had a pickup truck specially set up for this sole purpose.

Sean Little was picked up by Colonel John and driven to the landing site. Sean stayed back from the helicopter and remained in the Jeep. Colonel John took the bullhorn.

"To the occupants of the helicopter: you have trespassed on federally restricted airspace and property. You will exit the helicopter and place your hands above your heads. Once out of the helicopter, you will kneel on the ground, at which time my men will handcuff you. If any of you are holding a weapon, I have given orders for my men to fire."

The backhoe up against the pilot's door moved back, and the pilot exited. He kneeled down and was immediately handcuffed. The others, falsely claiming that they were invited, were likewise handcuffed. Colonel John contacted the local police, who picked up these trespassers at the main gate. As before, Colonel John had people taking videos of the helicopter, the trespassers being handcuffed, being led away by the guards, and being put in their cells.

Once the helicopter was empty and drained of fuel, Colonel John inspected the interior of the helicopter for any personal items. Colonel John looked at Sean, and Sean nodded. Colonel John then gave the order, and the operators of the two backhoes proceeded to crush the Bell 407GX helicopter. Several guards took pictures on their cell phones. Colonel John then asked anyone who had pictures to please forward them to the website company.

The video appeared on the website and was quickly picked up by the local news networks. Again, people thought that Sean had gone too far, and others felt that he had the right to protect his own privacy. Sean didn't care. No better deterrent than watching a brand-new helicopter being destroyed to keep others from visiting me, he thought. Sean laughed when he watched the news footage of the trespassers being formally charged and yelling that Sean should give them money because they were nice people. This never ends. Everyone wants either money or the secret.

As expected, weeks later, Wendy received an invoice from the "Federation" for $1.8 million dollars to replace their Bell 407 GX helicopter. Sean wrote on the invoice in black magic marker, "Kiss my ass, Sean Little." And handed it back to Wendy.

Wendy asked, "What if they sue us?"

"Great," said Sean. "Bill's not doing much anyway. It'll give him something to do." And they both laughed. Later, Colonel John reported on the incident.

"It would appear that their "Foundation" is a fraud and was only set up last month and funded by some outside source. The helicopter they had was a new one that they had recently purchased with a $200,000 deposit. We searched but did not find any weapons in the wreckage of the helicopter.

"The people we arrested say they want to meet you and have you fund their environmental efforts. I suspect they were here to gain your friendship, give them money, or do you harm. My belief is that they were here to do you harm. All four of them seemed extremely physically fit for environmental executives. That's all we know, and it's good that we stopped them before they got to you. They are still under arrest and are being formally charged with trespassing on government property."

"Thank you, John. I appreciate it," said Sean, and Colonel John got up and left.

Another Visit from the Vice President

Colonel John came in and told Sean that Vice President Vince Rogers would be flying in to see him tomorrow. As always, anyone who wanted to see Sean wanted one of three things: money, to get Sean interested in their pet project, or the secret. At least with the government, it was always one thing: they wanted the secret.

The next day, Vice President Vince Rogers arrived, flanked by his bodyguards. Sean greeted him as best he could. The Vice President took a seat and said, "Sean, we in the government are taking increasing heat over you and you alone having this secret. Many world leaders think that it is unfair that you are charging fifty million dollars per application when there are deserving people who should have it. The President and I think that you've had your fun trying to save the world, and now it's time for us, the professionals, to take over."

"Well, isn't that great?" replied Sean. "And I bet the first deserving people for my process would be you and the President. Am I right? You probably lay awake at night licking your lips, thinking about how you could control the world by dangling my secret in front of world leaders and getting them to obey your every word."

The Vice President replied with, "No, with the American government in control, we could decide which projects to promote and which ones to delete."

Sean, getting angrier, replied with, "Is that how you would help the world? You'd stop all of my environmental projects and stop funding the payments to the war vets, police officers, and federal agents. Can't you see what I'm doing? The entire world is lopsided. I have the means to make the two percent of the world population that controls fifty percent of the world's wealth voluntarily hand it over so that I can improve this world, a world you would prefer to destroy.

"We live in a society where people live in fifty million dollars houses with garages full of two million dollars cars living down the road from children who go to school with nothing to eat. Billions of people around the world have no access to clean water, sanitation, health care, education, or food, and all you do is try to find out more ways to wage war and kill people. Can't you see that you are killing this planet and everyone on it?"

The Vice President was having a difficult time controlling his anger.

"Look here. Your secret is confined to this compound, and as long as we protect you, you're safe. The minute you leave, here you know you'll be kidnapped and tortured to reveal your secret. We own you, and you know it."

Sean exploded, "Own me. You own me. You bastard. That's only if I wish to remain alive. I will take my own life before I let some piece of shit like you have it. Maybe I should publish the secret on my website and let the whole world know. What would you do, then? Everyone would have it. But no, you want it for yourself to bribe the other world leaders and take control of the world. Wow, you could have an entire race of superhumans who wouldn't age, ruling over everyone else living in poverty."

The Vice President went to speak, and Sean, boiling over, interrupted him.

"I will never give you this secret, never. You can kill everyone I know and torture me, but I won't tell you. Everyone I hold dear has stated that if they are kidnapped, I am not to reveal the secret. Our lives are not more important than this secret. You came here to threaten me. I'm helping to clean up the world and even paying war vets, police officers, and federal agents, and you still despise me. Now put a bullet in my head or get out of here and take your hired goons with you. You make me sick. Now get out."

At this, the Vice President left in a huff with his guards trailing behind. Sean thought, *I'm truly starting to despise this man.*

The World Turns Against Sean

Somehow, Sean noticed that the news medias were slowly starting to turn against him. The issues were muted at first and then grew louder. The local news media, with nothing else to report on, became obsessed with reporting about Sean and his applications. They started to turn against Sean using interviews with disgruntled employees, especially with Marlene Forbes, the lady who said that Sean refused to save her mother-in-law.

The local news channel interviewed Marlene, and with her yelling into the camera and saying, "Sean Little has the means to cure all our ills and make us live forever. He refuses to use it except on his friends and on anyone who can pay fifty million dollars. He is holding the world for ransom. He could have saved my mother-in-law but no, greedy Sean Little wouldn't do it because she didn't have fifty million dollars. Rot in hell, Sean Little."

Colonel John, seeing this, immediately contacted Nellis Air Force Base and talked to Marlene Forbes's commanding officer. The commanding officer said that he would see what he could do about keeping her quiet, but both agreed that the damage had already been done.

Somehow, this interview was the trigger that made the other news agencies respond with their own criticisms. The foreign news agencies started complaining about Sean Little, saying that his focus was only on the US when he should be helping the world. It didn't matter that he was funding major world environmental projects. The news agencies were condemning Sean, saying he wasn't doing enough.

Sean decided to make a statement at the upcoming Sunday's sermon. On that Sunday, Sean took the podium.

"Ladies and gentlemen, for reasons unknown to me, I am taking increasing heat from the world press for not doing enough for others. To date, my worldwide efforts include solely funding the Fresh Water Initiative, which tries to produce fresh water from salt water. I have stopped the worldwide whale hunt, and I am solely funding the cleanup of the Great Pacific Garbage Patch. But somehow, worldwide news agencies are saying

I haven't done enough.

"I have not sought individual contributions nor sought government aid. In the United States alone I would easily estimate that there are thousands of persons directly employed in my environmental efforts.

"Earlier this week, I was again visited by Vice President Vince Rogers, who again threatened me with handing over my secret to the US government. I told him, and I tell you now that I will never hand this secret over to the US government or any government, ever. This secret should be for the benefit of all mankind, not just a single government determined to control the world with it. I swear to you, and I swear before God that I will take this secret to my grave before I allow others to use it for their own evil purposes."

The World Responds

As before, on the website, people posted this speech, and the world reacted. Some of the world news agencies apologized to Sean for any inferences that they were being critical of his environmental efforts. The New China News Agency, the voice of the People's Republic of China, made an announcement, "Mr. Little, we herald your peaceful efforts to improve this world. We are grateful for your work in the Pacific Ocean and look forward to assisting you in your future environmental efforts. We deeply apologize if any of our comments have offended you. To us in China, you are a hero."

The announcer then continued, "We, the people of the People's Republic of China, again say that any effort to obtain Sean Little's age-reversing secret and to use it as an international bargaining chip will be viewed by us as an act of aggression deserving of a military response."

Sean and Jennifer watched this on the CNN news. Jennifer said, "You really know how to get a response. Do you think they will ever give up trying to get your secret?"

"No, Jennifer, I don't," replied Sean. "It's just too important to them. It must drive them nuts thinking that this secret is on their own soil, but they can't control it. Why people wish to use this for evil and to control others is something I will never understand. The world spends over two trillion dollars each year on military spending, money that could be spent on health care, education, or feeding their people. But no, the government types must have the latest and greatest weapons. Why humans love to kill each other is beyond me."

After this, the news agencies stopped seeing Sean as a scapegoat for all their problems. The flow of people through Ralph's lab was as strong as ever. There just didn't seem to be any end to people who had fifty million dollars who wanted to be five years younger. For the time being, they felt safe.

Is the Papyrus the Clue?

Every night, Sean pondered why the other laboratories could not duplicate his success. Why could he achieve these results when the others could not? *These are the best-equipped labs in the world, staffed by the best and brightest, but they still can't duplicate my results.*

He knew that the FBI had examined his aluminum case back at the lab in Boston, knew its ingredients, and photocopied his instructions. *They've recorded my every move when applying the applications but still, they can't duplicate my success. Why?*

He pondered the differences between himself and the others applying the formula.

The only difference could be that he and he alone had handled the papyrus. He knew the papyrus was covered with an oily substance, but he thought it was merely to preserve it. *Maybe the oil is the clue. Could it be that my being in contact with this oil activates the ingredients, allowing them to reverse the aging process in living cells? Am I the missing ingredient? No other factors made any sense.* But now with the papyrus gone, even Sean knew that he would never know for sure. Then he drifted off into a deep, restless sleep.

Chapter 50
Project # 13 – National $15 Minimum Wage Initiative

For any further major projects, Sean knew that his capital requirements would be growing. He got Barry Leibowitz, Ralph Barns, and Wendy together for a meeting and stated his intentions.

"Thank you all for showing up today. As everyone can see, our existing projects are costing a lot of money, and any of my new projects can only be funded with a radical increase in our revenues. At present, we are doing ten applications every two weeks, giving us about twenty applications per month for a revenue stream of about one billion dollars per month. As the medical building was originally designed to do twenty applications every week, I am asking you three what has to be done to do twenty applications every single Monday, fifty-two weeks a year. This increase in our monthly application rate from twenty to eighty or more per month would increase our monthly income to about four billion dollars per month.

"I realize that this will entail additional staff, additional housing, and maybe an additional medical building. You three decide. Wendy, I leave it up to you to coordinate so that Barry and Ralph have everything they need and to see to it that these additional procedures are completed.

"Wendy, I would like your finalized report on this by the end of the month. Plus, after today, you do not need to consult with me on this, just get it done."

And to everyone's surprise, Sean got up and nodded his head, left the boardroom, and shut the door behind him. The three just looked at each other and smiled. Wendy spoke first. "Well, we just heard it from the man. If he wants to go to twenty applications every Monday, fifty-two weeks a year, he gets twenty applications every Monday, fifty-two weeks a year."

Ralph spoke next. "I think we have the capacity to do twenty applications per week with the present medical building we have. All we need is an increase in our staff. But with what we are paying our people, I don't think that should be a problem. We already have a backlog of applications from former and existing military medical staff who want to work here."

Barry spoke next. "Yes, the present medical building should accommodate the increase in application traffic. If you do decide on an additional medical building, it would be best done without disturbing your existing procedures. If needed, I propose that I build an identical medical building right next to your present one and, when completed, join them with an exterior glass walkway where the guests can be wheeled over to the application room.

"Plus, you will definitely need an additional apartment building, most likely similar to the existing two-bedroom apartment building we have now. Once you approve, the nice thing is that we don't have to wait for municipal approval as this is a federal military establishment. I can proceed immediately with this new apartment building.

Wendy spoke next. "Great idea. Let me get you a ten million dollars deposit check to get the new apartment building underway. You have my permission to start on the additional medical building once the new apartment is completed. I think Sean has something big planned, and I don't want to disappoint him. Barry and Ralph, anything you need, let me know." Then the three broke away and agreed to get together tomorrow for lunch.

As requested, Wendy had the final report on Sean's desk for the end of the month. Pretty difficult not knowing what was going on as Barry already had the foundations of the new apartment building being dug.

"Looks like everything is coming along nicely," Sean said to Wendy as she placed the construction plans on Sean's desk.

Wendy then replied with, "I went ahead and asked Barry to build us an additional medical building joined to our existing one after he's finished with the new apartment building. I hope that meets with your approval."

"Absolutely," replied Sean. "There seems to be no end in sight of people wanting the application, and heaven knows we'll need a lot more money for any new projects. Plus, you didn't have to ask for my approval. You have the authority."

Wendy simply smiled, said, "Thank you" and left. She later mused to herself if Sean would even care to look at the report. And in the pit of her stomach, she knew that he had something big planned.

On one of their nightly walks and viewing the new construction, Sean said to Jennifer, "It's amazing how much work can get done if you put enough money and people behind it."

The construction on the new apartment building was started immediately, with the crews working two eight-hour shifts per day, seven days a week. The crews were being very well paid, along with free accommodation and meals. No one complained, especially when they heard there was a ten thousand dollars bonus check waiting for them at the end of the project. Sean really liked the offer of the "end of project" checks, as this seemed to get everyone motivated. Once the new apartment building was complete, Barry confirmed with Wendy and immediately started the foundation of an additional medical building.

With the new medical staff hired and settled in, it took another month of training. The existing medical crews were split up, with half being experienced staff and the other half being new recruits. This seemed to be working out well. And on Ralph's insistence, he wanted to ease into the new increased applications by only doing ten applications every week for the first month. Plus, he insisted on having only female patients scheduled for the next thirty days. Ralph explained to Wendy, "We don't need the new people having to deal with the screaming world leaders or businessmen on their first day. It is best to ease them into their positions by working with the females first. I'm afraid that if we started them out with the men first, the staff would all quit." Wendy laughed, and she couldn't help but agree.

The first month of applications every Monday was working out smoothly. Then, for the next month, Ralph agreed to go to the twenty applications per Monday as directed by Sean. Everything was working out well, especially since they were only doing female applicants at the time.

Sean's "National $15 Dollar Per Hour Minimum Wage Initiative"

As decided long ago, all those persons receiving applications were given forms to fill out explaining their suggestions on how Sean could:

Clean up the world.

Clean up their own country.

Help out their own people.

As promised, Sean read every single form. He even had a large trash can near his desk to throw out the ridiculous ideas. Most suggestions were for the usual—new hospitals or new schools to be built in their country. Then there were the annoying "If you and I got together, we could rule the world" suggestions.

Sean would often muse to himself, *Why some people only see this secret as a way to dominate others is beyond me. What is it in mankind that we wish to control others and bend them to our will? Little wonder that the world is always in turmoil and there is constant warfare. Somehow, mankind just loves killing each other. Why, I'll never know.*

But months ago, one suggestion caught his eye. It was from Alycia Cromwell, the daughter of a billionaire oil tycoon, who suggested to Sean that he should use his resources toward establishing a national minimum wage throughout the United States. She explained that she volunteered at a local soap kitchen and that many people who used the kitchen also had jobs, but at their present rate of pay, they could not afford housing or food to feed their families.

One comment she wrote, Sean kept replaying in his mind, "Establishing a national minimum living wage would be the greatest thing you could do for:

Helping families and finally breaking the cycle of poverty where the children who grow up poor always remain poor.

Restoring pride to the wage earners, as they could now provide housing and food for their families.

Reducing the "missing fathers" problems as more fathers would remain with their families instead of abandoning them.

Sean called Alycia, and Sean invited her to return and visit him at the compound. She arrived two days later, and Sean and Alycia spent an enjoyable afternoon viewing the compound and talking. Alycia explained that, though rich herself, her volunteering at the soup kitchen made her sympathetic toward the plight of the underprivileged, especially those who had jobs but still could not afford to provide for their families. She made a passionate plea that only by forcing the individual states to raise their minimum wages could we eventually relieve these people from the cycle of poverty they were in.

At the end, Sean thanked Alycia for visiting him and said, "You have given me lots to think about. Thank you." They both parted ways as friends.

Sean closeted himself in his office for the next several days. He read everything he could about the issue of raising the minimum wage. Then Sean finally called Wendy in to see him and said, "Wendy, I am going to put in place a national campaign to raise the minimum wage for every employee to Fifteen Dollars per hour across the United States. I am well aware of the pushback I will be receiving, but I'm confident I can pull this off. It doesn't make much sense that one state has a minimum wage of Fifteen Dollar per hour when the state next door has a wage rate of only $7.25 per hour. The States must be forced to start paying their people a living wage, and I have some ideas that will force them to do so willingly. Any refusal to pay an employee less than a living wage is nothing short of economic slavery."

Wendy could see that Sean was becoming upset over this issue. She saw the look in his eyes and knew that if he committed himself to this program, neither hell nor high water would stop him. When Sean set his mind to a task, it was all or nothing. Wendy replied, "I couldn't agree more. When a parent goes to work and doesn't even bring home enough money to feed their family or keep a roof over their head, something is wrong. Plus, it always makes me mad to see billionaires on TV saying that raising the minimum wage will bankrupt their companies and ruin the nation. Guys worth billions of dollars are saying that employees wanting a wage increase are greedy and don't deserve the extra money. What for? So the billionaire can afford a newer, larger luxury yacht or another two million dollar sports car? I'd love to see those billionaires get along for a month on only the minimum wage."

Then Sean replied, "Yes, and what gets me is the movie stars and pro athletes making a million dollars a month, and the people paying to watch them make less than eight dollars per hour. The pay structures in America are out of balance, and I am going to do my part to help out the low-wage earners in this country."

Sean Saw This as a Multi-Step Process

#1: He would need members of Wendy's staff assigned to discovering the minimum wages of each of the American states.

#2: He would have Wendy research the heads of all organizations dedicated to raising the national minimum wage.

#3: He would need a Program Director.

#4: He would hire news reporters to interview all state and federal politicians on their opinions on this topic. Plus, interview the heads of the nationwide food, restaurant, and hotel chains.

#5: He would have Wendy select four couples from the compound staff who could visit all the States and do some research for him.

#6: He would pledge one billion dollars in projects to any state that raised its minimum wage for all workers to at least Fifteen Dollars per hour. To those states that already had such a minimum wage, he would grant the one billion dollars in work projects immediately. These would be handled by his Program Director, Retired General Braeden Gordon.

Staff Meeting

Sean called a formal open discussion meeting with Wendy, Bill Fryer, Program Directors Retired General Braeden Gordon and Curt Kurnes. After explaining his new initiative, it was Bill Fryer who spoke first, "But many economists are saying that an increase to the national minimum wage will result in increased unemployment and an increase in poverty."

Sean quickly replied with, "That's BS, and you know it. I remember when the tobacco companies paid researchers to say that smoking was good for you, and they even went so far as to hire athletes to advertise the benefits of smoking. All the while ignoring the evidence that smoking is harmful and killing thousands of Americans per year.

"Plus, wasn't it the same economists who said that the American economy would collapse if the price of oil hit seventy dollars per barrel? Well, in June 2008, the price of a barrel of oil hit almost one hundred and fifty dollars per barrel, and we're still here. Now the price of a barrel of oil has exceeded hundred dollars per barrel numerous times, and today it hovers between seventy dollars to ninety dollars per barrel, and the economy is doing just fine. We have to stop putting our faith in these "the sky is falling," say so-called experts, and start using common sense. Something I think that economists have in very short supply." Sean continued, "How can you expect people to provide for their families when the wages they make don't even cover the necessities of life? Rent, heating, taxes, and gas are all going up, and we expect people to survive on less than ten dollars per hour wages. The biggest problem I see is that by not paying our employees a living wage, we're creating a class of people destined to remain in poverty for the rest of their lives. No matter how hard they work or how many hours they put in, they just can't seem to get by. Now their children are growing up in poverty, they end up taking low-paying jobs and the cycle of poverty repeats itself over and over.

"Across the United States, we have the highest minimum wage rate in Washington D.C., and this has not caused the economic disaster as predicted. Likewise, in other states, paying half of what Washington D.C., employers pay and they cry the blues that any increase to the minimum wage will spell economic disaster. It's all hogwash.

"Yes, I am quite sure that some businesses will close. We are the greatest nation on earth, but we refuse to pay our people enough money to keep a roof over their heads and food on the table. We should all be ashamed of ourselves.

"I especially like watching the billionaire national business owners claim that their employees are greedy and don't deserve more. The same ones that come here and pay us fifty million dollars just to be five years younger. I'd like to see them keep up with their lavish lifestyles for under ten dollars per hour. Besides, how much more money do these rich people need? Another billion, another ten billion dollars—where does it end? We have to start taking care of our own people, and the best place to start is by establishing a national minimum wage across the US.

"Big deal if the hamburger and fries I buy cost me a little more if I know that the person making it actually takes home a decent paycheck and can provide for their families. The lowest-paid workers tend to be in the hospitality, food preparation, and farming industries. Why can't we pay these people more? I've read that in some areas, it's legal to pay waitresses less than five dollars per hour, forcing them to rely on tips to get by. How would anyone in this room like to start making five dollars per hour? Please raise your hand, because I'll be happy to lower your income to that.

"I am going to see this project through. There are already organizations dedicated to this cause, but most seem to be aligned with one or the other national political parties. I refuse to get bogged down with the politics involved and will spearhead my own efforts. I will be looking for a non-politically aligned Program Director and will let you know when I locate one. And my last point, I will be making a formal announcement of this new initiative at my church this coming Sunday, so please keep this conversation to yourselves until then."

Even though Wendy knew of this upcoming new initiative for weeks, she was still taken aback by Sean's force and determination. She knew that not all of Sean's strategy had yet been formalized, but he was well on his way. Tackling an issue, Sean was a bulldozer on the move. Nothing could stop him. He had the determination, the resources, and the ears of all the politicians and business leaders. If anyone in the world could force the United States into establishing a national minimum wage, it was Sean Little. When Sean was like this, you either got on board or got out of the way. There was no middle ground.

Sean Meets With Braeden Gordon, Program Director of Infrastructure Projects

Sean arranged for a private meeting later that day with his Program Director of Infrastructure, Braeden Gordon. Sean got right down to business, "Braeden, I would like you to drop all the projects that you have not yet signed for. I am considering a reassignment of your duties."

Braeden was taken back. "Have I done anything wrong? I have followed your instructions to the letter."

Sean replied with, "Absolutely not. Your work has been exemplary, and I am proud to have you on my team. It's just that I have created this new national minimum wage program where I'm prepared to spend one billion dollars per state on infrastructure and other projects. This you will be in charge of."

Braeden replied, "Wow, and I thought I was getting fired. I really don't want to go back to organizing functions at the bingo hall." And both he and Sean laughed.

Now, back at Sean's office, he laid out his plans.

"As you can tell from today's meeting, I haven't gotten all the bugs worked out yet, but I am going to force the individual states into raising their minimum hourly wage rate to Fifteen Dollars per hour. Now, this is where you come in. I plan on bribing the individual states into raising their minimum wage to Fifteen Dollars per hour by offering to fund one billion dollars in infrastructure projects for their states. Even if this wage increase can be done by a federal mandate, I will still be offering this one billion dollars incentive. Pretty difficult for a politician coming up for re-election to be opposed to raising the minimum wage, especially since it comes with one billion dollars in funding. I would think that anyone opposed would certainly lose their next election.

"We, of course, will honor all of the projects you have committed ourselves to or are presently underway. But from this point on, I want you to visit every state and get an idea of, if we were to offer them one billion dollars in funding, which projects should we undertake?

"I would think that you would have to notify every state governor of your intentions so they can start putting their plans together. As I am aware, all the states have already been putting together plans for you to review. It's a simple matter to include more projects.

"Plus, where you have already started working, the other state governors are looking at those projects with envy and want to get some of our money. But please do not mention my intentions of raising the minimum wage until after this Sunday, when I make my formal announcement at my church. Now, with you reviewing these projects but not committing, my incentive is to get them to agree later on. Like I say, pretty hard going up for re-election when your record shows you are against raising the minimum wage and accepting one billion dollars in project funding."

Braeden replied. "Sean, I've got to hand it to you. Once the state politicians get a smell of one billion dollars funding, they'll all start drooling. Even the ones dead set against raising the minimum wage will come on board. Like you say, they will have to, or they'll never be elected again. I am in favor of this initiative and will follow your instructions to the letter.

"I will immediately contact every single state governor and mention that you are considering funding projects for up to one billion dollars and that they are to assemble the plans for my inspection. Believe me, every state governor knows about my visits and the projects I have approved to date. They all want in on the action. And I'll keep this conversation to myself. I agree, the less they know, the better."

Sean continued, "I suspect that this new project will take years to clear all the legal loopholes, which will give you time to visit all the states and meet with the governors. This is a major, long-term project. And one other thing, I will be meeting with Curt Kurnes to inform him that he is not to commit to any other environmental projects unless cleared by you. In short, Curt now reports to you, and his projects now fall under the one billion dollars state grant program."

Braeden said, "No problem. Curt and I enjoy working together. You talk to Curt, and I will get right on sending out those letters to all the state governors. One billion dollars in funding is guaranteed to get their attention." Both he and Sean laughed, and then they parted company.

Meeting with Curt Kurnes, Program Director of Environmental Projects

Sean called Curt into his office for a chat. Curt was impressed with Sean's minimum wage initiative and wanted to do anything he could to help. Sean got down to business. "Curt, I am happy with your work to date on my environmental projects. But like Braeden, I have to ask you not to commit to any more projects. Yes, we will continue to fund those projects already underway and those that you have already signed for.

"I wish you to continue investigating environmental sites for cleanup and the Mississippi River project, for example, but not commit yourself to any additional funding.

"From this moment on, you are to coordinate your efforts along with Braeden's to be included in the one billion dollars in grants I am giving those states that raise their minimum wage to at least Fifteen Dollars per hour. So, to put it in a nutshell, you now report to Retired General Braeden Gordon, who will approve your work in those states that meet our minimum wage requirements. Any questions?"

Curt replied with, "No, none at all. I totally agree that by dangling these major projects in front of the politicians will finally make them raise their minimum wages, giving everyone in their state a decent standard of living. I totally agree that working with Braeden is the right way to go. We are meeting for lunch later, and I'll talk to him then." Then Sean and Curt parted company.

Later that week, Sean met Wendy and the four couples she had selected.

"Thank you for coming here today. I appreciate that all of you have agreed to leave the compound for one month to do some traveling and research for me. What I want you to do is get an accurate indication of the cost of living in each state. I want you four couples to visit every single American state in North America except Alaska, and I want you to go to the capital of each state and one other city and make purchases for me:

–From the large national hamburg chains:

–One cheeseburger, one large fries, and a large pop.

–From the large national pizza chains:

–One large meat lover pizza.

–From the large coffee shops:

–One box of twelve donuts.

–From the large sub sandwich shops:

–One twelve inch assorted sub.

"I want you to keep and catalogue the receipt and take a photo of each meal. I don't care what you do with the food—eat it yourself or give it away; I don't care. What I need is an accurate cost of living in each state. And I want you to keep all your receipts so that we can compare food and housing costs between the states. Plus, I want you to bring me back a copy of the capital city's newspapers along with its apartment rental section so we can try to get an idea of the cost of renting an apartment in each state.

"The four couples here should be able to cover the US in one month. If this is not enough time, just let Wendy know. For example, my suggestions are that:

–Team #1 can go to California and then north.

–Team #2 can go east toward Florida and then north.

–Team #3 can go north-east to cover the mid-west.

–Team #4 can drive up and start in Maine and cover the North-Eastern Seaboard States.

"And yes, you are welcome to drop off and spend some time with some family and friends. Wendy looks after everything and will assign you a company vehicle and a credit card. I think she will likely be assigning a member of her staff to deal with yourselves directly, but that's up to her.

You have your assignments. Any questions? Take them up with Wendy." Then Sean said goodbye and exited the boardroom.

Wendy, in her efficiency, already had the credit cards made up, and the vehicles assigned. She asked the couples which routes they would like, and they selected those routes that would allow them to spend some time with their relatives. Everyone was happy, and they left the following day.

CBW News

Sean then contacted his friend, Nick Palmer of CBW News, and outlined his plans. Nick was eager to help. Sean then stated, "I need you to set up some teams of reporters and cameramen to interview every state governor, state senator and state members of the House of Representatives.

"I want your people to formally interview them and get their reactions to raising their state minimum wage on tape. Plus, I want a separate team to interview and tape the CEO's of the nation's largest restaurant, food, and hotel chains. I want their opinions, too.

"Please do not do anything with these interviews and forward them to me, as I may need them in the future. Besides, before I start, I want to know who exactly is in favor of this idea and who is opposed. I will cover all of your expenses and will have my Executive Secretary, Wendy, issue you a check for ten million dollars to get you started."

Nick answered, "Great idea, Sean. I will write up an agreement that you own the interviews and tapes and get going on this right away. I personally feel quite strongly on this issue, and anything else I can do to help you, please ask."

Former Vice President John Harper and Kevin Sander's Join Sean

Sean then looked over Wendy's research on those organizations dedicated to raising the national minimum wage. Sean then drafted up a letter to the head of each organization, asking for their advice on how he could assist them. Sean had his own ideas but thought it best to get some additional input before proceeding.

In the coming months, Sean and Wendy interviewed candidates from these organizations for the Program Director's position, but to no avail. Then it occurred to Sean, *What about former Vice President John Harper, along with Kevin Sander's his assistant?* Sean contacted Kevin Sanders himself and invited them both down to the compound for a chat. On the date of their arrival, Sean met John and Kevin at the main gate and greeted them like old friends. Both marveled at the improvements to the compound. After the customary tour of the compound, Sean brought them into his office and got down to business.

Sean started out by asking them, "What are you two up to now?

John Harper, knowing of the friendship between Kevin and Sean, let Kevin speak first, "Well, to be honest, Sean, we both are up to very little. All past Presidents and VPs have a yearly allowance to keep certain staff and security personnel, and I'm one of them. Life sure is boring after leaving the Oval Office."

Then John Harper concurred with, "As the President has gone back to being an oil company executive, that left Kevin and myself out on our own. Being out of power is like driving a sports car at hundred miles an hour and then being stuck in a traffic jam for twenty minutes. All this energy and no place to go. For four years we were running the most powerful nation on earth, and then one day you're moving back to your old home to write your memoirs. Kevin is right, Sean. One day you're in charge of forming national policies and talking to the most important people in the world, and the next day you're leaving Washington basically unemployed. Sure, would like to get back into action again. Sean, what's up? You didn't call us down here to discuss the weather."

Sean replied, "No, I didn't. Gentlemen, I am planning my own initiative to achieve a nationwide Fifteen Dollar minimum wage for all employees. So far, I have set in motion my friend Nick Palmer from CBW News, who is using teams of reporters and cameramen to interview all state governors, state senators and state members of the House of Representatives and ask their opinions on this issue. Plus, a separate team is interviewing the CEO's of the nation's largest companies, especially those in the food and hospitality industries. Before putting any national campaign together, I want to make sure who is with us and who is against us.

"John and Kevin, I liked working with you before and believe that we can work together again. I would like the two of you to consider being my

Program Directors on this issue.

"First, I feel this is a very highly politically charged issue, and having you as my directors would help this along.

"Second, your work would be non-partisan and not represent the efforts of a single political party.

"Third, as you will be acting independently of all the political parties, you may not endorse any party, candidate, or platform. You will also be acting independently of all other organizations already working on this issue.

"Fourth, I will be funding all expenses, and you will report only to me and no one else. Understood."

Ex-Vice President John Harper replied with, "Understood. Your work to date in forcing through your own initiatives, especially the clean-up of the Great Pacific Garbage Patch, was nothing short of pure genius.

"No one, including myself, believed that you could achieve the level of international cooperation to clean up that mess.

"Plus, your other projects, from helping out the disabled war veterans and others to buying up all the junk firearms and your environmental projects, mean that you are now seen as a national hero, willing to help the common man. I am sure that Kevin and I will be proud to be associated with you on this. We both feel that raising the minimum wage is a necessity for bringing people out of poverty.

"While in the Oval Office, the President and I tried to pass such legislation but were shot down. Even with all our best efforts, some states did raise their minimum wages, but not nearly enough. We just couldn't get our bills past the Senate and the House of Representatives. We are in; we're both in." And Kevin nodded.

Sean stated, "All right, from this moment on, I'm making you my Program Director and you Kevin his Executive Assistant for my National Fifteen Dollars Per Hour Minimum Wage Initiative. As with my other directors, John, your pay is fifty thousand dollars per month and Kevin, your pay as his assistant is twenty-five thousand dollars per month. Wendy will set you up with a bank account here and a couple of million dollars to help with expenses.

"My intentions are to offer each state that raises its minimum wage to Fifteen Dollars per hour one billion dollars in infrastructure projects. Pretty difficult going up for re-election if you have been opposed to raising the minimum wage and refusing one billion dollars in funding for your state.

"All projects will be approved by Retired General Braeden Gorden, my Program Director of Infrastructure Projects, and myself. We approve the project and guarantee its funding. The state proceeds to complete the project, and once completed and inspected, I will reimburse the state for all costs plus interest. Upon any evidence of graft or corruption, the contract will be considered null and void."

The former Vice President replied, "Sean, if anyone in the world can pull this off, it is you. Your works to date have made you a national hero and a person that everyone in the world sits up and listens to.

"I agree it's best that this be seen as your initiative, independent of any single political party. Kevin and I will present ourselves as your representatives and as members of the American people, away from my former political party.

"And for your information, in the United States, we have a two-tiered minimum wage system. In any project where the federal government is involved, the minimum wage is set at a base rate of Fifteen Dollars per hour. For example, the fellow sweeping the floors at a fighter jet factory is making the minimum federally mandated wage of Fifteen Dollars per hour, while the fellow making the pizza down the road is likely only making $7.25 per hour.

"As you well know, the lowest-paid workers tend to be in the food, restaurant, hotel, and farming industries. These jobs lie outside of the federal minimum wage mandate and are set by the individual states themselves. So far, most states have been very resistant to increasing their hourly wage rates, but with one billion dollars in funding hanging over their heads, I think they will start to see the light. And I agree with you; any politician refusing to raise the minimum wage rate and thereby refusing one billion dollars in funding would be doomed at the polls."

Sean replied, "Great, put together your plans. As mentioned, my Project Director, Braeden Gordon, will be speaking with the individual state governors, and you two will be working with the members of the Senate and House of Representatives. I will now introduce you to Wendy, whom you already know, who will set you up with your bank accounts and company credit cards. She will also be reviewing our standard list of Program Director guidelines that she will expect you to sign.

"As with all my other Program Directors, you are not to call me. If I want to talk to you, I will call you. My attitude is that if you have to call me, I hired the wrong person for the job and will replace you. So you two are on your own in convincing Washington and the individual states to back this initiative. Plus, I expect a written report on my desk by the 20th of each month outlining your progress to date.

"As you are already aware, you may never imply that I will meet with someone, and never even attempt to bring anyone with you to meet me. Never. Plus, the concept of a free application of my age-reversing process is not on the table. And the last thing, Program Director Braeden Gordon reports directly to me and not you, and you are not to interfere with his efforts. Only he and I will decide on what projects will be undertaken. Understood?

"I am not totally sure of how I will be using the recorded interviews of the national politicians and business leaders just yet, but I will let you know who will be supporting our efforts and who will be opposed. These interviews should be in my hands in the next month or two.

"And my last point: I will be making a formal announcement at my church this Sunday, so I would appreciate you keeping this conversation confidential until then.

"As my announcements at my church are monitored by all the national news networks, this will help to establish this as an independent initiative, separate from any political party. Agreed?" Both John and Kevin nodded their heads in approval.

Sean then said, "Now I'll bring you over to Wendy, who will set you up with what you need. And as I always say, "Be nice to Wendy. She writes the checks!"

At that, Sean got up and took both the former Vice President and Kevin over to Wendy's office and made the proper introductions. After shaking both John and Kevin's hands, Sean turned, walked back into his office, and closed the door.

Wendy, being totally aware of the new initiative, was prepared for them. Wendy set them up with their own credit cards and a bank account with ten million dollars in it. She then handed them each a list of the Program Director's guidelines and made sure she covered every point. She then insisted that they sign their copies. The former Vice President and Kevin were obviously a little put out that they were being treated as mere employees and being talked to by a secretary like this. But the tone in

Wendy's voice left little doubt that she was in charge and that these two men would have no more authority than any of Sean's other Program Directors.

Kevin then asked, "Why can't we come and go in our own helicopter? I used to before."

To this, Wendy sternly replied, "Sean has a real problem with helicopters, and I agree with him. If we let one in we let in a hundred tomorrow. Everyone from our Program Directors, people showing up for their applications, spouses dropping in to see how their partners are doing, every person wanting Sean to invest in their pet project, and lastly, every single news agency in the world would be landing here. So if you really want to piss Sean off and likely get fired, show up here in a helicopter. He's pretty firm on this, so don't do it. Very few people are allowed in by helicopter like you were when you held an official title."

When Wendy was finished, she pressed a button on her desk, and two heavily armed guards appeared out of nowhere. Wendy then asked the guards to escort John and Kevin out of the building and to take them to the airport. As Sean's office door was closed, it was obvious that he was not coming out to say goodbye.

Now being led out of the building, both the former Vice President and Kevin knew where they stood. Sean and Wendy were the boss, and they would have to work within the guidelines set down by Sean, or he would simply get someone else. He had the resources and the international reputation to see this project through, and knowing his determination, they both knew that he would be successful. *Better to work with him and not against him,* they both thought.

Staff Researching the Cost of Living

All of the couples gathering data on the cost of living in each state, arrived back, and their reports were made. Now Sean could easily compare the typical cost of living from one state to another and compare it to that states minimum wage.

It quickly became obvious that those states that already had a Fifteen Dollars or so state minimum wage did not face economic disaster once they brought in the higher minimum wage. He compared the cost of takeout food between those states that had a high wage rate and those that had a lower wage rate. It became obvious that, for example, a cheeseburger, large fries, and a large pop were only seventy-five cents higher in the higher wage rate states as compared to the lower wage rate states. Similar results were found on the price of a large meat-lover pizza or any other takeout food. He had the fresh data.

He asked Wendy to assign a staff member to set this out in a chart form for the website company to place on the site, along with the title showing the minimum wage rate for that state and the costs of the takeout food in each state. This took about a week to accomplish, and Sean was pleased with the results. Anyone with a brain could see that those states with the higher minimum wage did not decline, but their economies flourished under the higher wages.

The Church Announcement

That following Sunday, at the end of the Chaplan's Furlong's excellent sermon, Sean took the podium.

"Ladies and gentlemen, Today I wish to speak of my latest initiative. After careful consideration, I have concluded that my efforts and resources should be directed toward helping the common working man.

"In the United States, it would appear that we have a two-tiered minimum wage system. At the high end, you get the federally mandated higher minimum wage of usually Fifteen Dollars per hour if you are working on a project either funded by or where the federal government is involved. But for all the other workers, especially in the restaurant, hotel, food preparation, and farming industries, the pay is much lower, usually around $7.25 or so.

"Ours is the most powerful and wealthy nation on the face of the earth, yet we pay our employees a wage that doesn't allow them to keep a roof over their heads or put food on their tables. We have enforced a position of poverty on these people, where they are poor and their children growing up poor will likely remain poor as they grow older. This is nothing short of economic slavery.

"I am now letting every business owner, large or small, and every state government official know that I, Sean Little will be directing all of my efforts into forcing every state to enact a state-wide minimum wage law of Fifteen Dollars per hour for all employees with no exceptions.

"Yes, I am aware that there will be some economic difficulties to start and that some businesses will close. But the resulting benefits of putting more buying power in the hands of the average American will only make our people and our country stronger. And to ensure that this does take place, I am offering one billion dollars in infrastructure projects to those states that currently have a state-wide Fifteen Dollars minimum wage and one billion dollars to those states that will enact a state-wide Fifteen Dollars minimum wage in the future. This will all be carried out by my Program Director of Infrastructure, Retired General Braeden Gorden." Then Sean started getting upset and smashed his hand on the podium.

"I, Sean Little, swear to yourselves here before me. I swear to every American that here, in the church of my parents and before God, I will see a nationwide minimum wage of Fifteen Dollars across America. I have sworn, and I have committed my life to this. It will be done, so help me, God."

The congregation erupted in applause and cheering. When Sean came down from the podium, people mobbed him to congratulate him. Everyone could see that he was crying, and they knew that once committed, there was no holding him back. Like a dog on a bone, Sean would see that every American would soon have a living wage.

Within the hour, every single TV news agency replayed Sean's speech to the rest of the nation. The reaction was mixed. The people applauded his efforts, and the business owners cried the blues, saying that they were going out of business. But the networks were unanimous in their support, saying that such an initiative was long overdue and that Sean Little was just the man to pull it off.

CBW Staff Interviewing Government Officials and Business Leaders

Later that month, CBW News sent word that all the video-recorded interviews with all of the American state governors, state senators, members of the House of Representatives, and major national business CEOs were finished. His friend Nick Palmer, CEO of CBW News, called Wendy, and she approved of him delivering the documentation personally.

Nick arrived in two days and was met by Sean. Sean was appreciative of the efforts and even asked if he needed any more money. Nick replied with, "No, Sean, your generous check for ten million dollars more than covered our expenses. I and my staff are totally in favor of your efforts to raise the minimum wage. Anything else we can do for you, please ask. The benefits to our people and the nation will be incredible when you pull this off, which I am sure you will. You are the only person everyone has to listen to. Great success to you."

Sean thanked Nick for his friendship and his support. Then, after a casual lunch, they parted company.

Sean felt that this was so important that he himself and two of Wendy's assistants reviewed every single taped interview. It started alphabetically, with Alabama being the first state to be reviewed. They reviewed the interview of the state governor then the interviews of the state senators and the House of Representatives. They all kept their own notes as to the individual government officials' support for a Fifteen Dollars national minimum wage. Basically, the states were then divided into four groups:

Group #1: Those states already having a Fifteen Dollars minimum wage.

Group #2: Those states whose government officials were favorable to raising their minimum wage.

Group #3: Those states whose government officials were undecided.

Group #4: Those states whose government officials were opposed to raising their minimum wage.

After two days of reviewing the interviews, Sean and the two staff members sat down and compared notes. They reviewed each response and came up with a list of all the government officials who were in favor, undecided, or opposed. For Group #1, Sean came up with these states that already had a Fifteen Dollars minimum wage:

–California
–Connecticut
–Massachusetts
–Washington, D.C.
–Washington State

He then contacted Kevin Sanders and explained that he wanted both him and John Harper to make a big media splash, announcing their one billion dollars in infrastructure grants, starting with these five states and beginning with California. Sean felt that once this hit the news networks, every single other state official would sit up and take notice.

He told Kevin that he would be calling Braeden Gordon and that he would like him to be involved in the announcements in the state.

Later that day, he contacted Braeden, and Braeden thought that the large media announcement was the best way to get those in opposition to sit up and take notice. Sean then asked Braeden to speak on his behalf and to make a strong announcement that he was determined to see a National Fifteen Dollars Minimum Wage become a reality.

The California Announcement

One month later, John Harper, Kevin Sanders, and Braeden Gordon all met in Sacramento, California, with the state governor, state senators, and members of the House of Representatives. With all the TV crews in place, the state governor started out to announce the important news coming from Sean Little. Next, he introduced Former Vice President John Harper, who took the stand, "Ladies and gentlemen, I stand before you not as the former Vice President of the United States but as a private American citizen. I, along with my assistant Kevin Sanders, have been asked by Sean Little to spearhead his National Fifteen Dollars Minimum Wage Initiative. For your information across the United States, all projects either funded by the Federal government or to be purchased by them, the minimum wage is the federally mandated Fifteen Dollars per hour. All other employees are covered by the state legislation minimum wage laws, many lower than the federal rate.

"Therefore, to encourage the individual states to raise their minimum wages to that of the federal level, Sean Little is offering one billion dollars in infrastructure projects. And the states of California, Connecticut, Washington, D.C., Massachusetts, and Washington State already have wage rates of Fifteen Dollars. These states will automatically be getting the one billion dollars Sean Little grants.

"Now I would like to introduce Retired General and Engineer Braeden Gordon, Sean Little's Program Director of all Infrastructure Projects."

Braeden Gordon took the stand. "Ladies and gentlemen, I am Retired General Braeden Gordon, and some time ago was asked by Sean Little to be his Program Director of all his Infrastructure Projects. I am excited about being involved in raising the minimum wage across the United States. Later, I will be sitting with the officials of the State of California and reviewing their suggestions on the projects that will be covered and funded by the Sean Little one billion dollar grant. (Everyone cheered)

"Ladies and gentlemen, I have been involved with Sean Little for some time now, and I can guarantee you that once he puts a plan of action in motion, there is no turning him back. He is totally committed to providing a living wage to every single working individual in the United States. Hear me and hear me now. Sean Little will not stop until every single state in the United States has raised its minimum wage to the point where the employees can keep a roof over their heads and food on the table.

"I am proud to be associated with Sean Little, John Harper, and Kevin Sanders on this worthwhile project. By the grace of God, we will be successful and provide a living wage for all Americans." The crowd erupted in cheers and applause.

Sean loved the newscast and immediately contacted all three of them to tell him how happy he was with the announcement. He then requested that they now make the same announcement in Connecticut, Washington, D.C., Massachusetts, and Washington State.

In his phone call to Kevin Sanders, it was Kevin who reminded Sean, "Sean, Washington, D.C., is not technically a state but a federal district. You still want Washington, D.C., included?"

Sean replied with, "Yes, Kevin I do. What better way for the members of the Senate and House of Representatives to see that we are serious about funding infrastructure projects than by seeing these projects being conducted in their own backyard? Even better if they got into a traffic jam caused by one of our highway projects. Pretty hard to ignore us then, don't you think?"

"Yes, you're right," replied Kevin. "Any projects taking place in downtown Washington are likely your best advertising. I have to hand it to you; you're right again." And both Sean and Kevin laughed.

The media caught this and ran with it. By the time all four states and Washington, D.C., were given their announcements, every other State's legislature was discussing raising the minimum wage. The lure of the one billion dollar grant was doing its job. As Sean always said, "It's pretty difficult for a state official to go up for re-election when they oppose raising the minimum wage and therefore denying their state one billion dollars in additional funding."

After reviewing the government officials' recorded interviews and his staff notes, Sean came to the conclusion that:

Group #1: Those five states already have a Fifteen Dollars minimum wage:

–California

–Connecticut

–Massachusetts

–Washington, D.C.

–Washington State

Group #2: Those states whose government officials were favorable to raising their minimum wage (Sean felt that there were fifteen states favorable).

Group #3-: Those states whose government officials were undecided (Sean felt that nine states and officials were undecided).

Group #4: Those states whose government officials were opposed to raising their minimum wage (Sean felt that there were twenty-three states and officials that were opposed to raising their minimum wage).

Once Sean's research was finished, he called John Harper, "John, as stated in my email, now that you are done with your presentations in the five states that already have a Fifteen Dollars minimum wage, I want you to concentrate your efforts on those states in Group #2. These, I feel, are the most likely to quickly implement a higher minimum wage, especially once they see the projects being done elsewhere. And once these new states increase their wage rates, I want you, Kevin, and Braeden to make a big presentation on each states Capitol step outlining the one billion dollar grants. This will get everyone else's attention."

John was quick to reply. "Sean, ever since you made your announcement at your church and mentioned the one billion dollars in Infrastructure grants, my phone has been ringing off the hook. Braden had already set in motion that you were funding large-scale projects, and with an announcement of one billion dollars in grants, you got everyone's attention.

"As you know, the United States evolves around money, and for any politician to deny their state, this funding is doomed at the polls. Plus, the media is hundred percent behind this effort. Government officials can ignore the media and the electorate in non-election years. But in an election year, no official can ignore the money, especially one billion dollars. My compliments to you. I believe that within the next two years, every single state in the United States will have a Fifteen Dollars minimum wage. They will have to. You're ramming it down their throats."

John and Sean laughed. Then Sean calmly replied with, "Thank you, John. And once we get these next fifteen states on board, we can then turn our attention to those states and politicians who remain undecided on the issue. And I agree with you, the one billion dollars in grants will help change their minds."

Sean, let the media carry the ball. With CBW News at the forefront, all the national news networks were totally in favor of this initiative and constantly ran talk shows, promoting the benefits of raising the minimum wage. Plus, those states still holding out looked at the projects being done in neighboring states with envious eyes. State legislatures were constantly debating raising their wages, and Sean felt that they would all come over to his side, one by one.

Sean always encouraged Braeden to include a lot of smaller projects in the one billion dollar grants. Sean wanted to see road construction, bridge building, highway overpass building, and environmental cleanups as compared to one giant project. His reasoning was that he wanted to create as much employment as possible and basically spread the wealth around. Plus, roadworks, bridges, overpasses, and environmental cleanups are very highly visible examples of his grants.

Plus, Braeden was able to keep an eye on any cost overruns on these smaller projects. For example, fifty miles of road construction had to have the same costs regardless of the state it was in, and the same for bridges and overpasses. Braeden already had stock plans for any bridges and overpasses already drawn up and encouraged the States to use his plans. Few, if any, officials objected.

Six Months Later

As expected, the turmoil caused by Sean's announcement and his lure of one billion dollars in infrastructure projects was constantly being replayed by the media. It even went so far as one major restaurant chain took out television ads saying that any increase to the minimum wage would bankrupt their companies. Those in favor of this initiative called Sean a saint, and those opposed called him the devil.

As always, Sean's policy of "no questions, no interviews" served him well as he let John Harper and Kevin Sanders take all the heat from those opposed to raising their states minimum wage. This they handled with grace and dignity, something Sean didn't think he could do.

Regardless of how you looked at it, the lure of one billion dollars and the media attention were doing their jobs. No state politician could ignore this issue, especially since the media was constantly breathing down their neck, showing video of major projects being done in neighboring states that raised their minimum wage. The media onslaught was relentless. One by one, those states that Sean felt would raise their minimum wage joined in. Sean saw to it that John Harper, Kevin Sanders, and Braeden Gordon all made similar big presentations on the State Capitol Hill steps. The media soaked it up.

Now with twenty states on board with Fifteen Dollars minimum wages and with the much-called "economic collapse" not happening, this took the "wind out of the sails" of those opposed to raising their minimum wage. But a surprising thing did happen. Those states that raised their minimum wages saw an increase in overall economic activity as more money was now going to those who needed it the most. News networks were quick to interview those who were elated about getting a larger paycheck at the end of their week. It seemed that only good came to those states that raised their minimum wages.

Gradually, John Harper and Kevin Sanders set their sites on the nine states where Sean felt government officials were undecided about the minimum wage increases. One by one, these states caved in and joined. Was it the grant money, the media pressure, or they're coming up for re-election that made them accept the new wage rates? No one knows. Now there were twenty-nine states with a minimum wage rate of Fifteen Dollars or more, as compared to the twenty-three states that were opposed to raising their minimum wages. Sean called John Harper and Kevin Sanders and asked them not to press the remaining states too hard.

"Let's let the dust settle from the last nine "undecided" states joining. The media and public opinion are now on our side, and they will eventually see the light of day. They will join up, and they know it. It's only a matter of time." Both John and Kevin agreed.

Little did both of them know that Sean was secretly funding through his friend Nick Palmer, CEO of CBW News, major documentaries on the benefits of the States raising their minimum wages. Sean was paying for all their expenses and even paying for their airtime. He even arranged for the other news networks to use these documentaries free of charge. They did a wonderful job. It was almost difficult to not find a news program that didn't mention the benefits to the common working man of the increase in their state's minimum wage. Nationwide, public opinion was building like a tidal wave, and eventually these "holdout " states raised their minimum wages.

Likewise, as in every state capital, Sean ensured that a major presentation took place with much media fanfare.

Mission Accomplished

Just shy of two years into the initiative, every single State in the United states had installed a Fifteen Dollars minimum wage. Sean contacted John Harper and requested that he arrange for a major formal announcement to take place in Washington, D.C. As all of the other state announcements had taken place on the State Capitol steps, Sean asked that this presentation take place on the steps leading to the White House.

Sean personally called the President of the United States, who, wanting to get as much publicity out of this as possible, agreed wholeheartedly to the presentation and its location. The date was set.

Presentation on Capital Hill

It was a beautiful day in July for the presentation. All the major news networks were in attendance, as were many members of the Senate and the House of Representatives. To start, the President of the United States took the podium.

"Ladies and gentlemen, members of the Senate and the House of Representatives, I stand before you to make an important announcement.

"I am here today to tell you that an important dream has been accomplished. Across this great nation, every single state has enacted a

Fifteen Dollars minimum wage for its citizens. Because of this, there is now more buying power in the hands of our most underprivileged citizens. More money for the family breadwinner to keep a roof over their heads and food on the table. The American dream will now be shared by everyone, not just a select few.

"I sincerely thank all those who have helped Sean Little and myself with this initiative. I now call on Sean Little's Program Director for this initiative, former Vice President John Harper."

John Harper took the podium. "Ladies and gentlemen, this is a proud day for us and all Americans. Slightly less than two years ago, I and my assistant Kevin Sanders were hired by Sean Little to head up his "National Fifteen Dollars Minimum Wage Initiative." And with the help of his Program Director of Infrastructure Projects, Retired General Braeden Gordon, and to the individual state governors, members of the senate and the House of Representatives we now have a living wage available to all citizens of America. A dream realized. Thank you."

Everyone stood up, applauded, and cheered for at least ten minutes. Now, with this Fifteen Dollars per hour minimum wage a reality, every single politician wanted to make sure that they were seen as supporters of this idea from the beginning.

Sean and others watched the presentation on the large screen in the restaurant. Sean mentioned to Jennifer, "Now that this is a reality, everyone, even those totally opposed to the idea, are now trying to make themselves out as its greatest supporters. I bet if I go back over my notes, those politicians who are now beating their chests about pushing through this initiative years ago were totally against the idea. And the President—I don't seem to remember him giving us much support. Oh well, that's politics, I guess."

Sean stood up and walked outside to talk to the staff who had assembled outside of the restaurant.

"Ladies and gentlemen, a little under two years ago, I started my National Fifteen Dollars Minimum Wage Initiative and am proud to say that we have been successful. This success could not have been possible without the steadfast help of my staff. This is a proud day for all Americans. Thank you."

Wendy, standing right behind Sean, took the mike out of his hands and, in a booming voice, said, "Let's get something straight. This was totally

Sean's doing, and we all know it. The world knows it. Sean set a goal, laid out his plans, put the right people in place, put his money where his mouth is, and bulldozed his way through this issue until its success. Not once did he waver. Not once did he move his eyes off the goal. He single-handedly made every single politician in the United States sit up and realize that this goal would be achieved, come hell or high water. They would join his cause of achieving a national minimum wage or likely be on the unemployment line come the next election. There was no stopping Sean Little, and today the entire nation can rejoice that we have achieved a "living wage" for all Americans nationwide. All thanks to Sean Little."

The people in the crowd were cheering and crying. Sean had done the impossible.

Everyone looked to Sean for a comment, and all he could say was, "Job done, mission accomplished. I think it's time for a beer."

Chapter 51
Project # 14: World-Wide Nuclear Arms Reduction

The Proposal

At the latest Program Directors meeting Sean didn't say much and just let Wendy handle the proceedings. At the end of his speech, he complimented his staff for their work on these truly long-term, important projects. He felt that everything was going smoothly and that he had the right people in place. He also expressed his appreciation for everyone's support for his National Fifteen Dollars Per Hour Minimum Wage Initiative

But everyone knew something was up. Sean, when faced with an issue, would rarely speak business and remain lost in his own thoughts for days at a time. Even Jennifer confided in Wendy that she thought Sean was up to something big. He was paying little attention to the projects at hand and would lock himself in his office most days and refuse to take phone calls. Then he called a formal meeting with Colonel John, Wendy, and Bill Fryer. Sean started out the meeting.

"Thank you all for attending. As everyone can tell, our programs are all running smoothly with the directors in place and the watchful eye of my Executive Secretary, Wendy Rawlings.

"Allow me to finish my presentation before commenting. Ladies and gentlemen, this is the big one. I am now going to place my efforts and resources toward eliminating the spread of nuclear weapons and reducing the world's present nuclear stockpiles." Everyone sat in shock.

Sean continued, "To date, it would seem in the forefront of these efforts is the "International Campaign to Abolish Nuclear Weapons", ICAN, centered out of Geneva, Switzerland. This seems to be the most credible organization dedicated to this cause, and they were even awarded the Nobel Peace Prize in 2017 for their work on nuclear disarmament. The UN and ICAN were successful in establishing the "Treaty on the Prohibition of

Nuclear Weapons" in July 2017 and putting it into action in January 2021. This treaty is designed to stop the spread of nuclear weapons to non-nuclear states. The only problem is that none of the existing nuclear power countries signed this agreement.

"So how I see it is that the UN and ICAN organizations have only been successful in forming a consensus with everyone except those states that actually possess nuclear weapons. It appears they are lacking a way to get direct access to or influence, the nuclear power leaders.

"At present, we have the ears of the world. All of the world leaders have to come to us and have been under our complete control for roughly four days. We have shown our success in cleaning up the Garbage Patch and I think we can do the same for nuclear arms reduction. We have the influence, we have the money, and we have the credentials. I am positive that the leaders of the nuclear-armed nations will talk to us, therefore, we can succeed where the others have failed. I have committed my life to this goal. We will succeed."

Wendy, Colonel John, and Bill Fryer knew that once Sean had formulated a plan of action, he was impossible to deter. He was unbreakable in his resolve. They knew that Sean's determination was like a bulldozer tackling a mountain. He goes right for the heart of the problem and attacks. But it was Wendy, the most outspoken of the three, who spoke first.

"Sean, that's impossible. The entire world knows of the horrors a nuclear war would cause, and all the world-wide attempts to influence the nuclear powers to eliminate their stockpiles have met with stonewalling. Heaven knows people and governments have tried, but getting the nuclear superpowers to give up their nuclear armaments will be impossible. Somehow, for some reason, mankind loves war and killing each other."

"Yes, and I agree with you, Wendy," stated Sean. "The intense level of distrust and anxiety in the world has doomed any such cooperation in the past. But look, the world has about thirteen thousand nuclear warheads in existence, with little consensus on what to do with them or how to eliminate them. Diplomacy to date has stalled the spread of nuclear weapons to non-nuclear powers, but no government or organization can coordinate with all the nuclear-armed nations to dispose of the nukes they presently have." Sean then went to the easel pad and flipped over some sheets to show his chart.

List of Countries with Known Nuclear Weapons

Country-Known   Nuclear-Potential   Weapons   ten   percent Reduction

Country	Known Nuclear Weapons	Potential 10% Reduction
Russia	5977	597
USA	5478	548
China	410	41
France	290	29
UK	225	22
Pakistan	165	16
India	160	16
Israel	90	9
North Korea	43	4

12,838

"I propose to set up a single agency dedicated to talking directly to the nuclear-armed world leaders and to offer to dispose of ten percent of their nukes at an agreed-upon international site. This agency would act independently of all other agencies and will not get bogged down with the endless rounds of useless diplomacy and diplomatic luncheons. They will direct their efforts and speak to the world leaders themselves, going over the heads of their state departments, so to speak."

"Great idea, Sean," replied Wendy. "But any attempt from yourself and the US will meet with the same stonewalling, and the talks will go nowhere. I do not suspect that China, North Korea, India, Pakistan, and Russia will allow an American initiative to even get off the ground. Any American government initiative is doomed to failure."

"Yes, I have thought of that," replied Sean. "I propose that this become my initiative, supported hopefully by the People's Republic of China and their leaders. This initiative will be totally independent of all other nuclear disarmament efforts and directed by myself hopefully with the support of the Chinese government.

"When the President of China, Mr. Chen Song, was in for his application, in the brief time that we spoke, he said he was appreciative of my efforts in the Pacific Ocean. I mentioned to him that I was considering ways to assist the world powers in eliminating some of their nuclear weapons and asked him if I could count on his support. He said that he would be open to any ideas that I had.

"My opinion is that without President Chen Song and the Chinese government's involvement, there is no chance that North Korea, India, Pakistan, and Russia will even sit down at a table and talk about nuclear disarmament. I will personally talk to the President of China, Chen Song, and ask him to select a representative of his government to be my Program Director. As this is my initiative, I will be directing the operations and paying for hundred percent of all expenses.

"I am sure that, bolstered by the international cooperation achieved in cleaning up the Great Pacific Garbage Patch and with my efforts sanctioned and supported by the Chinese government, I can get these nuclear-armed powers talking and come to an agreement. To start, the director's job will be to contact the leaders of each nuclear-armed state and determine what has to be done for them to relinquish ten of their nuclear armaments to us for disposal.

"For disposal, I propose to select an international site where the nuclear weapons can be stored in lead boxes, placed in the ground, and then covered with concrete. I have eliminated the idea of having the stockpile on American soil and like the idea of finding a deserted island with, hopefully, an abandoned mine where the nuclear warheads could be stored.

"An uninhabited island, away from other inhabited islands, would be perfect as it would be difficult for terrorists to get to and can be easily guarded to ensure that the stockpile is not being tampered with. My idea is to purchase the island from its present owners, and once the storage facility is full, turn its ownership over to the UN for constant monitoring."

"Well, Sean," replied Wendy. "Your worldwide credentials for cleaning up the Garbage Patch certainly allow you direct access to all the world leaders, and with the potential backing of the Chinese government, you might just pull this off. Heaven knows that all other attempts have failed."

Sean then flipped over to the next chart to review the points covered:

–The world leader's doors are open to us as we have proven our sincerity in undertaking efforts to improve our world.

–We have proven that the direct approach is the best. With previous projects, we never asked or sought out anyone's permission to act. We acted. We silenced the critics by stating what we were going to do, and above their criticisms, we went right ahead and did it and succeeded.

–Asking permission from the world's governments simply means that our good intentions will get bogged down in endless rounds of diplomatic talks and nothing will get done. Talk, talk, and more talk and no action.

–I believe that an outside organization, us, working outside of regular diplomatic channels with the influence to open the world leader's doors be heard, can eventually shame all the leaders of the nuclear-armed states into reducing their nuclear arsenals.

–My intention is to request the cooperation of the Chinese government and hopefully have a Chinese national from their Atomic Division be my Program Director. My opinion is that if this is seen as an American initiative, Russia, China, North Korea, Pakistan, and India will resist the efforts and the program will fail.

–I and I alone will select the suitable storage site based on:

–an uninhabited island distant from other inhabited islands

–hopefully one with an abandoned mine on it and

–which I can purchase from its present government owners and then turn it over to the UN once completed.

All three in the room realized that this was what had been keeping him occupied for the past several months. Plus, each knew that once he laid down his plans, he was impossible to deter. This project was a go. Colonel John spoke next.

"Sean, you know the US government is going to hit the roof when they hear that you have asked the Chinese government to become involved, not themselves.

"I totally agree that without the Chinese involvement and influence, that North Korea, India, Pakistan, and Russia will never even consider cooperating."

"Yes, John, you are correct," replied Sean. "Their complaints are merely a side issue I will have to deal with. My plan is to inform our President of my actions after talking to President Chen Song of the People's Republic of China."

Now it was Bill Fryer's, the lawyer's, turn to speak.

"Sean, I can see thousands of reasons why it won't work. The deep-seated distrust of the nuclear-armed powers will be almost impossible to overcome. But even with seeing a thousand reasons why it won't work, your influence and direct access to the world leaders you have the greatest chance of making it work. Plus, if you can get the Chinese to support your efforts, you are halfway home. I think that I speak for all of us, we're all for it. And to quote Wendy, if anyone can pull it off, it's you." Everyone laughed.

"Thank you for your support," replied Sean. "I will draft up a letter to the President of the People's Republic of China and ask for his support and to have him select a candidate as my Project Director. I will keep you informed on how I make out. I will then include a letter to the President of the United States to keep him informed of my efforts. And as always, this is in strict confidence, and you are to mention it to no one."

Everyone agreed. They then broke up and went back to their duties. Each was deep in thought on what looked like an impossible mountain to climb.

Letter to the President of the People's Republic of China

Mr. Chen Song,

It was my pleasure to meet you when you were in for your application of my age-reversing formula. I hope you are feeling well and that the procedure has received your approval.

Thank you for your cooperation in my efforts to clean up the Great Pacific Garbage Patch. The world has marveled at the level of international cooperation involved in cleaning up this environmental problem.

During our brief chat, I mentioned that I was looking for ways to encourage the world's nuclear-armed powers to allow me to dispose of some of their nuclear weapons. You generously asked me to consult with you, and you also shared my vision.

Mr. Song, I propose…

–I would appreciate you selecting a member of your atomic energy department to be my Program Director. His task is to head up my international effort to reduce the existing world nuclear weapons stockpiles by ten percent.

–This group, totally funded by myself, would deal directly with the world leaders of the nuclear-armed nations and would remain independent of all other nuclear disarmament agencies and independent of any UN actions. This group will report to only yourself and myself.

–I will investigate and purchase a yet to be determined uninhabited island site with an existing abandoned mine where the nuclear weapons could be stored. I will pay for this site and all accommodation and testing facilities myself. Once completed, this site will be turned over to the UN for their constant monitoring.

–My idea is to encourage the existing world nuclear-armed powers to relinquish ten percent of their arsenal to be stored on this safe island site. My intention is to have a team of scientists, one from each of the nuclear-armed states, oversee the storage of the weapons themselves.

–I look forward to meeting the representative you forward to me. My only request is that this representative be presently actively involved in your own nuclear agency and be fluent in English to ease my conversations with them.

Thank you
Sean Little

Reply from The People's Republic of China

Mr. Little,

I wish to again express my sincere appreciation for your efforts in cleaning up the Great Pacific Garbage Patch. Your insistence that this be an international effort directed and paid for by yourself is a stroke of pure genius. The level of international cooperation that has been achieved in this environmental cleanup is a credit to yourself, your vision, and your efforts. We, the People's Republic of China, and myself are forever in your debt.

We, the People's Republic of China, are eager to assist you in your efforts to reduce the world's nuclear weapons arsenal. We totally agree that an outside agency, directed by yourself, is the proper way to proceed in discussions with the world leaders. Your desire to reduce the world's atomic arsenal by ten percent is an honorable one. I pledge my efforts and the efforts of my country to help you with this initiative.

For this, I have selected Mr. Hing Zoi as my candidate for your

Program Director. Mr. Zoi is a high-ranking member of our atomic agency, and my instructions is to follow your instructions to the letter. I believe you will find him fluent in English, as you requested, and a quality member of your team. He will be arriving in the United States shortly. Again, I and the People's Republic of China thank you for your environmental efforts and pledge our support for your nuclear arms reduction initiative.

Chen Song

President

People's Republic of China

Immediately upon receiving the Chinese President's reply, Sean sent copies of this cover letter to the President of the United States. Sean was fully aware that this was going to be a "tough pill to swallow" for the President and Vice President but he didn't care. He was determined to commit his life to the initiative and see it through.

To Mr. Samuel Walker,

President of the United States

From Sean Little,

I am sending you this letter to inform you of my intentions to influence the world's nuclear-armed powers to relinquish ten percent of their nuclear weapons to me for safe storage. My procedure is laid out in the letter I have written to the President of the People's Republic of China. I have included a copy of my letter to him and a copy of his reply.

I hope that you realize that if I were to involve the US in this initiative, the nuclear power nations of China, North Korea, Russia, Pakistan, and India would refuse to cooperate. Therefore, I have asked for and will be receiving the aid of the Chinese government.

I look forward to your support for this nuclear arms reduction plan.

Thank you

Sean Little

The Arrival of Hing Zoi

Sean arranged for Colonel John and Wendy to greet Mr. Zoi at the airport. Wendy suggested bringing along Dr. Cindy Marshall, their Chinese-American compound doctor. Sean's reply was, "Whatever you think is best."

After settling Mr. Zoi in his room at the Parkway Hotel, the three took him out to an elegant restaurant in Las Vegas as a diplomatic courtesy. Having the beautiful Dr. Cindy Marshall there easily relaxed and impressed Mr. Zoi. Mr. Zoi now had a dancing partner, and the four of them got along famously. *Good move,* thought Wendy.

The next day, Mr. Zoi met with Sean Little at the front door of his office complex.

Mr. Zoi was exactly what Sean expected. His suit, his hair, and his politeness were impeccable. Sean took Mr. Zoi for a courtesy tour of the compound. Once in Sean's office, Mr. Zoi handed Sean a letter outlining his credentials and then stated that President Chen Song had ordered him to follow Sean's instructions in the letter. He also stated that President Song was eager to assist Sean in his nuclear arms reduction plans. After thanking Mr. Zoi, Sean laid out his plans.

"Mr. Zoi, it is my intention to reduce the present world stock of nuclear warheads by ten percent. This initiative will be directed by me, you, of course, and the People's Republic of China. You will remain independent of all other governments, government agencies, and other nuclear reduction organizations.

"You will talk to and deal directly with the leaders of the world who now possess nuclear weapons. Dealing with anyone else except the leaders themselves will just frustrate our efforts and lead to endless and futile diplomatic discussions. I am confident that, with my influence and the influence of your President, the various world leaders will welcome you. But please, in your discussions with other world leaders:

–You may never imply that free applications of my age-reversing formula are available

–You may never imply that I will be visiting another country. Recent events have shown that I am only safe within the confines of this compound, and to leave it certainly spells my doom.

–You may never offer or pay a kickback or cash payment to any person, government official, or government to get them to comply. I will not be purchasing these warheads, but expect them to be given to us for free storage. I will pay for all transportation costs to the island.

"I will arrange for another organization to scout out suitable storage sites. The ideal storage site would be an uninhabited island away from other inhabited islands and not one presently under the control of one of the nuclear-armed countries. Ideally, this island would have an abandoned mine on it where the weapons could be stored. I will select the island myself and purchase it from the government that owns it. I will then have living accommodations and nuclear testing facilities installed.

"Before storage, all nuclear weapons will be inspected by a team of scientists, one from each of the nine nuclear-armed states before it is placed in an additional lead-lined box and placed underground. Once in the shaft, the weapons will be sealed in concrete. Once this site is full, I will be handing the island's ownership over to the UN for them to monitor and inspect."

Sean continued, "Mr. Zoi, you will be receiving a standard director's pay of fifty thousand dollars per month and ten million dollars in US funds to be placed in an American bank account to cover your expenses. If you need more, just let my Executive Secretary, Wendy, know.

"As with my other directors, you are hundred percent in charge of this initiative. Unless it is very important, please do not call me. You are required to have on my desk by the 20th of each month a full written report of your progress. If I have any questions, I will call you.

"I request that your first task is to meet with the nuclear-armed world leaders themselves and inform them of our plans. This is a long-term commitment, so I do not expect success overnight. I have already informed the President of the United States of my intentions.

"You are welcome to make presentations on our behalf to the UN, but your efforts will remain independent of their influence and efforts. As mentioned, many others will want to become involved with your efforts, but you will refuse their assistance. The more involved with other governments and agencies, the more you lessen your chances of success."

After a respectful pause, Mr. Zoi replied with, "Mr. Little, I am honored to be involved in such a worthwhile initiative. I will set my sights on interviewing each of the nuclear-armed world leaders and discussing with them relinquishing ten percent of their nuclear arsenal to be stored in a safe, internationally monitored site. As requested, I will report back to you in writing on the reactions of the world leaders whom I meet. I am sure that with your influence and the influence of my government, I will be successful."

"Thank you, Mr. Zoi," replied Sean. "It is my hope that your Chinese government will support this effort by being the first to offer up ten percent of their nuclear stockpile for storage on this island. This effort would encourage other nations to participate, especially the US and Russia. This in turn will convince the others—France, the UK, Pakistan, India, Israel, and North Korea to in turn offer us part of their nuclear stockpile."

Mr. Zoi replied with, "Mr. Little, as you can appreciate, that is not a decision I can make. I will certainly mention your suggestion to President Song when I meet him again."

"Thank you, Mr. Zoi. I appreciate that," replied Sean. "Plus, I expect great protests from the American government once they know that China will be assisting me in this initiative. Their protests are to be expected. Please pay no attention to their complaints.

"Plus, unless I authorize it, you are not to meet with the President of the United States or make presentations to the American government. The hardliners in this country opposed to this program will state that the US would be caving into Chinese interests and our efforts here will fail. I will personally direct the efforts in this country. Plus, once you are successful in reaching an agreement with the other nuclear-armed states, I am sure the US will comply.

"The entire procedure of picking up the weapons, their transportation to the site, their testing, and then their disposal are to be totally video recorded and placed on my website for the entire world to see. I am confident that once the world sees the sincerity of our efforts and that these nuclear weapons can be stored in an international safe site, the pressure on other world leaders to relinquish part of their arsenal will increase and silence the skeptics."

Both Sean and Mr. Zoi reviewed the list of director objectives so that there was a clear understanding of what was expected.

"Mr. Zoi, while in the compound here, you are welcome to go where you please and talk to whomever you please. We have no secrets here, just good intentions. It is not necessary for you to have accommodations or an office here as these will be in your home country of China."

After fully explaining his intentions to Hing Zoi, Sean introduced him back to Wendy, who set him up with his bank account and a deposit of ten million US dollars. Then they both left for a bit to eat. After a cordial handshake, they parted company, and Colonel John and Wendy picked up Mr. Zoi for his drive to the airport. Somehow Wendy arranged that Dr. Cindy Marshall to be in the vehicle to accompany Mr. Zoi. This pleased them both.

Later that day, meeting with Sean, Wendy asked, "Sean, do you really think you can pull this off? You will be tackling head-on the hatred and animosity between the world's superpowers. Hatred and animosity that people hold true to their hearts and help them define their identity. You will meet opposition on all fronts, even from our own government."

"Yes, you are correct, Wendy," replied Sean. "Someone once said that all great ideas start out having to overcome great opposition, and this effort is one of them.

"Under my direction and with China's approval and backing, we are starting out with a great deal of confidence and credibility, especially with those nations that distrust the US.

"I believe that China can place considerable influence on Russia, Pakistan, India, and North Korea to reduce their nuclear arsenals. This in turn will heavily influence the US to not be left out of this worthwhile cause, and who likewise will influence the UK, France, and Israel to reduce their nuclear arsenal. So to answer your question, yes, I believe it will happen—likely not soon, but in the future. I have dedicated my life to seeing this through."

The International Campaign to Abolish Nuclear Weapons (ICAN)

The next day, Sean contacted the ICAN offices in Geneva and spoke to their Executive Director, Helmut Zimler. Mr. Zimler was well aware of Sean's environmental work and the astonishing international cooperation he achieved in cleaning up the Great Pacific Garbage Patch. Sean thanked him for his compliments and then briefly outlined his course of action to reduce the world's stockpiles of nuclear weapons.

Mr. Zimler was delighted that such a high-profile individual as Sean Little was directing his efforts toward nuclear arms reduction. Sean told Mr. Zimler that he was impressed by his efforts to date and that his organization had an important role to play in this initiative and invited him to visit him at the Nevada compound at his earliest convenience.

Mr. Zimler agreed to meet with Sean at the compound the following Monday. Once Mr. Zimler arrived and Sean gave him his courtesy tour, they went to his office and got right down to business. To inform Mr. Zimler of his plans, instead of explaining his intentions, he gave him copies of his letter to the President of China, their reply, and the letter informing the President of the United States. Sean patiently waited for Mr. Zimler to read the three letters. Mr. Zimler replied, "Sean, this is impressive. You have what we lack. Your worldwide influence and your success in getting major world powers to assist you in cleaning up the garbage in the Pacific Ocean are just the tickets needed to succeed in reducing nuclear arms stockpiles around the world.

"I totally agree that an outside agency like yours with the ears of world leaders can convince them to reduce their nuclear arsenals. My organization has worldwide coverage and support, except for the nuclear-powered nations themselves. Yes, their representatives talk to us, but nothing ever gets done. We have been ineffective in getting to the leaders of the nuclear-armed states themselves or in having any leverage to get them to dispose of their weapons. We just end up getting bogged down in endless diplomatic talks that never go anywhere. To date, the major nuclear powers listen but do nothing.

"You, with your influence, can be successful. But I am alarmed and question your involvement with the Chinese. The Chinese have frustrated my people at every turn. They talk and they smile, but they do nothing. I think you should reconsider."

Sean had anticipated Mr. Zimler's opposition to his being involved with the Chinese and was quick to react.

"Let me get something straight. I did not invite you here to ask for your permission or your opinions on my course of action. I have told you what I am going to do, and I am going to do it. You have been invited here to play a role in this initiative, or I will find someone else who will. It's up to you."

Mr. Zimler was shocked at Sean's quick rebuttal of his comments. Mr. Zimler, knowing of Sean's quick temper and steadfast determination, wisely settled down and replied with, "Yes, on second thought, you're getting the Chinese involved opens the doors for talks with those nations who distrust the US, most notably North Korea, India, Pakistan, and Russia. We at ICAN are always seen as a European or American agency, so we have been frustrated at our attempts to influence those five world powers."

"Yes, I agree with you," stated Sean. "Everyone agrees we have the nuclear capacity to turn the entire world into a smoldering ember thousands of times over, but getting them to agree to even a partial arms reduction is impossible. Every world leader thinks the other governments should reduce their arsenal first, but not them."

"So, Sean, how can I help you?" asked Mr. Zimler.

Sean replied, "While Mr. Zoi is discussing with the other nuclear-armed states to relinquish ten percent of their nuclear arsenal to us, I need your world-wide connections to scout me out a suitable island storage facility. Once you have selected some sites, my people will investigate each site, and I will make the final decision. An island is preferred because it is difficult for others to get to and can be easily monitored by the UN once I turn the island over to them. I think the suitable island site would be:

–an uninhabited island a distance from other inhabited islands

–the island would have an abandoned mine on it

–an island that is not part of the ownership of any of the existing nuclear-armed nations and is as far away from such states as possible.

–a site that all nine nuclear-armed states could agree upon

–and that I would be able to purchase this island and eventually hand it over to the UN as an international storage facility

Once you have given me about ten suitable sites and confirmed their government will sell their island to me, I will have my people inspect the sites and report back to me. The final decision about the site will be mine and mine alone.

"Here is a check for ten million dollars to cover your expenses in scouting out these islands. And the last point is that you are not to contact or interfere with Mr. Zoi's work under any circumstances. He reports to me, the President of the People's Republic of China, and no one else. Your involvement with him would only harm his efforts. Are we clear on this?"

"Yes, Sean, perfectly clear," replied Mr. Zimler, who was obviously disappointed that he was not playing a larger role in this initiative. "I will get my people on this right away. Thank you." And then he left.

Hing Zoi at Work

With the high-profile influence of Sean Little and the encouragement of Mr. Song, the President of the People's Republic of China, Mr. Zoi was able to meet directly with the world leaders and not be delayed by talks with their subordinates. Naturally, the heads of the other nations were cordial and listened to his plans. This delay was to be expected.

As promised, Mr. Zoi stayed away from the international diplomatic channels and those persons and organizations who wished to become part of his disarmament efforts. Such high-profile projects always attract those who wish to "ride on your coattails" and get involved to increase their own importance and self-image. This Mr. Zoi wisely avoided.

As expected, all the nuclear-armed world leaders expressed approval of Mr. Zoi's plans to reduce the world's nuclear arsenals. But somehow they all wanted the other nations to hand over their weapons first while they retained their own. No one wanted to be the first to cooperate.

Nuclear Storage Site Selected

Sean invited both Colonel John and Wendy to join him and Jennifer for lunch.

Sean explained, "Mr. Zimler, Executive Director of the "International Campaign to Abolish Nuclear Weapons," after three months, has handed me a list of ten suitable island sites that could be used as our nuclear arms storage facilities.

"Wendy and Colonel John, I have a very great favor to ask of both of you. I need you both to clean up the work on your desks and take a month off to inspect each and every island site and determine its suitability as a nuclear storage site. Plus, you must confirm that these islands can be purchased by myself with the intention of handing the islands and the storage facilities over to the UN. My conditions for a suitable island site are:

–this island must be uninhabited and as far away as possible from other inhabited islands

–this island cannot be presently part of the nuclear-armed states or under their influence

it would be preferred that it had an abandoned mine on it for storage

–the island must be large enough to install a deep-water docking facility, accommodation, and nuclear testing facilities

–you will also have to meet with the host government to confirm that I can purchase their island, store nuclear weapons on it, and then turn is ownership over to the UN.

"I think a month is about as long as I can survive without Wendy being here. Without her here for two weeks, the place starts to fall apart, and the whole compound would be a disaster if she stayed away longer than a month. I know that leaving us for a month to explore deserted islands is a tough decision for both of you to make, and I hope that you can find something to do while you are there."

Then Jennifer yelled out with a smile on her face, "Yeah, right. Frolicking on pure ocean beaches on deserted tropical islands. What a tough job, but I guess someone has to do it." And everyone laughed. Wendy couldn't control herself.

"Are you kidding me? Spending a month with John on deserted tropical islands!" She then jumped out of her chair, hugged Sean and Jennifer, and then kissed Colonel John.

Sean with a smile, then said, "I suppose by your actions that you both approve of going away to these deserted islands together." Everyone laughed as Wendy was wiping the tears from her eyes.

Wendy then asked, "When do you want us to leave?"

"As soon as you have the work on your desk caught up to where this place won't immediately fall apart while you're gone," replied Sean. "Plus, I do not want to hear from you while you are away. Naturally, you can communicate with your staff, but you do not have to contact me. Just give me a written report on each site you visit when you return. Do a good job, and if these inspections take more than a month, you will just have to go back again. Obviously, you will have to meet with and inform the host governments of your intentions and maybe have them ferry you to the island or rent your own transportation. You decide."

Wendy hurried herself to clean up her duties and assign important tasks to members of her staff. She was so excited to go that she and her staff worked late every night. Plus, she made sure that all the checks for veterans, police officers and federal agents were made well in advance.

With a farewell to Sean and Jennifer, Colonel John and Wendy departed for the airport to start their inspections. Everyone in the compound was jealous of their "tough job of having to go and explore uninhabited tropical islands." As expected, Wendy, where possible, kept in touch with her staff on a regular basis but did not talk to Sean.

But one week into their trip, Wendy called Jennifer. Wendy was crying. She was so excited. Jennifer exclaimed, "Wendy, what's wrong?"

Wendy, through her tears, said, "John proposed to me last night, and we had a chaplain flown in and got married this morning on a deserted beach. It was beautiful."

Jennifer immediately started crying. She was so happy.

"Oh, Wendy, I wish I was there."

"I know," said Wendy. "But I wanted to do it before he changed his mind." And they both laughed. "I just had to tell you. I'm so happy. Now you have to promise that this is a secret and no one is to know."

"Okay, okay, I'll keep it a secret," promised Jennifer.

The truth is that if you ever wanted something to become common knowledge, just tell Jennifer it's a secret, and the whole world will know within an hour. Jennifer immediately contacted Sean and told him the good news.

"Let's plan a party for when they arrive," explained Jennifer.

"No problem, you see to it," replied Sean.

Upon their return, Colonel John and Wendy were met at the airport as expected by the guards and escorted back to the compound. The guards were instructed to deliver both Colonel John and Wendy directly to the restaurant, regardless of what the Colonel ordered. Arriving at the compound, Colonel John asked to be taken to their apartments, but the driver ignored his request and instead delivered them to the restaurant instead. Colonel John immediately knew something was up.

Inside the restaurant, Jennifer had the place lined with "Congratulations on Your Marriage" banners, and everyone stood and cheered when the beautifully tanned married couple of Wendy and Colonel John entered. *Tough keeping a secret around here,* thought Wendy.

Jennifer and Wendy's female staff were all crying; they were so happy. Hugs and kisses abound, and everyone made toast to the newlyweds. Everyone marveled at how good both Wendy and John looked.

"Did you ever get any work done, or did you just lie on the beach for the last thirty days?" one of Wendy's staff said, and everyone laughed.

The next day, Wendy and Colonel John presented their reports to Sean. Sean, after a few days and with numerous international calls, decided on an unnamed deserted island in the Philippines that was set apart from the others and had a deserted iron mine on it.

Plus, it also had a large deep-water docking facility already in place. Sean contacted the President of the Philippines and settled on a price of thirty million dollars for the island. Sean then contacted Bill Fryer and told him of his intentions to ensure that the purchase went through.

Sean then contacted Mr. Zoi to inform him that a storage facility was being purchased and to inform the world leaders that the site would quickly be available as a storage facility. His next step was to employ the massive American construction firm Zenco Inc. to construct accommodation facilities and a nuclear testing facility on the island. They were also instructed to prepare and improve the mine as a nuclear warhead storage facility.

Six months later, with the ownership of the island in hand, the accommodation and testing facilities in place, and the mine prepared as a storage facility, the now-nicknamed "Nuclear Island" was open for business.

China Disposes of ten percent of its Warheads

And as Sean had hoped, it was Chinese President Song who started ball rolling. Premier Song ordered that ten percent of his nuclear arsenal of 410 warheads be selected for transport and storage at the new island facility.

On instructions from Sean Little, Mr. Zoi was to conduct the entire process, and that National Geographic would accompany Mr. Zoi and the weapons to the island and make a complete program out of the storage procedure. Mr. Zoi himself did a wonderful job of showing the nuclear weapons being loaded onto the ship, delivered to the island, inspected by representatives of the nine nuclear powers, then the weapons being placed in the mine shaft and covered with concrete.

Once this program was aired around the world in multiple languages, the worldwide roar of support for Sean's disarmament efforts was deafening.

Mr. Zoi was then invited to speak at the UN. Sean naturally approved of such a speech. Mr. Zoi's speech was broadcast throughout the world by enthusiastic world news agencies.

Mr. Zoi started out his speech with the customary thank-you's and words of appreciation to the UN General Assembly. He also mentioned the involvement of Mr. Zimler, Executive Director of the International Campaign to Abolish Nuclear Weapons, who assisted Sean Little in finding a suitable storage facility.

"Ladies and gentlemen, my name is Hing Zoi, and I stand before you as a representative of the Sean Little Nuclear Disarmament Program and the People's Republic of China. I am proud to present to you the first act of nuclear disarmament under the Sean Little's plan.

"If I could direct your eyes to the screen beside me. To start, you see forty-one Chinese nuclear warheads, or ten percent of China's total nuclear arms, being selected and transported to the Sean Little Nuclear Storage Facility on this deserted Philippine Island.

"Now you see each warhead being fully inspected by scientists from each of the nuclear-armed states, Russia, the United States, France, the UK, China, Pakistan, India, Israel, and North Korea. This inspection is to ensure the world that these are, in fact, nuclear warheads. Now you see the lead-lined crates housing these nuclear warheads being transported into the abandoned mine shaft, placed at the end of the shaft, stacked, and then covered in concrete.

"I am here to speak to you on behalf of Mr. Sean Little and Mr. Chen Song, the President of the People's Republic of China. Both Mr. Little and Mr. Song are totally dedicated to the reduction of the world's nuclear arsenal and this is just the first step. I now call on the world's nuclear powers to support Sean Little's nuclear disarmament efforts and to follow China's lead and relinquish ten percent of their nuclear capacity for safe storage.

"The reduction of the world's present nuclear weapons capacity is a just and noble cause. It has to be done and will be done. Mr. Little has dedicated his life to see this project through. Mr. Little requests your support, the People's Republic of China requests your support and the people of the world request your support. Thank you."

The entire UN General Assembly arose in a roar of cheering and applause. The only delegates not standing and cheering were those from Russia and North Korea. Likewise. Mr. Zoi's speech was broadcast on every news channel in every nation around the world. News announcers around the world were unanimous in their praise, "Finally, something is being done to deter us from this nuclear madness."

The Rest of The World Complies

As Sean expected, once the films of the storing of the Chinese nuclear weapons became public and Mr. Zoi made his speech at the UN, the world-wide clamor for additional weapons to be stored filled the airwaves. This had the desired effects on the US, the UK, France, and Israel as their people argued for their nations to join in disposing of part of their nuclear arsenal.

As one major American news reporter put it, "Even if we in the US give up just ten percent of our nuclear warheads that still leaves us with over five-thousand nuclear weapons, able to wipe everything off this planet a hundred times over. We don't need so many weapons, let's get rid of them."

And to the world's surprise, the next nation to offer up ten percent of its nuclear arsenal was North Korea. Sean assumed that the North Korean's were under pressure from the Chinese and wanted to increase their stature as a peace-loving country. Plus, Sean thought they likely hoped that this gesture would deter South Korea from creating their own nuclear arms program. The North Korean's made great fanfare of giving up four of their warheads for storage on the island. Mr. Zoi and the President of North Korea made a speech urging the other world nations to give up ten percent of their nuclear arms.

Chinese President Song, using his diplomatic pressure, later had the heads of Pakistan and India visit him in Peking and with Mr. Zoi as master of ceremonies, made a big diplomatic show of both the leaders of Pakistan and India agreeing to and signing a declaration to give up ten percent or sixteen of their nuclear warheads each. These were all to be removed on the same date and to be picked up and delivered by Chinese transport ships. This likewise was done with much fanfare and the world news agencies broadcasted the removal of the warheads simultaneously for transport to "Nuclear Island." The world-wide cries of admiration for Sean Little and the Chinese efforts to reduce the world's nuclear weapons were like an ever-growing tidal wave.

Within the month, the UK, France, and Israel, pressured by their media and people, all agreed to join and relinquish part of their arsenal. *Pretty difficult to say that you are only keeping these weapons for peaceful purposes when other countries around you are giving up theirs,* thought Sean.

Mr. Zoi made presentations in each of the UK, France, and Israel, declaring his appreciation to Sean Little and the People's Republic of China. The more fanfare he got, the more the world got on the disarmament bandwagon. Now it would appear that the only holdouts were the United States and Russia.

Sean Is Invited To Washington

Sean Little then did the one thing he promised he would never do. At the President of the United States request, he agreed to leave the safety of the compound and visit Washington to speak to the combined members of the Senate and the House of Representatives in two weeks time. The President even graciously invited Sean to stay overnight as his guest in the White House. Sean, after a long pause, accepted the President's invitation. Sean then mentioned that he would likely be bringing along his Executive Secretary and her Colonel husband, his head of security. President Walker assured him that they were also welcome to stay in the White House as his guests.

Sean informed Colonel John and Wendy of his plans and invited them to come along. He knew that Jennifer would feel more comfortable with Wendy, so it was a perfect fit. Two days prior to their departure, Colonel John visited Sean.

"Sean, I fully understand your desire to keep helicopter visits to the compound to a bare minimum. You are correct that once you allow one, one in a hundred will follow. But Sean, as your friend and responsible for your security, I have ordered a military helicopter from Nellis to pick the four of us up. There will be a military jet waiting for us at Nellis when we arrive."

"But John, I don't want any more helicopters here," replied Sean.

"Yes, and I appreciate that. But I can't have you taking an hour's drive through Las Vegas to Nellis and guarantee your safety. This is the first time you have left the compound in years, and it would be so easy for someone to either kidnap you or put a bullet in your head. The potential for problems is just too great," argued John.

"Okay, okay, you win. As always, I place myself completely in your care," answered Sean. Colonel John then thanked Sean and left.

In Washington

The four arrived in Washington a day early. The President asked Sean to have lunch with him the day before his addresses to the combined Houses of Government. Jennifer and Wendy, accompanied by a full contingent of White House security, naturally went shopping.

As expected, the President questioned Sean's insistence on having the Chinese lead the nuclear arms reduction initiative, and Sean outlined his plans. Sean would not budge and reminded the President that in no way was he seeking out the President's approval or permission to follow through on his plans. To quieten the President's objections, Sean said, "I have stated my plans, and I will follow through on them. All previous attempts to get the nuclear-armed nations to reduce their stockpiles of nuclear weapons have failed, so I would be a fool to follow in their path. I have committed my resources and my life to this effort, and I will succeed."

The President knew of Sean's quick temper and his steadfast resolve once he put his mind to a course of action. The President even thought to himself, *You know, he just might pull this off.*

On the appointed day, the security was so tight that a fly could not get into Washington without being questioned. Sean insisted that Colonel John, Wendy, and Jennifer were seated near the podium when he spoke. He knew that visiting Washington meant that every single elected official would want to talk to him, which he wished to avoid at all costs. He informed Colonel John to have his helicopter ready for departure immediately upon the completion of his speech.

Sean knew that the entire success of this effort would rest on this one speech, and he was ready. At the appointed hour, the President of the United States himself introduced Sean Little. "Ladies and gentlemen, I would like to introduce to you a man who everyone knows from the work he has accomplished in a very short time. Sean is responsible for the direct payments to our physically disabled veterans, police officers, and federal agents (the President had to stop as everyone was clapping). He is also responsible for establishing a Fifteen dollars per hour minimum wage throughout this great country. He is also assisting individual states with their infrastructure and environmental projects (more clapping) and has single-handedly managed to get the entire world to coordinate their efforts to clean up the Great Pacific Garbage Patch (more clapping again). Mr. Little has graciously accepted my invitation to speak to us today."

Sean Little Addresses the American Government

Sean shook hands with the President, and everyone clapped as Sean took the stand.

"Thank you, Mr. President, and members of the American Senate and House of Representatives, for your warm welcome.

I will be blunt and to the point. I, Sean Little, have devoted my life and my resources to this most ambitious task: the reduction and eventual elimination of the world's nuclear weapons stockpiles. I have committed to ending the world-wide lunacy that we now call mutually assured destruction.

"The nine countries of the world with nuclear weapons have a combined nuclear arsenal of about thirteen thousand weapons. To date, the countries of China, France, the UK, Pakistan, India, Israel, and North Korea have each given up ten percent of their nuclear arsenal, and I am proud to say that 137 nuclear warheads are now safely entombed in lead and concrete on my island in the South Pacific. As stated, once this nuclear arms initiative is finished, I will be handing over the ownership of this island to the United Nations for their constant monitoring and security.

"But still, even with these efforts, the world is still threatened by a world-wide arsenal of over twelve thousand nuclear warheads. I am telling the world that I will not rest until we start coming to our senses and start reducing our nuclear capacity. This lunacy has to stop.

"I am hereby calling on the last two holdouts, the United States of America with its estimated 5478 nuclear weapons, and Russia with its estimated 5971 nuclear weapons to put down their levels of distrust and allow ten percent of their nuclear arsenal to be placed in safe, international storage.

"I ask you to support me in my quest. Generations to come will look upon this moment as a time when the world sat up and realized the lunacy we were creating, or look upon it as a time when the world stuck its head in the sand and refused to see the path of destruction we were on.

"Ladies and gentlemen, the citizens of the United States and Russia and the other nations of the world, the time for talk is over. It is a time for action.

"My plans are made, and my plans are set. Follow me in my quest to see a nuclear-free world. A world safe from total annihilation. Thank you."

The roar of applause for Sean's speech was deafening. Sean shook the President's hand, and then he, Jennifer, Colonel John, and Wendy, known to only a few others, were led off the platform to their awaiting helicopter. Plus, on Colonel John's request, once in the air, an additional four fully armed Apache helicopters escorted them to the awaiting airfield to their military jet. Likewise, in the air, four fully armed F-14 fighter jets escorted them to the Nellis Air Force Base in Nevada.

Sean's speech hit the international airways like a tidal wave hitting a sandy beach. The public outcry to end this nuclear lunacy was too great for any political party or government official to ignore. Sean was counting on the support of the American news agencies, and they supported his cause perfectly. The airways were being flooded with countless news programs showing the horrors of nuclear war and countless talk shows hosting people favorable to nuclear arms reduction. With seven of the other nuclear-powered nations already having given up ten percent of their nuclear weapons, the public pressure on the American government to do the same was relentless.

Finally, something had to break. The President of the United States introduced the "Sean Little Nuclear Arms Reduction Bill," which, after months of debate, the Senate and House of Representatives finally agreed that for every nuclear weapon that Russia gave up, America would do the same. Now the only holdout was Russia.

Convincing Russia

By this time, everyone agreed that without the direct involvement of the President of the People's Republic of China, Mr. Chen Song, little could be accomplished. Now the world prayed that Mr. Song and Sean would likewise be able to influence Russia to sit down to nuclear arms reduction talks.

Somehow, nothing was ever said, but it just seemed that any Russian individual request for the age-reversing application was being ignored. Regardless of how often they sent in their money, their applications were always refused for the slightest error.

As more and more of the world's elites received applications, the aging politicians in the Russian government and business leaders began realizing that they were being denied this procedure.

Likewise, Mr. Zoi was making constant trips to Moscow to present his case for a 1:1 nuclear arms reduction with the Americans. He assured them that the Chinese would handle all of the transportation of their nuclear weapons and that no Americans would be landing on Russian soil.

Mr. Zoi informed Sean that President Song was also keeping up the pressure on Russia to accept nuclear arms reductions with the Americans. With the worldwide clamor to reduce the nuclear stockpile even further, Mr. Zoi received letters of intent from the other seven nations stating that they were prepared to reduce their stockpiles even further once the Russians and Americans began reducing theirs.

Months went by, but the worldwide cries to rid our world of nuclear weapons never let up, never stopped. It was like the constant beating of a drum. twenty-four hours a day, seven days a week, fifty-two weeks a year. Every day, the news media promoted the benefits of a nuclear-free world. Never before in the history of the world have all its people been so focused on a single issue. People talked about little else, and the news media reported on little else.

Mr. Zoi, on Sean's instructions, hosted an international news media tour of "Nuclear Island," similar to what Sean arranged for promoting his plans for the cleanup of the Great Pacific Garbage Patch. Films of this island and its secure storage facilities were constantly being shown around the world.

The world could sense it. This goal could be realized, the dream fulfilled.

In every church, every synagogue, every mosque, and every center of religious worship, prayers were being sent to heaven, asking for the world's leaders to work toward a total nuclear arms ban.

The drum beat for nuclear arms reduction never stopped, never quietened. The worldwide heartbeat for a nuclear-free world was relentless.

Known only to Sean, Chinese President Chen Song was becoming impatient with Russia's refusal to sit and talk about these nuclear arms reduction plans. Somehow, important Chinese exports to Russia were being diverted to other countries. Food and medicines were also being diverted and these shortages could be felt on the streets of Moscow, affecting every Russian citizen. Likewise, countries around the world were shunning Russian exports and manufactured goods. Russian diplomats were constantly being booed whenever they appeared in public.

Then the dam broke. The President of Russia, Igor Popov, personally called Mr. Hing Zoi and invited him to speak. Mr. Zoi was cordially welcomed into Russia and given an audience in the Politburo. During his speech, he outlined the worldwide benefits of a nuclear arms reduction and the increased international prestige afforded to Russia by reducing its nuclear arsenal.

The Moscow Nuclear Arms Reduction Summit

Two weeks later on Russian national television, President Popov announced that in the coming weeks, he would be inviting Mr. Samuel Walker, the President of the United States, and Mr. Hing Zoi of the People's Republic of China to come to Moscow to come to terms on how many nuclear weapons they and the US would send for storage.

The date was set, and the President of the United States and Mr. Hing Zoi of the People's Republic of China arrived in Russia. After two days of customary speeches and diplomatic luncheons, the three dignitaries were closed in a boardroom.

The world held its breath. Every major news agency in the world waited eagerly outside, nervous over the results. Years of countless hours of work for a nuclear arms reduction treaty were hanging in the balance. Could the world pull itself back from annihilation? Then, after three hours of intense deliberations, the doors of the boardroom were opened.

Mr. Hing Zoi took the podium and spoke first. "Ladies and gentlemen, and the people of the world. Today marks a historic turning point in the nuclear arms race. We, the People's Republic of China, are proud of the Presidents of both the Russian Federation and the United States of America for finally coming to an agreement on nuclear arms reduction. I now turn the podium to the President of the Russian Federation."

Then, President of the Russian Federation, Mr. Igor Popov, spoke. "Ladies and gentlemen, and the people of the world. Today marks a significant turnaround in the nuclear arms race. I, the President of the Russian Federation have now agreed with the President of the United States to relinquish five-hundred nuclear warheads for storage at the international nuclear storage facility in the South Pacific.

"I have also agreed to halt all further research and production of nuclear weapons and will allow agencies of the UN total access to inspect our facilities to ensure compliance. I now turn the podium over to the President of the United States."

The two Presidents shook hands, and the President of the United States spoke. "I, the President of the United States, have now agreed with the President of the Russian Federation to relinquish five-hundred nuclear warheads for storage at the international nuclear storage facility in the South Pacific.

"I have also agreed to halt all further research and production of nuclear weapons and will allow agencies of the UN total access to inspect our facilities to ensure compliance."

At this, the two Presidents stood together and hugged each other. The President of the Russian Federation took the microphone again.

"Today heralds a new day for nuclear arms reduction and a step closer to world peace. I also wish to thank the President of the People's Republic of China, Mr. Chen Song and his representative, Mr. Hing Zoi, for making this possible.

"The American President and I have agreed to accept their generous offer to have these nuclear warheads transported on Chinese ships to the nuclear storage facilities."

The roar of cheers from those in attendance was deafening. Around the world, people celebrated. A new day of international cooperation was finally upon us.

President Popov was immediately flooded with phone calls of appreciation. President Chen Song of the People's Republic of China's phone call was immediately put through to Mr. Popov. Mr. Song expressed his appreciation for Mr. Popov's acceptance of nuclear arms reduction and expressed his willingness to help the Russian people in the months to come.

Shipment of the Nuclear Arms

True to both their words, the Chinese sent transport ships to the Russian and American ports and loaded each with five-hundred nuclear warheads. News services around the world showed the loading of the ships and their departure for the South Seas.

The nine scientists, one from each of the nuclear-armed states waited patiently for the ship's arrival. The ship loaded with American warheads arrived first and waited for the ship with the Russian warheads to arrive.

On the island, it was determined that for proper unloading, testing, and storage, they could handle twenty nuclear weapons per day. Therefore, ten Russian warheads were brought ashore, along with ten American warheads. These were then inspected in turn by all nine of the scientists to prove that they were, in fact, genuine. Once approved, the warheads were placed in additional lead-lined boxes and taken down the mine shaft for storage. Once all twenty crates were stored in the mine shaft, specialized concrete pumping equipment sprayed them completely with concrete. Along with the various world news agencies, National Geographic was there filming everything.

This procedure took fifty days, with twenty warheads per day being inspected and stored. Hardliners from both the United States and Russia were forever stating that the other countries were sending in fake warheads. But with the warheads being individually inspected by nine independent atomic scientists, this quietened the skeptics.

On the final day, when the last of the warheads were inspected and stored, the two Presidents decided to address their own nations. With a seven-hour time difference between Washington and Moscow, it was decided that five p.m. Washington time and ten a.m. Moscow times would be the time for the simultaneous broadcast. The world waited in anticipation. Every television station around the world broadcasts these presentations.

The Presidents of both nations spoke at exactly the same time and said exactly the same thing. The American President spoke in English, and the Russian President spoke in Russian with English subtitles.

"Ladies and gentlemen, today marks a great step forward in the reduction of nuclear arms. Each of our countries, Russia and the United States, has relinquished five-hundred nuclear warheads each, for a total of one-thousand warheads that have now been safely stored in the international nuclear storage facility in the South Pacific. These warheads are now stored alongside the 137 additional warheads placed there by China, France, the UK, Pakistan, India, Israel, and North Korea.

"I would like to thank all those who have made this historic day possible. First, I would like to thank Sean Little for his tireless efforts and for providing the international storage facility in the South Pacific. I would now like to personally thank Mr. Chen Song, the President of the People's Republic of China, and his representative, Mr. Hing Zoi, for making this historic day possible. I look forward to further talks in order to further reduce nuclear arms. I am willing to talk."

Every person around the world cheered and slept a little easier that night.

The Peking Nuclear Arms Reduction Summit

A year went by, and Sean was content with his successes to date. He didn't want to press his luck and put more pressure on the world leaders until the dust settled down from the Moscow summit. Mr. Zoi continued with his diplomatic visits to the nuclear-armed heads of state to gently suggest an additional summit of all the nine nuclear-armed nations. Mr. Zoi, with Sean's and Chinese President Chen Song's encouragement, continued with the endless rounds of gentle persuasion and diplomatic luncheons. As expected, these talks always went nowhere.

Mr. Zoi informed Sean of President Song's intention to have an international nuclear arms reduction summit in his capital city of Peking in a years' time. President Song introduced this summit to the world.

"I, Chen Song, the President of the People's Republic of China, hereby cordially invite the leaders of the world nuclear-armed nations of Russia, the United States, France, the United Kingdom, Pakistan, India, Israel, and North Korea to a nuclear arms reduction summit to take place in Peking, China, in one years' time.

"This invitation is only open to the world leaders themselves and not to any delegates or subordinates. This entire summit will be canceled if any one nation refuses to participate.

"With the international cooperation shown in the clean-up of the Pacific Ocean and with the success of the recent nuclear arms reductions by all nuclear-armed powers, it is time that we walk back from the threat of total world annihilation and create a safer world for all of us and our children.

"My delegate, Mr. Hing Zoi, will be meeting with each world leader in turn and securing their promise of attendance. We, the people of the world, must not miss this opportunity to reduce our nuclear arms and foster world peace."

The world reacted as one. The cheers and applause for the Chinese President filled the airways. Finally, a world leader has taken the steps to end the arms race and save mankind.

Sean Little, well aware in advance of this announcement, ordered that additional mine shafts be dug on "Nuclear Island". Fortunately for him, "Nuclear Island" was just one really big island composed of pure bedrock and little else. *No need to find an additional storage site. Just make this one bigger,* thought Sean.

This, he wisely decided, would be done by a combination of Chinese workers, Russian workers, and American workers. Sean was generously paying for all the expenses, and the work proceeded admirably. Workers were being paid thousand dollars per week with an additional bonus of one hundred thousand in US dollars at the end of their six-month contract.

Caving into protests from the other nuclear-armed nations, Sean decided that the crews would now rotate every month allowing mining crews from France, the UK, Pakistan, India, Israel, and North Korea to participate. Generously, Sean decided to increase the pay to two thousand dollars per week with a month-end bonus of twenty thousand dollars in US funds, so there was no shortage of workers.

The mining crews worked three eight-hour shifts per day, seven days a week, for thirty days straight. When not working, they ate their meals in the well-stocked restaurant or lounged on the beautiful white sandy beach, a short walk from the living accommodations. Sean even has boats provided for those who wish to go on ocean cruises or go fishing.

The work proceeded without a mishap and with exceptional cooperation. No supervisor or mine worker wanted to create a fuss for fear of being rejected from the island and missing their month-end bonus. The work proceeded remarkably well. The entire island was now a honeycomb of mining shaft tunnels capable of housing tens of thousands of nuclear warheads.

The Peking Summit

Finally, the week arrived for the summit. Obviously, the major world powers put diplomatic pressure on the other nations to attend. Even the President of North Korea, who steadfastly refused to join the summit, agreed after being pressured by the Chinese government. Plus, the world news media did their part in pressuring all world leaders that this is a once-in-a lifetime opportunity to actually make a difference in nuclear arms reduction. There was no getting out of it. All the world leaders of nuclear-armed nations had to attend.

The Chinese capital city of Peking was decked out in all its splendor. The visiting world leaders were given three days to be shown the city and to be wined and dined.

All the major news networks were also invited. Then, on the fourth day, the summit began. All the world leaders, accompanied by a sole associate, entered a great hall at the urging of President Song. Here, they took their places.

The world will never truly know what took place behind those closed doors. It is known that Mr. Hing Zoi thanked every delegate in turn for attending. But what is not known is that once the discussions began, it was President Chen Song who directed the debates and forcibly stated that a nuclear arms reduction treaty would be finalized this week.

Known only to Sean, Mr. Zoi later told him that after the first day, the President of North Korea decided to leave, and that President Song ordered him to tell him that if he were to leave, he would not be leaving Chinese soil alive. Naturally, the President of North Korea complied.

Sean was also told that, along with the President of China, every world leader addressed the group and pledged to form a binding agreement to reduce their present stockpile of nuclear weapons and not to produce any further nuclear weapons. There was no escaping it. The consensus of making a nuclear arms reduction treaty was going to happen regardless of how much economic pressure the major world powers had to exert on the holdouts.

After three days of intense negotiations, an agreement was reached. The world would hear the news on the fourth day.

Mr. Hing Zoi made a statement to the press. Standing at the podium in front of the nine heads of the nuclear-armed powers, he proudly showed the set of documents signed by all the nine leaders of the nuclear-armed states.

"Ladies and gentlemen, an agreement has been reached. First, all nine leaders of the nuclear-armed nations have agreed to relinquish ninety percent of their remaining stockpile of nuclear weapons to be stored at the international nuclear storage facility in the South Pacific. The transportation of such weapons will be conducted by ships provided by the Chinese government and will commence immediately.

"Second, all nine world leaders have agreed to stop the research and production of nuclear arms and will allow agencies of the UN to inspect any and all nuclear facilities.

"Third, in a three-year time frame, all the remaining stockpiles of nuclear arms will be relinquished for safe storage. From this date forward, all nine nations have agreed that they will not research, manufacture, or again possess nuclear weapons.

"Fourth, this agreement is not a sign of weakness, but of strength. All nine nations are of one mind that if any nation, those that have signed this agreement or not, if any nation dares to research or produce nuclear weapons, this will be immediately considered an act of war, and their nuclear facilities will be bombed and eliminated.

"The combined efforts of Russia, the United States, China, France, the United Kingdom, Pakistan, India, Israel, and North Korea have decreed that the world will shortly be a nuclear-free world."

Mr. Zoi then invited each of the nine leaders to speak and verbally ratified the treaty. All voiced their pledge that they and their countries are now committed to this agreement.

Not since the time of VE Day in Europe has there been such rejoicing in the streets. People left their places of work and their homes and ran outside, rejoicing.

All businesses and government offices were closed. The specter of nuclear annihilation that has hung over the world since 1945 is now coming to an end. The entire world that had lived its entire life with this "Sword of Damocles" hanging over their heads had now been lifted.

Sean Little immediately called a party for all off-duty personnel to meet in the restaurant. He had the closing speeches of the Peking Summit replayed on the large flat-screen TV in the restaurant. Sean spoke over the cheering and clapping.

"My friends, I stand before you, happy with the world's final decision to put to rest the nuclear arms race. I am proud of the small part I played and hope that this agreement lasts forever."

Wendy, with a few glasses of wine in her, marched up to the microphone and started to speak, "Everyone in the world knows that it was Sean Little himself that got this ball rolling. Without his insistence on working tirelessly toward this nuclear arms reduction goal, world leaders would not have come on board. It was he who contacted President Chen Song of the People's Republic of China and told him of his intentions. He then hired Mr. Hing Zoi as his Program Director to see his vision through.

"It was Sean Little who addressed the combined Senate and House of Representatives and single-handedly forced the issue of nuclear arms reduction to the forefront until an agreement was reached. Everyone here and every single person on the planet Earth owes a debt of gratitude to the vision and perseverance of Sean Little. He has made our world safer for us all and for generations to come."

Everyone cheered and clapped for at least ten minutes. Then a voice rang out from the crowd, "But your name was not mentioned anywhere in the announcement."

Sean replied, "That's okay. I got the world focused on this issue, and the others finished it off. And I think it was former President Ronald Reagan who said, It's amazing how far one can go when they don't care who gets the credit."

The people could not stop cheering. Even Sean, who seldom drinks, had too much that night. Later that night, in bed with Jennifer, he said, "Jennifer, I think I did good."

Jennifer replied with, "Yes, Sean, you did. The entire world thanks you, and I thank you. Then they both fell off to sleep.

Chapter 52
The Final Attack

The evil ruler of the oil-rich kingdom in the Middle East, frustrated, pondered his options. He was infuriated at Sean's world-wide fame and his success in getting the world to reduce its stockpiles of nuclear weapons. Plus, he was now painfully aware that the Peking Agreement would keep him from developing his own nuclear weapons program. He wanted desperately to be the head of a nuclear-armed nation, and all his plans were now being met with failure at the hands of Sean Little.

He mentally reviewed his actions to date. His first operative, Amir's attempt to kidnap Sean at the lab in Boston, had failed. His second attempt was with Nybar, who successfully kidnapped Ralph Barns, but in the FBI rescue, he was killed, along with his countrymen.

His mind immediately turned to his trusted associate and third cousin, Jamal, who was secretly observing and assisting the previous two failed kidnapping attempts. Jamal was a very thin, nervous intellectual type who was totally devoted and loyal. *Jamal is my last and best chance, he will succeed,* the evil ruler thought to himself.

He contacted Jamal to have himself or another operative pose as a news reporter and question the Middle Eastern couple to whom Sean did his age-reversing application. They confirmed what they already knew. It was Sean Little who knew the secret and administered the formula. No one else.

The Russian's botched attempt to gain access at the main compound gate infuriated the ruler. Not only were there others after the secret, but these were amateurs that now made any of his further kidnapping attempts even more difficult. Watching Sean Little's General Meeting on the National Geographic network and his speech to the American government infuriated him even more. He yelled, "I must have this secret for myself. I and I alone must possess it, and I will control the world. World leaders would bow to my every command. I must have it, and I must have it now."

He immediately called Jamal and gave him instructions on how to act.

The ruler knew that the helicopter landing from the fake "World-Wide Environmental Foundation" gave them all the information they needed.

Jamal was in constant contact with his countrymen, who had obtained jobs working on the various sites in the compound. They confirmed that the compound was heavily guarded on the perimeter, but loosely guarded in the interior. They estimated that it took the first group of guards under one minute to get in their vehicles and reach the landed helicopter. They arrived in two SUVs with four men in each, for a total of eight guards.

Based on the times and distances estimated by the workmen, Jamal determined that they would have one minute before the first guards arrived and another fifteen minutes for the other guards to arrive from the barracks. Jamal estimated a window of sixteen minutes to kill the first set of guards, enter the office tower, subdue any guards found there, kidnap Sean, and leave. Jamal believed they could land, get Sean, and leave all in under fifteen minutes, a full two minutes before the next guards would arrive. Jamal was given the order to act now, and he must obey.

Jamal thought to himself, *Sean must not be harmed. He is of no value to us dead, and I fear the consequences of my failure. I must succeed. When we return, my men and I will be heroes in our home country.*

Jamal and his men were located some twenty miles from the compound in Saint George, Utah. Jamal took this position as being outside of the jurisdiction of the Las Vegas police and being far enough away to avoid suspicion. With the oil kingdom ruler's money, Jamal purchased two-thousand acres of desert land and set up a dummy filming studio on the property. *The perfect disguise,* he thought. As long as we have cameras running, we can practice our drills without interference. Even our helicopters will not be noticed. He rented an abandoned airstrip fifteen miles from the compound for use later on.

Jamal gave each of his countrymen working on the compound job sites one thousand dollars to call as soon as Sean Little entered his office tower. Two days later, the construction workers called to say that Sean Little had entered the office building.

The two helicopters immediately took off. Each helicopter was staffed with six heavily armed and dedicated soldiers. They approached the compound and veered off, as to act like they were headed to Las Vegas. Then they immediately turned into the compound and landed. The first batch of compound guards noticed that the sides and bottoms of the helicopters overhead had been painted CBZ NEWS, and they rolled their eyes and said, "Oh boy, don't these news people ever learn?"

The two helicopters landed directly in front of Sean's office tower. The group of soldiers in the first helicopter started running toward the office tower's front door, and the men from the other helicopter took up positions along the ground. When the first two SUVs loaded with compound guards arrived, they were immediately killed upon their arrival. The kidnappers were firing armor-piercing bullets which cut through the SUVs like butter.

Inside, Jamal and his men easily overtook the surprised reception guards and killed them both at their stations. The one dying guard was able to sound the alarm, but Jamal still thought they had time. One lone kidnapper entered the security camera area on the left and had the men lie on the floor. The other kidnapper entered the bank branch on the right and, likewise, had everyone lying on the floor. On the other floors, everyone hearing the alarm sought cover.

The four remaining kidnappers hurried up the stairs to the sixth floor, and two went into Sean's office and two went into the financial offices. The two kidnappers entering the financial offices immediately had everyone lying down on the floor. Then one kidnapper took Wendy at gunpoint and marched her into Sean's office. Sean was standing there with his Smith and Wesson pistol raised against Jamal, and the other kidnapper had his automatic rifle aimed at his head.

Once the kidnapper with Wendy arrived, Jamal spoke, "Sean Little, your position is hopeless. If you do not put down your weapon and come with us right now, my man will kill this woman, and then we will kill everyone else in this building. Are you ready to see everyone else die? You have fifteen seconds to put down your gun, and I promise this woman will be released."

Sean, seeing the look of terror on Wendy's face, threw his gun on the floor. The kidnapper released Wendy and yelled at her to get out. She ran for the door. Sean was led down the stairs and was met by the other two kidnappers. They all ran to the awaiting helicopters. Sean was shoved in, followed by the kidnapper holding his case, and the first helicopter took off, followed shortly by the second. They flew away from the approaching guards and exited the compound's air-space.

The helicopter carrying Sean and Jamal landed briefly at the abandoned airstrip, fifteen miles away from the compound. Here Sean was unloaded, and he and his case were put into the awaiting single-engine Cessna along with Jamal and one guard. Along with them was an identical Cessna, also preparing to take off. Once out of the helicopter, the helicopter immediately took off and proceeded westward with the other helicopter. The plane carrying Sean and Jamal taxied down the runway, took off immediately, and traveled due east. The other Cessna followed right behind them and, once airborne, turned directly south toward the Mexican border.

In Las Vegas, small planes were a familiar sight, and Jamal was counting on his helicopters and the additional airplane diverting attention away from them long enough for them to escape. His plan was working flawlessly. All government and police resources were directed toward the escaping helicopters as they headed westward toward the mountains. Plus, any and all aircraft flying anywhere near the Mexican border were being hailed and asked to identify themselves.

In thirty minutes, the helicopters arrived at their landing spot, and the guards quickly got into the awaiting trucks and took off. One lone police helicopter caught up to them at their landing location and radioed ahead that the men were getting into white commercial vans and escaping into the mountains.

The police quickly had the mountain highways closed and waited for federal government backup. Police helicopters swarmed the skies, and finally, the kidnappers were spotted. Wanting to keep Sean alive, the agents were ordered not to fire but to block off all the roads near where the kidnappers were traveling. The two white commercial vans were speeding down the small highway, only to be greeted by a full police roadblock and two Las Vegas police helicopters landing behind them.

The police hailed them on bullhorns, only to be met with a round of gunfire. Two officers were hit, and then all hell broke loose. Everyone opened fire, including the two police helicopters in the air. Within seconds, thousands of rounds were expelled, and the ten kidnappers lay dead. On examination, it was discovered that Sean Little was not with them. This was immediately reported to the FBI.

"Sir, I believe that Sean Little was offloaded by the helicopters shortly after they took off from the compound. They could either be in vehicles or have used one of the small airfields."

The FBI notified all air traffic control towers to ask if they noticed any aircraft leaving any small airfields nearby. One sharp-eyed air traffic controller stated that two small planes appeared on his screen about fifteen miles from the Nevada compound. He said that neither of the planes would identify themselves. That was all the information he had.

The FBI focused their attention on the small plane heading southward. That must be it, they thought. Every local military airbase was notified. Every small plane identified itself except for one heading directly southward toward Mexico. The military sent up aircraft and helicopters from their airfields to intercept. The small plane was located and quickly surrounded by military aircraft. They again hailed the pilot and warned him that if he did not respond, he would be shot out of the sky. He responded and was immediately told to land at the military airfield just ahead.

Upon landing, the pilot was surrounded by armed FBI agents. He quickly said he was being paid twenty thousand dollars to take off behind another identical Cessna, fly directly to Mexico, and deliver this plane to the tiny airstrip right across the Mexican border. He was told that if he was hailed by other aircraft; he was not to respond. While waiting to take off at the airfield, he said, a helicopter landed and three men got out. One he felt was being led at gunpoint and forced to board the other Cessna. The other fellow was carrying a large silver case. Once that Cessna was airborne and heading eastward, he said he took off immediately and flew toward the Mexican border, as instructed. The FBI contacted the air traffic control towers again and had them look for a single-engine Cessna heading east.

Jamal's plan was working flawlessly. I will be a hero when I deliver Sean Little to my countrymen in Mexico, he thought. His plan was for the FBI to follow the helicopters and to either have his men escape or be involved in a gunfight. His next diversion was the identical Cessna that took off after him and headed toward Mexico. He believed that the US military would shoot down this plane before allowing it to cross the border. By the time this happened and they checked the wreckage, he would safely be in Kingsville, Texas, and on his way to his boat ready to go to Mexico.

Landing at an abandoned airfield outside of Kingsville, just west of Corpus Christi, Texas, Jamal was met by his countrymen. The kidnapper carrying the case and Sean quickly exited the plane and was loaded into one of the three awaiting blacked-out SUVs. They immediately split up to confuse the police, and the SUV carrying Jamal and Sean headed toward the Gulf and their awaiting ship. By this time, the police had been searching all the airfields east of Las Vegas, and another sharp tower operator observed that the Cessna that would not identify itself fell off his radar west of Corpus Christi. He quickly notified the FBI, and they discovered the parked Cessna at an abandoned airfield just outside of Kingsville, Texas. This is our guy.

With the three SUVs all heading in separate directions, Jamal almost made it. But his luck ran out. On the highway ahead, there was a transport truck accident, and they were quickly locked into traffic. Jamal started to panic. He ordered the driver to go around the accident. As he did so, a police officer waved him down to stop, and Jamal took out his gun and shot the officer in the shoulder. The other officers hearing the shot came running, only to find their fellow officer on the ground and the blacked-out SUV racing down the deserted highway. This was immediately radioed in, and the police and military were informed. Police were notified to arrest the driver of the black SUV, and police helicopters were dispatched.

Jamal's driver, now on an empty highway, quickly made it to the marina and the awaiting boat. Jamal's countrymen cheered upon seeing Jamal and his captive. But just as Jamal was exiting the SUV, he could hear the sounds of the police helicopters overhead and the following police cruisers and their sirens. The kidnappers carried Sean's case, and Sean quickly got onto the boat, and the boat took off for international waters. The FBI already notified the Coast Guard to be on alert, and several Coast Guard vessels entered the area. Reaching the dock, the police did not fire, as they wanted Sean alive. The police helicopters followed Jamal's boat into the Gulf and guided the Coast Guard vessels to them.

Within fifteen minutes, the first Coast Guard boat caught up to the kidnappers and immediately cut them off. The small thirty-six-foot fiberglass boat the kidnappers were using was no match for the seventy-foot steel-hulled Coast Guard pursuit boats. Other Coast Guard boats joined in. They hailed the occupants of the smaller boat, but with no response. Then, by surprise, the occupants of the smaller boat started firing on the Coast Guard vessels. The Coast Guard men took cover behind the iron bulkheads and were safe.

Suddenly there was a lull in the firing, and the men watched as Jamal walked Sean out onto the deck with a gun pointed at his head. Jamal shouted over a bullhorn that unless they let them pass and reach Mexico unharmed, Sean Little would be killed. Then, in a surprise move, while Jamal was yelling into the bullhorn, Sean grabbed the gun out of Jamal's hand and

437

started shooting him. The men on the closest Coast Guard vessel couldn't believe their eyes. The kidnappers all cried out and started shooting Sean. Knowing that Sean was dead, the entire Coast Guard boat opened fire with everything they had. The men who had now cut down Sean were cut down themselves from the .50 caliber machine guns mounted on the top of the Coast Guard vessels. The kidnapper's vessel then burst into flames and exploded, killing everyone on board.

The Aftermath, Sean Is Gone

The world reacted in shock to Sean's death. His efforts had touched hundreds of thousands of lives and given millions of people hope. Every person on the planet knew the name Sean Little and mourned his passing. When once people looked forward to the future with hope, they now looked in despair. What would become of the projects he started—those same projects that no government would admit to or tackle? The Great Pacific Garbage Patch was an issue even the United Nations would not touch. His work forcing the nations of the world to relinquish their nuclear stockpiles made him not only the savor of the environment but also the savor of the world.

Wendy was interviewed about her ordeal with the kidnappers. Wendy, in tears, said, "Sean Little gave himself up for all of us. He knew he was going to die, but he gave himself up so that we could live. He was a great man. He saved our lives."

In the following days, the government, directed by Vice President Vince Rogers, had the FBI scour the compound looking for anything that would give them a clue to the secret that only Sean held. Every single item that Sean ever touched was examined, his pens, notepads, desks, everything. They took apart everything in his office, even his desk. Nothing was left untouched. When they were finished searching, another crew came in and searched again. Jennifer had to move into another trailer because of their constant searches. They rechecked his house in Crystal Falls and found nothing.

"He must have left a clue somewhere," was an often-heard statement from Vice President Vince Rogers.

Bill Fryer arranged for the reading of Sean's will. The FBI examined the will itself, looking for clues, but found nothing. At the reading of the will, these were the main issues:

Jennifer Little, Sean's wife, would receive fifty million dollars and all of Sean's property and possessions in Crystal Falls, Michigan.

Ralph Barns would receive fifty million dollars and most important, Wendy Rawlings, his trusted Executive Secretary, would now be in hundred percent control of "Sean Little Inc.", with all its funds and properties to continue with the projects as she sees fit.

Everyone expressed relief that Wendy would be in charge and would continue on with Sean's world-wide initiatives. Meeting with Jennifer, Ralph, and Colonel John later, she felt that with the eighty-seven billion dollars in the bank, she could keep up the environmental efforts for at least another ten years. Hopefully, many of these projects will have reached a conclusion, most notably the Fresh Water Initiative and the cleanup of the Great Pacific Garbage Patch.

Bill Fryer and Wendy arranged for a large funeral to take place in Sean's church for the ten guards who had died in the attack, plus the families of the guards who were killed while protecting Ralph in Boston. Wendy saw to it that these family members were brought down at company expense and put up at the Parkway Hotel. And without anyone else knowing, she wrote out checks for two hundred and fifty thousand dollars each to the families of those guards who were recently killed and gave them to their families at the end of the service. Wendy had already given the families of the two guards killed protecting Ralph in Boston two hundred fifty thousand dollars. *Better to do this now because who knows what constraints will be placed on Sean's bank accounts in the future?* As before, she contacted the Tax Department and notified them that she would be paying any tax applicable to this money.

Bill Fryer also looked after finding Sean's remains and arranging for the funeral the following week after the guard's funeral. After the large funeral the week before, Bill and Wendy tried to make Sean's funeral a small private affair, but with the prominence of the Sean Little name, people from all over the globe asked to attend. Wendy had no choice and made arrangements that the funeral would be on an invitation-only basis. Even on an invitation-only basis, she expected a large turnout. She increased the gate security, and the guards had lists of all those to allow through. Plus, Wendy had the portable fencing moved to surround the church to ensure that no one entered who was not invited.

Security was tight as dignitaries from around the world arrived. High-ranking government officials, especially those from the nuclear-armed nations, attended along with the President of the United States, Samuel Walker, and Mr. Hing Zoi of the People's Republic of China. Each in turn expressed their condolences to Jennifer and their appreciation for the work Sean did. Mr. Zoi, on behalf of Mr. Chen Song, invited Jennifer to accept his invitation to visit Mr. Song in China.

The program directors were all invited and attended. Wendy assured them that their projects would be continued and promised to meet with each of them, likely in a few months.

The chaplain had a beautiful service and commended Sean for his generous work in cleaning up the planet and prompting the world to reduce its stockpiles of nuclear weapons.

"Now he will rest with his parents, whom he so dearly loved," concluded the Chaplain.

Later that day, in the small cemetery on the outskirts of the compound, Sean Little's casket was lowered into the ground. At Sean's request, his grave marker was covered with a cloth, only to be removed once he was laid to rest.

With Sean comfortably interned, Bill Fryer removed the grave marker covering.

The tombstone read:

Here lies
Sean Little
1980 to 2023

There is hope
For mankind,
I did my best.